THE
GLASS PRISON

THE KINGDOM OF GEMS TRILOGY

THE KINGDOM OF GEMS TRILOGY

~ BOOK 3 ~

THE

GLASS PRISON

Jasper Cooper

Illustrations by Jasper Cooper

SILVERWELL PUBLISHING

For more information on Jasper and his books, visit:

www.TheKingdomOfGems.com

or

www.JasperCooper.com

First Published in 2010 by SilverWell Publishing
8 College Road, Canterbury, Kent CT1 1QX   UK

Reprinted in 2011

3 5 7 9 10 8 6 4 2

ISBN
978-0-9551653-2-0

Printed and bound in Great Britain by
CPI Bookmarque Ltd, Croydon, Surrey.

CONTENTS

~ BONUS STORY ~

 The Somon   499 *(i)*

This is a story from the KOGworld™
Membership website. See all the details
on the inside back cover.

TIMELINE

Covering events that happened in and around The Kingdom Of Gems

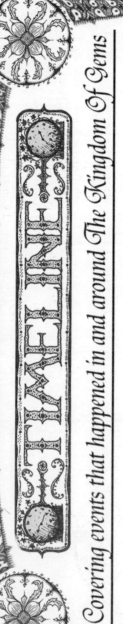

931 Or Ramoy Korum explores tunnels in The Kingdom of Sanseem. (Later renamed The Kingdom of Gems.)

962 Or King Karadan the Great builds a castle on Keill Island in Summertime Kingdom.

14 Sn THE GUGEOL RAIDS - Gugeol begins a series of daring raids into other kingdoms causing great suffering and lasting over 150 years.

42 Sn WIZARD CANDARA IS BORN in Tarr Kingdom.

102 Sn WIZARD CANDARA presents The Candara Gems to The Kingdom of Sanseem.

111 Sn The Kingdom Of Sanseem is renamed The Kingdom of Gems.

131 Sn WIZARD CANDARA DIES.

His life is celebrated at a twelve day gathering in Chymyn where his ashes were sprinkled in the Great Delgardi River.

Age of Orseter (Or)

← 950

1,000 / 0

Age of Stellen (Sn) →

50

100

150

200	
201 Sn	GUGEOL ARISES and invades the surrounding kingdoms of Gliyfild, Bortell, Urlom, Fantem South and Hesteri.
227 Sn	GUGEOL occupies many kingdoms between the two Great Oceans but not The Kingdom of Gems which is protected by the Candara Gems.
250	
259 Sn	ARAM & HALO awaken to protect The Kingdom of Gems against an invasion of evil Troublers sent by Gugeol.
300	
308 Sn	THE FIRE CREATURES OF RUDDHA join forces with Gugeol.
339 Sn	THE TWENTY DAY HAROOR UPRISING in the Kingdom of Mardice is quashed by Gugeol. 132 prisoners taken.
350	
376 Sn	Widespread famine caused by a massive volcano eruption in the Heldfore Mountains in the Kindom Of Aguita. The Kingdom Of Gems is protected from this by the Candara Gems.
400	
447 Sn	THE GREAT INVASION - Gugeol is defeated and forced back. The Fire Creatures return to Ruddha deep beneath the earth. The Dark Ages end.
450	
470 Sn	The FORENTONE BEARS attack the wolves in Juran Forest in Summertime Kingdom, and start their territorial war.
500	
511 Sn	THE GLYIFILD BELL is cast by Gugeol in the iron mines of Glyifild
528 Sn	GUGEOL INVADES SUMMERTIME KINGDOM and casts a spell with the Glyifild Bell.
550	
553 Sn	THE MUNDEN REBELLION led by Hawkeye. Gugeol retreats.
567 Sn	The Dark WizardTroubler captures The Kingdom of Gems.

201 - 447 Sn
The Dark Ages
called
The Thousand Seasons
of Night
(Known by Gugeol as The
Mighty Age of Gugeol.)

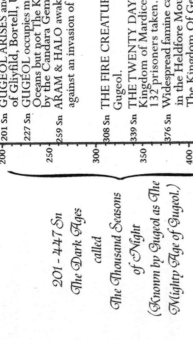

The 7 Eras of Known History

each lasting 1,000 years.

Shair Era
Tenair Era
Salume Era
Ealume Era
Punat Era
Obster Era
Stellen Era

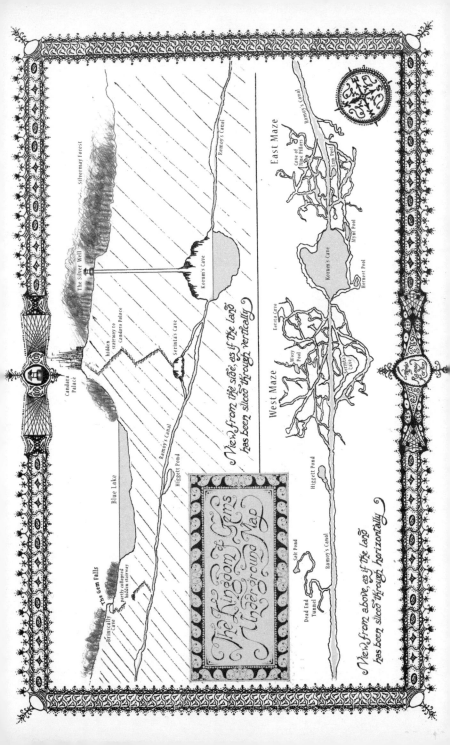

The Kingdom of Gems
Underground Map

View from the side, as if the land has been sliced through vertically

View from above, as if the land has been sliced through horizontally

Silvermay Forest

The Silver Well

Candara Palace

hidden stairway to Candara Palace

Blue Lake

The Gem Falls

Brinscall Cave

partly collapsed hidden stairway

Ramoy's Canal

Higgett Pond

Serinta's Cave

Korum's Cave

Ramoy's Canal

West Maze

East Maze

Cave of the Pillars

Ramoy's Canal

Eretta Cave

Woss Pool

Serinta Cave

Korum's Cave

Horsett Pool

Mynt Pool

Sim Pool

Higgett Pond

Salt Pond

Dead End Tunnel

Ramoy's Canal

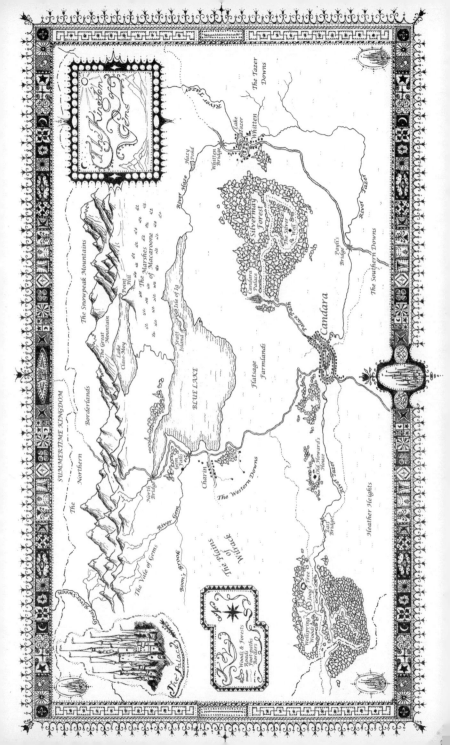

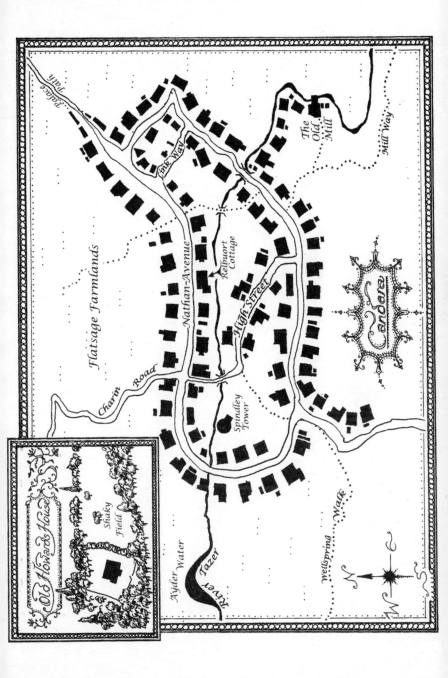

This book is dedicated to Rebecca and Joseph,

my wonderful children.

Chapter 1

~ The Hadia Stick ~

The grounds at the back of Wizard Elzaphan's castle were cloaked in the darkness of a still night. Looking down from above, the moon tenderly shed its pale light on the high turrets and front walls, leaving the garden at the back in deep shadow. The black sky was studded with a thousand stars, a wondrous sight to lift the spirits of anyone with their eyes raised above.

There was someone gazing upwards, but the star-scattered display did nothing to lift his spirits. He was lying on a bed, staring up through a small window. Such a dark mood consumed him that his eyes were glazed with the hue of heavy thoughts. He felt he was the most unfortunate man alive and was wallowing in his misery. It was Old Howard.

He was in a sturdy wooden hut. There were two small windows in the room and an oil lamp rested on a bedside table, lighting up the room with a yellowish light. His muddy boots were lying untidily on the floorboards and he was stretched out on the bed in his tattered clothes. One of his big toes was poking out through a hole in his sock.

Old Howard had been escorted to this hut in the grounds at the back of the castle by Cedric the gardener. He was reluctant to follow Cedric and even more reluctant to live in the hut. His frustration exploded into violence when he heard the key turn in the door to lock him in for the night. When he realised that escape through one of the windows was impossible for his rotund body, he punched the wall in temper and then collapsed onto the bed with his hand throbbing. This pushed him into a somber sulk but there was something else that sent his mood tumbling to the depths of gloom. The Hadia Stick.

Wizard Elzaphan had forced him to take hold of the Stick before casting a spell and now it lay beside him on the bed with his hand clasped around it. Old Howard rolled his head on the pillow and looked at it.

It was a beautiful object, skilfully made from strong hazel wood and decorated with three bands of silver. A silver tip capped the base for walking. At the other end a curved silver handle continued down the Stick for a couple of inches and was engraved with Wizard Elzaphan's coat of arms. The third silver band wrapped around the Stick in the middle. This was delicately engraved with a poem in beautiful lettering.

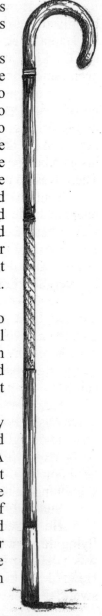

Old Howard scowled and turned away, looking blindly upwards and out of the window again. He hated the Hadia Stick so much that he could not see its beauty at all. Looking at it was almost unbearable, so he did not even notice the poem.

He had already tried to be free of the Stick by letting go of it and had experienced pain so intense that he had grabbed it again immediately. Since then he constantly kept it in his hand. Now, as he lay on the bed, he released his grip but kept a finger touching it to see what happened. There was no pain. Perhaps the spell had ended now.

Tentatively, he drew his hand away. Nothing happened. He rose from the bed and stood up. All was well. Then he cried out as he felt a sharp pain and reached out to grab the Stick again. He stopped with his hand poised when he realised it was his injured ankle. He lifted his weight off the ankle and the pain eased.

Beads of sweat glistened on his forehead catching the lamplight as he moved. A couple of drips ran down around his eyes so he shook his head and then wiped his hand across his face. Then he took a step towards the door and glanced back at the stick. It looked harmless. His fear subsided. He was free.

He crept, limping on his bad ankle, as slowly and as quietly as he could across the wooden floor. At the door he reached out, grasped the handle and turned it just to check. As he expected, it was locked, but it still angered him and he shook it violently in frustration. He glanced around for something he could use to smash the door open.

Suddenly a sound behind him made him jump.

He jerked his head around. The Hadia Stick was flying through the air towards him. As if an invisible hand was wielding it, it paused and then rose in the air. Old Howard put his hands up to protect himself as the Stick swung down at him. With a swish it whacked him on his hand. He yelped in pain like an injured dog and pulled at the door, trying in vain to open it. Suddenly another pain, far worse than the last, filled his body, and this time it made him scream.

He knew it was the Stick and so he grasped at it, desperate to stop the pain, but it lurched away. He lunged after it, hobbling on his bad ankle, but once again it dodged his swinging hand and he overbalanced, crashing heavily to the floor. As he scrabbled to his feet, the Stick floated towards him but when he reached to grasp it, it darted away again and hid under the bed.

Old Howard shouted in anger, "Come 'ere!"

He dived under the bed and stretched out for it but the Stick escaped on the other side.

This comical scene continued for a few minutes. The Hadia Stick would always stay just out of reach, dancing cleverly in the air, and then it would hide somewhere. When Old Howard found it, he would pounce on it like a cat after a mouse but it would always dart away at the last moment. Old Howard grew more and more cross.

Old Howard's pain continued to throb through his plump body. He was breathing heavily now but carried on trying until he collapsed onto the floor and leant against a wall. He thumped his hand on the floor in frustration.

"Please... please," he cried.

He was sobbing now. Great tears rolled out of his eyes to mingle with the sweat running down from his brow.

"Please... come 'ere! Oy'll be good, oy will. Oy promise. Oy promise."

The pain was too much and he closed his eyes in despair.

Then he felt the most wonderful touch he had ever felt. It was the cool of silver as the Hadia Stick slipped into his hand and the pain disappeared.

"Thank you," he said softly, "Thank you."

Old Howard had not said 'thank you' since he was a boy many years ago. He sat there for a while recovering from his ordeal and when he felt better he opened his eyes. To his surprise, the door was open, and looking at him out of the darkness was a brown rabbit.

"Hello, Old Howard," said Feeni.

She hopped inside and kicked the door closed with her back feet. One of the ornaments on her necklace flashed in the light of the lamp. It was the small piece of gold that Old Howard had used to pay her for helping him. Beside this hung a very small piece of deep red garnet gemstone, and a tiny silver skull. She smiled.

"That was quite a show," she said.

"What are yer doin' 'ere?" Old Howard growled.

"Nothing really. I heard all the noise you were making and came along to see what was going on. I'm glad I did! That's the best entertainment I've had for ages!"

"Not for me it wasn't," he grumbled.

Feeni shook her head and laughed.

"If you're doing it again, let me know! I've never seen anyone dance with a stick before. I'll sing along!"

Old Howard glared at her. "Oy won't be doin' any more dancin'. 'Ow did yer get in?"

She sat up slightly with pride.

"I have ways," she said, "Locked doors don't stop me. I often come in here."

Feeni hopped closer and looked at the Hadia Stick in his hand. She turned her head on one side.

"That Wizard Elzaphan…" Old Howard groaned, "I hate him! He made me hold the Stick and then he cast a spell... it's a terrible thing!"

"Ah," Feeni nodded, "And it hurts when you let go?"

Old Howard nodded reluctantly. He was still sitting on the floor and slumped against the wall.

"I've seen this before," she said, "It's a Hadia Stick... they carry spells. You see... I watch and I listen. I know things that he doesn't think I know. I've seen him do this Hadia Stick thing to others. It's so mean... so evil. He's got it in for you, hasn't he?"

Old Howard just sighed.

She took another step and looked more closely at the Stick.

"You know there's writing on it," she commented, "And it's a poem... it's always a poem he puts on them... but don't read it! You musn't read it!"

"Woy not?" he asked, "Wot's it say then?"

"Bad words," she replied, "With bad meanings. I wouldn't read it even if I could read."

"Oy won't," he said, "Oy hate poems... oy hate that wizard..." his voice rose in bitterness and he lifted the Hadia Stick and banged it hard on the floor, "An' oy hate this Stick. Oy've got to get away from 'ere some'ow."

There was silence for a moment, then Feeni spoke.

"Well, I hate all those things too. That's why I'm leaving here."

Old Howard suddenly looked interested.

"Leavin' 'ere?" he asked, "This 'orrible island?"

She nodded.

"When?"

"As soon as I can. Now is as good a time as any. It's a dark night... perfect for it."

"But, 'ow?"

She looked smug.

"It's either by boat which I haven't got, by air if you're a bird which I'm not, or through the tunnel. So, the only option is through the tunnel and as I don't want to be seen, it's the best way anyway! For most the tunnel would be impossible... 'cos everything is locked, as well as the entrance to the tunnel."

She paused and looked at Old Howard who was listening intently and then she continued.

"But for me, locked doors are no problem. I can get into anywhere."

"Oy'll come with yer," Old Howard said, "We can work together."

"Ha!" she laughed, "I can help you escape, but how can you help me in return?"

Old Howard thought hard. He must think of something. Suddenly he reached out, grabbed her by her long ears and pulled her across the floor to him.

"Ow!" she screeched, scrabbling with all four legs to wriggle free, "Get off!"

He grabbed her necklace, let go of her ears and lifted it over her head. He grabbed her ears again and shook the necklace in front of her so that it rattled.

"Take me with yer," he shouted, "Else I'll keep this."

"Let go of my ears!" she cried, "I've got a much better idea."

Old Howard loosened his grip but kept holding her.

"Let go!" she commanded crossly.

He let go.

"Good," she said, "Now give my necklace back."

"Woy should oy?" he demanded.

"Because…" she said, "because then I'll tell you my plan… for your freedom."

"No," he insisted, "Tell me your plan first."

Feeni sighed. "Alright," she agreed, "Now, here's the deal. I get you out of here, through the locked entrance to the tunnel, to freedom... and you help me by carrying me."

"Carry you?!" he exclaimed, shaking his head, "Oy don't know about that."

She hopped to the door and turned to face him again.

"Alright then," she said, "Keep the necklace... I'm off to freedom!"

She turned to go.

"Wait!" Old Howard exclaimed.

Feeni turned back.

"Last chance," she said, "Come on! I'll ride on your shoulder. I'm very light. My legs get tired and I don't like walking much. So, take it or leave it."

Old Howard was desperate to get away from Wizard Elzaphan and suddenly here was an opportunity. Carrying a rabbit was a small price to pay for freedom. Of course he still had the terrible Hadia Stick but there was nothing he could do about that at the moment. Perhaps it would lose its power the further he got away from Wizard Elzaphan.

"It's a deal," he said.

Feeni hopped to him and stretched up ready for the necklace. Old Howard dropped it over her head.

"Good," she said, "Let's go then."

Old Howard got to his feet. He put on his old coat which hung by a hook on the back of the door and grabbed his canvas bag. He threw a few things into it; some food, a bottle of water, a woolly hat, an oil lamp. He put it on his back and lifted Feeni up to place her on his shoulder.

Circumstances had thrown together these most unlikely of companions and together they moved out into the night.

Harris, the golden eagle who guarded Wizard Elzaphan's Castle with Quint, had left the castle just after dusk, jumping off the highest turret and spiralling upwards on the warm currents of air. The fringes of his dark brown plumage tremored in the breeze as he rose with a perfect combination of power and agility. The rising moon hung yellow in the black, star-filled sky.

He ascended gracefully upwards, his brown eyes looking down at the castle which perched on top of Keill Island. Surrounding the cliffs lay the smooth, ebony surface of Lake Beautiful. He saw the great wizard looking up at him and waving, his face lit by the light of the flaming torches fixed to the battlements.

He levelled off and felt the warm air rush past him as he sped swiftly through the night. He was following Wizard Elzaphan's instructions and heading directly south. He was high above Summertime Kingdom now which was spread out beneath him like a colourless map, a nocturnal world painted in shades of grey. He flew swiftly above the Forest of the Fairies, over the Clungberry Fields and past Lake Burney to his left, and then he saw The Great Crack to the Centre of Ruddha.

The dawn was approaching now as the darkness gradually softened, and the stars lost their sharp crystal brilliance. As the light grew and the horizon glowed with the promise of dawn, the world below became clearer. The sun appeared as a star point of fire and spread to form a golden curve of blazing light.

The early morning sunlight glanced off the feathers on the nape of his neck and glinted brightly in gold. Now he could see more clearly and his fears were confirmed. Ahead and some way below, he could see the raven army, a mass of swirling, black, angular shapes heading for the border. He had witnessed their ferocious fighting and knew he could handle two or three, maybe a few, but a whole army of over one hundred would overwhelm him in a moment. He must keep his distance.

He realised he had a choice. He could hold his altitude and follow from high above, or he could drop to the land and continue to the border from there. Dropping to ground level was dangerous; he might be seen. He decided to stay above.

To his left he noticed another group of ravens. They were far below, flying in an arrow formation towards the border. He quickly counted them as best he could from the distance; there were at least twelve, maybe more.

He could see the border now. It was a strange sight; a wall of falling snow rising high up into the air. Across the border in The Kingdom of Gems, the cloud cover and snow-filled air was keeping the dawn at bay and so it was still dark. Harris looked down again at the ravens as he followed them, alert and ready for action.

"Amalek!" shouted Simron, gripping her around her shoulders from behind and shaking her, "Listen to me!"

Amalek was staring straight ahead and across the border where the blizzard was whipping the snow past in streaks of white. Her eyes were fixed on the black eyes of the Dark Wizard Troubler who was standing in a cloud just above the deep-lying snow.

"Don't look at him!" Simron pleaded.

He moved alongside her and tried to step in front and turn her away, but she lunged forwards. He tried again, but she seemed immovable; the wizard's power was already taking her. All he could do was grasp her by the arm.

She felt trapped, unable to resist the Troubler's power. She had been drawn into his shadowy world, ensnared like an animal falling into the trap of a hunter. She could hear his voice echoing in her mind as he whispered commands.

"Come here," he hissed, his black eyes glaring, "Come to me across the border. You can help me rule here... and then you can have your brother back."

She tried to fight against the eerie pull of the wizard but she felt she was sinking into his dark world. She twisted free from Simron's grip.

"Come here and get your brother back," the wizard whispered, "Come here now!"

The voice was irresistible. She stepped towards him, held in a trance, like someone sleep-walking.

"Stop!" shouted Simron.

She took another step.

"Step across," whispered the evil wizard to her, "It's easy... your brother needs you..."

She took another step. One more and she would be moving across into the spell-bound kingdom. The wizard leant forwards, reaching out a hand, his long sinewy fingers trembling with excitement. Amalek stepped, her hand stretching towards his and her fingers moving into the falling snow.

He smiled with glee and hissed, "Ah, yesss."

Simron grabbed her shoulders again and jerked her back. Suddenly, Tally jumped in front of her, his back right against the snow, and leapt up, his strong hind legs pushing into the ground and springing him into the air. He hit Amalek in the stomach and winded her. She fell back and into Simron, doubled over with the blow and collapsed onto the grass. Her eye contact with the wizard had been broken. She felt free again but the ordeal had drained her and all she could do was to lie on the ground gasping for breath.

Aram was still some distance away and observed what was happening. He was ready to gallop towards them and help, but the falling snow became thicker, gusting and sweeping on the wind in a mass of white. It blew into his face with force making him blink and turn away, and stagger sideways. When he turned back, the view was blanketed by the fierce blizzard. Unsure which way to run he pointed his alicorn to make a path, but even this was not enough to see his friends. He began to run not realising that he was heading back towards the mountains.

"Seph!" cried Joog.

Simron and Tally, followed by Lazuli, ran towards Seph who was hanging in mid-air halfway across the border. He was frozen by the spell. Joog glided above. Seph's head and shoulders were now covered with snow. At the same time, on the other side of the border, the Dark Wizard Troubler floated in the cloud towards him and got there first. He reached out, grabbing Seph by his arms and pulling.

"Say goodbye," he sneered at them, "I've got him now."

He pulled Seph's arms until his body was completely across. His legs were following when Simron reached the border just in time to grasp his ankles. They were only a few feet from the wizard. His presence was stifling, almost unbearable. Simron struggled to keep his mind on his task.

"Pull!" exclaimed Tally as he looked up at Simron from below.

"Help me, Lazuli!" shouted Simron.

Lazuli was a couple of steps behind and Simron was losing the tug of war. His hands were now right next to the border. The Troubler glared at him with hatred.

"Let go!" he snarled, "Unless you'd like to come too!"

He pulled harder and with a jerk Simron's hands slipped over the border and into the falling snow, leaving only Seph's feet in Summertime Kingdom. Simron felt a dreadful freezing tingle through his hands as he tried to fight against the spell. His grip loosened.

Lazuli hooked her trunk around Simron's waist but even with her great strength pulling, Simron was being dragged through.

"My hands are frozen!" exclaimed Simron, "Pull harder, Lazuli!"

Suddenly, they heard hooves pounding the ground. Amid a whirl of snow, Aram appeared, galloping along the border towards them. In a second he was there, stabbing his alicorn toward the Troubler's hands. There was a flash.

"Ahh!" cried the wizard, his hand wracked with pain as he was forced to let go, "No!"

He was left gripping Seph's arm with one hand - the hand with the finger and thumb missing.

"No!" cried the Troubler again, screwing up his face with sheer anguish.

He was now being pulled. If he crossed the border his spell would dissolve and this was too much to lose, so with another cry of frustration he let go and fell back into the cloud. Seph was immediately pulled back across the border and collapsed to the ground. Simron shook his hands and the life began to flow back into them.

Amalek had recovered now and tried to help Seph to his feet, but he was too weak. He looked at her in a daze, unsure where he was and what was happening.

"Seph!" she shouted at him, shaking his shoulders.

"Ammey," he said sleepily, "What happened? I feel weird."

"You did a stupid thing," she snapped, "That's what happened."

"What?"

"Never mind now," she said quickly, "Look there!"

She pointed at the approaching raven army.

"What shall we do?" she blurted out in a panic.

She looked back at the Troubler and then hauled Seph onto his feet.

"He can't cross," said Joog quickly from above their heads, "Remember? Otherwise his spell ends... but we'll have to fight the ravens. Get ready!"

"Follow me!" cried Tally.

He started hopping as fast as he could, away from the border and towards a small wood. The others immediately ran after him, first Simron, followed by Lazuli, Amalek and Seph. Joog flew past them and entered the woods first. The others quickly followed.

As they disappeared into the wood, the ravens arrived overhead and carried on to the border. They swooped down towards the Dark Wizard Troubler. Most of them landed on the grassy side of the border but the General and Colonel Gerr flew into the falling snow and were immediately caught in the driving blizzard. They struggled to control their flight but managed to turn into the fierce wind and darted into the cloud where the Troubler stood. While the stormy blast whipped the snow past, it was completely sheltered inside the cloud. They landed at his feet.

"Master," began the General, bowing his large head. The black compass hung around his neck. "We are honoured to..."

"Get them!" the wizard screamed above the howling sound of the blizzard.

"Who?" cried the General. His compass was now twitching with little jumps, "Get who, sir?"

"The Prince and Princess, of course!" he shouted.

The General and Gerr started jerking their heads this way and that as they looked for them.

"You idiots!" the wizard screamed in frustration as he pointed across the border, "There! Over there in that wood! I saw them run in there! Now... go!" Then he shouted as loud as he could across the border, "All of you!"

Some of the ravens, the ones who had heard, immediately replied, "Yes, sir," and the others gradually joined in although they did not know why they were saying it.

The General and Colonel Gerr took to the air and flew across the border where it was now light.

"Follow!" the General shouted as he passed above the army.

"Follow!" shouted Gerr still wallowing in the pride of being appointed colonel.

There was a bustle of black flapping wings as the whole army took off and rose in the air to follow the General.

"Listen!" the General shouted, turning his head to look back as he flew, "The enemy are in that wood down there."

There was an uproar of excited cackling.

"Listen!" he boomed.

"Listen to the General!" screamed Gerr.

The cackling faded out.

"We fly above first!" the General commanded, "All together... understand?"

"Yes, sir!" they all replied.

"We scan for them. OK?"

"Yes, sir!"

"Then... we get them. If they're hiding like cowards then we will fly in there and search that wood until they are unearthed. OK?"

"Yes, sir!"

They were now right above the wood when they were joined by the group of fourteen ravens led by Sergeant Forr. They mingled in with the others hoping that the General would not notice how late they were.

"Sergeant Forr?" shouted the General, "Come here... now!" He turned to Gerr and asked, "Where have they been?"

"I don't know, sir," began Gerr, "But shouldn't we hunt the enemy first?"

"Of course," the General snapped, "But we know we've got the enemy, don't we, because we know where they are? They're in that wood... so we've got them trapped. Think about it, Gerr... if they try to run out we'd see them."

Forr was beside the General now.

"Yes, but..." Gerr began.

"Where have you been?" the General snapped at Forr.

Forr opened his beak to speak but couldn't think what to say, "Er... er... we... er..."

"I'll hear about it later," the General said crossly, "And you'd better have a good reason."

He could feel the black compass pulling on his neck, as if urging him to carry on with the hunt for the enemy.

"Scan the wood!" the General commanded to the whole group, "The first one to spot them gets an official commendation from me. Now scan!"

The army became a swirling mass of cawing birds, all flying at the same level and scanning the wood below with their heads pointing down.

Suddenly there was a swishing sound as something shot through the flock of ravens. Several ravens were pulled together by the rapid movement. Their wings became tangled as they bumped together and they started falling. They soon fought themselves free again and rose back up to the others.

"What was that?" one of them cried out.

"Something fast," replied another, "Very fast."

"It was an eagle," called out Sergeant Forr.

"An eagle, eh?" said the General with interest as he looked down, "Well where is it now? Can you see it Gerr?"

"No sir," Gerr replied brightly, "It could be anywhere by now sir, the speed it was travelling."

The General rose slightly and looked down at his army. "Drop lower now," he boomed, "We'll search among the trees. Work thoroughly and let me know when you find the enemy."

The army of ravens dropped into the wood below and began searching among the trees. After they had hunted in and around every tree and every possible hiding place, the General landed on the top of the highest tree.

"Gather!" he screamed.

Within a minute the whole army had landed, perching all around the General. Some were below him in the same tree and some in the trees close by.

"OK then!" he bellowed, "So I presume that since I have heard nothing from you, the enemy have not been found."

There was no answer.

He looked around at them with a superior look that told them that they were all failures. "Well!?"

'They're not here," announced Akk.

The General glanced back nervously towards the border where he could just about see the Dark Wizard

Troubler through the falling snow. He knew the wizard would be looking in his direction waiting for news and expecting it to be good news.

"But the Master..." began the General, "The Master told us they were in here. Therefore they must be here!"

"Well they're not," said Razz from the next tree.

"Who said that?" demanded the General, looking across.

"It was Razz," replied several birds.

"Razz! I could've guessed. In spite of what you say, we need to search again because they *are* in there."

"Oh, what's the point?!" sighed Razz, "They're not here."

"I don't like this rebellious attitude of yours," the General snapped, and then he raised his voice, "Don't ever contradict the Master... or me!"

There was complete silence now. The light from the rising sun shone in metallic purple on the General's shiny black feathers. A light breeze rustled the leaves. The black compass turned gently as it nudged the General on his chest to calm him down.

"You will go down again Razz, with everyone, and search again. The enemy went in there and therefore they *are* in there. They are hiding. Search again... thoroughly this time! Colonel Gerr will organize the search. Now go!"

The ravens all dropped out of the trees and began to search again. After a while Gerr returned and landed in the tree just below the General who looked down at him with disdain from his lofty position.

"I assume," he began, "That you have failed again. That is right, is it Gerr?"

"We can't find them," Gerr confirmed, "But we're still trying, sir."

"Then, Gerr, you should have found them. Because..." he shook his head in frustration, "Because they went in there. They can't just disappear like that! Have you searched everywhere?"

"Yes sir," Gerr replied perkily, "They're not there, sir."

"Gerr," the General sighed, and then grumbled, "You're getting on my nerves. Why are you always so bright and... chirpy? We are facing a disaster!"

A few ravens had seen Gerr land and so they landed discreetly on the branches just below him.

Gerr tried to be more serious. "We can still find them, sir."

The General suddenly thought of something and lifted his head.

"Where's Iker?" he said looking around jerkily, "Have you seen him?"

"No sir," Gerr shook his head.

"Strange. Did he return with Sergeant Forr and the others?"

"I don't know, sir... I don't remember seeing him, sir."

"Look out for him, Gerr, and let me know. He may be sleepy and slow but he is my nephew."

"OK, but what shall we do now, sir?" asked Gerr.

The General shook his head again, "We'll have to call this mad hunt off soon and tell the Master."

This statement sparked off a wave of frightened mumblings among the birds below.

"Send a bird to go and tell him, Gerr."

The ravens below heard this and slipped off the branches and disappeared below. Gerr looked down.

"There's no one to send now," he said.

"They're better off searching anyway," the General snapped, "You'll have to go."

"Me, sir?" asked Gerr nervously.

"Yes, you, Gerr," the General snapped, "You're my colonel, so you go."

Gerr stayed still. Then he started looking down for the other birds.

"Can't you send *someone* else, sir?"

"Keg!" called out the General, "Come here!"

Nothing happened.

"I can see you hiding behind those leaves!"

Keg emerged very sheepishly and flapped up to a branch just below Gerr.

"Don't ever hide from me again!" the General snapped, jerking his head downwards. Then he suddenly screeched so loudly that Gerr cowered down on the branch and then fell off. "Go now, Gerr, and take Keg with you!"

As Gerr turned in the air Keg joined him and they headed off together towards the border.

"You're right, Tally," said Simron, "Look... there."

It was dark and the only light was a dim glow which came from Seph's oval magic box. He was holding it with the lid above a map and the light was streaming out from inside. Simron was crouching down and pointing at the map with his finger. The rest of them huddled around, the children kneeling, and Lazuli looking down from above through their circle of heads. The map looked old; the faded paper was tattered at the edges and creased where it had been folded.

"It must go under the border there," continued Simron, "See where it ends... right at the border. I wouldn't have thought it just stops there. It must continue into The Kingdom Of Gems."

"We'll take it and see," commented Joog, "It's not far so we'll soon find out."

"Wait!" exclaimed Amalek, "We must all have some ink from the magic pens on us before we cross the border. Who needs some?"

"I do," answered Lazuli.

"And I definitely do!" smiled Seph.

They needed magic ink on them to protect them from the Dark Wizard Troubler's spell. Lazuli held out her trunk to Amalek who took a magic pen from her pocket and put some on. She dabbed some on Seph's ankle and then checked everyone to make sure they were all protected.

The magic box cast a pale golden light around them and threw their shadows in rippled shapes on the roughly-hewn rock walls of the tunnel. Beneath them the floor was uneven and damp in places, so they had found a dry patch to open out and flatten the map. Behind them, stretching up into darkness were about forty steps which descended from the surface above in a straight line.

A short while earlier Tally had led them into the woods, paused to take a quick look at his map, and then found the hidden entrance to the tunnel. He knew there were many secret tunnels in Summertime Kingdom and had noticed this one when he was looking at the map earlier. As soon as the hidden entrance was opened they all rushed in, jumping down onto the wooden-boarded floor at the top of the steps. When Lazuli's turn came she jumped down heavily throwing up clouds of dust around them. They quickly closed the sliding entrance above their heads and descended the steps to the tunnel below.

After studying the map Amalek folded it carefully for Tally and put it back into the pouch on his belly.

"I'd love to see them now!" said Seph, smiling, "The ravens... and the Troubler... imagine it... when they can't find us!"

Amalek nodded and laughed.

Simron shook his head, "But they might. What if they do find the entrance?! What then? They may be stupid but they've got sharp eyes and there's so many of them."

"Simron's right," Joog agreed, "And if they get in here then we'd be finished... they'd have us trapped. So let's stop talking about it and get going."

Seph walked in front. He clutched the magic box in front of him to light the way but he could only see about one step ahead by its dim glow. With the uneven rock floor it was not safe to move faster than walking pace. The others followed with Lazuli's great bulk last.

Chapter 2

~ The Kingdom of Moone ~

By the time Gerr and Keg had swooped across the border into the driving snow, and then into the cloud to land at the Dark Wizard Troubler's feet, they were both shivering. It was not only the freezing cold that penetrated the warmth of their black feathers but also the grip of fear; they had to report the bad news to the evil wizard and they were terrified.

The wizard was clutching his hand. Aram's attack had left the skin blackened by the flash and badly bruised by the impact of his alicorn. A jagged gash on the back oozed blood. He glared down at the ravens.

"Well?" he demanded urgently, his voice as icy as the weather, "I've been waiting all this time for news. What *have* you been doing?"

"We... we... we..." Gerr stammered.

"Yes?!"

"W…we've been hunting in the wood, Master."

"Yes?" he questioned, "And you've found them?"

"We..." Gerr tried to control his fear and get the words out that he knew he had to say. "Well... no, master... we can't find them, sir."

"What?!" the wizard exclaimed.

"Sorry, M... Master," Keg forced the words out, "We've looked thoroughly... thoroughly, master, and they're not there."

"I *saw* them go in!" the wizard snapped, "Are you telling me that they've escaped somehow?"

"Yes... Master," Keg responded.

The wizard screwed up his face in anger. In temper he lifted a black boot and swung it at Keg as if kicking a football with all his might. It hit Keg in the side and sent him flying out of the cloud and falling out of sight. The wizard watched him go and then glared down at Gerr.

"Right," he said, carrying on as if nothing had happened, "Right then. So... alright... it seems they've escaped. While you thought they were hiding in the wood they've sneaked out the other side... cunning. They could be anywhere by now! You've been hunting in the wood and they've escaped. Did no one think that they might do this?"

Gerr was too afraid to answer. He opened his beak nervously but no words came out. The wizard lifted his leg to kick Gerr who cowered down, half spreading his wings and closing his eyes ready for the blow. The Troubler controlled his anger and placed his foot down again, clutching his injured hand and wincing in pain. Gerr opened his eyes.

"On your way here," the wizard said, "did you see that unicorn?"

"No, Master."

"Are you sure?"

"Yes, Master, no unicorn," said Gerr, "There's too much snow to see very far, Master."

The Troubler thought for a moment. This was puzzling. He knew he had trapped the two unicorns, the silver one and the gold one, in the cloud over Candara. Now there was a third unicorn.

"Take a message back to your General..." he continued, "I want the enemy killed. You must find them and kill them. Tell him to search the surrounding area to the north of that wood. They must've run right through the wood and out the other side." Then he suddenly raised his voice and Gerr cowered low again, looking terrified. "Find them and kill them!"

"Yes, Master."

With a quick jump Gerr took off and was about to plunge into the driving snow when the wizard shouted at him.

"Stop! Come back!"

Gerr turned and fell back at the wizard's feet, his black beak dotted with snowflakes.

"Did I say you could go?" the wizard snapped.

"No, Master," replied Gerr, his voice grovelling to the dark figure above him.

"I hadn't finished with you," he growled. He bent down until his face was close to Gerr's. "With a whole army of ravens after them they are *still* free." He shook his head in disbelief. "When you find them and kill them you must let me know straight away... bring me evidence."

"We will, Master," said Gerr bowing his head.

"And bring the evidence to Old Howard's House. I am going there now... I have something I *must* attend to there."

He looked out through the driving snow and into Summertime Kingdom. This time Gerr waited to be dismissed.

"Now go," the wizard hissed.

Gerr was greatly relieved that the conversation with the Troubler was over. He took off and flew out of the cloud. The blizzard swept him sideways and along the border and he dropped down to look for Keg. The snow was deep and he spotted him lying on his back on the surface with wings outspread and snow beginning to cover him.

"Keg!" he called out.

There was no response. He swooped down beside him and landed, his feet slipping into the snow but his body holding, like a seabird sitting on water.

"Keg!" he shouted, blinking as snow blew into his face.

Keg's eyes were open and unseeing. His feet were pointing up, the claws curled in tension. The snow was whitening his feathers and beginning to cover him. Gerr dropped his head closer and saw Keg's chest heave. He was alive.

The chest dropped again, the claws relaxed and then he was still. Keg had breathed his last breath. The blow had killed him.

Fighting the fierce icy wind, Gerr took to the air and managed to turn towards the border. In a moment he was in the still warm air of Summertime Kingdom and speeding back towards the wood.

The Troubler watched him go. Then he turned, whispered a few words of command to the cloud and in a moment it was rising rapidly and carrying him back to Old Howard's House.

At this moment Iker awoke. He was the General's nephew and the youngest bird in the army. Although he was fully grown, his black plumage still displayed the slightly fluffy look of a fledgling. He had been sleeping soundly in a giant redwood tree at the edge of Duran Forest since the group of thirteen ravens, led by Sergeant Forr, had left him there. He was astonished to find that he was alone and jerked his head this way and that looking for the other ravens.

His breath caught and shallowed. He was beginning to panic. His mind flashed with thoughts. Why did they fly off without him? Could they have left him here by mistake? He was puzzled.

"What's going on?" he said aloud and then he called out, "Where are you? Forr? Razz? Akk?"

There was no answer.

"This isn't funny!" he called out.

Silence.

The truth gradually dawned on him and he shook his head in dismay. They had flown off without him and left him behind on purpose. He remembered the mistakes he had made when they were carrying the great dog Jamaar on the blanket and they had been very cross with him then, but these were just mistakes; he had tried his best.

He flapped up to the top of the tree and gazed around, wondering what to do.

When Gerr arrived back at the wood, he was gliding above the tree tops when suddenly he heard a huge outburst of cackling from below. He swooped down through the branches towards the great commotion. The ravens were swarming around a tree and just above the ground.

"What's happened?" he called out.

"We've found the entrance to a tunnel!" replied a raven.

"Gather!" screeched the General.

This created even more commotion as they did not know where to gather so they twisted and turned in the air, bumping into each other. Several of them called out, "Where?"

The General was standing on some grass by the tree.

"Down here," he commanded.

They descended like a mass of black falling leaves and in a moment they were surrounding the General, transforming the green grass into a carpet of black. Gerr landed beside the General who walked towards the exposed roots of the tree. The other ravens moved aside to form a pathway as they walked through. The General hopped up onto a root and Gerr followed.

"Who found the entrance?" demanded the General.

"I did," replied Razz proudly.

He was standing near the front of the great crowd of birds. The other ravens looked at him and murmured to each other.

"Well?" asked the General, "Where is it then?"

"Here," replied Razz, "Right here."

He pecked the grass twice with his large bill. The General's compass swung as if in excitement.

"Where?" demanded the General.

"Look," said Razz, pointing down with his shiny black bill, "There's a line, I can just see it under the grass, and it's straight until there." He pushed a few ravens out of his way. "Then it goes along there. It's a rectangle. It's an entrance for certain... the entrance to a tunnel."

"I can't see it," the General said.

"No, not from there you can't," Razz stated.

"Go and have a look, Gerr," said the General.

Gerr jumped off the root and flapped down beside Razz.

"I can see it!" he exclaimed walking in a straight line and then turning a corner, "It's like a line in the grass... Razz is right."

"Excellent," the General nodded, "It explains how they disappeared. They are down there... no doubt. So... quick... open it up and let's get after them. They'll be trapped like rats in a sewer! Open it!"

"How, sir?" asked Gerr.

"Female Squadron..." the General boomed, "Who's the leader?"

"They haven't got one, sir," Gerr replied.

"What!? Why not?"

"Because you haven't appointed one since Searle deserted, sir."

"Oh, yes," the General nodded, "All that stupid business with Searle and Urrg... OK then, appoint someone, Gerr."

Gerr puffed out his chest with pride and looked around with a superior air.

"Tull," he announced. Tull looked up at him timidly. "I appoint you leader of the Female Squadron and your first duty is to get that entrance open... and make it quick!"

Tull looked stunned.

"Yes sir," she said hesitantly, "Females..."

"You can't command from there," interrupted the General, "Up here... on this root. And speak louder!"

Tull hopped up reluctantly onto a root just below the General and Gerr.

"Females," she said in a slightly louder voice, "Line up beside the entrance rectongle."

"Rec*tangle!*" corrected Gerr loudly.

After a bustle of activity the males had moved back and the females, over fifty of them, had taken up their positions around the entrance. The General snapped crossly at them.

"Not on the door... get the other side of the line! How can you lift it if you're standing on it?!"

They quickly hopped across the line and then Tull continued nervously.

"Females... er... females... dig away some of that earth around the entrance."

"Quickly now!" shouted Gerr.

Bits of earth and grass flew into the air as they dug furiously with their beaks and clawed feet.

"Stop!" shouted the General.

The General and Gerr both looked down at Tull who looked up at them.

"Go on then!" snapped the General at her.

"Oh... yes..." she said, "Good... good. Now... er... beaks under the... um... the... um... under there."

They forced their beaks under the door.

"Now... all together... *lift!*" she said.

Nothing happened.

"Try harder," the General shouted, "Now... *lift!*"

The birds strained even harder but still the door would not budge.

"It's too heavy," said one bird pulling her beak out quickly, "We'll break our beaks."

The General scowled at her and then screeched at them all.

"Try harder... now, all together..."

"Stop!" interrupted Razz from the crowd of males, "Try sliding it across."

"What?" exclaimed the General, and then crossly "Who interrupted me?"

"Me," stated Razz, who seemed to have no fear of the pompous General, "It may be a sliding door... try sliding it."

Tull put her head on one side and looked quizzical for a second before announcing to her squadron, "It may be a sliding door... try sliding it. You lot, at that end, push."

The door jerked and slid open smoothly and the ravens on the other side scurried out of the way. One was not quite fast enough and lost a tail feather as the door caught it.

"Excellent!" exclaimed the General, "Gerr you lead the male squadron in. Find the enemy and show no mercy. Then report to me!"

Gerr jumped off the root and glided down through the open entrance followed by the great mass of male ravens. In a few seconds they were gone, leaving the females chattering and complaining to each other about why the males always got the best jobs. A moment later the male ravens tumbled out of the tunnel in a muddle. Gerr emerged from the centre of them and landed beside the General again.

"What's happening?!" the General blurted out.

"It's too dark," replied Gerr, "Can't see a thing down there, sir."

At this the General's black compass hanging around his neck jumped excitedly and began to glow. The General was still unaware that living inside the compass was a small two-tailed scorpion. Now the compass was shining brightly and he looked at it with surprise.

"I'll lead," the General announced.

He swooped down into the tunnel and all the males followed like a great swarm of bees.

Harris descended from high in the clear blue sky. The warm morning sun graced the land below like the gentle massage of soft hands soothing the darkness of night away. As he fell towards Wizard Elzaphan's Castle he was feeling pleased that he was carrying good news. He knew that the great wizard was concerned about the group of travellers he had dispatched on a journey which was both perilous and challenging.

The golden eagle glided towards the front entrance of the castle, skimming just above some trees, over the drawbridge and then landing on his guard-post by the door. Quint greeted him from her post.

"Harris," she said warmly, "I'm glad to see you back safe and sound."

"I hope you never doubted," he commented.

"I never doubted you, Harris," she said, "But I kept thinking of you fighting with over a hundred ravens... did you see them?"

"Yes, and I flew through them! Ha! They are stupid birds... cunning, yes... evil, yes... but stupid. I was gone before they knew what had happened!"

"And what about our travelling friends?"

"They're alright," said Harris happily, "They're fine. They found a tunnel entrance and I saw them entering it and closing the door. I must report it to Wizard Elzaphan... he'll be pleased."

"Yes," agreed Quint, "He's waiting for you and hoping for good news."

At that moment the door opened and tall figure of Wizard Elzaphan appeared. His deep blue robe fluttered slightly as the breeze caught it. He stepped out.

"Hello, Harris," he said, looking at him from under bushy white eyebrows, "It's great to see you back. Did you find them?"

"Yes, I did," Harris nodded.

He then described everything that he had seen.

"That sounds promising," the wizard commented, "So they found a tunnel did they? That must have been Tally... his grandfather Hawkeye gave him a tunnel map of the kingdom. But do you think the ravens saw them?"

"No," answered Harris, "I'm sure they couldn't have seen them from where they were. They were way above the trees."

"Good... good," said the great wizard, "The perfect escape! As long as they know where the tunnel leads. We just have to trust and hope. But thanks Harris, you've done a good job."

"What shall I do now, sir?" asked Harris.

"Could you look out please from the East Turret? And check on Cedric every so often... he's on the West Turret. You know his eyes are not so good now, although he has his squirrels Relly and Ho with him, and they both

see well. Let me know if you spot anything unusual...
anything at all."

The General led the male Squadron through the
gloomy darkness of the tunnel. The tunnel was wide
enough for three or four ravens to fly side by side, so the
General had organized them into a block. There were three
across, four downwards and four to five behind each other.
The black compass projected an eerie glow which lit the
grey rock walls dimly in front of them. Gerr was beside
the General. The close mass of birds flew like a shoal of
fish in water with the swish of their wings echoing along
the tunnel.

They flew quickly. Many of them grumbled and
complained because the light was dim and they kept
bumping into each other, but they were so skilful they
could correct their flight with tiny movements of their
wings.

All went well until the tunnel narrowed slightly at
one point and one raven clipped a wing on the wall. He
veered into the pack which instantly caused chaos, sending
another raven into a spin who then crashed into several
others. With the chain effect the whole group dropped
quickly and nearly hit the floor, but somehow they
managed to swerve upwards just in time.

"Get back in formation!" boomed the General.

"Back in formation!" echoed Gerr.

In a few seconds order was regained.

"Who did that?" asked the General.

Several ravens piped up, "Yug did, sir," they said.

"I'll see you later, Yug," the General snapped crossly, "Now, no more mistakes!"

They flew on in silence.

After a while the General spoke, "Where are they, Gerr?"

"We'll find them soon, sir," Gerr replied, "Maybe around the next bend..."

"You're right, Gerr, and so we must be ready... but keep quiet so they don't hear us coming."

He turned his head back and announced in a soft voice to the birds right behind him, "All ready for attack! Pass it on."

The message was passed back through the flock.

"Message from the General: All ready for attack!"

It finally reached the last row of ravens at the back.

"Sausage from the General for the teddy bear's snack!"

"What?!" asked several of them together.

"Teddy bear's snack?" queried another, "What does *that* mean?"

"Doesn't matter," said another, "If we're getting a sausage who cares?"

They flew on around next turn and then the next. After a few more turns the General was getting anxious.

"I can hear sounds," said Gerr softly.

"What?" asked the General.

"I can hear sounds, sir. Around that next bend."

The General slowed and listened.

"You're right, Gerr," he whispered turning his head to speak to his army. The birds behind bumped into each other again and for a moment there was confusion.

"Sort yourselves out!" he snapped crossly, "And brace yourselves for attack. This is it!"

"What about the sausage?" called out one raven from the back.

"Be quiet," snapped the General, "No talking in the ranks!"

"What if..." Gerr began, now whispering, "What if it's a trap, sir?"

"But, Gerr," the General whispered back impatiently, "They don't even know we're coming!" The compass jiggled around his neck. "But... OK... just in case we'd better take care." He turned to the birds behind him, "Land!" he ordered in a whisper.

The message was passed back and after a lot of jostling for position all the ravens had landed and were waiting eagerly for action. The General and Gerr were close to the bend.

"The sounds have stopped, Gerr," whispered the General, putting his head on one side.

"That confirms it then. It's them... just around that bend. But they've probably heard us."

The General jerked his beak forwards to instruct Gerr and the others to follow him. They walked as quietly as they could. The only sound was the soft clicking of their claws on the rock floor. As they approached the bend they slowed and then stopped when they got there. The General stretched his neck and peeped around. The compass shed its dim light.

"What!" boomed the General.

All the ravens jumped in shock. They had been waiting on tenterhooks for the shout of 'attack' and when they heard the General's shout it sparked them into action. The ones at the back pushed forwards, some taking to the air, and suddenly there was a great mass of ravens flying around the bend.

"Stop!" shouted the General.

"Stop!" shouted Gerr.

But it was too late. The squadron was on the move, like a wave on the ocean driving forwards. A moment later there was an explosion of confused cackling. They had flown into some steps which led up to the way out at the end of the tunnel. The ones at the front cried in pain as they hit the steps while the ones behind bumped into them. The scene was a muddle of black flapping wings and tumbling ravens just visible by the light of the General's glowing compass.

The General and Gerr looked on in astonishment.

"Where are they?" the General snapped, "Where are the enemy? And what were the sounds you heard?"

"I don't know, sir."

The General shook his head, "Useless. Those sounds must have been something."

Razz appeared out of the mass of ravens who were mostly on their feet now, some on the steps and some on the floor preening their feathers.

"The sounds were an echo," Razz stated sulkily, "The echo of our own sounds. They must've got out... up there." He nodded his head up the steps towards the door above.

The General looked up and immediately took off. The compass swung around his neck and seemed to glow even brighter. He landed on a wooden-boarded area at the top of the steps and gazed up at the door above his head. Gerr landed beside him followed by Razz, Sergeant Forr and a few other ravens.

"How does it open?" asked the General.

They started walking around looking for a lever or something to open the door.

"You lot," shouted the General to the ravens below, "Some of you come up here and help."

They flocked upwards. The General looked alarmed.

"No!" he shouted, "Not all of you!"

This again caused a scramble as they fell back and jostled for places on the rock floor, flapping their wings and cawing at each other.

"Sergeant Forr," called out the General, looking for him in the mass of birds below. The black compass glowed brighter. "Select a dozen birds and send them up here."

A few seconds later twelve ravens flew up and landed underneath the door. They tried in vain to find the way to open it.

"OK," announced the General angrily looking down at the ravens below who all looked up at him, "OK. This is a waste of time. They have escaped through there," he jerked his head crossly upwards, "And now we find that the enemy have damaged the lever or whatever to open it so that we can't follow. Cunning. So we'll have to fly back. We'll fly back and out of this stupid tunnel... then we'll hunt them down."

He paused and looked down at them expecting a response.

"Well?" he asked.

"Yes sir!" one of them said and gradually the others joined in, which just made a muddled noise.

"Try again," the General snapped.

"Yes sir!" they all said together.

"That's better. But I'm not happy with the general level of conduct in the Male Squadron. I expect obedience and higher standards... your flying has become sloppy. You came through the tunnel like a flock of clumsy geese. It's ridiculous! What would the Master say?"

A few of them shifted uncomfortably on their feet.

"OK then. Be told... and learn. Now, we'll fly back in an orderly fashion..."

"But sir..." began Razz from below.

"So, follow me," the General commanded as he jumped into the air.

Gerr was right by his side and the others on the wooden area flapped into the air behind him. They were followed by all the rest.

"When we get out..." began the General to Gerr.

"But we won't know..." said Razz who was just behind the General.

The General glanced behind and snapped impatiently, "You! Stop interrupting me all the time. And call me 'sir'."

"The trouble is..." Razz continued, "We won't know where to look, will we?"

"At the end of the tunnel, of course," the General snapped.

"And where's that?" asked Razz.

"We don't know yet," the General replied, trying to cover up his mistake, "We have to find it, don't we? Work out where it should be. Gerr... what do you suggest?"

"Let's try and remember the direction, sir, as we fly."

"But it's so bendy," the General complained, "It's frustrating. But, yes, we must try."

They stopped chatting and tried to concentrate on the direction as they twisted and turned along the tunnel.

Further along the tunnel, in front of them and around several bends, a crack of light pierced the darkness. The pale golden ray spread to flood the tunnel with a gentle light which glinted here and there on the damp rocky walls.

"They're gone," whispered Amalek.

Seph had opened the lid of his magic oval box, first a little and then fully, letting the light shine out again. Lazuli had been filling the entrance to a tunnel which forked off the main one. She was sideways on, and her grey wrinkled side looked just like a rocky wall. The gap through her legs looked like a dark, shadowy hollow.

It had been Simron's idea. He was concerned about the possibility of the ravens finding the entrance and then following them. As soon as they came to the fork in the tunnel he thought of it. He stood in the tunnel and weighed up the situation, looking first at the wall and then at Lazuli. He was a Master of Disguise and this was his art. His talent for disguising himself or others was stunning.

With Lazuli filling the entrance they had all waited behind her, looking out through her legs into the pitch black darkness. After a while they had heard the ravens approaching, at first a distant swishing of wings and then their voices. By the dim light of the General's compass they had watched them fly past; ghostly black shapes in the darkness. The ravens were totally unaware that they had been passing another tunnel entrance.

The six friends waited again until they were sure the ravens were not returning. Amalek poked her head out underneath Lazuli's belly. For a moment she listened.

"There's no sign of them at all," she said.

Lazuli relaxed and stepped away. The light grew.

"We'd better get moving then," said Joog, "The sooner we leave those ravens behind..."

"Sshh," whispered Amalek, "Hang on..."

She looked to her left along the dark tunnel and listened.

"I can hear something," she whispered to the others behind her, "I think I can hear their wings."

She stepped back.

"Quick," whispered Joog to Lazuli.

At that moment the swishing sounds became louder as the ravens came around a bend.

Lazuli moved forwards and Seph closed his magic box. The light dwindled to nothing.

"What was that, Gerr?" asked the General.

"What, sir?"

"I saw something," the General said, "A light... ahead... there. It's gone now... but I'm sure."

The compass hanging around his neck glowed brighter.

"Land now," ordered the General.

"Land now," echoed Gerr.

The ravens at the front descended and the others followed until they had all landed just past Lazuli.

"There's nothing here," said the General looking around, "But... I'm sure I saw a light... search the area, Gerr."

Gerr turned to all the ravens behind him, "Search the area!" he commanded.

The ravens started jerking their heads around and walking in all directions. Sergeant Forr was following the wall back when he stopped suddenly and tilted his head sideways. He was gazing at Lazuli's foot. Simron put his hands on Amalek's and Seph's shoulders and gave a gentle squeeze. The friends were looking through the gap in Lazuli's legs and could just see the raven by the light of the General's compass. They held their breath. Amalek and Seph felt their hearts pounding.

Forr stepped closer and pecked at the foot, hitting a toenail. Lazuli did not move. Forr pecked again. Then he lifted his head and looked straight through the gap at Amalek. He squinted his eyes, trying to see into the deep darkness.

"Complete waste of time!" announced Razz loudly.

Forr turned to look at him and so did all the others.

"There's some sort of..." Forr began.

The General was further along the tunnel and did not hear him, but he had heard Razz.

"Call me *sir!*" he boomed, "And keep searching."

"Sir?" shouted Razz, "All this searching is a complete waste of time. It was just a reflection."

The General was seething with anger at Razz upstaging him but nevertheless he was interested by the idea.

"Reflection, eh?" the General looked thoughtful, "Well, maybe, but a reflection of what? If we find that out we may find the enemy."

Razz sighed. "We're in a tunnel... there's nowhere to go!" he exclaimed sarcastically, "Where are they?" and he looked up and down the tunnel mockingly, "They aren't here at all... they are up there somewhere." He jerked his beak upwards.

"OK... OK," the General said slowly.

He could not allow Razz to treat him with such disrespect and he would deal with that later. At this moment, the most important thing was to find the enemy. He could not deny the sense of what Razz was saying and his compass had started jiggling excitedly around his neck.

"We'll search first just to make sure."

The ravens turned away and began looking again. Forr peered again into the darkness, which he thought was a hole in the wall.

Razz began shouting again, "But... this is ridiculous." All the ravens stopped once more. "There's nowhere for them to be, is there? There's just rock. Why are we looking here? Are you mad? See that damp bit there?" He nodded at the tunnel floor in front of them. "It was the light from *your own* compass reflecting."

"OK," the General snapped, "That's enough!"

"Which means," Razz continued, "That if we waste any more time here the enemy will be harder to find when we get out and start *really* looking for them. Right now they are getting further and further away!"

The General lifted his voice, "All ravens continue to the end of the tunnel..." and then he shouted so loudly that it echoed for a few seconds around the tunnel, "In an *orderly* fashion."

Sergeant Forr was still standing right next to Lazuli. He turned and stared unseeingly into the darkness and at Amalek. Then he was gone, joining the back of the group of ravens as they took off.

Old Howard's House was cold. The ever-deepening snow lay thickly on the roof and window sills as well as piling up against the window panes. Icicles had gathered along the guttering, long frozen fingers stretching downwards. The relentless descent of snowflakes had smoothed the garden to gentle curves and gifted the trees with winter coats of white.

Inside the downstairs room at the back of the house, it was almost silent. The only sounds were the slow breathing of the Dark Wizard Troubler and the muffled howl of the fierce wind outside.

The wizard sat in Old Howard's shabby armchair with his head resting on the high back. He was still. His breath clouded from his nostrils and momentarily hung in the cold air, dispersing a second later. The chill in the room seeped in from the arctic conditions outside but it was also the result of his cold, mean heart which was constantly intent upon his desires.

He was tired. It had drained his energy to travel in the cloud. He tried to sleep but his mind was turning excitedly with thoughts of something that stopped him relaxing. He was waiting for a visitor.

Suddenly he lifted his head to listen; he heard something moving outside. He gripped the arms of the chair and pulled himself onto his feet. After pausing to listen again, he strode out of the room, up the stairs and into a back room, his heavy boots echoing on the wooden floor.

He put his face close to the window until his nose touched. He squinted but still he could not see out clearly through the swirling, frosty patterns so he grabbed the handle and pushed. It was stuck, frozen by the icy conditions. He rattled it angrily but still it would not open. Glancing behind him, he stepped back, grabbed a nearby chair and swung it into the windowpane. The glass smashed and immediately snow swept in like a swarm of white bees. He stepped forwards again, his boots crunching on the splinters of glass, and looked out of the window and into the blizzard. He caught his breath with excitement; his visitor was here, struggling through the thick snow in the garden and towards the house.

In a few seconds he was down the stairs and flinging the door open. When he saw that his visitor was carrying something he smiled; a cunning twisted smile of selfish glee.

"Come in," he said.

Jamaar came round with the sound of the sea in his ears and felt confused. He lifted his head, felt a sharp pain in his jaw and dropped his head down again. Where was he? He opened his stinging eyes for a second but the light dazzled him, so he quickly closed them again.

He was by the sea. He heard the sound of waves, the great waves of a mighty ocean washing up on a stony beach then falling back and dragging the pebbles against each other. The smell of salt filled the air which rushed by on the off-shore wind, blowing hard in his face. The side he was lying on was cold and wet but on his other side his fur had dried and he felt the warmth of the sun.

He tentatively moved his jaw and felt the sharp pain again.

Where was he? How did he get here? He forced his eyes open and lifted his head.

After a few moments he became used to the light, and looked up at a high chalk-white cliff which towered above him. He tried to stand up but he felt weak and fell back again, closing his stinging eyes. He lay there and tried to gather his strength together. Then he tried again.

This time he managed it and stood unsteadily with his padded paws on the pebbles. After a few moments he felt stronger and shook his wet fur.

He tried to remember what had happened. His mind was blank.

Then it gradually came back to him. He had fallen into a well, although he could not remember how. Had he slipped accidentally or had he been pushed?

"Think," he said aloud to himself, "Think."

He was with his master, the Dark Wizard Troubler, and they had thrown the King and Queen down the well. He remembered the snow, lots of snow, and the silver walls of the well; yes, it was The Silver Well. But the last thing he could remember was slipping off the edge of the well, and then... nothing. He must have hit his jaw as he fell in.

He had become victim to the same fate that he handed out to the King and Queen, and now he was in this strange place having somehow survived it. But where was he and how had he got here?

He wondered if the King and Queen could have survived too. But then no, they were trapped in the spell whereas he was free. He looked around for them but all he could see was the pebbly beach sloping down to the vast expanse of rough ocean which stretched out to the gently-curving horizon. He turned back to the cliff and looked up, squinting into the bright sun. The wall of chalk rose majestically above him with scattered patches of grass and other plants.

He looked back and straight out to sea. He could see an island on the horizon. Looking further north he could see what looked like mist hovering above the water and dispersing as it rose into the air. He realized he had been here before.

He looked up at the cliff. Yes, he had been up there, at the top, and looking out to sea. He remembered seeing the island and the mist. This was the Great Synamian Ocean and he was in the Kingdom Of Moone. The mist was actually steam rising from the Great Crack to the Centre of Ruddha which ran from Summertime Kingdom, across the Kingdom of Moone and then under the ocean.

He knew he had a journey to make. First and foremost he needed to get back to his master. The bond between a dog and his master is very strong and he felt the pull of this more than anything else now. He had to go west to find the wizard again and would head inland using the sun to navigate.

Then he noticed that something was missing; the black compass that had been hanging around his neck before he fell into the well was gone. He was disappointed because he was just getting to know it and what it could do; it had become his guide. He was sure there was more to discover about it, more powers that he had not found yet. Now he may never find out.

Looking around, he thought at first he was trapped on the thin strip of pebble beach with the cliff towering above him on one side and the huge powerful ocean on the other. Then he noticed a zigzag path which worked its way up the steep chalky rock. Jamaar walked over the pebbles and began to climb. He was still weak and had to rest every so often but gradually he worked his way up the cliff.

At the top he sat down to rest. The offshore wind blew harder here, ruffling his fur from behind. In front of him, beneath the clear blue sky, was an extraordinary scene. This was not how he remembered the Kingdom Of Moone. When he was here a few years before, it was a green land with many trees, bushes and grass everywhere.

He stared in amazement at a desolate desert landscape. Gently undulating waves of sand swept away from him and into the distance. It was a windswept, barren place which looked uninhabited.

There were occasional trees dotted here and there in the sand but they bore no leaves. They were dark lifeless trunks of rotting wood, crumbling away under the severe elements. What was left of them was leaning away from the sea winds at extraordinary angles. There were a few thin prickly cacti also tilting away from the prevailing wind.

Close by, just along the cliff edge, were the ruined remains of a building. It was just a pile of rubble with one line of decaying wall left standing only three or four bricks high. As he looked the wind gusted, catching some of the powdery remains and throwing up a small cloud of dust. The wind whipped it away.

He felt possessed by two strong urges. Firstly he wanted to be back with his master, and secondly he was hungry and thirsty. His stomach rumbled loudly, complaining that a meal was long overdue.

He was feeling stronger now so he stood up and as he did, something caught his eye. Something moved. Anything that moved might be food - a small animal maybe. In one movement he turned and instinctively pounced. He was already jumping when he saw that it was a small two-tailed scorpion spreading its wings. He knew how dangerous they could be but it was too late to stop. His front paws landed first, his heavy weight pushing into the sand and spraying it up in front of him. He lifted his front paws carefully one by one and looked all around the area. He could see nothing. It must have buried itself under the sand.

He turned back and looked across the great area of desert. His powerful legs were energised by his desire to return to the Troubler. He broke into a trot and headed west.

He felt the nagging feeling in the back of his mind that someone or something else was here; that he was being watched. He paused to glance nervously all around but saw nothing, so he began to trot again.

His paws kicked sand up behind him as he headed off across the wide lonely expanse of pale yellow sand dunes.

The Female Squadron had waited around the entrance to the tunnel while the males were gone. They sat down on the grass and grumbled about being left behind. Tull perched on the root above feeling very nervous about her new appointment. She watched the others and tried to look as if she was in charge.

A few of the female ravens stood right at the edge of the entrance looking down and so when the Male Squadron shot out of the tunnel like a mass of black bats swarming out of a cave, they jerked their heads back to avoid being hit. A couple of them were too slow and cried out as they were knocked out of the way.

The Male Squadron circled around the tree and then landed, the males mixing in with the females and the General pushing Tull off the root to make room for Gerr and himself.

"Now, Gerr," said the General, "Which way?"

Gerr looked around, "Which way for what, sir?"

The General shook his head in frustration and then shouted, "The enemy!"

At this the ravens on the grass glanced around in alarm thinking that the enemy was nearby. A few of them took to the air and started flying away and calling out, "Look out... the enemy!"

Some called out "Where?!" and "I can see them in the trees!" and "Get them!" and "Where are they?!"

"Stop!" boomed the General.

They all stopped and the birds in flight landed again.

"What are you doing?!" he shouted at them, "The enemy isn't *here*. I haven't given any orders, have I?"

Meanwhile Gerr was looking around nervously in a random way.

The General glared at Gerr, "Come on, Gerr. I'm relying upon you. Where is the other end of that tunnel?"

"Er..." Gerr began, "Er... that way, I think... no, that way..."

"Well," the General snapped, "Make up your mind!"

"Where's the enemy?" called out one of the females.

The General looked down at his army spread out on the grass. Some of them were now under another tree and pecking the ground for bugs to eat.

"Has anyone seen Iker?" he shouted.

No one replied.

"Sergeant Forr... where are you?"

Forr's heart dropped with fear and he huddled to the ground. Several ravens around him shouted, "He's here, sir."

Forr realised he could not hide and bobbed his head up.

"Where's Iker?" the General asked him abruptly.

Forr looked around innocently, "Isn't he here, sir?"

Razz's voice rose again from the group, "Shouldn't we search for the enemy now? They'll get away again."

"He's right," said Gerr.

"OK, OK," the General agreed, "But Gerr, I want Iker found... you investigate and let me know."

"Yes sir," said Gerr.

While the General was still trying to work out how to proceed and was discussing it with Gerr, Sergeant Forr shuffled over to the entrance and thought about what he had seen in the tunnel. He wondered about the dark hole in the wall. Perhaps it was more than just a small hole; maybe it led into a cave and the enemy was hiding in there. He had needed more time to look but then the General shouted his order to leave the tunnel and he had obeyed.

On an impulse he decided to go back and have another quick look just in case. He would not tell anyone. If he found something then he would report it to the General and he would be a hero. He was in trouble with the General already for losing Iker and he was afraid of being demoted but if he was the one to find the enemy, it would make up for it.

After a quick glance around to make sure none of the others were looking at him he dropped into the entrance and disappeared.

The rest of the army were still looking like an untidy shamble of birds rather than an organised army. The compass jiggled around the General's neck. He realised he needed to regain control.

"All of you," he screeched, "Males and females... the whole army... gather together as before."

They all looked at him. He grabbed the black chain in his beak and the compass hung in front of him. He flicked it with a claw. It made a ring and then spun, flashing in the sunlight. The compass had become a symbol of his power as leader and this ritual was his way of reminding them. It worked perfectly and in a few moments they were all gathered in front of him and looking up. He surveyed his army for a moment and when he spoke he sounded calm and matter-of-fact.

"Now... that's better. Never forget you are in an army under *my* command. What happened just now was... ridiculous... a ridiculous display of unnecessary panic... a total waste of time and energy." He was starting to get angry again and his voice was rising, "Always... *always*... wait for my commands!" Then he shouted, "Understand?"

"Yes sir!" they chorused.

This response satisfied him. He felt under control again.

"We should be searching," Razz called out.

"Quiet in the ranks!" blasted the General.

He took a deep breath and then he continued calmly.

"So, what do we do now? The enemy have somehow escaped again... it seems incredible, but yes, they escaped into that tunnel." He pointed to the entrance with his beak.

"Are you sure?" called out Razz.

"Of course I'm sure," the General replied crossly, "Where else could they go? Think about it. And don't interrupt... *and* call me 'sir'!"

There was no response from Razz so the General glared at him and then, feeling he had made his point, continued addressing them all.

"And then... and then the enemy slipped out at the other end. Now we don't know where they are." He spread his wings in an expression of despair. "We don't know where the entrance is because Gerr's memory is too poor to remember."

Gerr looked upset at being blamed. The General continued.

"We'll have to..."

He stopped suddenly because the compass around his neck had started jumping around excitedly. All the ravens looked on in wonder. Then something happened that had never happened before. The compass made a small high-pitched screech. The General jumped with shock.

"What's that, Gerr?"

Gerr was staring at his compass and so were all the ravens. The screech had not been loud but because it was so shrill they had all heard it.

"It's that, sir," replied Gerr nodding at the black compass.

"I know that!" the General snapped.

As they all watched, the compass stopped jiggling around and began to swing.

"What's it doing, sir?" Gerr asked.

"It makes movements to help, you know, to tell me what to do. But why did it make that noise?" The General looked down at it swinging as it hung around his neck, "It's never done that before."

"It sounded urgent, sir. Perhaps it knows where they are."

"Well, that's good *if* you're right," the General nodded, "But that ridiculous noise, Gerr?" Then he snapped crossly, "I hope it doesn't do that again."

"Look..." said Gerr excitedly, "It's swinging to the north... is it telling us to go north, sir?"

"I don't know..." the General replied.

"Maybe it means south!" Razz shouted out, "Or east... or west... who knows?"

The compass was swinging to and fro.

"OK," the General said looking down at it, "We'll start searching anyway... and we'll go north *and* south and spread out as we go. That should cover it. We'll split up... the Male Squadron south, across the border, in my opinion unlikely, but we'll try... and the Female Squadron, led by Tull, go north."

"Tull," the General called out, "Take your squadron and search to the north." He looked around for Tull and then spotted her trying to look as if she had not heard him. "Tull, get up on this root!"

Tull flapped up sheepishly.

"Er... Female Squadron," she said, "Attention! Let's go!"

The females all took off with Tull following and trying to catch them up. They rose between the trees and headed north.

"Male Squadron!" screeched the General, "Our task is more difficult... more challenging, because we are heading across the border and into the snow. We need to stay in close formation. OK?"

"Yes, sir," they shouted.

"Attennnnnnnnnnn...tion!" the General's voice was so loud that it echoed around the wood, *"Let's go!"*

With a hurried flapping of wings the great cloud of ravens rose above the trees. They were excited and ready for action and a minute later they were passing across the border and plunging into the driving snow.

Chapter 3

~ Gratch ~

Sergeant Forr had flown swiftly back down the tunnel. When he turned the first corner, the darkness began to deepen and when he glided around the next, he could see nothing at all. He quickly landed and wondered what to do. He was not far from the hole he had seen earlier, so he decided to follow the wall around the next bend and try to find it. If they were hiding there he would hear them.

He walked carefully with one wing lifted slightly and touching the wall until something made him stop still. He heard voices!

He crept on. The voices grew louder. He turned the next bend, saw a pale light ahead and stopped. At that distance it was hard to hear what was being said. He listened for a while, straining to pick out words but the echo muffled the speech into a blur.

Suddenly a head poked out from the hole and looked one way and then the other. It was the enemy! His heart thumped with excitement. He must tell the General.

He crept back until he could see again and then took to the air. He flew out of the tunnel, excited by the information he was carrying and ready for the General's praise.

They had all gone.

He landed on the grass to work out what to do. He had just found the enemy. This was the most important thing he had ever done. But now the army had gone, so there was no one to tell. The enemy might be on the move right now, escaping along the tunnel. He had to make a snap decision; either he could try to find the army and maybe lose the enemy or he could track the enemy before they got away.

Impulsively, he flew back into the tunnel again. He turned the bends and began walking in the same place. Then he saw the light, now paler than before and gradually dimming. He jumped into the air and flew towards it. When he landed he was amazed at what he found. The light was shining from a tunnel leading off the main one. Where had this tunnel come from all of a sudden? Earlier there had been just a small dark hole.

Looking towards the light he saw silhouetted figures; an elephant, a bird in flight, a child. It was definitely the enemy. They were moving away. To attack by himself would be foolish, so he decided he would keep his distance and keep them in sight.

He crept into the tunnel and followed them.

High up, at the top of the massive redwood tree, Iker was watching. He had seen the Female Squadron rise out of the wood and fly north. He was just about to fly towards them when the males took off and headed south. He decided to follow the males and so he left his high perch and flew after them as fast as he could. He was desperate to catch up with them but they were moving too fast. Just when he thought he was closing slightly, they hit the wall of falling snow at the border and disappeared.

Iker followed them in. The blast of the icy blizzard took him by surprise. He was not as strong as the others yet, and in a moment, the wind caught his wings and he was swept along the border. He tried to regain control, struggling, flapping and fighting the blizzard as he tumbled. It was a battle he could not win.

He cried out as he felt a sharp pain in one of his wings as the wind forced it back and across his body. Then he hit a tree. His head glanced off the bark and he fell as limp as an autumn leaf into the deep snow. He lay there unconscious.

"You've done well Gratch," said the Dark Wizard Troubler leaning forward in Old Howard's armchair with his black eyes fixed intently on his visitor.

The wizard's injured hand was wrapped tightly in a white bandage. Blood was seeping through from the cut which showed as a plume of dark grey in the dull room, muted to a colourless gloom by the wizard's evil presence. His twisted craving to possess the kingdom infected his surroundings wherever he went. Cold gripped the air, touching everything with icy fingers.

"You've done very well," he continued, "It's a long journey... how long did it take?"

The answer was a deep rumbling, as if coming up from the very centre of the earth.

"Days. But you were expecting me?"

The wizard nodded. "Yes... I have scouts you know; ravens. You were seen by one yesterday in Toblar heading in this direction. And it saw what you were carrying. It's just as well you had that with you, otherwise you'd have been frozen by my spell at the border."

The wizard glanced across the room and laughed with glee. The corner was absorbed in an unnatural darkness, a dull glow of black, and just like a mist that shrouds a field or a wood, the corner was completely hidden from view.

"I thought I may never see it again," he said, "But how did you get it?"

The Komodo dragon smiled with sinister pride. His forked tongue flicked out of his huge mouth. Bacteria-filled saliva dribbled out and onto his scaly skin and a line of it hung down and shook as he spoke.

"I knew where to look. Before you left, Horrik told me what had happened."

"Ah..." the wizard nodded, "Of course... Horrik. But Horrik was tethered... when did you talk to her?"

"Just before you both left," replied Gratch in a deep growl, "You left her tied up outside before you started your journey. Remember?"

The wizard looked thoughtful, "Yes... yes. I do remember."

"I wanted to work for you then," Gratch growled, "And that's why I stole it for you. But then, when I'd got it, you'd already left. So I decided to follow. I want to work for you, Master."

"You can... and you've proved your worth already."

The wizard thought for a moment. Eerie silence filled the room.

"And Horrik told you where we were going?" he asked.

"Yes," said Gratch, "She was very upset you know, when you accused her of trying to escape from you and you wouldn't believe her story. Then you punished her and tethered her with that black chain. She hated you for that…"

The wizard glared crossly and raised his voice. "Are you criticizing me?"

"No, Master," Gratch grovelled, his tongue snaking out and in again.

"Good," the wizard hissed. Then he leant forward, his icy stare fixed on the dragon. "Good. Because you're working for me now and so you treat *me* with respect."

"Of course," Gratch replied, shifting uncomfortably, "I am fortunate to be in your service. I would never criticise you, Master. But Horrik was speaking the truth. She didn't try to escape from you. She was trying to help, as she said. But where is she?"

"Gone," the wizard replied coldly, "She's gone."

"Do you know where she is now?"

The wizard spread his hands. "No idea." He shrugged and shook his head, "It's a shame because I could use her… but now I have you instead… an excellent replacement."

He looked at Gratch and admired his massive frame. He was well over three metres long; a powerful bulk of muscle with strong legs and razor-sharp claws. The wizard glanced again at the corner of the room, blackened with the eerie glow of darkness.

"Was it difficult to steal?"

"No," Gratch answered, "They were not expecting a theft at all and I used some rats to do the job. They moved silently and fast. They were in and out of there quickly and without being seen."

The wizard stood up and moved to the corner of the room, the black glow darkening his thin pale face. He reached his hand into the murky black haze and grasped something. As he walked back to his chair the darkness faded, like mist in the dawn. He was carrying a wizard's staff with a massive deep garnet gemstone sitting on the top, clasped in a silver metal holder that held it like a hand. The red of the garnet was the only colour in the room and it glowed gently against the dull greyness of everything else.

The wizard returned to the chair and sat down, still holding the staff. He ran a finger tenderly down the wood, caressing it with the gentlest touch. Then he tapped it twice on the floor. Yellow and white sparks flew up from the impact.

"I've been missing this, Gratch," he hissed.

He lifted it and slammed it down with a loud thud. This time a flash exploded around the dingy room as if lightening had struck. The wizard disappeared. The dark glow weakened and dissolved and the wizard gradually appeared again.

"You're a great wizard, Master," Gratch said.

"Stick with me and you'll see much more than this," said the Troubler in a deathly whisper that echoed around the room, "I've only just begun."

The party of friends had journeyed at a steady pace. Amalek and Seph were in the front, side by side, with

Seph holding his oval magic box with the lid open. Tally was hopping beside Seph with Simron behind them. Lazuli came next while Joog flew above, one minute ahead and the next at the back, listening and watching in case they were being followed.

Sergeant Forr was still trailing them. He had judged it exactly right. He was close enough now to hear what they were saying but far enough back down the tunnel to stay unnoticed. He would run for a few steps and then hop off the ground and glide. Then he would run again. The only sounds were the clicks of his claws on the rock floor and the soft swish of his wings but both of these were out of earshot of Joog, even with his acute hearing.

The light from the magic box was not strong enough to shine along the tunnel but did show the group of friends the area in front for a couple of steps.

"It's so dark," said Amalek, "I wish we could see further. I keep imagining ravens!"

"It's alright, Ammey," said Seph, "They've gone... we fooled them...." he smiled, "Again!"

"I know, but I'd feel safer if I could see better."

"I know what you mean," agreed Seph, peering into the darkness ahead, "But at least we can see the ground in front."

"Enough for the next step," commented Simron, "Step by step and we're moving along nicely."

Joog flew above Lazuli as the tunnel widened and became taller.

"It's like a poem I know," he said, now landing on Lazuli's head, "It's about how something small leads to something big."

The children stopped walking to turn to Joog, and so Simron had to stop and then Lazuli as well. Forr stopped too.

"What do you mean?" asked Amalek.

Joog's eyes reflected golden in the dim light. "A long journey is made up of lots of small steps... of flaps in my case!"

"I see," Amalek nodded, "Can we hear the poem then?"

"Of course," Joog replied, "I hope I can remember it all."

He started reciting it.

"One small breath at the time of birth
And half a billion prove its worth.

One bright star that shines so small
Twinkles above to guide us all.

One drop of rain on a thirsty flower
And the dry earth is dampened in the following
                                                    shower.

One cautious step falling in the right place
Begins a journey too long to face.

One tender smile that comes from the heart
And in that small moment a friendship may start.

One ray of sunshine at the break of day
Dispels all the darkness of night-time away.

One tiny word strong and true
Can fill a weak heart with strength anew."

They found the poem uplifting and encouraging. The dangers they were bound to meet awaited them somewhere in the future, like an approaching storm that could not be avoided. Each step would take them closer to

ONE CAUTIOUS STEP

"One small breath at the time of birth
And half a billion prove its worth.

One bright star that shines so small
Twinkles above to guide us all.

One drop of rain on a thirsty flower
And the dry earth is dampened in the following shower.

One cautious step falling in the right place
Begins a journey too long to face.

One tender smile that comes from the heart
And in that small moment a friendship may start.

One ray of sunshine at the break of day
Dispels all the darkness of nighttime away.

One tiny word, strong and true
Can fill a weak heart with strength anew."

confrontation, an inevitable clash that was terrifying just to think about. They were aware that somehow the power of the Troubler was growing. They were moving into the unknown.

Amalek opened her rucksack and took out a packet.

"Who wants some Mayan beans?" she asked.

"Just the job," answered Seph.

Lazuli stretched out her trunk and sniffed them, "Smells lovely... but what are they?"

"They're very sweet... and they give you energy," said Amalek pouring some into her hand, "You'll love them."

She gave some beans to each of them.

"Is that all we get?" Seph joked as he finished.

"Yes it is, Greedy," replied Amalek, laughing, "I'm saving some for later."

Seph launched into a pretend raid on Amalek to get some more beans. Amalek responded by hiding behind Lazuli, and Seph chased around to try to catch her.

Sergeant Forr was huddled against the tunnel wall, watching all this with interest. Should he attack? He could take them completely by surprise and kill the owl before they realised what was happening. He could see it perched on the elephant's head and facing the other way. Quickly he thought of a plan; he could fly in low, then rise suddenly and stab the owl hard with his beak. He could easily escape; flying much faster than any of them could run.

Forr braced himself, took a deep breath and bent his legs ready to jump into action.

"Let's go," announced Joog, turning his head to look behind them down the tunnel. Forr stayed completely still. Had he been seen?

The children had stopped running around now and Amalek had the remaining Mayan beans safe in her bag.

"We must press on," continued Joog, "We want to cover as much distance as we can."

The party of six friends moved off again. Joog flew at the back, turning frequently to look behind him and along the tunnel. They did not know for certain where the tunnel was heading because it twisted and turned so much. They hoped it was taking them into The Kingdom Of Gems and according to Tally's map this seemed to be so. On first entering the tunnel, it was cool and damp and they found that every so often their feet were splashing in shallow puddles. Water dribbled down the jagged walls. As they travelled further, the temperature dropped until the puddles turned to ice and they had to be careful not to slip.

Simron's gentle voice echoed in the tunnel.

"It's so cold that we must be going in the right direction. Tally, what do you think?"

Tally was hopping beside Seph.

"Yes," he replied, "I'm sure we're travelling southwards."

Seph looked down at Tally, "We must be in The Kingdom Of Gems then."

They paused to get some warm clothes out of the bags that Wizard Elzaphan had given them. There were hats, coats and gloves as well as thick warm socks. They quickly slipped them on and then continued walking. They started looking for a way out, hoping to come across one soon.

A short distance behind them Sergeant Forr followed, running and gliding as before. He knew he had missed his chance. He would follow and wait for another opportunity.

After Aram had stabbed the Troubler's hand, he had galloped along the border. He pointed his magic alicorn forwards to clear a pathway and the snow flew up around him in the wake of his mighty gallop. He skidded to a halt and then turned to watch from a distance. When the snow settled he found he was well-hidden by the deep snow which was halfway up his body. From here he watched and had seen everything that had happened.

He was right next to the border so he was able to see his friends when they ran away and into the wood. He wondered about Flop and Miriam. Where *were* they? Then he watched the ravens dive into the woods and he feared the worst. Soon after, the Troubler flew off in the cloud, leaving no one in view.

He waited for some time, wondering what was happening in the wood and whether he should do anything. Then suddenly, the ravens rose out of the wood, a black swirling cloud of cackling birds, and they flew off as well. Some flew to the north and some to the south across the border. Now everyone had gone.

The blizzard was blowing from behind him, shaking his golden mane forwards and around his face. He was completely still, his proud head held high with ears alert and facing forwards. His brown eyes were intent. Power filled his golden body. But for his fluttering mane and tail, he looked like a statue, stately and strong, with a layer of snow on his back turning gold to white, as if a blanket had been cast across him.

He wished he could cross the border, run into the wood and find his friends but the laws of magic forbade him; if he crossed the border he would instantly be turned into a statue again. He was a creature of The Kingdom Of Gems.

His heart was heavy with fear. He kept imagining a terrible scene in the wood; his friends lying bloodied and dead, covered with terrible wounds from the beaks of the mass of ravens. It would have been impossible for them to hide from such a fierce hoard of birds and survive an attack.

This deathly vision hit him like a hammer-blow and he dropped his head in sadness. Suddenly he felt cold and began to shiver. His eyes glazed with despair and the strength drained from him. What could he do now? Again the terrible image of his dead friends flashed into his mind.

Then he thought of Halo, trapped in the cloud above Candara. How could he fight the Dark Wizard Troubler alone? He had tried already and failed. It was hopeless now.

Although despondency gripped him, he realised that there was still a choice, like a spark of light in deep darkness. He was caught between two powerful emotions; despair and hope. It was like hesitating at a crossroads and not knowing which way to turn. But his golden heart was beating strongly and with a great inner effort he turned to hope. Maybe his friends were still alive. At least Halo was alive and perhaps he could still save her. He felt strength arise in him again and ripple through his golden body.

He shook the snow off his back and then, not knowing where he would go or what he would do, he stepped forwards, pushing into the deep snow.

"Look!" cried Seph.

He pointed ahead and up at a thin line of light.

"What?" asked Lazuli whose eyesight was the weakest of them all.

"Light!" answered Seph, "It must be the way out."

A moment later, the dim light of Seph's magic box revealed the first of some roughly hewn rock steps leading upwards. They began to climb. After twenty steps they were all standing on a wooden-boarded platform peering up at what looked like another sliding trap-door in the ceiling above. There were several ways of getting out. Halfway between the platform and the ceiling was another smaller platform. Then there was a rope for climbing as well as a ladder fixed vertically to the side wall.

Dropping down into the dark, away from the steps they had just climbed, were more steps. Tally noticed them first.

"The tunnel must go on," he said, "Look... down there."

They all looked down the descending steps.

Meanwhile Sergeant Forr worked his way up the steps behind them and then stopped about half way up. From here he could not see much but he could listen.

"Maybe," Amalek said thoughtfully and pointing down the other steps, "Just maybe... that's the lost Mularn Tunnel! It's a tunnel that leads under the Snowpeak Mountains and no one knows where it is anymore."

"If that *is* it," said Seph, "Then it's perfect. It's exactly what we need."

"So..." Tally said looking up at the others, "Do we carry on down there or... use that door to get out?"

They all looked up again. The line of light above their heads traced a thin gap along one side. Seph held his oval magic box up and they could see that the door was the same design as the one they had used to enter the tunnel. A mechanism of weights hung down on one side to help it open smoothly.

"Something concerns me," Simron said, his deep voice echoing slightly around the rock walls.

They all looked at him. As he spoke they could see his breath in the cold air by the light of the magic box.

"It may be nothing... but why can we see light up there when there should be a deep layer of snow above to make it dark? It makes me think that this tunnel may have been used recently and someone has cleared the snow from the entrance."

Joog flew up to land on Seph's shoulder, fanning the air with silent wings. He looked up at the line of light again. His yellow eyes seemed bright in the dim light of the magic box.

"I see what you mean," he said, "But we need to get out to see where we are. If someone has used this recently they've probably gone. If we are moving in the right direction then we can come back in and carry on through the tunnel down there... and if it *is* the Malarn Tunnel... well that will be perfect for us. Also... what about Aram?"

"We can blow his magic whistle again," said Amalek.

"Right then," said Joog, "That decides it. Let's open up and see where we are."

Forr was still listening on the steps below.

"Who is Aram?" he thought, *"And what is the whistle for?"*

Although he could not understand it all he tried to remember what they were saying. It could be useful information to pass on to the General. This was not the right time to attack. Looking up the steps he could not see them well enough so he dipped his head down, kept still and listened.

Lazuli's trunk snaked up to grasp the handle of the sliding door. It jerked into motion and immediately a few small snowflakes swirled in and around them. The weight mechanism clicked into action and the door slid smoothly across.

Seph stepped onto the ladder and climbed up until his head was through the entrance. He looked around cautiously.

"It's sheltered here," he said, climbing out, "That's why there's not much snow." He looked around again. "It looks like the mouth of a cave."

Joog flew out next while Amalek picked up Tally, mounted the ladder and stepped out. Lazuli hauled her great bulk up and out, using the smaller platform and her trunk. Simron was last, climbing the ladder with smooth, lithe movements.

The mouth of the cave was sheltered and protected from the blizzard by a dense group of pine trees, their long trunks stretching upwards to a mass of overlapping branches above. The cave was the size of a room but roughly round and with an uneven sloping floor. A thin layer of snow had drifted into the mouth of the cave, like the sprinkling of sugar on a cake, but it had not reached the entrance to the tunnel. Outside, under the shelter of the trees, the snow was a couple of inches deep.

Joog was looking down from a branch. "I'll take a look around," he announced.

He flew through the trunks of the trees. A minute later he was back.

"We're at the foot of the Snowpeak Mountains!" he exclaimed, "There's too much snow falling to see far... I can't see the border. Seph... blow the whistle."

Seph was already clutching the tiny unicorn whistle in his gloved hand. He lifted it to his lips and blew.

Aram was walking through the deep snow, his alicorn clearing a pathway for him. His golden mane was now matted with frozen snow and he knew he had to keep moving to stay alive in this arctic weather. Despair loomed within him, like a fierce animal ready to strike and bring him down, but so far he had been too strong for it, keeping his hope alive by thinking positive thoughts. Maybe, just maybe, his friends had found a way to hide in the wood. maybe they were still alive. He must stay close to the border in case they suddenly appeared; he must be there for them.

He moved steadily eastwards for a while and then turned west again, like a soldier on guard. He paused for a moment to look carefully across the border, out of the driving snow and into the peaceful sunny day that bathed the lands to the north.

They were not there.

He had just begun walking again when he heard something. His heart missed a beat. Could it be? He had heard the faint sound of a whistle, the whistle he had given to Seph, but it had been mixed in with the wind howling in his ears.

He stopped to listen and held his breath. The excitement was almost unbearable. All he could hear now was the wind. Had he imagined it? Had his hope been so strong that his mind was playing tricks on him?

He needed to hear it again, so he waited. Then it sounded, and this time he could pin-point where it came from. It was them! They were alive, or at least one of them was.

He shook his golden mane, spraying the frozen snow off and into the fierce wind. He shook it again and this time fine golden sparks flew in all directions. All his strength filled him now. Pointing his alicorn in the direction of the whistle he trotted into the parting snow. A few seconds later he accelerated into a gallop.

Sleeping in a tree on the northern slope of a mountain were the two elderly ravens, Crayle and Jum. They were close to the trunk and well-sheltered from the driving blizzard by the snow-laden leaves on the branches above. They found that flying in the driving wind was extremely difficult because they were so old and frail, but they discovered that as long as they stayed close to the ground where the wind was less fierce they could just about manage.

In this way they had struggled on, battling through the snowstorm, until they had reached the first of the great range of Snowpeak Mountains. The journey exhausted them so much that they stopped to rest as soon as they could, shook the snow off their feathers and had immediately fallen asleep.

Crayle woke up first.

"Jum!" he said, nudging her with a wing, "Jum, wake up!"

Jum opened her eyes and blinked. For a moment she felt free and then, a second later, she remembered their situation and the burden of it descended upon her like the sudden arrival of an unwelcome guest. Although she wanted to leave the raven army and live a quiet life in a tree near Munden in Summertime Kingdom, Crayle obstinately refused. He had always been strong-willed and he imposed his idea with such determined force that she had given in to it. They would leave the army and they would become spies.

"Crayle?" she asked.

"Good," he said sharply, "You're awake. We need to get on. We have important work to do."

She looked at him kindly, "Listen, dear. Let's not rush into this…"

"Rush into what?" he asked, turning to her so he could look at her with his one eye.

"This business of being spies. I can't see how we can do it... or why we should do it. At our time in life we should be taking it easy, not taking on new jobs... especially difficult ones like this."

He shifted uneasily on his feet.

"But, Jum, it's not difficult now is it? Think of it like this: we are leaving the army... and taking on something a bit more challenging than just doing what the General says." He began to get cross, "I hate the General," he snapped, "This way we can prove to him that... that... that we're at least as good as he is... or better..."

"But why bother?" she sighed.

"It's in my bones," he replied, "Being in the army is who I am. We can't just stop can we? What would we do? Nothing? No, not me. So, it's obvious, isn't it? Spying on the enemy... what an opportunity!"

She knew trying to change his mind was a hopeless task so she sighed again in resignation.

"Good," he said firmly. He knew he had won the argument, at least for the time being.

He stretched his wings as if getting ready for action and did not notice that he accidentally pushed Jum. She nearly overbalanced and had to flap her wings to stay on the branch.

"Right then," he announced, "We need to cross the mountains first and then start spying on the enemy."

"But we don't know where they are, Crayle," she objected, "We don't know if they are here... there... or anywhere." She nodded her head in random directions. "We don't even know if they've crossed the border do we? We don't know anything."

She glared at him. Crayle avoided her gaze and looked around uncomfortably as he thought about the truth of Jum's words.

"I know that," he replied, "But we must be ready."

He suddenly jerked his head forward.

"What's that?!" he exclaimed.

Jum looked out through the branches and into the falling snow. Some distance away, where the land levelled off into the Northern Borderlands, they could see a cloud of snow being thrown up.

"It's moving, that is," said Crayle, "What is it?"

"It's snow," Jum replied, "It's a cloud of snow... and something is making it. Something is moving fast and throwing up that cloud of snow. *And* it's coming straight towards us."

"The enemy!" concluded Crayle, his voice filled with excitement, "It's the enemy! There you are saying we don't know where they are... well, now we do!"

"What now?" asked Jum.

Crayle puffed out his chest feathers with pride, "What happens now is that we begin our life as spies. OK? We spy on them. We spy on the enemy!"

"How?"

"The role of a spy," Crayle began, "Is to watch, secretly, and to obtain information... er... information of the enemy's secret plans and intentions... to discover their whereabouts and movements. Then the information is passed on and acted upon."

"But who do we pass it on to... the General?" asked Jum.

"Not the General!" replied Crayle looking shocked, "We will be reporting to the very top of course... the Master."

Jum shook her head.

"I don't know about that," she muttered, "Is that wise?"

"We need to go," Crayle announced enthusiastically, ignoring her question, "Come on."

"Wait!" cried Jum.

It was too late. Crayle had jumped off the branch. He flew out through the branches into the full blast of the blizzard and was immediately blown sideways and disappeared.

"Crayle!" Jum called out as she jumped off the branch to follow him.

She was swept sideways too but dropped at once towards the ground. As she descended she saw Crayle sprawled on his back in the snow below.

"Crayle!" she called out again.

She landed beside him and sat on the top of the deep snow. Crayle was scrabbling with his feet and wings and trying to turn the right way up. Jum tried to help but some snow thrown up from Crayle's frantic efforts hit her in the face like a snowball and knocked her back. A moment later Crayle had succeeded and was sitting beside her on the snow. Jum looked at him with concern.

"Are you OK?" she asked.

"Of course I am!" he snapped.

"Remember your age, Crayle," she said, "You're not a young bird any more."

Crayle gave his head a little shake as if to dismiss her words completely.

"Right," he said, and turned to use his good eye, "Where's that cloud of snow?"

It had moved quite a distance towards them now. It quickly loomed closer and for a moment they thought they were about to be engulfed in it.

"Crayle!" screeched Jum, "It's going to hit us!"

Just then it turned past some trees and stopped just along the mountain from them. They watched the snow-cloud settling.

"It's stopped," said Crayle, "Now our spying begins. We need to check that it is the enemy... although I'm sure it is... and then we look and listen."

Jum nodded.

"Let's go!" he commanded.

He took off. Jum caught him up and flew beside him. They were flying into the wind, so progress was slow. They hugged the ground, weaving around rocks and trees until they neared a small group of pine trees where they had seen the snow-cloud stop. They landed in one of the trees and then hopped and fluttered quietly from tree to tree until they heard voices.

"Look!" whispered Crayle, "It *is* them... the enemy!"

They gazed down with excited glee from their hiding place among the high branches. Just a few snowflakes were finding their way through the canopy of branches and pine needles above their heads.

"Look at that!" whispered Jum, "They've got an elephant with them now."

Aram stood in the shallow snow with the others all gathered around him. Seph had Joog on his shoulder and was patting Aram on his side. Amalek was stroking his golden mane.

"It's *so* good to see you," she said.

"And I'm very relieved to see you," said Aram, his rich voice comforting and strong, "I was worried about you." Then he looked puzzled. "But how did you get here?"

"It was easy," began Seph, "You see we were running into the wood and it was Tally's idea..."

"Tally?" asked Aram, "And who's Tally?"

"I am," said Tally, who was still in Amalek's arms.

"And he saved us!" stated Amalek, stroking Tally's ears with affection, "He had a map of tunnels and that's how we got here... through a tunnel. And as it carries on we're going to use it, hopefully under the mountains." She frowned. "Where's Halo?" she asked.

The golden unicorn tapped a hoof gently in the snow and bowed his fine head before answering slowly, his voice grim and serious.

"*He* caught her, I'm afraid... the Troubler... and he's trapped her in a cloud... but now that you've returned maybe we can rescue her."

"Of course we can," said Seph pluckily.

"And the Candara Gems have gone!" Aram continued, "They've been stolen."

They were half-prepared for this news but it still came as a shock. Their minds swirled with thoughts.

"The Troubler," concluded Seph, nodding, "But how did he...? Did you see him take them?"

"No," Aram replied calmly, "I looked into the Brinscally Cave and they've gone. That's all I know. But the spell is stronger..."

Joog raised a wing, "We need to hear more about it... but right now it's important that we get going. We can talk as we travel. We need to hear more about the stolen gems... and talk about rescuing Halo... but now we *must* get going."

"Joog's right," Simron commented, looking around as he spoke, "The sooner we get going the better."

Together they walked towards the cave, their feet crunching in the snow and Lazuli leaving two rows of large round footsteps.

"What are these special gems?" asked Jum.

"I don't know," replied Crayle, he tried to look around a branch, "Where have the enemy gone? I can't see with this branch in the way."

"I can't see either," replied Jum.

Crayle leant sideways to turn his one eye in the right direction and then craned his neck as far as he could. He began to topple off and flapped his wings to regain balance. Then he leant back and turned to Jum.

"There's a cave and they're going in," he said quietly, "I'll have to fly down there and take a closer look."

"Wait a bit, dear," Jum said, "They'll see you, or hear your wings flapping."

"But they might get away," Crayle snapped, "It could be a big cave..." he cocked his head as he suddenly thought of something, "Or a tunnel! We don't want them getting away down a tunnel. I'll just take a quick look."

He jumped off the branch and dropped through the air. In a moment he was back.

"Can't see them," he said, "They've gone right into the cave... or tunnel if that's what it is."

"What shall we do then?"

"I'll have to take a look inside," he replied.

"No," she said firmly, "Not with that magical unicorn with them... you might get killed!"

"I'll be careful," said Crayle, and he jumped off the branch again before Jum had time to stop him.

He swooped towards the cave and Jum immediately followed.

They looked into the empty cave with astonishment and then landed just outside.

"They've disappeared!" exclaimed Crayle, "They've completely gone."

"It's impossible!" Jum said, shaking her head with complete disbelief.

They gazed into the cave for a moment and then walked into it and looked around.

"They're gone," said Crayle, "But there's nowhere to go! I don't understand...."

"Magic?" asked Jum, "It must be some kind of magic... *must* be."

They walked towards the mouth of the tunnel until they were actually standing on top of the hidden doorway.

"Well," said Crayle, "They've definitely gone... and it must be magic, clever magic. But... at least we now know that they are here, in this kingdom, although where they are now is anyone's guess. *And* we know who is in the group. So that is good. That is spying."

"What shall we do now?"

He thought for a moment.

"We'll fly deeper into the kingdom," he said.

"What!" exclaimed Jum, "We'll have to cross the mountains!"

"Yes," Crayle said decisively, "It's the only way."

"But at least let us rest first," Jum said just as decisively.

He sighed, "OK then, just for a few moments."

They huddled together to keep warm and gather their energy for the treacherous journey.

As Jamaar padded across the hot sand he was growing weaker again. The sun blazed down relentlessly from a crystal, clear blue sky and the wind blowing off the sea had dropped to a light breeze. The desert landscape lay in front of him like a vast yellow blanket dotted with cacti, withering trees and the occasional derelict building.

It was hard work trotting here; his heavy paws pressed into the sand and slipped slightly as each step pushed off. He was panting in an attempt to cool down but he found that the heat of the sun on his wide back was gradually draining him of energy. After a while he began to feel dizzy and nauseous, his eyes began to sting and his vision kept moving in and out of focus. His bouncy trot slowed to a swaying walk. He desperately needed some water.

Chapter 4

~ The Thief ~

Summertime Kingdom was bathed in warm evening sunlight, lending a magical beauty to the calm surface of Lake Burney. Small ripples sparkled on her waters with a million star-points of light which would capture the imagination of any passing poet. Just north of the lake, in the cluster of trees which crowned Burney's Hill, the evening sun was playing on the feathers of over fifty ravens. The sunlight flashed in purple, green and blue on their jet-black plumage. Some pecked at the branches and leaves for bugs to eat while others were cackling noisily to each other as they preened their feathers.

The Female Squadron had been searching thoroughly for the enemy and had covered every possible hiding place. They were all gathered now except for two, who had been sent to search in the Forest of the Fairies but had not returned yet. Tull was perched in the centre of the group and was looking around at all the birds now under her command. She was very uncomfortable being the leader. She had always shied away from such positions of responsibility and found it very difficult to control so many ravens.

"Females," she said hesitantly. Then, after clearing her throat she repeated it much louder, "Females!"

Most of the ravens still ignored her.

"Females!" she screeched.

This caught all their attention and they stopped pecking and preening and looked at her.

"Females," she said slowly, "Er... I believe, I think, that the enemy are not here. We have tried to find them... er... we have looked everywhere possible, I think you'll agree about that." There were mutterings of agreement. "I think it is probably certain now that they may have gone. We have searched to the north of where they were last seen... er... and they are not here. Therefore, somehow, they have gone south... they must have sneaked off to the south. They have probably crossed the border by now."

She paused.

A few ravens sighed and whispered complaints about Tull.

Tull opened her beak to speak and then closed it. Some ravens started pecking again and a few closed their eyes to go to sleep.

Then a raven called Jekka suddenly called out loudly, "I'll bet you my granddad's tail feathers that the General knew!"

"Knew what?" asked Tull.

Jekka looked around at the others. "That they'd gone, of course! He gave the best job to the males again 'cos he thought the enemy were over there... across the border!"

The other ravens cackled in support. Tull held up her wings in an attempt to get their attention.

"Stop it!" she shouted, "We don't know... do we?!"

The ravens stopped chatting for a moment and then began grumbling about the General.

"What shall we do now?" shouted Jekka above the commotion.

Tull turned her head to one side and thought.

"Er..." she began, "Er... "

"Yes?" shouted Jekka.

"We'll..." began Tull slowly, "Er... we'll... cross the border... yes, that's what we'll do..."

"When?" snapped Jekka.

"Well... er... now, I suppose," stated Tull.

The ravens shifted on their feet and grumbled again about needing to rest.

"OK... OK," Tull said, "OK... OK... In that case we'll rest first and then go."

All the ravens immediately sank down onto the branches and shook their feathers ready for sleep. Tull continued speaking but now no one was listening.

"We'll have a good rest and then... er... leave... and... er... cross the border."

It was not long before they were all fast asleep.

The night closed in and stars appeared in the growing blackness of the sky. When they had been sleeping soundly for over an hour the two missing ravens returned from The Forest of the Fairies and landed in one of the trees.

"Wake up!" shouted one of them called Ontim, "Wake up!"

Some of the ravens stirred, lifting their heads, opening their eyes and looking around sleepily, while many of them remained asleep.

"We found something!" shouted Himmi, the other raven. She puffed her chest out in pride and looked around. "We found something near the forest!"

The ravens were gradually waking up and started mumbling and complaining, saying things like, "What's happening?" and "I've only just gone to sleep," and "What's all the fuss about?"

Tull was still on the highest branch and looked down on the others. In the night shadows of the trees below, they were just dark shapes. She shook her head to try to wake up and see more clearly.

"Where are you, Himmi?" she asked tentatively.

"I'm here," she replied.

"Good, good," said Tull, "So... OK, you've found something... is it... er... well... is it?" she tilted her head on one side, "What is it?"

They all looked at Himmi.

"Old Howard," she said.

Tull was surprised.

"You saw Old Howard?" she asked.

An excited buzz filled the trees.

"Yes," joined in Ontim, "And he was carrying a rabbit."

"On his shoulder," added Himmi.

"But..." said Tull slowly, "But Old Howard... he's not the enemy is he? I thought he was on our side."

At this Jekka flapped up a few branches until she was just under Tull. She nudged another raven off and took her place. She glared crossly at Tull as if she was stupid.

"Of course he's on our side," she said loudly.

She looked down at Himmi.

"Did you talk to him?"

"We did," replied Himmi, "He saw us and called us down. He said he's escaped from Wizard Elzaphan and is going back to the Master. Then the rabbit said that the Master wants us to carry them back."

"Carry them back?" repeated Tull, "But..."

Jekka interrupted, "But how do they know that?"

"The rabbit said," began Ontim, "She said that the Master *told* her that he wants them back in the Kingdom Of Gems as soon as possible."

"When we carried him before," commented Jekka, "We did it easily."

"I don't know about all this," said Tull, "How do we know that what this rabbit is saying is true?"

Jekka sighed impatiently.

"Listen," she said, "Old Howard works for the Master, yes?"

Tull nodded.

"He's escaped from Wizard Elzaphan... yes?"

Tull nodded again.

"Therefore, he's going back to the Master. Now that makes a whole load of sense to me. If we carry them back we are helping the Master, yes?"

"OK, OK," said Tull, "So... er... OK, we'll do it. This will be... our first proper task under... er... my command."

She paused. The ravens were all wide awake now and keen for action. All they needed was the order to take off and get on with the job and some of them were ready to jump. Others had actually lifted their wings.

"Ravens," said Tull, "We have... a job to do... and... er... we want to do it... er... well. So..."

"Oh, come on!" said Jekka impatiently and she took off.

All the other ravens started following her and Tull quickly shouted, "Take off!"

"Himmi," shouted Jekka, "Lead the way!"

In the night they looked like a great cloud of bats as they followed Himmi to The Forest of the Fairies.

Seph, Amalek and Simron were all riding on Aram's strong golden back. The tunnel was lit up clearly now by the unicorn's alicorn which was shining brightly. It shed a golden light which was much stronger than the soft glow of Seph's magic box.

The lively clip-clopping of Aram's hooves on the rock floor echoed along the tunnel. His trot was carrying him along at a good pace but not too fast for Lazuli to keep up. She was padding behind him at a run with her strong young legs working hard and Tally riding on her back. The young hare was just behind her head. At first he found it difficult to balance and nearly fell off twice but he soon got the hang of the motion and began to enjoy his ride. He had to sway slightly with the movement and soon his skill grew until he could even keep his balance as he stood up on his back legs.

A long strap crossed Lazuli's broad back, hanging down on either side to carry the two bags of food and clothes that Wizard Elzaphan had given to them. They swung in rhythm with her steps.

Joog flew silently between Aram and Lazuli.

After they had descended the steps and started moving along the tunnel they exchanged all their news. Aram explained everything that happened to him and described the plight of poor Halo.

"What about the gems?" asked Joog.

"I knew something had happened when I felt a terrible pain," he replied, "And that must be when they were stolen because straight after the pain, everything fell – everything that was frozen by the spell – people and animals overbalanced. Also, the birds were gone… they were all frozen in the air and when I looked they were gone. So I checked and found some under the snow. Then I checked in the cave for the gems and they were gone too."

"I don't understand it," said Joog, shaking his head, "Because we are still alive and free, the Troubler *cannot* steal them. But we have to face it… he must have found a way. And that makes the situation much worse."

This lay heavily in their hearts as they told him about their journeys in Summertime Kingdom. After this they were silent and thoughtful as they moved along the tunnel.

The tunnel had been virtually straight since they started travelling again and so they were sure they were under the mountains. Fortunately the roof was high, rising to twice the height of Lazuli in most places. Every so often Aram's hoof would crunch into a frozen puddle, shattering it into hundreds of pieces of ice.

After travelling for a while they stopped for some food and drink. Aram and Lazuli were breathing heavily and their breath clouded out in the cold air, hanging momentarily in the golden light and then dissolving to nothing.

Back along the tunnel, in the darkness, Sergeant Forr stood near to the wall and watched. His black feathers were the perfect camouflage and he was sure that he had not been spotted. He had been flying to keep up with the travellers and the swish of his wings was drowned by the echoing sound of Aram's hooves.

He watched them eating and drinking and realised that he too was hungry and thirsty. There was ice under his feet but he knew that one peck would give him away. He would have to wait.

"How far do you think we've gone?" asked Seph, who was sitting cross-legged.

Aram dropped his head to reply. "We must be right under the mountains now," he said.

"It's getting colder," remarked Tally, as he chewed on a carrot.

Lazuli was just lifting a roll of bread to her mouth with her trunk. She paused to speak before she put it in.

"So that means there will be no way out for some time."

"That's right," Joog joined in, "We'll have to sleep in here... but we can travel some more first."

Simron leant towards the others and spoke softly to them. Forr strained to hear but he was not close enough and he wondered who this man was. He watched as they gathered the remaining food into the bags and got ready to move on.

Amalek, Seph and Simron had now mounted Aram who started walking for a few steps and then broke into a trot. Once more, the sound of his hooves clattered in the tunnel. Lazuli followed behind him and built up speed to a comfortable run with Tally standing on her back like a charioteer. Joog flew between them.

Sergeant Forr took to the air and followed. All that he could see through the semi-darkness was the back of the elephant. If only the owl would fly at the back then he could carry out his plan and attack. He would have to be patient and wait for the right opportunity.

Gratch stirred in his sleep and then woke up. The long journey had tired him and sleep had come easily, descending upon him like a soft warm blanket. His huge scaly body was stretched out along one wall and where his head was resting on the floorboards his bacteria-filled saliva had dribbled out leaving a yellowed decaying patch.

The room was cold, dull and colourless and was lit by three black candles which flickered pale light around the walls.

The wizard was still asleep, his head tilted back against the back of Old Howard's tatty armchair. His thin hands rested on the arms of the chair. The hand with the thumb and finger missing was now completely healed but the other one was singed black by Aram's attack. It was swollen and bruised. The jagged gash had stopped bleeding and there were no bones broken.

Gratch looked up at his new master, his profile silhouetted against one of the candle flames. The wizard's mouth had fallen open and each breath puffed out rhythmically in a small, murky cloud only to fade in the wake of the next one. In one corner of the room the wizard's staff was hidden in the black haze that surrounded it.

Gratch looked at it and wondered. When he was carrying it he could feel its power. It seemed to give him added strength for the journey. He also felt that it was drawing him along, pulling him in the right direction.

It was this power, this attraction, which he had become aware of before the journey, only dimly at first, but undeniably there. It made him steal the staff and set off to return it to its rightful owner. The power had then grown stronger as he moved, day by day, closer to the wizard.

Gratch felt contented. He had hoped to be in the service of a great wizard for some years and now he had found one. He felt he deserved it and eagerly took his chance when it came his way. He had followed his instinct until he had ended up here.

He mulled over his good fortune as the darkness deepened towards midnight; his favourite time. He was feeling so good that he growled in contentment. The wizard jolted at the sound, his mouth closing as he sat up in the chair.

"Gratch?" he asked, "Was that you?"

"Yes, Master," growled Gratch.

His long forked tongue slipped out of his mouth, twitched in the air and then hid again.

The wizard leant back and closed his eyes to think for a moment. Jamaar and Horrik were both gone now so it was perfect that this Komodo dragon had turned up to take their place. Gratch was a worthy replacement. He would make good use of him.

The Troubler opened his eyes and turned to look at Gratch.

"We need to get working," he said.

The snowstorm gripping The Kingdom Of Gems had transformed it into one of childhood's favourite dreams; a winter wonderland. The streets in Candara were steadily filling with snow as the blizzard persisted, flinging great multitudes of flakes down from the clouded sky and through the icy air to gust around the houses and cottages.

Normally, during the day, the people of Candara would have been out to clear paths and doorways, and animals of all kinds would be helping. Shouts of glee and excitement would have thronged through the happy town and snowball fights and tobogganing would have been the essential priority of the day. Children and young-hearted adults would have been having fun.

When there was a fall of snow it was a favourite passtime of the children to slide down a hill on the back of an animal. Otters and badgers enjoyed it the most and would spend hours playing with the children on the snowy slopes.

All this would happen on a normal day when the arrival of snow would release a surge of energy for all these joyful activities. The last few days, however, Candara had been like a ghost town. It was as silent as a graveyard at night. The Dark Wizard Troubler's spell held everyone in its icy grasp, freezing them in utter stillness; all life, every human, animal and insect was caught in a terrible limbo somewhere between life and death.

Inside each house, away from the driving blizzard, an eerie silence hung in every room. They were as silent as tombs. The people living there were now motionless. It was as if time had given up on them. Their unseeing eyes stared at a point somewhere, like someone in a day-dream. A white frost coated their ashen faces, turning their hair and eyebrows to grey, and making them all, even the children, look old. Before the Candara Gems had been stolen, many of them were balanced precariously in some task they had been busy with. But since the theft of the gems from the Brinscally Cave, the spell had deepened and these people had now toppled over, falling like heavy stone statues.

Midnight brought the depth of icy darkness. Then someone stirred and woke. A candle was lit and flickered into life in the musty attic in The Old Mill. The thief moved, disturbing puffs of dust which were lit up in the yellow light. The hooded figure stood up and walked to the middle of the room, stooped to lift one of the floorboards and then reached in for something. A second later the hand was drawn out clutching a folded piece of cloth. It was placed on the floor and then opened. A sharp intake of breath and a gasp of delight. The room danced

with the sparkle of many-coloured lights. It was the Candara Gems.

Dawn was slow to come, creeping over the land like a silent snake. The Flatsage Farmlands stretched away to the north of Candara. The low-hedged borders of the fields were hidden now by the white expanse of snow and each tree was decorated with a thick layer of white fur on every branch. Beyond this, Blue Lake's white covering was as flat as a table-top, with only the high-cliffed Sratt Island and the tiny Isle of Ig rising above.

Further north lay Lake Clase-Moy. It was draped with a sheet of untrodden snow at the foot of The Great Mountain. Forested slopes rose into the haze of snow and cloud. On a tree, perched on a branch and close to the trunk were the two old ravens, Crayle and Jum.

They huddled together for shelter from the blizzard. Snow caked the other side of the trunk but where they were, the bark was bare. They were extremely tired after their journey through the mountains but they would never have managed it without the good fortune of the wind blowing behind them. With this and frequent rests, as well as Crayle's fierce determination to spur them on, they had worked their way right through the mountains.

"This weather!" exclaimed Jum, shaking the snow off her feathers, "It makes travelling so difficult."

"Difficult, yes," replied Crayle, "But not impossible."

He felt very pleased about the journey so far and puffed out his neck feathers with pride. Jum glanced at him and shook her head in disapproval.

"But, Crayle," she said, "We should have taken more rests. Then we wouldn't be as tired as we are now."

He tried to turn so that his good eye was facing her but only succeeded in tapping her head with his beak.

"It's no good," she said, "Swap places."

He tried to scramble past her but pushed her off. As she flew back up she was suddenly exposed a blast of snow-filled wind. It caught her wings and she had to struggle and fight to land again only to find that they were still in the same places. He tried again to move past her on the branch.

"Careful this time," she said, her black feathers dotted again with white.

With some careful shuffling they managed it.

"Can we rest now, dear?" she asked.

"Yes," he replied, "But after that we've got to get on. We have important work to do."

"I *still* don't see why it's so important," she grumbled.

"Do I have to go through all that again?" he sighed, "Listen. Being a spy is good work. It requires cunning... and guile... and cleverness... and, well... er... those are the sort of things I'm good at."

Jum just shook her head again and looked out through the branches and into the driving snow. She straightened up slightly in surprise.

"It's changed here, hasn't it?"

He turned his head so that he could look out with his good eye.

"Yeah," he agreed, "The snow's deeper now."

"Of course it is, Crayle," she said impatiently, "But it's not that. When we were here before... before we flew north with the army... there were birds all frozen still in the air. Remember?"

Crayle nodded.

"Yes," he said slowly, "And...?"

"Well, they were all over the place then. Now they've all gone, haven't they?"

"Hmm... yes," he acknowledged, and began to work it out as he spoke, "The birds were frozen by the spell... and now they've gone... therefore... that *must* mean they've escaped the spell... therefore... *that* means..." He hesitated and then, turning back to look at her, he triumphantly reached his conclusion, "That means the spell has ended!"

For a moment neither of them spoke as the impact of this sunk in.

"Then it's over!" exclaimed Jum with a joyful ring in her voice.

The reaction from the two birds could not have been more different. Crayle looked deeply disappointed and slightly confused, whereas Jum lifted her wings in celebration, accidentally nudging Crayle sideways and making him lean and move a foot to keep balance. Then she made another announcement.

"So we don't have to be spies any more!"

Crayle felt he had been hit by a sledgehammer. The whole meaning of his life had suddenly been snatched away from him. He pecked at the branch in sheer frustration.

"Crayle, dear," she said tenderly as she put a wing around him.

He jabbed his beak at the branch again. It hammered in and stuck there.

"Nnnnnnnnnn!" he cried as he tried to pull it out.

It suddenly jerked free and he toppled back off the branch. A few seconds later he was back, his feathers flecked with snowflakes.

She tried to comfort him.

"It's not that bad," she said, "We can do what we want now."

Now he was sulking.

"But I want to be a spy," he groaned.

For a few moments they looked out again through the branches in silence.

"Crayle?"

"Yes," he answered grumpily.

"I've just realised something."

"What?"

She looked at him with a sparkle in her eye.

"It's still snowing!"

"Great... great," he mocked loudly, sitting up to imitate enthusiasm, "That makes everything OK again. Let's celebrate! It's snowing! It's snowing! It's snowing! It's still snowing!" Then he slumped down again, "So what?"

"Don't you see?" she urged, "If it's still snowing, and still so cold, then the spell must still be here. Perhaps it's just weakened."

Then something dawned on her. She was so sorry for him in his despair that she was now happy the spell might still be working. Only a minute ago it was the last thing she wanted.

Crayle gazed out at the blizzard.

"You're right!" he exclaimed, "Jum, you're right! The spell is still here and *that*," he nodded at the view, "that snow is the proof. OK, so it might have weakened... but that is for us, as spies, to find out. That is our first assignment. Has the spell weakened or not?"

Jum was thinking of other things.

"Shall we rest now?" she asked.

"OK," he said, sounding bright and perky again, "We catch a quick sleep and then on with the assignment."

They ruffled up their feathers for warmth and leant against each other. Jum closed her eyes and as she drifted off to sleep she thought about the tree near Munden where she would like to live. These thoughts comforted her so much that very quickly she fell into a restful sleep.

Meanwhile Crayle had closed his one eye. He was so tired that he went to sleep within a minute and then had a wonderful dream. He dreamt he was a young bird again with shiny new feathers and a strong beak, spying on the enemy from a tree and finding out all their secrets. He reported to the Dark Wizard Troubler who was so pleased that he promoted him to General and gave him the black compass.

In this way they both slept happily in their sheltered place as the blizzard raged fiercely around them.

Sergeant Forr was feeling very pleased with himself. While all the other ravens were hunting for the enemy above ground, he had found them and now he was tracking them in the tunnel.

He could see the rounded outline of the elephant as it ran along the tunnel in front of him, a dark shape silhouetted against the light of the unicorn's shining alicorn. Forr was trying to keep just the right distance; he needed to stay in the dark in case one of them looked back but he also wanted to keep them in his sight. The loud clatter of the unicorn's hooves were still echoing through the cold rocky tunnel and drowning any chance of them hearing him. He had got it just right.

Suddenly, something happened that took him completely by surprise. He felt something grip him powerfully from above. His body and some of his wing feathers were held as if in a clamp. He immediately panicked and struggled as hard as he could, flapping wildly so that his wings pulled free. Then the grip tightened and he felt the pierce of sharp claws into his skin. The pain was too much and he knew he had to keep still. He managed to twist his head around and saw what he had feared. It was the owl.

He had been totally outwitted, bringing a sharp end to his smug feelings. He must have been spotted earlier and the owl then hid from him in the shadows. The most annoying part was that he must have flown straight past it.

He let out a screech of anger and all his energy burst out in another determined effort to wriggle free. The talons squeezed harder piercing further into his black skin. Forr realized his struggling was in vain and gave up.

The others were all staring back along the tunnel as Joog swooped towards them with his prey. They passed above Lazuli and landed in the middle of the group. Forr was now pinned to the ground. He glanced around for a way to escape.

Simron took a step towards Joog and Forr.

"Now," Simron said decisively, "You can struggle and try to escape if you like but it will do no good. Aram here could take away all your feathers with one nod of his head. You would never fly again. Understand?"

Forr did not answer but looked at him defiantly.

Aram nodded at him, pointing his glowing alicorn. One tiny black feather pulled out from his neck and flew to the ceiling of the tunnel. Forr watched it as it floated down slowly, turning beautifully, until it touched down beside him.

Forr was shaking.

"Understand?" asked Simron.

"Y... yes," stammered Forr.

"Let him go," Simron instructed Joog.

Joog let go and flew onto Seph's shoulder. Forr shook his feathers and stood up, glancing around uneasily at the circle of faces looking at him.

Simron knelt down in front of Forr, "Now some simple questions... needing simple, honest answers. What's your name?"

"F...F...Forr... Sergeant F...Forr," he replied nervously. The threat of having no feathers had terrified him.

"Sergeant?!" exclaimed Simron, "I'm impressed!" Then he looked around at the others, "We have captured a special prisoner here... a sergeant no less." He looked back at Forr. "Who sent you?"

"No one."

"Now... Sergeant Forr," said Simron staring intently at the raven, "Do I need remind you about the simple, honest answers?"

"But it's true," Forr said quickly in a raised voice, "I came down here by myself and found you and then I went up to tell the others but they'd all gone... so no one knows..."

"Are you sure, Sergeant?" asked Simron.

Forr cowered down in fear.

"Yes, because it's true! Honestly! They were gone. No one knows I'm here and no one knows I've found you."

"Well," said Simron, standing up, "It's surprising for a raven... but he's telling the truth."

Forr looked relieved and stood up again.

"So," Simron continued, "What else do you know I wonder? But we can hear it all as we travel."

"I've told you all I know," complained Forr, "Let me go..."

"You can tell us more..." said Simron calmly, "about what the ravens are doing. I want to hear about the General and that compass he wears around his neck. And other things too."

"But..." pleaded Forr, "I don't know anything... I don't even know where they are... let me go. I'll just fly away..."

"No!" snapped Simron, "You're coming with us. Now stop talking."

Forr opened his beak and then closed it again. Simron had spoken with such authority that Forr realised that no amount of begging would make any difference. He resigned himself to being a prisoner, at least for the time being.

Simron parted his cloak to reveal a belt around his waist hung with all sorts of pockets and tools. He drew out a small knife and then opened one of the pockets and took out a roll of twine.

"Right," he said.

He knelt down again beside Forr. He found the end of the twine, unwound a length of it and then cut it with the knife. He reached out towards Forr who took a step back and cowered down again.

"Keep still," ordered Simron.

Forr obeyed as Simron wound the twine around the frightened raven until his wings were tightly held by his sides. Then he tied it firmly.

"That should do," he commented.

Joog flew down from Seph's shoulder and landed beside Simron. His white feathers were tinted with the gold light from Aram's alicorn.

"You're really making sure, aren't you?" he asked.

"Yes," Simron nodded, "Because if he escapes then we'd be in trouble. He'd tell the other ravens, or the Troubler... and down here we'd be an easy target."

Amalek and Seph had been watching all this. Amalek pulled a packet of Mayan beans out of her bag.

"There's probably enough for everyone," she said and poured all the remaining beans into her hand, "Come a bit closer, Aram, so that I can see."

Aram's hooves clattered on the rock floor as he moved. She counted the beans.

"Twelve," she announced, "One each for the humans... that's *three*... then three for Lazuli because she's so big and she's working so hard running... that's *six*... three for Aram because he's big and he's running as well... that's *nine*... one each for Tally and Joog... equals *eleven*. And one left over."

At this Forr lifted his beak slightly to glance at Amalek.

They all looked at him. He was a pitiful sight. His black feathers were untidily ruffled, his wings were strapped to his sides and he was looking very sorry for himself.

"And one for Forr," said Seph, "As bad as he is, we want him well enough to answer more questions."

The others nodded their agreement. Amalek handed round the beans and they were quickly eaten. After a drink of water they were ready to go. Simron sat again on Aram's strong back but this time held Forr in front of him. The two children were between them and Aram's neck. Tally sat on Lazuli again and Joog glided above.

They moved along with renewed strength, gradually accelerating until Lazuli was running at her top speed just to keep up. Simron peppered Forr with questions and he answered them truthfully. There was not much that

Simron did not know already but he did discover a few details that might prove to be useful later on.

The tunnel was a harsh, cold place. It was still absolutely straight which made travelling easy and quick. It also meant that they were confident that they were moving in the right direction.

They travelled on, not knowing whether it was day or night but growing more and more tired. They would have to stop soon to sleep and rest. But before this they wanted to cover as much ground as possible, so they sped on. The walls flashed by, lit up by Aram's golden light, as they journeyed on deep beneath the Snowpeak Mountains.

Chapter 5

~ Two Prisoners ~

orning broke in The Kingdom Of Gems like the slow creep of a snail. Beneath the clouds, where the blizzard swept across the land, the light grew cautiously until the dull day had finally arrived. White snow robed everything, while in the raw air the rushing flakes veiled the distant view in all directions. On the foot of the southern slope of The Great Mountain the trees were laden with snow, as if each branch had grown a layer of fur of which any white cat would have been proud.

It was mid-morning when the Male Squadron came in to land in a couple of large atlas cedar trees. Although they were buffeted by the powerful blizzard, they managed to keep reasonable control of their descent with their excellent flying skills as they swept down skilfully into the trees. They were angular black shapes in a white world of snow.

When they landed it was a buzz of activity. They tried to shelter as much as they could, and hustled for the best spots. They were all facing into the wind as they shook their wings and preened their feathers to get the snow off. Some of them started pecking at the snow to drink. Then a few of the younger ones kicked some snow off a branch onto the ones below. This caused a great furore of rage to break out from those below who retaliated by flying up and trying to knock the others off their branches. All of a sudden more ravens joined in until the trees rang with their harsh noises and flapping wings. The snow driving through the trees on the wind was joined by clouds of snow shaken off the branches.

"Stop!" screeched the General.

The fighting died down until they had all settled quietly. The General was on the highest branch with Gerr just below. He looked down at them through the falling snow with a look of disgust. He was fuming with anger.

"That was *disgraceful!*" he boomed, "All that noise..." he lowered his voice realising that his shouting was probably as loud as the noise they were making in the first place, "All that noise could have told the enemy where we are. And as well as that, it's a shameful way for an army to act!"

He paused for a moment for his words to sink in and to let his temper calm down.

"Now," he continued, "There has been no sign of the enemy all through the mountains... of course we could have missed them, especially with all this snow... but my compass here," he held it out with a claw, dangling it from the chain, "this compass has guided us here... to this place. Why? It does seem strange because the enemy could never have got this far by now."

Several birds shook their heads and echoed, "Never."

"Anyway," he continued, "We will search this area because this compass came from our Master." He pointed to it with his beak and there were some 'oos' from the army. "There is his coat of arms. So, you will search in pairs and I will stay here with Colonel Gerr. Report to us if you find anythi..."

A sound below made him stop abruptly. They all looked down but there were too many snow-laden branches for them to see much of the ground apart from tiny glimpses. They dodged their heads from side to side in an attempt to see more.

"What was that, Colonel Gerr?" the General asked quietly.

"Sounded like snow slipping off a branch, sir," replied Gerr.

The General was looking below but having to lean out past Gerr to see. Suddenly he overbalanced and fell. With a few quick flaps he was back on the branch again.

"You could be right, Gerr," he said as if nothing had happened, "On the other hand..."

"We ought to check," called out Razz.

"Sshh," said the General, "They'll hear us..."

"Who?" said several birds together.

"The enemy, of course," whispered the General but some of the birds could not hear him.

"What?" they asked.

"Sshh," said Gerr.

The ravens on the lowest branches who could not hear started chatting.

"What's going on?" asked one.

"I don't know," said another, "I can't hear."

Razz was near the centre of the mass of birds and was getting frustrated. He flapped upwards until he was on a branch just below Gerr.

"It's stupid just talking about it," he said, "Let's go down and look."

"Go on then," the General ordered, "You go... and take Akk with you."

Down below, right underneath the tree, was the entrance to Mularn Tunnel. The party of underground travellers had slept the night and then rushed on until they had reached this entrance. For them it was the way out.

They had opened the sliding door and a mass of snow had fallen in on top of them; this was the sound that the ravens had heard. When this happened Seph was at the top of the ladder. The snow almost knocked him off but he held tight and that's when he heard the ravens.

It was Razz's call of "We ought to check," that made him look up. Above him he could see the branches with cedar tree needles heavily laden with snow. But through that thick canopy he thought he saw some black shapes and as soon as one of them moved he knew that it was the ravens.

"It's them!" he whispered down to the others who were still brushing the snow off, "The ravens!"

"I'll close the door," said Lazuli, reaching for the handle with her trunk.

"But… hang on!" Amalek exclaimed, "They'll see the entrance. There's no snow on it now… it will stand out."

Simron took control.

"Put the snow on Lazuli's back… quick!"

In a few seconds her back was covered with a layer of snow.

"Now, up on the ledge," he said to her.

With some help from the others pushing her and keeping the snow on her back she was up with her snow-covered back filling the opening; the disguise was complete. It just looked like a slight bump in the snow.

At that moment Akk and Razz descended from above and landed at the foot of the tree beside the huge trunk. In the shelter of the big tree the snow was shallow so they could stand up with only their legs covered. The wind was less strong, but they still turned into it to stop their feathers being ruffled.

"You go around that way," whispered Razz, flicking his beak in the direction, "And I'll go the other… but be careful."

When they were half way around Akk heard Razz make a short squawk. He rushed around the tree expecting to see him but he was gone.

"Razz," he called.

He went around again to check.

"Razz," he called, "Stop messing around! Where are you?"

He ran around the tree in the other direction.

This was strange - very strange. He jerked his head this way and that, looking in different directions, and then tilted his head to look up. He ran around the tree once more, shook his head and spread his wings in disbelief, and then took off.

He landed just below Gerr and looked up at the General.

"Well...?" asked the General, "Anything?"

"No sir," replied Akk.

"Where's Razz?"

Akk suddenly thought that perhaps Razz had flown up into the tree although he could not understand why he had not seen him. He looked around the gathering of birds anyway to check.

"Razz, are you here?" he asked.

There was no answer. He looked puzzled and then turned back up to the General who was waiting for an answer.

"Well, I don't know sir," Akk said slowly, "Down there, sir, he... well, he just... disappeared sir."

The General shook his head and then tilted it on one side. The compass around his neck seemed very agitated and was jiggling around all the time.

"What do you mean, disappeared?" asked the General, "He can't just disappear like a somon in the night, can he?"

"No," agreed Akk, "But sir, he went behind the tree and then he was gone."

The General listened and then shook his head again.

"Deserted!" he concluded.

"Are you sure, sir?" asked Gerr.

"Think about it, Gerr," the General said decisively, "He can't have just disappeared into thin air, now can he?"

"No sir."

"And all the signs for desertion were there. I've been watching him. He was a rebel who enjoyed the sound of his own voice far too much for my liking. He was weak and couldn't take my discipline. To tell the truth, I'm glad to be rid of him."

He looked down at the black compass that was still jumping around.

"Keep still!" he snapped at it crossly.

The compass did as it was told. The General was beginning to get fed up with all its movements. He was also losing faith in it. They would search here and if they did not find the enemy then he would know that something had gone wrong with its guidance. He would still wear it because it showed his authority over all the other birds but he would make his own decisions and ignore the compass.

"Sir?" asked Gerr, "Should we organise a search party for Razz?"

"No!" the General snapped, and then remembered to lower his voice, "Definitely not! I don't want that rebel back in the ranks. Besides, we need to find the enemy. Male Squadron!" he said just loud enough so that they could all hear, "Atteeeeeeeeennnnnn...tion! Search the area in pairs and report back to me. Take off!"

Razz had had the shock of his life. He had been walking around the tree when his foot slipped into a hole. Immediately, he was pulled downwards by his leg, with a sharp jerk. Before he could do anything about it, he was through the snow and under the ground. He opened his beak to call out to the others but something snapped it closed so quickly that it hurt, and then gripped it tightly, turning his frantic cries for help into a soft muffle. He was bundled down some steps and then held. He could hardly move, with his head facing straight towards a tunnel stretching away into the dark, lit up by a dim light behind him. He was being held against something soft, and glancing to his right he had another shock; right beside him, looking at him with frightened eyes, was Forr.

"Be quiet and keep still," ordered Simron, lowering his head and whispering to them, "Both of you. Move or make the slightest noise... and I'll break your necks!"

Razz and Forr did as they were told.

After a few minutes, Lazuli whispered, "How much longer?"

"Not long," whispered Joog.

"Are you alright?" asked Amalek.

"Well, yes," she whispered, "Although my back is *very* cold." Then she joked, "And I would like a more interesting job next time... one that involves perhaps a *little* intelligence... and movement! First I was a wall in the tunnel and now I'm the ground at the entrance!"

"Next time..." began Seph, smiling, "you could be a floor or maybe... a ceiling..."

Joog was on Amalek's shoulder. He ruffled his feathers and looked down at Tally. "We could take a look up there now. Could you look Tally? Your white fur is perfect camouflage."

"Yes, of course," replied Tally, feeling very pleased to be given the task to do.

"I'll hold you up," volunteered Seph, "Tap your foot twice when you want to come down."

Tally nodded and said brightly, "Alright."

Seph picked up the young mountain hare, pushed him beside Lazuli and then up through the snow. His head popped out into the falling snow. He shook the snow off his head and then looked around, his long ears sticking straight up and flicking this way and that. There were no ravens in sight. Then his sensitive nose twitched; he sniffed and caught a scent. The ravens were still around.

Tally tapped his foot twice. Seph lowered him carefully to the floor and then quickly forced some snow up into the gap.

"They're still here," said Tally, "And close by. I could smell them."

Aram was standing behind the Princess, his alicorn lighting up the area and reflecting on his gold body.

"We can wait," he said, his voice deep and rich.

Amalek turned and affectionately ran her hand down his golden mane; it shimmered like the setting sun on the ocean.

They were in a small square room with rough and uneven rock walls. Under their feet, the wooden boards puffed up dust when they stepped which clouded in yellow only to settle again quickly, leaving a damp musty smell. The cold air nipped the children's faces and each frosty breath they exhaled faded within a second.

Aram's golden light paled into grey down the steps, where the dark, handsome face of Simron could be seen looking up at them.

"Well done, Tally," said Joog, "We need to discuss and decide what to do next, so let's go down there where we won't be heard." He pointed down the steps with a wing. "You'll have to stay here, Lazuli. Are you alright?"

"Of course," she said smiling, "It's the only job I've ever done where I can doze and still do a perfect job! I think I'm getting used to this."

Seph and Amalek laughed. They both patted Lazuli on her rough-skinned hide and then climbed down the steps, followed by Aram and his glowing alicorn. Joog overtook them, gliding effortlessly above their heads. At the bottom Simron was binding Razz with the twine. The two ravens looked extremely unhappy with their situation. Razz turned to face Forr, beak to beak.

"Forr!" he exclaimed, "How did you get here?"

"Long story..." answered Forr, "Where are the others?"

"Keep quiet," commanded Simron firmly.

He had spoken softly but his strong voice still echoed around the spacious tunnel, giving more power to his words. A few seconds later he had finished binding Razz's wings and when he lifted his hands away the two birds were also bound together. They struggled for a moment and then both stood up and tried to walk. They looked like a strange four-legged creature and only managed two steps before they began to stagger sideways and fell over into the wall.

"Well?" Razz asked Forr, "What happened? How did you get here?"

"I told you to be quiet!" snapped Simron, "Unless you want me to tie your beaks closed."

They stopped talking immediately and looked up at Simron with black eyes. Joog flew onto Amalek's shoulder and looked calmly around the group. He started the discussion with the question they were all wondering about.

"Why did the ravens land here?" he asked, "They've landed in the tree right above the tunnel entrance. It can't be just chance... and yet they don't seem to know about the entrance."

"Well..." said Simron, "let's ask *them*." He nodded at Razz and Forr, and stared at them. "Tell us why you landed there."

Razz turned and his black eyes shone brightly in the golden light. His feathers looked ruffled and untidy and he held his up head defiantly.

"Loosen this," he asked, pretending to gasp for breath, "It's too tight... I can't breathe... then I'll tell you."

Simron was firm again. "You are in no position to bargain. You can't fly... you can't even walk..."

Aram aimed his alicorn at the two ravens and a tiny feather was pulled out painlessly from each of the necks of the cowering ravens. The feathers spun around each other in front of them, as if caught in a whirlpool.

"So," said Simron, "Answer the question!"

Forr stared at the whirling feathers and stammered, "T...t...tell him, Razz... g... go on."

"OK," said Razz, "It's no problem. I don't like the General anyway. It was that compass he has around his neck. *It* knew."

"How?"

The feathers spun faster as if to threaten the two birds.

Razz looked up at Simron. "I don't know... *he* doesn't know either... it just jumps around... but he said it led us to that tree."

"What are they doing now?"

"Searching for you."

Joog stretched his wings as he sat on Amalek's shoulder, one of them brushing her ear and tickling it. Amalek smiled. Joog looked around the group.

"As we thought. We'll just have to wait then," he said, "Tally can check from time to time and when they're gone we can get out of here."

Seph smiled. "That will be good."

Crayle woke first. The blizzard howled just beyond their sheltered spot in the tree, but it was the shouting voices of some ravens very close by that jolted him out of a good long sleep. Then he heard the voices again.

"Shall we go back?" shouted one.

"Oh, I don't know," was the reply, "The General wants us to search the area well."

Crayle nudged Jum and she woke up sleepily.

"Sshh," he said softly before she could speak, "Listen."

The first raven shouted again, "Yeah, I know... OK then... we'll search a bit more first and then go back. It's so difficult in this terrible weather."

Crayle turned to Jum. "It's them!" he said.

"Who?" Jum asked.

"The army!" he said urgently, "I heard them mention the General. It's them!"

Jum was suddenly wide awake. "Then we must go! They're so close, Crayle. If they find us we're in *real* trouble!"

Then they heard the voices again.

"Come on!" shouted one, "What are you doing?"

"Just resting," the other replied, "Sorry. OK... I'm ready."

The sound of flapping wings sparked the two old birds into action. They were afraid of being seen and taken back to the General.

"Follow me," said Crayle as he jumped off the branch.

He left the shelter of the branches and just at that moment a particularly powerful blast of the blizzard was rushing by, which caught him and swept him away like a leaf in a hurricane. Jum was right behind him and got caught as well, and together they tumbled helplessly in the fierce wind. They were totally out of control. They rolled through the air with snow swirling all around them, and were swept back up the mountainside.

"Help!" cried Jum.

All of a sudden, the wind stopped and they both fell, landing gently in some snow. For a while they lay there recovering.

When they felt better they stood up and found that the snow here was shallow. They had been swept into a dense copse of trees where even the howling wind did not reach. When they looked around they saw why. A thick tangle of tall bushes was acting as a windbreak. It was a little haven of stillness.

"What happened?" asked Jum.

"We escaped from those ravens," replied Crayle, "And what an escape!"

"We were lucky," she said, "*Very* lucky!"

Crayle was looking pleased with himself.

"An escape is an escape, Jum," he said, "And that was one of the best! And against all the odds. It's all just a case of going with the flow of things. It's like..."

He stopped when they heard the sound of flapping wings. They looked up to see a raven swooping down towards them.

"Look out!" shouted Crayle.

Before they could do anything the raven had crash-landed beside them and tumbled over several times in the snow. It made a little whimper and then lay still.

Crayle moved cautiously towards it. The raven was fully grown but not quite an adult yet. Its feathers were jet black and splattered with snow, and with some fluffiness of babyhood still lingering on. Its body heaved rhythmically as it desperately drew air in and out. It looked exhausted.

"It's Iker!" said Crayle.

Jum joined Crayle and looked down at Iker. He was looking up at them with the innocent appeal in his eyes that all baby creatures have.

"Ah!" said Jum fondly, "Look at him... the sweet little thing." She bent over him and asked him gently, "Are you alright?"

"I... think so," Iker replied slowly.

Crayle stepped away.

"We'd better get on," he said, "We have important work to do."

Jum turned her head and spoke crossly to him.

"We can't just leave him here! Have you no heart?"

"But he said he's OK," complained Crayle, "We can't keep stopping for every waif and stray that..."

"He's not a waif," she snapped turning back to Iker and talking tenderly, "And you're not a stray, are you dear?"

Iker shook his head and said, "I'm... tired."

Jum leant over him and wiped a smudge of blood off the feathers on his head. She turned back to Crayle.

"He's injured, poor thing," she said.

Crayle sighed.

"I can't stand young ravens," he groaned, "Let's go."

"Don't be stupid!" she snapped, "You were a young raven once! We're not leaving him and *that's that!*" she announced, "And he needs to recover before we go."

Crayle knew that when she was in this sort of mood he could not change her mind. She would win in the end. It had only happened a few times before but he knew the signs, so he resigned himself to the situation. He settled down sulkily on the snow near a tree trunk. Jum helped Iker up and supported him as they walked across and joined Crayle by the tree. Iker slumped down in exhaustion and Jum stroked and preened his young feathers with her beak.

Tally's young nose twitched in the chilly air. For a mountain hare with an excellent sense of smell there were many scents drifting by, but he was only interested in one; the scent of ravens. Seph was holding him up again through the entrance to the tunnel so that he could check to see if the ravens had gone yet. It was the fourth time he had squeezed past Lazuli and poked his head out.

It was all clear. His smell told him that the ravens must have gone. The falling snow blew into his face and made him blink.

"KYWAY."

The sound made him jump. He had not heard it for a while. It was the kind voice of his grandfather, Hawkeye, and it felt as if the old hare was standing right next to him. He felt a thrill inside. Was his grandfather really here? How he would love to see him again, to talk to him and to hear some of his wonderful stories. He quickly looked around but he was not there.

"KYWAY."

This time it seemed to be clearer but really it was his listening that was clearer. The word seemed to cleanse him inside so that his mind was more alert, more present and more open to the surroundings.

"Tally, don't forget...KYWAY!"

Tally remembered the meaning of the words, 'Keep Your Wits About You,' but his senses had already sharpened. His nose twitched again and picked up a faint smell that he had not noticed before. He had to concentrate, but it was definitely there in the rushing snow-filled air. It was the scent of ravens.

"Thanks, Gramps," he said softly and then tapped his foot twice.

Tally told the others that it was not safe to leave yet. The next time he checked he could not smell even the slightest hint of a raven and so they all clambered out until they were standing in the snow above ground.

A few minutes later, they were on their way, dashing southwards across the snow at the foot of The Great Mountain. Aram led the way, pointing his magical alicorn now to clear a pathway through the deep snow. A white cloud flew up in front of them and surrounded them before settling in their wake to leave no sign of tracks. The children rode on Aram, holding onto his golden mane, and behind them was Simron with the two prisoners. They were now talking secretly in the quietest of whispers. Joog glided above.

Lazuli followed Aram, running as fast as she could with Tally crouching on her neck. From time to time he would stand just for the fun of it, skilfully swaying with the elephant's movements. Inside the snow-cloud thrown up by Aram, they were protected from the arctic weather.

It was warm and calm and they felt like boats in a sheltered harbour.

"Aram," called Joog, swooping just above his head, "I'm concerned about this snow-cloud around us... we might be seen."

"You're right," Aram replied, "I'll make it smaller and slow a bit."

The flat expanse of Lake Clase-Moy came and went, after which they passed between a winding river on their right and the Marshes of Macaroone on their left, both hidden under the deep snow. It was not long before they moved onto the frozen surface of Blue Lake.

Now they were out in the open again, they no longer felt protected by the tunnel which hid them from view. The frightening feeling of being vulnerable accompanied them; they could be attacked at any time and from any direction. As they travelled they became aware more deeply of the dull deadening presence of the Dark Wizard Troubler and his spell. They had felt it ever since they entered The Kingdom Of Gems but it lay in the background. Now it thrust itself at them from all directions. It hung everywhere around them and they could feel the terrible discomfort of it seeping into their minds and thoughts. It filled the whole kingdom like a bad smell that cannot be ignored. It was an atmosphere charged with the gloom of desolation.

Blue Lake was white and flat. It was a vast open area which dwarfed the travellers like ants. The snow-cloaked land stretched away in all directions; a wide arctic landscape that treated all visitors with contempt. Snow drove through the icy air and blew across the surface at speed. Below the smooth snow covering, the water had frozen rock-hard with a thick layer of ice.

They were shielded of course from all this bitter weather. However, the snow-cloud around them, although much smaller now, also meant that they could not see far and this made them feel weak and defenceless against a sudden attack.

"Ammey?" asked Seph, "Did you feel that?"

"What?" asked Amalek, glancing at her brother.

"Cold air," he said, "I felt it on my face… yes, there it is again."

"Oh yes," Amalek agreed, "And snowflakes… look."

"It's the spell!" called out Aram, turning his head slightly as he galloped, "Some cold air is beginning to get in… the spell is growing stronger."

Amalek shivered. They had been used to being protected from the cold and the snow.

"What shall we do?" asked Amalek.

Joog answered from above. "There's nothing we can do," he called out, "But the sooner we get to the palace the better."

Soon they were passing close to the cliffs of Sratt Island to their left, which were adorned in white like everything in the spellbound kingdom. Leaving the cliffs behind, they continued at a steady pace until they heard a change in the thudding of Aram's golden hooves and Lazuli's pounding feet. They had moved from the frozen surface of the lake to solid ground which took them onto the Flatsage Farmlands, where the rich fertile soil produced plenty of food for the creatures of the kingdom. Now there was no one to farm anymore and no one to eat the food; the Dark Wizard Troubler's spell had squeezed the life out of the land with sickening precision.

They had barely left Blue Lake, with Joog cutting through the cold air just above their heads, when they heard a noise above. It was the swish of feathers rushing through the snow-filled air and immediately the fear of the ravens hit them like a punch in the stomach. Aram stopped as quickly as he could, skidding on the snow and sending it spraying up in front of him. Lazuli was just behind him and slipped into Aram. With the jolt Amalek and Seph lost balance and fell off Aram, landing softly in the snow. They leapt to their feet and looked up.

The sound had gone. They could see nothing through the swirling whiteness. Joog flew up and followed the direction of the sound. Aram and Lazuli moved together and turned back-to-back ready for an attack. Simron dismounted and placed the two raven prisoners on the snow. They muttered and complained quietly. A glare from Simron was enough to silence them.

"Watch that way," said Simron to the children, pointing the direction, "And Tally and I will watch this way."

They waited in anticipation.

Nothing happened.

A few seconds later Joog returned.

"Nothing," he said, "Whatever it was, was too fast. It's gone. There's no point trying to follow... it's best to stick together."

"Ravens!" Amalek said shuddering, "Must have been them."

"Did you see them?" he asked.

"No, but I heard the sound of feathers, and what else could it be? The spell has trapped all the birds here."

"Yes," Joog sounded calm, "As you say... it must be ravens. But as we didn't see them they probably didn't see us. They've gone, for the moment anyway."

Simron picked up the captive ravens and mounted Aram and the children followed.

"We need to be more alert," he said, "We must be ready just in case something unexpected happens. The Troubler could be here."

They were all ready to go again. Aram lowered his alicorn and cantered into the pathway as it formed. This time they kept more alert. Tally remembered KYWAY and Seph and Amalek decided they would watch one side each. The unseen flight above their heads had already put them on edge but the thought that they could meet the Troubler at any moment had created a nervous tension in the pits of their stomachs.

They moved on for about ten minutes. Suddenly, above their heads they heard the same sound; birds swiftly passing through the air. This time it was speeding in the other direction. It was gone in a moment leaving the group of friends puzzling over what the ravens were doing.

"Keep going!" called out Joog from above, "And speed up! They may be going to get more ravens!"

Joog flew just in front to lead the way. Aram accelerated and Amalek hung on tightly to his fine golden mane. Seph held on to his sister with his arms around her waist. Behind him, Simron held the two ravens in front of him. They had stopped talking and were sulking at their present situation. They felt they were the two most unfortunate ravens ever to have lived.

The snow on Palace Path had been recently disturbed. Someone had moved up the hill towards the palace.

"Stop!" called out Joog, and Aram slowed and then came to a halt, "We're at the palace!"

The snow-cloud around them gradually settled and they began to be able to see their surroundings. They were standing in the shallow snow where Aram's alicorn had cleared it. All around there was snow everywhere, weighing down the branches of the trees and bushes, and deep-covering the ground in smooth waves of white. The palace towered up above them. It was a beautiful sight.

The Prince and Princess gazed up at it. The spires rose up high above, to fade into the thick falling snow which shrouded their tops. The snow was clinging to it wherever it could, filling some windows and half-filling others. Long icicles hung from every ledge. This was the children's home and mixed feelings of joy and pain welled up inside them as they thought of their parents, the King and Queen, frozen by the spell. They needed to see them.

Amalek dismounted Aram, jumping down into the snow. Seph followed and then Simron.

"Where are the others?" asked Seph, looking back.

"Sorry, I must have gone too fast for them," commented Aram, "But they can't be far..."

He was interrupted by the crunching of approaching footsteps but with the falling snow they could not see beyond a curtain of white.

"Here they come," said Amalek, and then doubtfully, "It *must* be them."

Fear of the Troubler leapt into their minds. They were beginning to think that every sound floating to them out of the snow-hidden surroundings was him. They sighed with relief when Lazuli appeared with Tally riding on her.

"Where have *you* been?" joked Seph.

Lazuli waved her trunk and then padded towards them, following the path in the deep snow made by Aram.

Tally stood up, balanced well for a moment and then slipped off. He landed in the soft snow and scampered after Lazuli, his powerful back legs springing him along and kicking up snow behind.

The back door, from which they made their escape, was still open as they had left it, and they could see that snow had blown in and piled up inside.

"Right, let's go in," said Joog looking at the others.

"It'll be great to have some food and shelter," said Amalek, "There'll be loads of food in the kitchen."

She took a step towards the door and then stopped. They heard a sound from inside the palace. They all turned and stared through the failing light at the great door.

Something moved the snow. They backed away slowly, trying to make as little noise as possible. Nothing should be moving here because all living creatures were trapped and frozen... except for the Troubler and those who worked for him; his ravens, the great dog and the Komodo dragon. Fear seized their minds.

Amalek panicked and tried to get away as quickly as possible. Her feet slipped and she fell backwards into the snow. Lazuli reached down with her trunk to pull her up just as Seph grabbed her arm. Together they got her onto her feet again.

Aram faced the door, his magic alicorn pointing at it.

They saw the snow inside the door shift again but through the thick falling snow it was hard to see. Something black moved and they knew this meant trouble. They turned and moved back, their thoughts set on retreat. They had to get away; they scrabbled and slipped in the snow.

"Stay together," stated Joog from just above their heads, "and don't panic!"

Amalek looked behind and back towards the door. She gasped with surprise when they saw who it was.

"It's Flop!" she cried.

They all turned now and saw him and watched with the mixed feelings of relief and delight. Flop stepped out from the doorway and shook his fur sending snow spraying off his body. Then he worked his way through the deep snow with a few huge leaps until he reached the cleared pathway. He ran to them with his fluffy tail up in the air and the black areas of his fur white-speckled with the falling snow.

"Flop!" shouted Seph, and he started running towards him.

He scooped Flop up in his arms and stroked him with his gloved hand as he turned to carry him back to the others.

Flop purred in Seph's ear and then greeted the others.

"It's good to see you," he said looking at them with his clear yellow-green eyes, "You didn't think I'd be beaten by a mere sting, did you?"

"We were worried…" began Joog, "We were very worried about you. But it's wonderful to see you back to your old self."

"I like the collar," said Amalek.

Flop had a new collar around his neck. Hanging from it was an ammolite gemstone which shone gently with green, blue and red.

"That's from Wizard Elzaphan," he commented, "They took my old one off when I was ill. This gem protects me from the spell."

"Miriam!" exclaimed Seph.

The little harvest mouse popped her head out of Flop's fur. She was nestled, as always, on Flop's neck just behind his head. She had just woken up. Her nose twitched as she looked around at the smiling faces. She also had a collar with a tiny ammolite.

The joy of the moment took over and for the reunited friends the danger seemed to dwindle in the excitement of meeting Flop and Miriam again. The light was failing now as they stood chatting in the falling snow at the back of the palace.

Simron, however, stood slightly apart from the chatting group. He could feel that something was not right. There was still the constant dull presence of the spell of course, the terrible atmosphere that hung like a mist throughout the kingdom was growing stronger. But there was something else. Simron knew they were being watched.

His head turned as he searched for something to confirm his fears.

"It's great to see you," said Amalek reaching out and scratching Miriam on her head with a finger, "But how did you get here before us?"

"An express flight!" Flop replied, "Harris and Quint carried us in a basket."

Joog nodded, and then asked, "And you've just arrived here?"

"Yes," Flop answered brightly, "Just a few minutes ago. Wizard Elzaphan thought I would find you here… at some time anyway... well, he was hoping you'd get through. He has a lot of faith in you, you know."

Then Miriam's voice squeaked, "It's great to be with you again!"

Joog noticed Simron and flew over to him, landing on his shoulder.

"What is it?" Joog asked quietly.

"I don't know..." Simron whispered.

Simron was still scanning the surroundings, his eyes alert and quick. He reached down and grabbed the two prisoners, Razz and Sergeant Forr who were lying on the

snow still bound up tightly. Forr opened his beak to speak
but Simron snapped it closed with his hand.

"No noise," he ordered.

Then he continued whispering to Joog.

"Someone else is here... I'm sure of it. We ought to
go in."

Joog flew back to the others and swooped around
them as he spoke.

"We're going in," he said softly, "Simron thinks
we're being watched."

They looked around in fright. It was so hard to see
through the driving snow. Everything faded into the grey
of the snow and the failing light of the evening.

Aram led the way as they walked towards the large
wooden back door.

Watching from one of the high trees close by, was
Gratch. To him they looked small and harmless, even the
elephant. He wondered why his new master had made
such a fuss about them.

"Go to the palace, Gratch," the evil wizard had
instructed him, "And find a place to watch..."

"I can climb trees, Master..." Gratch said with a
touch of pride because for Komodos of his size it was
usually too difficult.

"Up a tree, if you like," the Troubler said, and then
lowered his voice into a threat, "But don't be seen. I don't
know where they are but I *must* know if any of them get to
the palace. I've had no good news from my ravens so
that's not a good sign. The enemy may be in my kingdom

now… and I don't like trespassers. If they do get through they'll come from the north and they'll go to the palace because they'll be looking for the King and Queen. They'll approach the palace from the back. They are devious and dangerous… so take care. If the unicorn is with them then don't attack and report to me."

He was promised food for this job but at the first sight of them his mouth began to water. He remembered his master's instructions not to attack if the unicorn was with them so he restrained himself but it was not easy; he nearly gave in to his strong desire for food.

Climbing a tree was not easy with the great bulk of his body, but his claws were razor sharp and it was a skill he had practiced. He was soon high up and watching them from above. He saw the cat come out of the palace and then watched as the unicorn led them back in. The last to go in was the elephant, just fitting through the huge doorway.

His long, forked tongue snaked in and out of his great mouth where bacteria-filled, venomous saliva dribbled out and down his scaly skin. A drop fell on the bark of the tree and sizzled as it froze. He climbed down, jumping the last few feet and skilfully landing flat, his great bulk thudding into the snow. He headed across the back of the palace, pausing at the open back door and cautiously looking in. He saw the snow piled high inside.

He sensed with his tongue that they were not close; he could still smell them but they must have passed along the corridor. Again he was tempted. Hunger burned in his stomach and his huge frame ached for a good-sized meal to satisfy it. After all, he deserved a meal after fighting through the snow to get here.

He took a step towards the door. It would be so easy to run in, catch one of them, one of the children perhaps, and then drag the child out to eat. After the meal he would report back to his master and tell him he had killed one. His master would be pleased. The thought was appealing and pulled him forwards.

He walked to the door and put his head inside. He carefully placed one foot through the doorway. Then he doubted. What if it went wrong? His new master was too powerful to upset. He felt like a coward but he stepped back out. He would get another chance.

He began the difficult journey down Palace Path, through the deep snow back to Old Howard's House. It was easier now as he followed his way through the pathway that he had made as he ploughed his way here earlier. His body twisted with each step as his long tail dragged behind.

The icy weather had frozen the water everywhere. Streams, lakes and rivers were all thickly crusted and Gratch's deadly saliva was also freezing as it streaked off his scaly skin. Dribbles trickled down from his mouth and hung down in long, thin strands which shattered as they hit the ground.

He fought his way through the deep snow until he was clear of the palace and heading down Palace Path. His movement was slow but his great strength allowed him to plough through at a steady pace. He was eager to report to his master and receive the meal he had been promised.

In The Kingdom Of Gems there were two other creatures who were not caught in the spell but were nevertheless trapped. One was high above the land and the other was deep below. Both of them were desperate to escape but this is where the similarity ended. One of them was Halo and the other Horrik.

Halo was still trapped in the cloud above Candara. Every so often tears of despair trickled from her eyes as she thought of the helplessness of her situation. She worried about Aram and the others and repeatedly she would gallop right across the cloud as fast as she could, her silver mane flowing like a river, and with hope in her heart that she might break through and be free. But every time she reached the edge, the cloud would somehow turn her around and she would find herself racing back in the other direction.

It seemed that there was no answer to her sad predicament. She had tried but she could do nothing about it. She was waiting for a miracle.

Under the ground, Horrik had still been unable to find a way out of the labyrinth of tunnels. In her underground prison, she wallowed in her own self-pity as she lay in Serinta's Cave. She survived by eating bats and drinking from pools of water. By the light of the black compass she had tried to find a way out but had failed.

She was consumed with hate for Jamaar who she saw as the cause of all her problems. It was his fault that she was trapped down here and she was desperate for revenge. This made her even more determined to find a way out and she dreamt of being above ground again and hunting for Jamaar. Then she would put the score right. Jamaar deserved to die.

Inside the palace the group of nine friends were waiting for Flop at the foot of the stairs. They were out of the arctic wind now but inside it was still very cold. The children sat down on the bottom step and huddled together with their hats, coats and gloves still on. The stairway behind them curved up gracefully to a balcony which overlooked the hall. The stifling presence of the spell hung heavily around them and the daunting feeling that it was becoming stronger weighed upon their minds. As well as this, they were very tired after the journey and needed rest and sleep.

As soon as they were inside, Flop had dashed to the cellar to find his family. He knew they would still be frozen but he could not help hoping that perhaps Tilly and their five kittens had somehow freed themselves. As he ran down the stairs, hope had flared up in his heart.

He found them where they always slept, in the corner on a rug. Tilly was lying on her side with the kittens around her in various positions. It was a pain that was hard to bear. He had paused beside them and then tried to lick one of the kittens. Instead of soft fur, his tongue had scraped over icy spikes that were as hard as stone.

He shuddered, then turned away and quickly ran up the cellar steps as if he was being chased by a ghost. As he passed the kitchen, Miriam jumped off his neck and went to check on her family. She reappeared in a moment.

"Frozen?" asked Flop.

"Yes," Miriam sighed.

Flop held out a paw for her to climb up. Then he lifted her up until their faces were close together.

"What shall we do?" he asked.

"Carry on," she replied in her high squeak, "At least we know where they are... If we can stop the spell, then they'll be free again. Imagine that!"

Flop nodded, trying to convince himself. Although Miriam was tiny, she had been a great strength to him, especially when they were trapped together in the sack.

"Thank you," he said, "That's better... but the dark Wizard is so powerful."

Miriam climbed along his leg and sat on the back of his neck. They heard the sound of Aram's hooves and Flop trotted along the hall to join the group at the foot of the stairs. Joog and Simron were just returning from a tour of the ground floor where they had checked all the rooms. Joog landed on Seph's shoulder.

Simron looked around at the group and whispered, "All clear down here."

Amalek saw Flop arriving. She could tell straight away that he was upset.

"Oh, Flop... you found them?" she asked quietly, looking down at Flop as she sat down on the first step to be closer to him. He jumped up onto her lap and she stroked his soft black and white fur.

"Yes," Flop whispered, "They're still frozen... it's terrible."

"And your family, Miriam?"

"All frozen too," she replied.

"We'll free them," whispered Seph, "We'll free them all…"

"Yes," whispered Flop nodding, "That's what Miriam was saying... I just hope you're right."

"Before we go up," whispered Joog, "I'd better fly on ahead." He took to the air. "In fact, don't move until I've checked the whole palace first."

He flew off, gliding silently upwards. He could open the doors by just landing on the handles. They had been designed to be easy for animals to use. Each door had two handles; one in the normal place and a second close to the floor for smaller animals like cats to use.

The others knew there were many rooms so they settled down to wait for Joog to return.

The palace was spacious with high ceilings and wide corridors which meant that Lazuli, still young elephant, could move through the palace with ease. She noticed, however, that the doors to many of the rooms were too small for her.

They had already passed a few people. Some of these were standing like ghostly statues, greyed by a light coating of frost. Others had fallen to the floor in strange positions and one of these was an elderly lady lying on the stairs above them with her head facing downwards. Gripped in her frozen hand was a green jumper and some more clothes lay below her, strewn on the stairs.

"Oh, Habel!" said Amalek with compassion.

She reached down to touch her cheek. It was cold and rough with frost. She withdrew her hand quickly.

"She must have fallen," Seph said, "But when we left she was standing... remember?"

"Yes," agreed Amalek, "We ran past her."

They looked down at her still body and then they noticed her staring unseeing eyes. It was very strange; Habel was not dead and yet they could see no life in her eyes. Seph pulled at her cold hand.

"I can't move her," he commented.

Simron moved quickly up the stairs to help. His strong dark hands gripped Habel's arm and pulled with no effect at all. Then they pulled together.

"It's no good," said Simron.

They both crept down to the others.

"It's extraordinary," whispered Simron, shaking his head. "This spell is so powerful already and yet now, it seems, it's growing stronger."

"Yes," Seph whispered, "And that would explain why these people have fallen and why there are no birds in the air... the weight of the spell must've dropped them out of the air. I bet they're under the snow."

Amalek was gathering the clothes up and tying them around Aram's hooves to muffle the sound.

Joog had still not returned, so Simron turned his attention to the two unhappy prisoners. They were still bound tightly together with their wings at their sides. They looked as if all the sadness in the world had descended upon them.

"Right," said Simron looking at them. "What shall we do with you?"

"Let us go," pleaded Razz, "We'll just fly away somewhere."

"Yes," agreed Sergeant Forr, "We won't go back to the General... we don't want to fight anymore..."

"Please, let us go," repeated Razz, "Then you won't have to watch us all the time..."

"We'll definitely just fly away," said Forr, "Definitely."

Simron was ignoring their pleading and looking around.

"What's in there?" he asked Amalek, pointing to a door under the stairs.

"It's a large cupboard," she replied, "For cleaning things... you know brooms and stuff like that."

"Perfect," he said.

He picked up the ravens and strode over to it.

"What are you doing?" asked Razz.

"Yes, what are you doing?" echoed Forr.

Simron held them at arms length and looked at them. "Just putting you in a safe place for a while," he said, "Where you can't do any harm."

He opened the door.

"Not in there," complained Razz, "It's too dark."

Simron put the ravens down inside the cupboard.

"Stop," cried Razz, "You can't lock us in here... it's too dark..."

"It's too dusty!" cried Razz, "It's horrible in here..."

"We'll die," announced Razz, "You can't..."

Simron closed the door. There was a key in the lock which he turned while inside the two ravens still complained bitterly. Their voices were now muffled and at the foot of the stairs they could only just hear them. Simron walked back to join the others.

They waited until Joog returned with the good news that it was all clear. They were still cautious as they climbed various staircases leading up to the Round Room. Dust lay on everything. Just as a mist fills the air everywhere, so the spell had stretched out its icy power, seeping into all places in the kingdom. Even the bricks of the buildings had been infected and in the dull atmosphere dust was settling much faster than it normally would.

As they reached the foot of the final flight of stairs winding up to the Round Room, twilight was fading into the darkness. Lazuli found she could not fit so she stood at the foot of the stairs while the others went up.

At the top, they stepped onto the landing where the cook stood in the dim light, the frosty covering making her look like a stone sculpture. As they passed, their movement stirred the air and little clouds of dust puffed off her shoulders and head.

"Look!" said Seph, "The door's gone."

A few splinters lay on the floor where the Troubler and Jamaar had ripped it off its hinges.

They passed into the Round Room with Seph leading, Amalek next and then the others. Gold-framed windows ran right around the room, as well as one in the ceiling, making it lighter here. The wind blew through an open window and snow had piled up inside.

The children stopped and stood still, transfixed, staring across the room. The sudden shock of what they saw held them in a moment of timeless agony. The King and Queen had gone!

Amalek's legs crumpled as she fainted and fell to the floor. Tears filled Seph's eyes and began to trickle down his face.

"Oh, no," he said, dropping to his knees beside his sister.

"Ammey!" he said, shaking her.

Simron put a comforting hand on Seph's shoulder.

Amalek began to come round. Seph helped her to sit up. She stared at the place where her mother should be and then where her father should be, and then back again.

"What does it mean?" she asked.

Joog landed beside the children.

"It may not mean..." he began, "It may not mean they're..." he could not bring himself to say 'dead', "Maybe he's just moved them somewhere."

For a minute everyone was still. No one knew what to do next in the face of such a shocking discovery.

Simron moved over to close the window, stepping into the snow which had piled up on the floor. He reached out to pull the window shut. The glass was broken but it reduced the wind and snow coming in. The room was dim now so he lit two candles and headed over to the fireplace.

Aram turned to the children and when he spoke his voice was strong and calm.

"Children..." he said, "you'll have your parents back. I feel certain. In due course we'll free the kingdom and then we'll find your parents... don't lose heart. You musn't lose heart. Your parents would want you to serve the kingdom, wouldn't they?"

Amalek and Seph nodded.

"But now," Aram continued, "in order to be strong, we need to eat and sleep. There's food in the kitchen. You two go down and get some. We can eat here by the fire."

The children felt uplifted. They nodded again and Amalek patted Aram on his golden neck.

"I'll come with you," said Joog.

The children felt in a daze, numbed by the shock of the disappearance of their parents. It was a terrible feeling, like being lost, drifting aimlessly like a small boat on a wide ocean. Something had happened that they could do nothing about it and it had left them reeling. But there was nothing else they could do and it was best to get on with something useful.

While Simron was starting the fire, the Prince and Princess went down to the kitchen to get some food and drink. On the way back up they stopped to share some of it with Lazuli. Then they climbed the spiral stairs to the Round Room where the flames of the fire were licking up the chimney and giving a warm glimmering light to the room. Simron had blocked the broken window and the chill of the air was beginning to lose its bitter edge. They all gathered around the blazing fire and began to warm themselves. Amalek and Seph took their gloves off and held their hands out towards the fire.

The food and drink was passed around. Normally a meal like this, especially when they were so hungry, would be a jovial time with laughing and joking. Tonight the mood was sombre. The children looked glum as they ate with spirits dampened by the recent events. They felt heartbroken.

After they had eaten, Tally went down to keep Lazuli company and Joog followed to keep watch at the foot of the spiral stairs.

They all felt exhausted and settled down quickly to sleep on a variety of cushions, pillows and blankets brought up from the other rooms. The dull night closed in tightly, bringing with it an even deeper feeling of the dark power of the spell which was pressing in upon them. It lingered everywhere like a persistent headache, possessing, controlling, and deadening the life and happiness of the kingdom.

Chapter 6

~ The Magic Star-Box ~

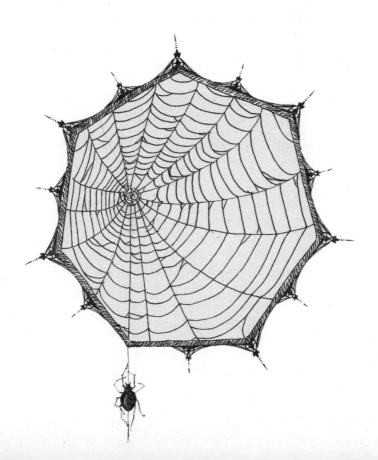

ratch was lost. When he started his journey all had been well because he could still see his tracks which he knew would lead him back to Old Howard's House. But as he ploughed down Palace Path, his tracks disappeared under the heavily falling snow. The night had deepened, closing in around him until he could hardly see anything. The snow was so deep that without knowing it he had left the path and now he was completely lost.

When he was travelling to The Kingdom of Gems, the wizard's staff had guided him; he wished he could have such guidance now, but he was on his own.

He began to panic. He feared for his life in the arctic weather conditions. Snow caked his scaly body and he could feel the cold creeping into him. He scrabbled through the snow, sometimes finding himself underneath so that he had to push his great body up to break the surface above. Most of the time, however, he was able to work his way through by making a channel in it. It was hard work.

After a while he came to a bridge. He did not know it, but he was underneath Payli's Bridge, to the east of Candara. It crossed the River Tazer which was now frozen and covered with snow. The snow lay thickly upon the bridge but underneath was partially sheltered. A little snow had blown under leaving a shallow layer. He crawled in with the idea that he could shelter and try to think more clearly.

He decided he would wait in the hope that the snow would ease so that he could see something he recognised and find his way. If this did not happen then he would stay there until dawn when he would complete his journey.

The attic room of The Old Mill was dusty and dirty. Cobwebs draped from the ceiling and on the walls. All the spiders were frozen by the spell, some on their webs and some lying on the floor. The darkness of night was heavy, weighed by the sinister dullness of the spell.

No one had been into the room for years and so it had remained empty and neglected. A smell of damp wood hung in the stale air. Only the spiders and insects lived here and they had been totally undisturbed - until now.

The thief crouched in the centre of the room and reached down to open a folded cloth. Light flooded out from the Candara Gems in a wonderful blaze of many colours.

Instantly the dingy room was transformed by the dazzling display which banished the darkness. The thief gasped with delight and reached down again, this time to delicately touch the red ruby with a finger. The colour flared brighter still, bathing the room in red.

Then the finger tenderly ran over the purple amethyst and again the colour gleamed more brightly. Finally the finger caressed the resplendent blue sapphire and clear blue glowed intensely all around the room.

The hand withdrew and tucked under a cloak. Settling into a cross-legged position the thief's eyes fixed on the three gems in deep concentration.

Gratch woke up and found himself shivering. He had not intended to fall asleep but somehow he must have drifted away. He had no idea how much time had passed. He looked out from his sheltered place under the bridge and into the darkness. Something had changed.

He moved forwards, pushing on his powerful back legs until his rounded snout was in the open air.

It had stopped snowing.

The cold had seeped into his great body and he knew he must get moving; if he stayed here he would die. He crawled out. The air was fresh and crisp. His foul-smelling breath clouded and dispersed. The view was gently lit by moonlight reflecting off the smooth snow and he could see into the distance now. He looked up. The clouds had cleared leaving a black sky sprinkled with stars, a vast multitude of silver points of light around a pale moon.

There was just one cloud still remaining and this was the one above Candara, and it was still snowing there.

He looked down again and across the snow. Not far away he could see Candara and he knew Old Howard's

House was beyond that. He could see where the snow dipped slightly and traced the line of the river and he decided to follow it. This would lead him through Candara and then close to Old Howard's House.

He forced his powerful body into the deep snow resting on the ice of the river. It was deep and again he found he was forming a tunnel as he moved and had to force his head upwards to break the surface. Travelling like this was slow and difficult and he felt very cold but he moved with renewed energy after his sleep.

As he ploughed along he began to think of the meal he would be given by his master. With this to drive him on, he progressed steadily until he was moving into Candara and into the falling snow. He passed Relbuort Cottage on his right and then the tall Spindley Tower on his left.

Fighting through the deep snow, the river opened out to become the small lake of Ayder Water where the sky was clear once again. He battled on under the clear sky and soon saw the group of trees surrounding Old Howard's House. He left the river and turned north.

High in a tree in Silvermay Forest a conversation vibrated in the still air. It was the only night-time sound in a forest bound by the deathly spell which held the whole kingdom prisoner. The darkness had lost its edge when the clouds had cleared and the silver moon looked down on a white view where the snow had refashioned the land. The crisp night scene offered a smooth landscape of fresh beauty where everything was clothed in gentle curves of white linen. However, the two ravens perched in the top of the tree had other things on their mind.

"Bind it up tighter," said Searle, "I keep expecting it to spring open any minute."

She was holding Amalek's golden, magic star-box which they had stolen. It was bound tightly with a mass of the strongest stems of plants they could find. They had made a loop which acted like a handle which was hooked around one of Searle's claws. Before they had stolen it, it snapped at them and then blew Urrg high into the air.

Searle managed to catch it in her beak and keep it closed until they had bound it up.

Now it hung down harmlessly but Searle was still nervous.

"Collect some more plants, Urrg," she said, "Climbers are the best… like ivy. It's strong. Go on."

Urrg sighed.

"But it's alright now," she said grumpily, "Look! It's not moving or anything."

"It's not moving *now*," said Searle, "But what if it did!"

"It can't with all that binding around it! The sooner we get it to our Master the better," said Urrg.

"Yes, of course," agreed Searle crossly, "But we'll bind it up a bit tighter first and then we'll go. I'll hold it here and you get the plants."

Urrg sighed again. "But it's so difficult with all this snow around."

"But it's stopped snowing," snapped Searle, "Stop complaining! Just go and do it!"

"Oh OK," she agreed reluctantly, "But next time there's some work to do it's your turn."

Urrg jumped off the branch and descended into the trees.

When Gratch arrived at Old Howard's House it was still night but the dawn was only one hour away. He opened the front door with his clawed foot and stepped inside. When his long body was halfway in, the Dark Wizard Troubler appeared in the hall and glared at him.

"Where have you been?" he demanded.

Gratch's rumbling answer was defensive. "It's hard to travel in the snow... very hard..."

Then the wizard noticed that it was not snowing.

"What's this?" he said, walking to the open door and looking out, "What's happened?"

"It's stopped snowing, Master," answered Gratch.

"I can see *that!* But what about my spell?"

The wizard shook his head and looked around and up, scowling at what he saw.

"It's impossible," he concluded.

His thin face looked pale and gaunt in the moonlight as he stepped out to look to his left towards Candara. "At least *that* cloud's still there… and my trapped unicorns."

He stepped back in.

Gratch had lowered himself to the floor to rest. The Troubler looked crossly down at him.

"Gratch, get up," the Troubler hissed at him with a cruel sting in his voice, "Get out there and dig around until you find a bird under the snow."

Gratch pulled himself onto his feet.

"Go!" shouted the wizard.

Gratch did what he was told and after burrowing in the deep snow he was back inside in a minute. The evil wizard looked intently at him.

"I found a bird," Gratch growled.

"Was it hard?"

"Yes, Master."

"How hard?"

"Very hard, Master... completely hard, and cold... it was frozen. I touched it with my tongue and then tried to move it. It wouldn't move at all."

The wizard sighed in relief.

"Good," he said, "Good... good. The spell is living. It's intact. But it should be snowing, Gratch. I don't understand it at all... there must be some reason."

He closed the door and walked to the back room with the Komodo following. Gratch was glad to get indoors although it was almost as cold. He slumped down flat on the floorboards. The wizard dropped into the armchair, leant back and closed his eyes in thought. Then he spoke his thoughts aloud as he tried to work it out.

"The spell is living... but the snow has stopped..." He shook his head. "Why has it stopped?"

Gratch was feeling impatient for his food.

"They're here," Gratch replied, his voice a deep rumbling growl, "I saw them arrive, Master."

The wizard's eyes opened wide.

"So," he hissed quietly with his words charged with venom, "They got through..." He frowned with irritation. "My ravens are not doing well. They let them get across the border and then travel all that way. But, Gratch, did you kill any?"

Gratch's tongue flashed out and a drop of saliva dribbled out and then hung down as if on string. The thought of killing the enemy made his hunger stronger.

"No," he growled, "The unicorn was there with them... and you said..."

"Yes, yes," the wizard interrupted, "That's good. And did they go into the palace?"

"Yes, they went in and that's when I left, Master. I came back to tell you."

The wizard thought for a moment.

"I see... with the unicorn... this mysterious unicorn... with that they could travel fast. What colour was it?"

"Gold," answered Gratch.

"So, another gold one," said the wizard, "I wonder if there are any more? But it's good... we know where they are. But what if they leave there, Gratch?"

"Won't they rest first, Master?" suggested Gratch.

"They will," agreed the wizard, "They'll eat and rest after their long journey... they're bound to. And also, they don't know that I know where they are, do they?"

"No, Master."

"They didn't see you, did they?"

"No, Master."

Gratch decided not to tell the wizard about how he got lost and slept under the bridge. He knew this would excite the anger of his master.

"They were there when you left, Gratch?"

"Yes, Master."

"Then they'll still be there resting, at least for a while." The wizard narrowed his black eyes. "They think they're safe. But I have a plan." He laughed. "I'm almost ready. Then I'll deal with them... and I have them exactly where I need them. It's perfect. When I'm prepared I'll do it... they'll be finished." He lowered his voice to a sinister whisper that hissed out into the dingy room. "Finished."

"Yes, Master," Gratch said very politely hoping that he would get his food soon.

The wizard brought his hands together and closed his eyes.

"And there's something else, Master," began Gratch.

The wizard opened his eyes with interest.

"You know that mill in Candara?" asked Gratch.

"No," the wizard said.

"Well, it's the other side of the town from here... to the south. I saw a light in the top room."

The wizard looked stunned and frowned.

"A light?" he asked, shaking his head in utter disbelief, "A light, Gratch? That's impossible. There's no one... unless... unless it's another unicorn?"

"Their horns do light up, Master," Gratch said.

"Then, it *must* be," concluded the wizard, "But where are they all coming from? That's four now. You'll have to go out and deal with it, Gratch. That will be your meal."

"Unicorns can't be eaten, Master," growled Gratch, "I'll go and kill it but I need a meal first."

"Alright then," the Troubler agreed, "I'll get your food then you go out and kill the unicorn... and bring me back its alicorn," he said greedily, "I can syphon off the alicorn's power. Then I'll deal with the enemy. And *then*... the gems."

"The Candara Gems, Master?" asked Gratch.

"The Candara Gems," confirmed the wizard.

He stood up and went to the kitchen to get the food for Gratch.

Dawn broke sharp and clear across The Kingdom Of Gems. It was a dramatic contrast to the days before when the fierce blizzard swept across the fleecy hills in a mad rush. Today the air was almost still with a gentle breeze blowing from the east. The rising sun was peeping over the horizon and tinting the snow with pink as it glanced across the whole land like a watchful eye. Every icicle hanging on the ends of branches captured a touch of the pink light, each becoming like a little lantern. The sky above was empty of clouds except for the one above Candara.

The Prince and Princess were looking out of a gold-framed Round Room window with a sense of wonder at the beautiful scene. The beauty was uplifting and strengthening. A moment later, however, the feeling was dampened when they thought of the Dark Wizard Troubler and how his spell had caused the snow. The heavy presence of the spell was all around them and the terrible feeling of the loss of their parents sat in their stomachs like a lead weight. They knew they must go forwards but they doubted that they had the strength.

Simron came up behind them and Joog swooped into the room and landed on Seph's shoulder.

"It's a fine morning," Simron said calmly, "Perfect for travelling."

"I feel as though I can't do anything," sighed Amalek, "With our mother and father gone. Can't we stay a bit before we go?"

"We have no time," Joog said, his voice serious but kind, "We have slim chance as it is... if we delay I think our chance will have gone. We need to leave here now. What would your parents want us to do?"

Amalek nodded slowly.

"He's right," agreed Seph, "We need to go."

"I know," said Amalek, "I know. But it's so difficult. I feel so weak now."

Simron smiled at them kindly.

"We have strength," he said, "More strength than we know. Remember what I told you... I think I called it a great secret at the time. That's because most people don't really know about it... and they don't live by it either."

The children spoke together.

"Real strength is found within," they said.

As they spoke they began to feel stronger.

"Right," said Seph decisively, "We'd better go then."

Amalek made an effort to shed her despondency and managed a smile.

"Let me at least comb my hair first," she said.

Simron chuckled, "Just one minute, that's all."

Joog felt admiration for the children. Seph was only twelve and Amalek thirteen but they were showing such courage.

They all descended the stairs to the ground floor. Aram had the clothes tied around his feet again to dampen the clatter of his hooves just in case. Tally hopped enthusiastically by Seph's side.

As they approached the front door, they felt the palace shudder. The children and Simron fell towards the wall and then clung to it to keep their balance. Lazuli thumped into the wall with the sound of cracking plaster. The floor shook again and then settled, and then the palace seemed to sway as if afloat on the rolling waves of a mighty ocean.

Near the front door, a table rocked and a pile of five or six books slid off and tumbled onto the floor in an untidy heap. Then the table skidded across the floor and hit the other wall.

"What's going on?!" squeaked little Miriam, "What's going on?!"

"I don't know..." replied Joog.

He flew to the door while the others moved towards it, clinging to the wall. The palace was still swaying. The Prince opened the door a crack and looked out. His eyes opened wide in astonishment.

"What is it?" asked Amalek who was just behind him.

"We're flying!" exclaimed Seph, "The whole palace has taken off!"

Seph opened the door wide and they all crowded around and peered out. It was true. The palace had left the ground and was rising steadily like a hot-air balloon.

"Let's jump!" cried Seph.

"No!" snapped Simron, "It's too late."

He was right. The palace was already too high to jump out safely. Terror gripped them like the vicious bite of a fierce dog that would not let go.

They rose rapidly, and after a moment they could see for miles. The palace turned gently so that the scene was ever-changing; it was a panorama of the wintery landscape. They could see Candara way below like a tiny toy village with the snow falling thickly and lying upon the roofs and streets. Across Blue Lake, the Snowpeak Mountains were still and majestic like silent witnesses to all the extraordinary events that were taking place in the kingdom.

The palace was still rising and heading due west, carried silently by the breeze, above the Flatsage Farmlands and heading for the Western Downs. They passed over Charin Road, just visible by the snow-covered hedge that runs alongside it. Then they were above the downs, and a moment later over the flat area of The Plains of Wilrack.

"We're going so fast!" exclaimed Joog, "What shall we do?"

"We're heading for the border!" cried Seph, "He's taking us right out of the kingdom!"

Suddenly, the palace lurched and slowed, stopped turning, and then tilted back. It took them by surprise and sent them all sliding away from the door and along the hall. As they passed the cupboard they heard the alarmed voices of the two prisoners.

"Help!" shouted Razz.

"Let us out!" screeched Forr.

The ravens had managed to work some of their bindings free, releasing one wing each but they were still bound together. They had no idea what was happening and this was sending them into a panic. They slid across the floor and bumped into the door.

Then the palace tilted back again, sending the ravens careering back across the cupboard. They cracked into the wall and cried out in pain.

In the hall, the tangle of friends slid back, as if on ice. Seph was first and slipped right out through the open door.

"Help!" he cried.

He swung out an arm in desperation. His hand smacked into the door frame and he gripped on for his life. His body swung down and he hung there precariously by one arm.

The palace levelled off, leaving Amalek a few feet away from the door with the others behind her. As she watched, she saw Seph's hand disappear. He had gone.

"Seph!" she shouted.

She turned to Joog with panic in her eyes, "Joog, he's fallen!"

Joog immediately flew out through the door.

Amalek scrabbled to the door and nervously looked over.

"Seph!" she cried.

Flop, Miriam and Tally rushed to the door and peered out. Seph had caught hold to a step just below the door and was hanging on to it. Amalek reached out a hand towards him.

"Lazuli!" called out Amalek, "Hold onto my legs!"

Lazuli wound her trunk around Amalek's legs and held her tightly.

Joog was clutching Seph's coat at his shoulder, gripping with his talons and flapping furiously to pull him up.

"Lower me out!" shouted Amalek to Lazuli.

Lazuli moved forwards and lowered Amalek out of the open door.

"I'm slipping!" shouted Seph.

Joog started flapping his wings even faster but Seph was too heavy. At that moment his weight became too much and his hand began to slip off the step.

Joog summoned all his strength and flapped furiously to support Seph and stop him plunging downwards. Lazuli swung Amalek towards Seph. Her hands met his arms and she gripped as hard as she could, but still his arms were slipping through. Then their hands met and the grip held.

The palace lurched again and Seph's coat was ripped from Joog's talons. Immediately, the children's hands slipped until it was just their fingers hooking over each other that kept contact. Seph's life was held in the fragile grip of their hands. They both strained but they were not strong enough and Seph's weight began to prise the fingers apart. Suddenly, Joog's taloned feet grasped around the children's hands and squeezed, locking the hands together.

Lazuli pulled. Amalek was hauled back to safety and Seph followed with Joog still holding their hands together. The children collapsed onto their backs. Seph shook his head in disbelief and then sighed with relief.

"That was close!" he said, "Thank you, Ammey."

He looked up at Lazuli's huge face, "And thank you Lazuli... and Joog."

The others were all on their feet again, with Tally and Flop by the open door. Simron stood behind them, looking out and down as well. Behind them the two ravens were rapping at the cupboard door with their beaks and occasionally one of them would shout, "Let us out!"

The palace had turned, changed direction and was passing over the Wellspring Woods. Joog saw his tree, his home, the wood where he lived and which he loved so much. Then he shuddered when he thought that all the creatures, all the life that made the woods busy with happy activity, were now trapped by the evil spell. The woods were no longer teeming with life. Would it ever be the same again?

"What can we do?" asked Flop.

No one answered. They were caught in the palace like flies in a spiders web with no way of escaping. They were victims of the evil wizard's power and they felt helpless. Then Flop heard Miriam's voice close to his ear.

"We'll think of something," she said.

The palace was now travelling south but arcing around towards the east. They were soon over the Heather Heights and then heading towards Candara. Aram had taken the clothes off his feet so that his grip was better. He tapped a hoof on the wooden floor and they all looked at him.

"I think I know what's happening here," he said, "The Troubler is flying this palace into the cloud above Candara. He wants to trap us there... like Halo."

"He's right," said Simron, with urgency in his voice, "That's it. So, we must get off the palace somehow, and soon, before it reaches the cloud."

Joog looked out again, his head turning 180 degrees. The palace was heading straight for the cloud. He wished he could help the others. He could fly but all his friends were in terrible danger.

The palace was accelerating and now it was clear that Aram was right; they were heading straight for the cloud which loomed larger every second.

The Prince and Princess looked at each other.

"Magic books," they said together.

They quickly took them out of their pockets and began studying them.

"I know where to look," Amalek said.

The Princess flicked over a few pages.

"Quick!" said Tally, "We're getting closer to the cloud."

"It's here somewhere," she said, and then exclaimed, "Yes!"

She looked up to see all the others staring at her. Her face was alert and she was keeping her panic at bay.

"There is a way," she began quickly, "We'll have to jump! Where's your box, Seph?"

He had his oval, golden magic box in his hand.

"Open it," she said.

He opened it.

"Quick!" said Tally who had turned to look out of the door.

"Take out the bells and hand them around," Amalek said.

He took out some tiny golden bells on golden threads and started to hand them around.

"There's only seven," said Seph, "You don't need one Joog, and Miriam you can stay on Flop. With the threads you can hang them around your necks."

Amalek looked into the magic book again.

"The magic box will catch us somehow just before we hit the ground," she said as quickly as she could, "But you must ring the bell."

Tally's young eyes were wide with fear.

"Are we going to jump?" he said.

"It will work," said Seph, "You have to trust it."

The cloud looked huge now as they sped towards it. Then they saw Halo in the cloud running towards them, a shining, silver streak in the morning light.

"Halo!" called out Aram.

"Jump now, Aram!" commanded Seph, "Jump now!"

Aram knew there was nothing they could do for Halo now; they had to jump. But they were so close to her.

Aram could see the tears in her eyes, like sparkling pearls in the sunshine, and his heart melted. He was tempted to leap across into the cloud and be with her again. At least they would be together. But he knew the others needed him.

"I'll save you, Halo," he called.

"Seph," said Amalek, "Throw the box out."

He tossed the oval magic box through the open door.

Lazuli closed her eyes, plucked up courage and jumped, followed by Flop who was fine with heights. Miriam was on his neck in a panic.

"Help!" she squeaked as they launched into the air and fell away.

Simron saw Aram hesitating and with all his strength pushed him out and then followed himself.

Tally was poised on the edge unable to move.

"KYWAY, Tally, KYWAY," said his grandfather's voice.

He felt the gentle touch of a paw on his shoulder and then the encouragement of a slight push. In front of him the cloud was rushing towards him and he knew he only had a few seconds. He had to do it. He closed his eyes tightly and jumped.

"I'll keep an eye on them," Joog called out to Amalek and Seph as he glided out. He circled around the others as they fell.

Amalek and Seph felt a wave of mist from the cloud touch their faces. Halo was watching them, so close and yet so far from freedom. Amalek hesitated in the doorway. Suddenly, the fear of jumping out and falling from such a height had flooded her mind. Then she saw Halo and wished she could do something for her.

"Come on!" shouted Seph.

Another second and the palace would plunge into the cloud.

"Halo!" shouted Amalek as she threw her tiny golden bell towards Halo while grabbing Seph's hand. They jumped together and fell hand in hand. As the palace rushed into the dark cloud just above Halo's head, Seph shouted to her.

"Jump!"

On Halo's alicorn, wrapped around the silver spiralled pattern, was a golden thread, and on the end of the thread a tiny golden bell.

In Old Howard's House, sitting on a chair and looking out from an open upstairs window, was the Dark Wizard Troubler. His hat was resting on the floor and his black cloak was wrapped tightly around him. His jet black hair, contrasting with his pale skin, was swept back harshly, lying tightly against his head. It was long and unkempt and fell down beyond his hunched shoulders. He was clutching his staff and pointing it toward Candara. The great garnet gemstone was glowing deep red.

He had sent Gratch out to investigate the light in the Old Mill and expected him to kill the unicorn and bring back it's alicorn as a trophy. He knew he could harness the magic of the horn for himself.

He had used his staff to make the palace float up from the hill and then watched with excitement as it headed for the border.

He had intended to fly them across the border and right out of the kingdom. Then he would let the palace crash to the ground somewhere and hope that they were all killed. But then he had changed his mind. He had a much better idea which would keep him in control. He would fly them into the cloud, his prison-cloud.

He turned the palace in the air and rushed from window to window to perform his magic as the palace circled over Heather Heights and then north-east, towards the cloud. Then something small and bright fell from the palace and he wondered what it was. But the important thing for him was that they were in the palace and the palace would soon be in the cloud.

"Good," he whispered to himself, wallowing in sinister glee, "At last!" His lips turned up in a mixture between a smile and a snarl.

He stood up to witness the final moment of glory.

"What?!" he exclaimed.

A moment before the palace entered the cloud he had seen them falling to the ground. They had escaped! The smug feeling of success had vanished like a feather in a hurricane. He sat down in shock and leant forwards and out of the window, thumping his fist on the window frame in fury.

Seething with anger he watched as they fell.

It was too far away to see what happened to them and also there were some houses in the way, but he knew they would survive the fall. They must have found a way, otherwise why would they have jumped? It would be magic from Wizard Elzaphan. He would go out himself and find them. He turned away from the window and stood up. If he had waited a moment later he would have seen a silver unicorn fall from the cloud.

He strode out of the room and down the stairs.

Gratch followed his tracks along the river passing through the houses and cottages of Candara. He had left a channel in the deep snow and so the return journey was much easier. Snow fell steadily from the one remaining cloud in the kingdom.

He looked up at the tall Spindley Tower reaching up high above him. It was an extraordinary building, decorated with carvings which had collected snow in every nook and cranny. Icicles seemed to hang everywhere. The top section leant a little giving it a slightly comical appearance. He soon passed it, continuing through the town until he turned the first sharp bend in the river. There was the Old Mill clearly in view.

He approached it cautiously. Although it was daytime, he could still see the light in the attic. This puzzled him. Why was its alicorn glowing in the day? Also, how was it bright enough to shine so clearly in the daylight?

He paused to think about it and work out a plan. It was all very well for his master to send him out to kill the unicorn but this might not be such an easy task; he knew how dangerous they could be.

There was only one door to enter. The shutters were closed on all the windows downstairs. He reached the door, and being as quiet as he could, he pushed it open. It swung open with a creak. Inside it was dark. He stepped inside, dragging his long tail after him, until all of his great body was through. He could not see anything in the darkness and blinked as his eyes tried to adjust.

He heard a noise to his right and turned. Then he felt a sharp blow to his head and his world turned upside-down.

When the Dark Wizard Troubler was downstairs, he prepared himself for a journey. He hastily ate some food while getting ready to go out and thought about his plans. The main thing was to kill the Prince and Princess and the others with them. When they were all dead, then the Candara Gems would be his. It was simple.

He left by the back door and stepped out into the deep snow. He looked up at the clear sky. It concerned him that the snow had stopped falling, but he could do nothing about that at the moment.

As he looked up, he saw two ravens swooping down towards him. It was Searle and Urrg. They glided though the icy air and landed on the snow in front of him. The Troubler glowered down at them, looked around and then at them again.

"Why only two of you?" he snapped, "Where are all the others?"

Searle and Urrg had been confident about reporting to the wizard but now, as they looked up at him and his staring black eyes, they felt afraid. They knew he was powerful enough to do what he wanted with them.

"The others..." began Urrg nervously. She realised she should have prepared for this question and now she could not think what to say. Her mind was spinning in a panic. "The others are..."

The wizard looked down at her with disapproval, "It's a simple question," he snapped impatiently, "Where are they?"

Then he noticed that she was carrying something.

"What's that?" he demanded.

"It's a magic box," began Urrg, "We stole it from the Prince and Princess, sir. We stole it for you, sir."

"Where was this?" he demanded.

"Back there," Urrg jerked her head to point with her beak, "Way back there, sir... in Summertime Kingdom, sir."

"Good," said the Troubler with glee, "Good! Give it here."

He reached out his wiry-fingered hand and grabbed it. The loop of plant stem stayed hooked around Searle's claw and the binding began to unwind. The Troubler started unwinding it as well.

"Stop!" Searle called out.

The wizard looked shocked at the sudden order and frowned at her.

"What?!" he snapped.

"I mean... well... er… let me explain sir," stammered Searle, "I think it would be unwise, if I may say so, sir, to… to… open it. The last time it opened it blew… um… i…it blew like a wind coming out of it, sir, and it blew Urrg right up into the s…sky!"

"Stay here," the Troubler ordered.

He turned back and went into the house and returned a moment later with the star-box tied up tightly with thick black string. He studied it carefully.

"This came from Wizard Elzaphan," he hissed out the words hatefully, "Look, there's his coat of arms. It's good to have it but is the capture of a magic box really all we have? Is this all an army of ravens can do? Where are the others - the General and the rest of my army?"

Searle had had time now to work out an answer and was less nervous.

"We last saw them still searching in Summertime Kingdom, sir," she said, "But they're useless! We left them because they kept getting everything wrong and we couldn't stand it any longer. The General is hopeless, sir."

"What?!" the Troubler's black eyes flared with anger, but when he spoke his words were loaded with an icy calmness, "What do you mean? I chose my General personally to make the right decisions and lead with discipline! Are you questioning my selection?"

"No sir," began Urrg, frightened by the Troubler's anger, "He has good qualities, and your choice was good, of course sir. You chose well... very well. But, I think, after you chose him... *after* you chose him, sir... he has gone all wrong, sir... sort of... sort of... crazy, sir."

"Mad," added Searle getting more confident, "Completely mad! He doesn't know what he's doing."

"Has the power gone to his head then?" he glared at her, fixing his eyes on hers, "Is that what you're saying?"

"Yes sir," said Urrg, relieved that he was accepting what they said, "That's just it. Your choice was good, but he's changed... gone mad... since he's been in power, the power's gone to his head, sir."

"It explains a few things," he said, "Like why the army has failed completely under his command. Has he still got the compass?"

"Yes sir," answered Urrg.

"Alright then," he hissed, "Alright. I haven't time for this now... I'll talk to you later because I need to know more. But not now because the Prince and Princess are back and I'm going to finish them off... seeing that nobody else can." He glared at Searle and Urrg with such venom that they both felt weak inside, as if he had reached inside them, grasped every ounce of energy that they had and drained it out of them.

"Here are my orders," he snarled, "Stay here and guard."

He held out the star-box to Searle who took hold of it nervously by gripping the black string. "Put this in the house and then guard it with your lives," he commanded.

For a brief moment he glared at the two ravens to make sure he had imposed is iron will upon them, and then he turned and strode off purposefully, pushing through the deep snow.

Lazuli opened her eyes to find herself falling much faster than the snowflakes which fell from the cloud above her. At the same time she was tumbling over and over through the snow-filled air so that one second she was looking up at the dark cloud and the next she was seeing the snowy ground getting closer very rapidly.

She was drifting north-east on the breeze. As she approached the ground she shook the tiny golden bell with faith that the magic of Wizard Elzaphan would work. The bell rang beautifully in the chilly air and she saw a flash of silver. She felt herself being caught gently just before she hit the snow. She had landed in a fine silver net, both strong and supple, and it cushioned her fall.

Then she heard another tinkling bell and Flop landed beside her in the net with Miriam squeaking in fear on his neck. Aram had been followed by Simron and then Tally, Amalek and Seph. They had all rung their bells and trusted that the magic would catch them. The net had lowered the tangled group of friends gently into the deep snow. They had landed beside a house on the corner of Nathan Avenue and Link Way.

The snow was deeper in the town than elsewhere in the kingdom with the exception of the mountains, with deep drifts in the streets. Less snow had settled in the alleyways between the houses which were partly protected from the driving winds of the snowstorms.

The breeze swept large snowflakes down upon the group who rolled out of the net. They stood up, sinking into the deep snow which was up to the children's waists. They brushed the snow off and looked around. The children and Simron were wrapped up in coats, hats and gloves.

Amalek and Seph, however, were looking anxiously up at the cloud.

"Can she escape the cloud?" asked Seph.

"With the bell, yes," Amalek confirmed, "The magic bell will free her. Let's just hope she jumps."

Seph began frantically waving his arms to her, but the falling snow was to thick to see her.

"Jump, Halo, jump!" Amalek said quietly, wishing and hoping that Halo would follow them down.

Aram took a step towards them though the snow.

"What?!" Aram exclaimed, "What's happening?"

"We threw a bell to Halo," she replied, "So she can jump too."

Aram looked up and his heart leapt when he saw a flash of silver. Halo had jumped and was descending towards them. A couple of seconds later and she was almost down. Suddenly Amalek looked at her brother and grabbed his arm.

"She doesn't know that she's got to ring the bell!" she exclaimed.

Halo was almost down, falling upside-down, back first and legs pointing up when the Prince shouted.

"Halo!"

At the sound of his voice, Halo twisted her head around. The bell was still wound around her alicorn by the golden thread and it jingled. Immediately the silver net was there breaking her fall and catching her gently.

They all gathered around her and helped her out of the net. Aram gazed at her for a moment as she stood in the deep snow, her silver shining brightly in the dull morning light and surrounded by thickly falling snow. Aram moved to Halo to greet her, with a heart lifted with joy.

Seph looked for his oval, magic box and to his delight he found it was floating towards him. He picked it out of the air and then collected the tiny golden bells from everyone, putting them back into the magic box. Then he slipped it into his pocket and buttoned it up.

"The funny thing is..." he began, smiling, "Those two ravens are trapped up there in the palace!"

Amalek smiled too. "*We've* got away and he's trapped his own ravens!"

She felt Flop's paw on her leg.

"I can't see a thing from here," he said, "and my paws are cold."

The snow was too deep for a cat, and poor Flop was beneath the level of the surface.

"Oh, sorry, Flop," said Amalek, looking down.

She picked him up and Seph picked up Tally. They all pushed their way through the snow to the closest house in Link Way where they could shelter beside it from the falling snow. As they discussed their next move, the breeze dropped. By the time they stepped out again, large snowflakes were falling through the still air in a steady and quick descent to the smooth white land below. They moved into Link Way and then turned left into Nathan Avenue.

"Stop!" said Joog, "What's that sound?"

They all stood still and listened. It was the sound of footsteps; the rhythmical crunching noise of someone forcing their way through the snow. The steps were hurried and growing louder. No one moved. They gazed through the falling snow.

Then they saw a shape, a figure looking ghostly in the pale background and striding straight towards them through a channel in the waist-high snow. Another step and the figure was clearer to see, clad in a black cloak and hat, both covered with black stars, deeper than the darkest night, and dotted with snow.

The feeling of menace was intense. The dark presence that they had met before was now engulfing them again. It seeped into their minds and bodies trying to take them over, like icy hands gripping their beings with the chill of death.

The Dark Wizard Troubler stood still now and glared at them with hate. The bright white of the snow paled to a dull grey around him. His black eyes were blazing with a loathing that was tangible. His face twisted into a sneer as he lifted his staff. The garnet gemstone glowed red and then black, and then he disappeared.

Chapter 7

~ The Cloud ~

The group of friends were taken completely by surprise and stood in shock, with the snow falling all around and gently patting on their hats and coats, as soft as the touch of a feather. They all stared ahead in stunned silence, at the place where the Troubler had been before he disappeared. Amalek broke the silence.

"Where is he?!" she asked quietly with panic in her searching eyes.

"What shall we do?" asked Flop from Amalek's arms.

"He's still there," said Simron quietly, "He's invisible but he's still there..."

Then the snow moved, as if by itself, clearing a path through the snow towards them.

They heard his footstep crunch into the snow.

"Quick!" Joog said urgently, "Into the house..."

Joog was pointing with a wing and they looked towards the house. Then Joog changed his mind.

"No!" he said quickly, "The stable... over there... so that Lazuli can fit through those doors."

At Joog's voice they sprang into action. Aram led the way, dipping his alicorn to clear a path in the snow up to the door. They all rushed after him. The snow was less deep here than in the streets but it was still enough to block the door, so that when Seph grabbed the door handle and tried to pull it open, it stuck. Amalek helped him and it juddered open a little, and then stuck again.

They heard movements behind them. Tally was last and turned to look back. The shifting snow gave away the Troubler's position exactly. He was close behind them. Then Tally saw the sinister, black-cloaked figure of the wizard reappear.

"Quick!" urged Tally.

The children were pulling the door as hard as they could and trying to force it open. Simron grabbed Seph and pulled as well. Halo pointed her alicorn; the snow powdered into the air and the door jerked open sending Seph, Amalek and Simron tumbling backwards. At that moment the wizard lunged at them and they were engulfed in the dull feeling of his grey presence.

In his eagerness to get them, the wizard slipped and fell, but as he did, he desperately flung out a hand and caught hold of one of Tally's ears. The wizard tried to get up but in his frantic effort he slipped again. Tally cried out in pain and wriggled to try to break away.

Lazuli swung round and reached back with her trunk, grabbing Tally and pulling him free. The wizard was left holding a tuft of white fur in his hand.

The ten friends scrambled through the doorway, piling into the stable with Aram and Halo's hooves clattering on the straw-covered, wooden floor. Lazuli was last and she slammed the door with her trunk, and then locked it with two large bolts, one at the top and one at the bottom.

Two horses stood in the stable; frozen, frosty statues trapped by the spell.

"What now?" asked Amalek.

"Barricade the door?" suggested Tally.

"No," said Joog, "because then he'd have us trapped in here."

"You're right," began Simron., "We need to get out of here... and fast!"

He looked around.

"There."

He pointed at a door on the other side of the stable. Suddenly, the doors behind them rattled violently for a moment as the Dark Wizard pummelled them with his fists. They all stared, alert and ready for the wizard to smash the doors and burst in. The unicorns lowered their alicorns, pointing them at the door, but then the rattling stopped.

In the silence they heard something that sent a chill down their spines; it was the wizards's rasping breath. He was so close that it sounded as if he was in the room with them. Seph looked around for something to fight with and saw a broom leaning against the wall. He picked it up, held it in front of him with both hands like a heavy sword, and stepped forwards, next to Aram and Halo. Tally hopped up beside him.

Outside, the wizard was leaning against the doors to recover from all the efforts he had made. Sending the palace up into the cloud, followed by his hurried walk through the deep snow, had left him tired. After a moment of rest he felt better and stepped back. He gripped his staff tightly and lifted it.

"The door," whispered Simron, pointing across the room.

He urgently stabbed his finger towards the door, "Now!" he whispered, glaring at them, "Move!"

Aram and Halo turned leaving just Seph with his broom raised and ready to fight, and Tally beside him.

"Seph!" ordered Simron, "We're not fighting him now... not yet. Now... come over here!"

"Seph!" exclaimed Amalek.

Seph dropped the idea of fighting the wizard, let go of the broom and stepped away, with Tally following.

At that moment, the stable lurched. They knew what was happening and they rushed across the room to the door. Amalek pushed and Lazuli helped with her trunk, and it flew open into the snowy world outside. Falling snow blew into their faces. The stable was already in the air and swaying as it quickly rose higher.

Amalek dived out into the snow which was much deeper on this side of the stable. Flop followed, with Miriam in the fur on his neck. Seph and Tally were next; they jumped side by side. Simron ushered Aram and Halo out and then jumped himself. As soon as they landed, the Halo began clearing a channel through the deep snow with her alicorn.

Joog glided silently down through the falling snow to hover above the others. Tally joined in with the digging, using both his front and back paws with remarkable skill. The stable continued to rise.

Lazuli could only get her head in the door and she began to try to push through. The door frame cracked and splintered.

"Push!" cried Amalek, staring up at her.

Bricks and mortar began to crumble around the door. She pushed harder until there was enough room for her to get through. She got ready to jump but then hesitated. The stable had risen too high.

"I can't jump. It's too late..." she cried with her voice fading as she rose higher and higher, "Don't worry! Keep fighting... you can..."

The stable grew smaller as it sped upwards.

The children and Simron looked across the gap where the stable used to be. Standing there in the snow beyond, and glaring angrily at them, was the wizard with black eyes as cold as steel. The snow was up to his waist and his black robe was dotted and smudged with white.

Suddenly, he pointed his staff and a flash of red light cleared a path through the snow towards them. Then another flashed towards Seph, who instinctively held up an arm in defence. A golden flash from Aram's alicorn intercepted, making an explosion of sparks.

"Don't look at him!" cried Aram.

Halo and Tally were still digging a pathway into the snow with high walls on either side. They were working with amazing speed and Simron, Amalek and Seph turned and ran through it until they caught the others up. Aram fired a blast of light at the Dark Wizard who dodged sideways. The flash skimmed through the snow leaving a steaming pathway.

Aram rushed along the channel built by Halo and Tally, and joined the others. The unicorns turned and pointed their alicorns back, making the snow return and fill up the channel. Clouds of fine snow puffed up and drifted on the breeze like mist.

The black figure of the Troubler was running now across the snow-free gap where the stable had been. When he was across he met the deep snow like a wall in front of him. He held his staff out and with a flash snow began to clear.

The group of friends were scrambling away, the fear of the evil wizard spurring them on. Aram and Halo soon reached a house and cleared another channel through the snow to the door. The snow had blown up against the house to make a deep drift, much deeper than in the open road. It was so deep that it had almost covered the windows on the lower floor and reached up above the heads of the children to be even higher than Simron and the unicorns.

"Quick!" said Joog from above their heads, "He's coming!"

Joog looked back and saw that the wizard was striding so fast that it was too late for them to get away; in a few moments he would be upon them. Joog wheeled around and dived at the Troubler.

The evil wizard ducked and Joog reached out a clawed foot and scratched him on the cheek. With a cry, the wizard held his hand to his face and turned to watch Joog fly away. He lifted his staff and pointed it. A shaft of red light shot out. Joog swerved in the air just in time and the light singed a few feathers as it flashed by and plunged into a tree which burst into flames.

While the wizard was distracted, Simron was in charge.

"We can trick him here," he said, "Seph, open the door but don't go in... everyone else start digging another pathway there."

He pointed to a deep wall of snow that piled up high beside the door in a great drift. Seph opened the door.

"In here! Quick!" said a voice close by.

They all spun round. Where had the voice had come from? Tally started digging into the snow by the door. He broke through a thin wall of snow to come face to face with a mountain hare sitting inside the entrance to a snow-tunnel.

"Kendall!" whispered Tally in astonishment.

Kendall was pure white with a silver necklace around her neck and hanging on it was a small ammolite gemstone. It was translucent with green, red and amber blending into each other. It shed a soft glow which colourfully tinted her white fur behind it.

They all piled in. Simron was last and before he followed them in, he glanced back to make sure they were not being seen. He slammed the door to the house and then stepped in with the others.

"What are you doing here?!" Tally asked Kendall.

Kendall was too busy to answer. She was repairing the hole.

"Wait," ordered Tally, "There's still Joog to come."

At that moment, Joog swooped in, crashing into Tally.

Kendall and Tally filled in the hole and between them it was done in a few seconds.

"We've come to help," said Kendall, "Look, the tunnel goes along there and then right through the deepest snow drifts in the town!"

"Sshh!" whispered Simron.

He had heard the sound of the Troubler's footsteps approaching. The wizard had heard the door slam closed and was striding purposefully towards it. He paused and put his ear to the door. Then, very quietly, he opened it and went in.

They felt his evil presence intensify and then fade again.

Simron's trick had worked.

They looked along the large tunnel in wonder. A little way along they saw an old hare sitting up on his haunches on a sledge. It was Hawkeye. The sledge had been made especially for him so he could manage the journey from the Becci Mountains. Tally ran along the tunnel to him.

"Gramps!" he called out in his excitement and jumped up enthusiastically onto his sledge.

Hawkeye put a paw on Tally's shoulder. He looked old but his eyes were bright. Hanging around his neck was a similar necklace; a silver chain with a coloured ammolite gem. Tally looked at it with interest and tapped it gently with his paw.

"Gramps," Tally began, "How did…"

"Tally," said Hawkeye winking at his grandson and lifting a paw to his lips, "Sshh. We don't want to be heard. You're surprised to see me, aren't you? I thought you might need some help from an old-timer!"

Tally looked again at the ammolite. It looked similar to the ones hanging from Flop's and Miriam's collars.

"That protects me," said Hawkeye, "From the spell. It's from Wizard Elzaphan… isn't it beautiful? There's one for all of you too. He knew you had the magic pens but after you left he became concerned about them. Ink can come off… and so he sent these for you. They're more powerful anyway."

He pointed down with a paw and hanging on the side of the sledge was a collection of silver necklaces each with a shining, colourful ammolite hanging from it. He hooked one of them up with his paw and dropped it over Tally's head. It glowed brightly. Then he noticed the fur missing from Tally's ear.

"Ahh," he said, "You're learning already that to fight for what is good and right can be challenging! That will heal quickly. Now... run to the others and give them one of these each… quickly now."

Hawkeye made a quick calculation and then scooped up four other necklaces. Tally took them in his mouth and hopped off to give them to the others. A moment later Amalek, Seph, Simron, and Joog all had the silver necklaces draped around their necks which spread a faint coloured light around them. Aram and Halo were protected already by their own magic and Flop and

Miriam already had theirs. Tally scampered back to his grandfather.

"Gramps!" exclaimed Tally, hopping up onto the sledge and then lowering his voice, "I've had so many adventures. We... that's me and the others," he gestured back along the tunnel, "We came through a tunnel and... we fooled *all* the ravens... and we came out of the tunnel... and then we..."

Hawkeye laughed and held up a paw.

"I know, I know," he said kindly, his eye twinkling as brightly as the morning star, "And later on you can tell me all about it. But now we have things to do."

Tally looked at him with admiration.

"How did you get here?" he asked.

"On this sledge," replied Hawkeye, "And it was Wizard Elzaphan. He asked me... invited me really... and it's a great honour to help with this."

"I kept hearing your voice..." Tally said.

Hawkeye looked along the tunnel.

"Sshh," he said to Tally, lifting a paw to his mouth, "There'll be plenty of time to talk later."

The others were still gathered at the end of the tunnel. They could hear the Troubler moving around inside the house. A second later they heard him come out, close the door and stand by it. He was right next to them.

They felt the temperature of the cold air drop a few more degrees, and they huddled together in the chill. Everything around them paled to grey: their clothes, their skin, even the colour of their eyes. Only the ammolites kept their multi-coloured glow. The atmosphere that hung around him was so strong now that they felt they were being gripped by a thousand icy hands. They hardly dared breathe.

Then they heard his breathing again, slow and precise, but rasping like gravel. He was just the other side of the thin wall of snow. His breathing filled the still air like a whisper in a warehouse, a harsh echo of wickedness seeping everywhere. They felt as if a ghost was reaching into them and intruding into their beings.

Amalek shuddered. Then they heard a loud 'whoosh' and knew what had happened. The house was now soaring upwards to join the stable and the palace in the cloud. The Troubler lowered his staff and it crunched gently into the snow. Its red glow faded.

He looked across the space left by the house and wondered. What if they were not in the house after all? He had not seen them and this left doubt in his mind.

He sniffed the air hoping that he might catch their scent. If they were not hiding in the house which he had sent into the dark cloud, then where could they be? Perhaps they had slipped into one of the other houses. But which one? Nathan Avenue was full of houses.

The Troubler was standing right beside the tunnel where they were hiding. Amalek and Seph very quietly made two tiny holes in the snow and peeped through. When they looked through they had a shock. They could see the Troubler's black boots, the edge of his black cloak. They could see his sinewy hand with the finger and thumb missing.

Amalek gasped for air. She felt dizzy and faint, so she closed her eyes and clutched Seph's hand. He squeezed her hand twice to reassure her and put his finger to his lips.

The wizard's pale-skinned forehead furrowed as he tried to think things through. Then he decided. It would take energy, great energy, but it was the only way to be sure.

He tightened his grip on his staff and lifted it, pointing it at the next house in the street. The huge garnet gem on the top glowed with intense red. The house lifted into the air, slowly at first, and then gathering speed rose towards the dark cloud.

He pointed at the next house; up it went. Then the next, and all along Nathan Avenue. The air was filled with floating houses, drifting up and into the cloud like hot air balloons, gathering in speed as they rose.

When all the houses on one side of the street were gone, he cleared some snow with his staff and strode into the middle of the street. Amalek blew out some air in a sigh of relief.

They carried on watching as he began pointing at the opposite row of houses, starting with the furthest. One by one they rose, floating up in eerie silence towards the cloud.

"Wow!" whispered the Princess very softly to her brother, and then turning to the others, "He's sending *all* the houses up into the cloud!"

"Huh!" smiled the Prince, "to make sure he gets us. If only he knew!"

"Has he gone yet?" whispered Joog.

"No," replied Seph softly, "he's still there."

"Let's hope," Joog whispered softly, "that he really believes he's trapped us up in the cloud. That gives us an advantage."

Simron looked thoughtful and then spoke.

"Is there any way we could convince him we are up there?" he asked.

Amalek's face lit up. She pulled her golden magic book out of her pocket and turned to Simron.

"There's a chapter on mirages and reflections," whispered Amalek thoughtfully, "I saw it earlier..."

She started flicking through the pages and soon she found the right chapter.

"Here it is," she said.

They all waited, while outside the Troubler still stood in the street. He was looking intently all around, checking that there was no way they could have escaped, and nowhere else they could have hidden. Amalek studied the page quickly.

"Right," she whispered quietly, "Make a hole in the roof, please, and everyone gather around me... but I need some space in the middle here. Quick!"

Simron helped Seph onto Aram's back and passed him a knife from his belt.

"How big a hole do you need?" asked Seph.

Amalek looked up and pointed. "From there to there... and round."

Seph pushed the blade up through the snow ceiling just above his head and used it like a saw to cut a large round hole. The snow tumbled down on top of them and they brushed it off. Seph jumped down and joined the others who were circled around Amalek.

"Seph," Amalek continued, "Put your oval box here... in the centre."

He placed in on the snow-floor and opened it.

"The bells have gone!" he exclaimed, "And look..."

Inside the box was divided into three compartments. One contained a delicate golden spoon. The next had gold dust, and the third a liquid.

"Pick up the spoon," whispered Amalek reading the instruction for her book, "then mix three spoonfuls of gold dust with the liquid."

Seph did that.

Amalek continued, "Then pour it out."

Seph picked up the box and poured out the liquid. This formed into a puddle of liquid gold. It was bright, and so shiny and smooth that when they bent over they saw themselves perfectly reflected in it, just like in a mirror.

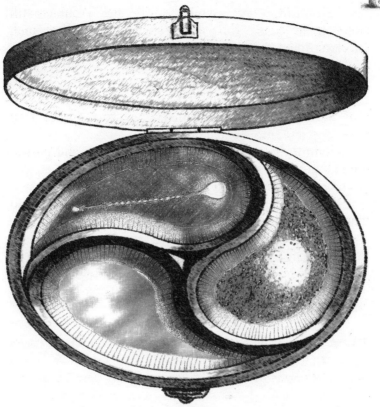

"Now," Amalek concluded, whispering, "We are ready. Tally, keep looking into the gold."

She looked up through the hole in the roof towards the dark cloud and all the others looked up too. They saw Tally looking down at them. He looked tiny high up in the cloud but they could still see his long ears.

"Look at that!" she said, "It works!"

Amalek looked down now and immediately they all saw her and Tally up in the cloud.

"It's amazing," whispered Seph.

"It's perfect," added Simron, "Just what we need. We'd better all look in now - and look alarmed and frightened! We need to really convince him it is us. And lift your wings, Joog, so he sees it's you and knows you haven't flown off somewhere."

They all looked into the magic pool of gold and their frightened, anxious faces appeared up in the dark cloud above, as if looking down.

The Troubler was still looking around, searching for the slightest movement. His black eyes scanned the surroundings for them. Nothing moved. Then he glanced up to the cloud. He almost missed them because they were so high up and small. When he saw them, his black eyes focused on the group of faces trapped in the cloud and a sinister smile twisted his thin face.

He laughed. It was such a relief to have finally beaten them. It was the sweet feeling of success that he had been after for so long. Now suddenly it was over.

"At last," he thought smugly, *"This kingdom is mine."*

Immediately, his thoughts turned to the Candara Gems. Now that they were his prisoners, he could steal them. His power would grow and he could move on to rule an empire, a whole group of kingdoms. He felt the thrill of perfect control.

His imaginings faded but he had glimpsed the future and he liked it. It was just a matter of time. He looked around, deciding what to do next.

"Do you think he's fallen for it?" asked Flop in a whisper.

"It looks like it," replied Joog, "But keep still. If he thinks we're up there… we don't want him to hear us now."

"Yes," Simron commented, nodding, "We need to complete the job. Everyone stay completely still... at least until we know that he's gone."

Dusk was falling over the kingdom. The Troubler stood still in the middle of the street then turned slowly and started walking away. His pale face was tired and drawn, drained of energy and power after raising all the houses into the cloud.

He left the snow and walked across the open space left by one of the houses. Then, suddenly, he turned again and headed straight for them. Joog was the first to hear his approaching footsteps.

"Keep still," he whispered, "He's coming back!"

Amalek looked alarmed. "What about the hole up there?" she whispered, "If he comes closer he will he see it?"

"No," whispered Joog, "The snow's too deep."

The Prince was looking out of one of the tiny holes they had made in the side. "He's coming this way," he whispered.

Amalek joined Seph to look through the other hole. The wizard's black cloak came into view and then he stopped, right beside them.

The wizard felt exhausted and decided he would rest for a moment before tackling the journey back to Old Howard's House. A block of snow-covered rock, which used to be the doorstep to the house, lay in front of him. He sat down on it.

Again, Amalek and Seph could see his black boots and the edge of his cloak. The breeze rippled the cloak and one of the black stars on it came into view. It was so black it seemed, in a strange way, to almost dazzle them. It began to suck them into the darkness. It was a hole of nothingness, a vacant abyss, and their minds began to swirl. They felt they were being drawn into something terrible.

Amalek could feel herself fainting. Her head began to fall and her eyelids drooped and flickered.

Joog saw her head drop and immediately flew onto her shoulder. He nudged her head with his to wake her up, pecked her on the cheek and she opened her eyes wide.

"Look away, Ammey," whispered Joog in her ear.

She pulled her eyes away and turned to Seph. His eyes looked glazed and so she tugged his arm. He looked at her as if waking from a dream. The world around them returned. It was still ghostly-grey but now they could see it clearly and they felt back in control.

They heard his boots move in the snow and then stride away. He crossed through the channel in the snow to the gap where the stable had been. It was speckled with white from the falling snow.

Inside the tunnel no one moved or spoke for a while.

"Relax," said Simron, still whispering, "He's gone... I can feel it."

Relief flooded through them, as fresh as a mountain stream. They breathed freely again.

"That was *so* close," whispered Amalek.

"But we fooled him," Seph whispered smiling, "He really believes we're up in the cloud."

"That was great!" commented Flop.

"Great!" squeaked Miriam in agreement., "Great!"

"But... what about Lazuli," whispered Amalek, close to tears, "She *is* up in the cloud. What can we do?"

"At the moment," replied Joog, "Nothing. Maybe later... but for now we must carry on."

Finding the tunnel was like an unexpected gift. They decided to stay where they were for a few more minutes, keeping still and quiet to make absolutely sure that the wizard had gone.

The Troubler was just moving around the bend in Nathan Avenue near Spindley Tower as he followed the pathway he had cleared on his outward journey. He had passed the empty gaps where the houses had been. From the corner of Link Way to the place where Charin Road and the High Street joined Nathan Avenue, all the houses had gone, leaving empty patches of land where the snow was already settling.

He was heading back to Old Howard's House. After his use of magic he was drained of power but now he knew, without doubt, that they were all trapped. Perhaps he would fly the cloud right out of the kingdom, across the Kingdom Of Moone and over the Great Eastern Synamian Ocean. There he would bring the cloud down where the waters were fierce and deep and this would end their lives.

But that would be later. First he badly needed to rest and then he would make another journey. This was one he had been keenly relishing for some time. It would take him to the Brinscally Cave behind the Gem Falls and there he could claim his well-deserved prize; the Candara Gems.

Horrik had made some real progress in her attempt to escape from the underground tunnels. She had heard again the terrible screech echoing down the tunnels. It was the most frightening sound she had ever heard; an awful combination of pain, frustration and intense fear. It sounded distant but the ghastly qualities in it sent a shiver down her spine and her immediate instinct was to get away from it. So she headed off in the opposite direction guided by the dim light of the black compass around her neck. This had brought her to Korum's Cave which cradled the still waters of Lake Merlode. She was an excellent swimmer so she plunged in and swam across.

She found the water on that side flowed out of the lake and she floated into a winding tunnel. She drifted with the flow.

After turning a bend she was surprised to see a dim light ahead. As she drew closer she was astonished; hanging from a rock by a chain and dangling just above the water was a black compass. She grabbed it in her mouth as she glided past. The chain jerked loose and rattled against her teeth.

The group of friends had moved along the snow tunnel to where Hawkeye was sitting on his sledge. Tally was still sitting beside his grandfather. Joog was on Amalek's shoulder.

"This tunnel saved us," Joog said to Hawkeye.

Hawkeye looked up at him. "It's a pleasure to help… but now we've got to beat him."

"Gramps," said Tally excitedly, "How did you make the tunnel?"

"I had some help!" he replied, "There are thirty-three of us here, thirty-four with you Tally…"

"But…" interrupted Tally, "How did you know? How did you get here?"

"Wizard Elzaphan sent Harris to me with a message," said Hawkeye, "He knows how good we mountain hares are at digging through snow and he asked us to come here to help you. He thought you could do with some help. We've already created a tunnel here for you so that you can move around without being seen."

"But how did you know where we'd be?" asked Seph.

"We didn't… at least not exactly. We thought you'd travel through the town," then he chuckled, "But it was a surprise to see you fall from the sky. I watched it all… from the palace taking off to you falling out. We'd already built quite a few tunnels between the houses and we thought there'd be a good chance you'd find one at least. If not I'd have sent Kendall out to find you."

Seph smiled at him, "We found it just in time. Where are the other hares?"

Hawkeye looked along the tunnel and nodded, "Along there," he replied, "They're all busy digging now; we're making a tunnel through the town. It zigzags a lot because we've kept to the places where the snow is deepest… where it's drifted. That was so that you can all fit, even Aram and Halo… just. It's designed to be big enough for everyone, except the elephant! We just couldn't make it that big! But unfortunately, she's in the cloud now, anyway. I had to persuade the other hares to come, of course, but when they heard that Wizard Elzaphan had called for them they soon came round!"

"Wonderful," commented Simron, looking around the tunnel, "You've done an amazing job. Let's get going."

"We'll lead the way," said Hawkeye.

Tally stayed on the sledge and Kendall positioned herself at the back, put her front legs on the sledge and began pushing. The snow on the floor of the tunnel was packed hard and it slid easily. The others all followed behind. The two children rode on Aram and Halo. Simron walked beside Flop and Joog flew.

Tally chatted to his grandfather as they were pushed along.

"But, Gramps," said Tally suddenly looking concerned, "You shouldn't have travelled yourself. You're too old now."

"You don't think I'd miss out on this, do you?" said Hawkeye, his eyes twinkling with youthful enthusiasm and reflecting the coloured light of the ammolite hanging around Tally's neck, "And I'm travelling like a king on this sledge! But how have you been getting on, you young scamp?"

"I've been following your advice!" Tally replied, feeling like a good student to wise teacher, "I've come through all sorts of things… and KYWAY really helped."

"It's useful, isn't it?" replied Hawkeye, "We all need reminders, Tally, to help us. The best reminders are always the simplest things… things like… listen… look… smell! But I knew you'd do well."

"And I kept hearing your voice reminding me of KYWAY, and it worked every time," he said.

"Of course it does," said the old hare.

They were moving at a steady pace and had turned several corners already.

"Now, Tally," said Hawkeye, "Would you like give Kendall a rest and push for a while?"

"Yes, please," said Tally excited at the thought.

He jumped off the sledge and took over from Kendall with lively enthusiasm. He gave the sledge a push. It slid more easily along the tunnel than he expected and he fell flat on his face. He scampered after it, together with Kendall. Unfortunately, the tunnel sloped and the sledge accelerated away even faster. They had almost caught up with it when it crashed into the wall of the tunnel and stopped abruptly. Hawkeye was thrown forwards and plunged through the wall of snow. Snow tumbled in behind him and the old hare was gone.

Tally and Kendall began digging frantically when they heard something that stopped them immediately. It was the harsh, cutting voice of the Troubler.

The evil wizard had seen the movement in the snow a little way in front of him, and had rushed to see what it was. Now he was stooping down and grabbing Hawkeye by the ears before he had time to move. He hoisted him up in the air and held him there.

"And why..." he asked, stabbing the words out like poisonous darts, "aren't you frozen too?"

For a few seconds they stared at each other. The wizard's eyes narrowed.

"Answer my questions," the Troubler demanded.

He gripped Hawkeye more tightly and brought him closer to his face. Hawkeye remained silent and stared fearlessly back.

"You look too old to cause much trouble, but you do need to answer my questions."

Hawkeye still remained silent.

"Alright then..." the wizard hissed with venom, "Lost your tongue, have you? Play it your way. You're up to no good that's for sure and I'll get the truth out of you later, if you can survive in here."

He pulled out a large black cloth from a pocket, wrapped Hawkeye in it and tied the corners together tightly with some string. Tally and Kendall listened to the wizard in horror, not knowing what to do. Tally glanced back down the tunnel where the others were catching up with them.

He decided he must act, and scrambled frantically through the snow and into the open air only to see the Troubler striding away. The makeshift black sack was hanging over his shoulder.

"What's happened?" said Seph, slipping off Aram's back and looking out through the hole.

"It's Hawkeye!" gasped Tally, panicking, "The wizard's caught him! He's taken him! What do we do?"

In a moment they were all there; Halo and Amalek arrived next followed by Flop, and finally Joog and Simron.

Tally looked distraught, with tears welling up in his large brown eyes. "I shouldn't have pushed him so hard!" he said, "What shall we do?"

Seph reached out and stroked Tally on his back. "It's not your fault, Tally," he said kindly to comfort him.

"It *was* my fault," Tally sobbed, "*I* was pushing the sledge."

"Come back in, Tally," said Simron kindly.

Tally hopped back into the tunnel.

"Tally..." Amalek began tenderly as she picked him up, "You didn't do it on purpose and you didn't know that there was a slope."

"She's right," said Seph joining in, "Don't blame yourself… it's just something that happened."

Their words were comforting and Tally felt slightly better, but still the burden of what had happened pressed hard upon him. He felt laden with guilt and regret.

"What are we going to do?" he pleaded

"We'll do our best," Joog said, "and the best chance we have of helping him is to stick to our plan."

Aram and Halo nodded their great heads in agreement and Flop moved beside Tally.

"He's alive," he said, "which means we still have every chance of rescuing him. Look what happened to me, and I survived, didn't I?"

Tally nodded, feeling that he was surrounded by friends. In his young heart, his deep love for his grandfather was now matched by the determined hope that he would see him again.

"Joog's right," stated Simron, "and we need to talk together about our plan. We'd better pause here and discuss it all."

The Dark Wizard Troubler felt drained of energy as he walked wearily through the snow. It was almost dark now and he had just left Candara to follow the River Tazer on his way to Old Howard's House. The snow continued falling when he left the town; somehow the clear skies had filled with clouds again and heavy snow swirled around him like a million white bees.

He was retracing his steps along the path he had already cleared in the snow. As he trudged, the icy chill of the weather was deepening around him. Underneath the snow, plants withered as he passed and as he walked beneath a tree, a branch cracked and fell, plummeting past his head and into the snow. He stopped and stepped back to dodge it, and then carried on, his mind was fixed on the possession of Candara Gems. With these he felt he would become an unbeatable force.

As he moved, he cursed the deep snow that was making his journey so difficult. Every frustrated step seemed to make his mood darker. He knew he must get back to Old Howard's House as soon as possible to sleep and rest, and regain his weakened magical powers.

Night had fallen upon the kingdom now, wrapping it in heavy darkness but around the wizard a dull light lit up the snowflakes. It was the black compass hanging around his neck and as he moved it tugged him in the right direction.

He neared Old Howard's House. Soon he would be indoors and able to rest. Tomorrow, when his energy had returned, he would steal the Candara Gems. The thought of it made him gasp with excitement as he imagined the power they would bring to him.

He needed to rest briefly before the final push to reach the house, so he stopped under a tree where the snow was shallow. He slipped the makeshift cloth bag off his shoulders and dropped it into the snow. He was unaware that Hawkeye could see through a small hole where the wizard had tied it up. He had been using the same hole to breathe in fresh air.

The Troubler paused to look down at the bag and then lifted his leg to kick it. As his leg swung through the cold air, Hawkeye saw it coming and hopped. The bag moved suddenly and the Troubler's black boot missed the target. He spun on the other leg, lost balance and his head glanced against the tree trunk. He fell face down into the snow.

The wizard lay there unmoving and Hawkeye seized his opportunity. He tried to widen the hole, pulling at it with the claws of his front paws, but the opening was tightly tied and would not move, so then he tried using his long incisors to tear it open. The material was too strong. So he hopped, kicking down hard with his powerful rear legs and huge feet, the legs that used to carry him in his youth at speeds faster than the deer in the forest. They were not so strong now, in his old age, but still the bag jumped out of the snow.

He hopped again and again, trying to put space between himself and the evil wizard. After a particularly good jump, he felt a sharp blow on the head and a wave of dizziness made him feel weak. His eyes glazed as everything went hazy.

He felt the bag being lifted up into the air. He hoped with all his might that it was a friend he would see when he looked out through the hole. His heart was beating hard in his chest. This attempt to escape had taken so much out of his already frail body that he now felt on the edge of falling unconscious. Cautiously he put his eye to the hole. Right in front of him, and staring at him, was the evil face of the Troubler with his black eyes glaring with anger.

"Do not," he ordered with a voice so harsh and penetrating that Hawkeye could feel it like a pain in his bones. He opened the top of the cloth just enough to look in. "Do not *ever* do that again!"

Hawkeye could take no more. He suddenly felt old. It was all too much for him and he felt that all his energy had now dried up. His dim eyes, once so clear and bright, were only showing him misty shadowy images and his mind swirled in confusion.

"What's this?" remarked the wizard as he noticed the glowing ammolite around Hawkeye's neck.

He reached into the cloth to grasp it. Just then Hawkeye's body went limp pulling the ammolite down with him. He collapsed and his sight faded completely like a fragile flame extinguished by a gust of wind. His aged body fell to the bottom of the cloth bag.

"Don't you dare die on me!" snapped the Troubler, "I need information from you."

He pulled the string tight again, slung it over his shoulder and walked back to the tree to sit down. After a short rest, he felt ready to complete his journey. He reached Old Howard's House, passed through the trees and into the garden.

He opened the front door and stepped in, slamming the door shut on the snowy world outside. He moved through the darkness, with his compass still glowing gently, and straight into the back room where he spent most of his time. Closing the door behind him, he carelessly threw the canvas bag on the floor. It landed with a thud and slid across the wooden floorboards to bump gently into the wall. He leant his staff against the wall, flopped down into the smelly old armchair and closed his eyes.

At last he could relax and sleep. He took a deep breath and exhaled slowly.

A low-pitched groan from the far side of the room made him jump to his feet in alarm and grab his staff. It glowed red lighting up the room like a sunrise.

"Who's there?" he demanded.

"Me, Master," growled Gratch.

"Gratch," said the wizard, relaxing, "You're back."

He gazed across the dark room to see the Komodo dragon's huge shape stretched along the wall. The red glow of the staff dwindled to nothing. The wizard leant it against the chair and lit a black candle, placing it on the mantelpiece. Yellow light grew and then flickered, reflecting brightly off Amalek's golden magic star-box which was on the mantelpiece next to the candle. It was still tightly bound.

The wizard slumped down into the chair again. He forced his tired eyes to stay open and looked across the room at Gratch.

"I've caught the Prince and Princess, Gratch," he said, "And all the others with them."

Gratch looked up, "How, Master?"

The wizard hissed his reply out with hate, "I put them in the cloud."

"All of them?"

"All of them," he confirmed, "Even the owl. And what about you? Did you catch the unicorn?"

"No, Master," Gratch replied grumpily. His head was still thumping after the blow he received in the Old Mill.

"Why not?" the wizard snapped.

"Because it wasn't a unicorn... at least I don't think it was."

The wizard frowned. Questions flashed through his mind.

"Who was it then?"

"I don't know."

"What?!" the wizard stood up again and stepped toward Gratch, "What happened then?"

The wizard stared at the Komodo dragon intently.

"When I went into the mill, Master, it was dark in there. I couldn't see anything... then something hit me on the head. I was knocked out and when I came round there was a rope around my neck and something holding me down. The rope jerked upwards and then this voice whispered in my ear..."

Gratch paused.

"Yes... yes," the wizard said impatiently, "Go on... what did it say?"

"It whispered..." Gratch shivered at the memory of the hissing whisper that held such force behind it that it filled him with fear. "It whispered... "Tell Kasimir…""

"What?!" exclaimed the wizard in shock, "That's impossible! How does it know me? Who was this?"

"I don't know," replied Gratch.

Then the wizard hissed his words out like spitting out poison, "Did you *see* who it was?"

"No," said Gratch, "It was dark in there and it was behind me."

"What did it say then?"

"It said... 'Tell Kasimir this: I am ready to take over here.'"

Gratch paused again and tried to control his fear.

"Take over?!" snapped the wizard, shaking his head and looking puzzled, "Take over?! And then what did it say?"

"It said, 'Tell Kasimir I have the Candara Gems.'"

The Troubler was stunned. His legs went weak and he collapsed again into the chair. This had shattered his plans. The pain of this was almost unbearable.

"Anything else?" he asked quietly.

"Yes, Master," Gratch growled, "It said that it is ready to take over here... this whole kingdom. But it would like to join forces with you for more power... but *it* would be the one in control. It said that if you won't join forces then it would take over anyway and you would be finished."

The Troubler swallowed uncomfortably.

"Anything else?" he asked.

"No."

For a few minutes there was silence in the room. The wizard was reeling under the blow of this message. His thoughts swirled chaotically. Suddenly his anger burst out and he thumped his fist on the arm of the chair. Then everything was still again in the room.

In the hall behind the closed door, Searle and Urrg huddled together on a shelf. They were listening to the conversation with interest.

After a while, the wizard made a big effort to think properly. He began to regain control.

"What shall we do?" asked Gratch.

"We do *nothing*," the wizard hissed out the words with sinister precision, "Let it come to us... and when it does then we must be ready."

"What about the gems, Master?" growled Gratch, "They're powerful."

"If it's got the gems then it's done my job for me, Gratch. It's taken them from the protection of the cave! And when it comes here I'll take the gems from it."

He grasped his staff and slammed it down on the floor. Again it flared up with a brilliant red glow and then faded.

"I doubt if it knows about this," he said, nodding at his staff, "It will be surprised by my power."

"Yes, Master."

The wizard paused to think, looking into the distance as he wondered about the Candara Gems.

"If it *has* stolen the gems, it must be from this kingdom... else how could it steal them? So, we wait, and it will bring the gems to me."

"But, Master," said Gratch, "What if it's bluffing about the gems and it hasn't got them?"

"Then that's good too," the wizard sneered, "And the more I think about it, the more I think that it is bluffing. If it is, then we carry on as planned and I'll steal them... as soon as the ravens get here I'll send some of them off to that cave to get them. I *want* those gems, Gratch."

Gratch nodded and his tongue slithered out of his mouth like a snake and then back in again. "That's good, Master."

The wizard leant forward and stared at Gratch with steely concentration.

"I've been waiting for a long time for the gems," he hissed, "And now I have them in my grasp. I *will* have them and I *will* have their power!"

The room fell still as though absorbing the ruthless intensity of the wizard's statement.

"I am *not* giving in to this wizard, or whatever it is," he continued decisively, "I will *not* be bossed around. I will *not* be threatened! This kingdom is mine so we will fight this imposter. Alright, Gratch?"

"Yes, Master," Gratch replied, too frightened of the intense mood of his master to even think about disagreeing.

The Troubler leant his head back and his eyelids drooped. The news had been so shocking that he had pushed his weariness aside for the last few minutes. Now deep fatigue was pressing hard against him with the inevitability of an incoming tide.

"I must rest now," he said, "And you will guard. Go upstairs and keep watch from the windows up there."

Gratch's head was still throbbing from the blow and he really wanted to go to sleep as well. Reluctantly he heaved his bulky body onto his feet, left the room and climbed the stairs.

When upstairs he heard a movement in one of the rooms. He paused to listen and then tried to creep quietly into the room. His claws were so noisy on the wooden floor that he abandoned his careful approach and rushed through the door. He was just in time to catch a glimpse of two black ravens flying through the broken window and out into the falling snow.

Chapter 8

~ The Creeping Desert ~

J amaar had continued his journey over the desert in the Kingdom of Moone but he was struggling. He was desperately thirsty. His panting helped to begin with but then his mouth became dry and the hot air burnt against his tongue and throat. His legs grew weaker and his head swirled with dizziness. In spite of this, however, his determination to survive was so strong that he was still able to navigate by the position of the sun. This was keeping him on a westerly course.

He had continued staggering along until he saw something ahead that brought extra strength to his exhausted legs. Still a little distance away, shimmering in the heat rising from the sand, he saw a tree. He forced his eyes to focus and the view became clearer. It was not just one tree, there was a group of them, a little copse with bushes as well. Just before the wood the sand ended; it was the edge of the desert. It was the best sight he had ever seen.

Knowing that he was almost there, he carried on tottering and swaying across the sand. He expected the desert to peter out gradually, so he was very surprised to see a clear line ahead where the sand ended and the grass and plants suddenly began. Then something made him prick up his ears. He heard a strange chorus of clicking noises up ahead.

The noise grew as he approached the edge of the desert, and it made him cautious. He sat down to consider for a moment and tilted his head to one side as he listened.

"What is it?" he thought, *"I must be careful..."*

He began walking again until he reached the line where the desert began, but stopped just before it and looked down to see what was making the clicking sounds. At first he only saw movements in the sand but then, gingerly, he dipped his head to take a closer look and sniffed at the sand.

He jerked back in shock. A small two-tailed scorpion jumped out of the sand and swung its stings at his nose. Jamaar was only just quick enough and barked a couple of times in retaliation. The scorpion ignored this and started busily digging into the sand. Jamaar stared at it and then noticed another one beside it, and then another. He looked along the line and saw more scorpions, all busily digging, throwing the sand and earth behind them, and changing the grass into desert.

The desert was being made by the scorpions. There were hundreds, maybe thousands, possibly millions, every one working hard with their claws clicking together as they moved the desert along. Slowly but steadily the desert was eating into the land, converting the earth into sand. It was a creeping desert.

Jamaar felt weak but noticing that the scorpions had wings folded on their backs stirred some energy in him. He did not want them taking to the air and attacking him; he imagined them swarming up in a great cloud and decided to move on immediately.

He jumped across the line, landing on the grass and then continued walking. A few more wobbly steps and he entered the shade of the trees. The sound of trickling water was like the sweetest music and he followed it to a little brook. He dropped his head above the cool water and lapped it up desperately in great gulps. His parched tongue was instantly soothed and he kept drinking for some time.

When his thirst was fully satisfied, he sank down onto the grass. With the sound of the brook babbling in his ears he slipped off to sleep.

Horrik hauled her huge body up the last few feet of the zigzag path up the cliff. She had unknowingly followed the same journey that Jamaar had made, drifting on the same underground stream and then out into the Great Symarian Ocean. She had swum on the same current to the small, stony beach. As soon as she clambered up the pebbles, she sank down to rest and sleep.

When she awoke it was dark. She now had two black compasses around her neck both of which had fallen into her possession, it seemed, by accident. The first had caught on her foot just before she fell down the Silver Well after the fight with Jamaar. The second was the one that Jamaar had stolen from Darsan Lopery's desk. Horrik had found it hanging in the tunnel as she was floating by.

She had grabbed it and held it in her mouth until she had reached the beach. Now both were glowing in the night as they hung around her neck, swinging and knocking together as she climbed the path up the cliff.

As soon as she left the path and was on the top of the cliff, she stood for a moment to survey the scene. The compasses shone more brightly now and the moon shed a silver light across the waves of desert sand which lay in front of her as far as she could see. Unlike Jamaar she had no idea where she was.

Some tracks in the sand led away from where she was standing and she dipped her great head over them to take a closer look. Deadly saliva dripped out of her mouth, sizzling as a few drops landed on the sand. She stretched out her long forked tongue and left it there for a few seconds to sample the air. Then she picked up a familiar scent which instantly shocked her. A flood of mixed emotions followed. It was the smell of Jamaar!

Her mind rushed. She felt the intense emotions of satisfaction and hate tumbling through her. She was set on revenge against this dog that had caused her so much trouble. Her mind flashed with painful memories.

She tensed with anger. While she had been trapped in the underground tunnels her mind had run over and over the things that she hated about Jamaar; the things he had said and the things he had done.

It seemed to her now that a miracle had happened. She was now on the scent of Jamaar, the dog that she wanted revenge against more than anything else. She would do anything to find him and kill him, and now she could follow his tracks. It was like accidentally finding the most precious buried treasure.

She felt strong after her sleep and ready to do anything necessary to find Jamaar. She began to follow the scent and with eager anticipation she ran across the sand.

The warm night air was perfect for travelling. As she ran her bacteria-filled saliva began to flow when she imagined the food that she would soon be enjoying. She would eat Jamaar and it would be the most satisfying meal she had ever eaten.

The Male Squadron of ravens which numbered about fifty, had left the Snowpeak Mountains some time ago. The General was now ignoring the movements and guidance of the black compass because he had lost faith in it. It was glowing slightly in the night and still bobbing around from time to time.

It was snowing heavily again making visibility poor and so they had to drop slightly until they could see the ground. After searching thoroughly over the Great Mountain they flew over the flat expanses of Lake Clase-Moy and then Blue Lake. The wind was behind them which meant that they could drift along without much effort while scanning the land below for the enemy.

Their black, angular shapes were bunched together and they made a rough arrow formation with the General at the front followed by Colonel Gerr. The white frozen scene of the Flatsage Farmlands lay below as deserted and still as the surface of the Moon.

"Pay attention!" shouted the General, hoping to be heard by the whole army, "We must find them this time! Keep scanning as you fly!"

At the back, as usual, they could hardly hear.

"Sir," said Gerr, nodding in the direction of Candara, "What if they're already there?"

"No problem. We'll be there soon and then we get them," said the General.

"But what if we've passed them sir?" Gerr said.

"Still no problem," the General was getting agitated, "Look, what's the matter with you?! It's obvious! Then we get them when they arrive. Either way we win and they lose. OK?"

"What about the deserters sir?" asked Gerr, "The spies... Searle and Urrg?"

The General twisted his head around to shout back to the whole army. "You keep an eye out for those two deserters!"

At the back there was some chatter, "What did he say?" said one.

"I'm fed up with this," grumbled another, "We can never hear what he's saying!"

"Sounded like 'If you see a hide-out then you alert us,' " replied the first, and they decided this must be it.

"I wonder what those deserting spies are up to?" asked the General.

"Perhaps they're…" began Gerr.

"Stop all this guessing, 'perhaps this'… 'perhaps that!' " the General snapped crossly, "We'll find them." Then he turned his head to call back to the following army, "We'll scan Candara first for signs of the enemy. Then we'll report to the Master in Old Howard's House. OK?"

They all chorused, "OK!" with the ones at the back who had not heard clearly joining in slightly after the others.

"Good," he shouted and then he boomed, "We'll search for the enemy as we go... and search *thoroughly*!"

Then he turned back and spoke to Gerr, "We might have to scout around a bit here and there. But I'm sure we'll find them."

"And then we'll kill them, sir," said Gerr brightly, "And then we can report to our Master."

"Exactly," agreed the General.

"With good news and evidence, sir!" added Gerr.

"Exactly!" said the General with glee, "It would give me pleasure... huge pleasure... to carry some evidence to our great Master and present them to him! I'm looking forward to that..." Then he added in frustration, "if only we could find them Gerr."

They stopped talking and concentrated on scanning the smooth, white land below them as they flew across the Flatsage Farmlands toward Candara.

"It's gone!" exclaimed Jum.

Crayle shook his head.

"Don't be silly," he said, "How can a palace disappear?" He turned so that his one eye was looking at Jum who was beside him. "We must be in the wrong place."

Crayle, Jum and Iker were perched in a tree in Silvermay Forest. They were sitting in a row with Iker huddled low on the branch and leaning against Jum. His young feathers were puffed out slightly to keep him warm and he was nodding off to sleep. Jum had been looking after him as if he was her own son. Crayle was sulking because Jum had insisted on taking Iker with them.

They all felt refreshed after resting in the sheltered spot on The Great Mountain and found travelling under the clear sky without snow falling was much easier. Now the snow had began to fall thickly again making visibility poor and hiding everything from view except the close surrounding area. The three ravens' black feathers were speckled with snow.

"It's not the wrong place," Jum insisted, "I recognise it... and anyway there's hardly any snow in it so it must have gone recently."

Crayle was reluctant to admit that he was wrong and looked doubtful.

"Hmm," he said shaking his head, "I think we're in the wrong place. And it means we can't use it for spying. We'll just have to find it."

"I don't see why," said Jum, "This whole spying thing is silly anyway."

"Spying?" asked Iker, suddenly waking up and looking interested, "Are you spies?"

"Yes," replied Crayle proudly at the same time as Jum was saying, "No!" indignantly. Crayle glared crossly at her and then continued talking to Iker.

"We're spying on the enemy."

Iker perked up even more.

"Can I be a spy too?" he asked.

"No," snapped Jum, "It's just Crayle's stupid idea. How is he going to find anyone to spy on anyway?"

She raised her eyes upwards in exasperation and shook her head.

"I want to be a spy," said Iker, "A spy, a spy, a spy."

"You can't," snapped Crayle, "It needs training, intelligence and a sharp eye... and as far as I can see you have none of these."

Iker tilted his head and made a soft high-pitched whine. He was crying.

"How could you!" Jum said crossly, "You've made him cry now."

She put a protective wing around him. For a few minutes there was silence but the atmosphere between Crayle and Jum was tense. In the end Jum spoke.

"You're so rude to him," she began, "You should treat him better."

There was another tense silence. This time Crayle spoke, blurting out the words crossly.

"OK... OK, then. I'll... well... I'll try to be nice to him... I'll teach him how to be a spy."

"No, no," said Jum "I didn't mean that."

Iker perked up again.

"Me... a spy!" he exclaimed.

"Calm down, Iker," said Jum, and then turning to Crayle, "Don't encourage him."

Crayle looked blindly through the falling snow. He hated the idea of having this young bird with them but if it had to happen then he would teach him to be a spy and he would make the most of it.

"If he wants to learn... then I'll teach him," he stated.

"Great!" called out Iker and he jumped up and down on the branch in excitement, shaking some of the snow off. "I'm gonna be a spy!"

"Ever spied on anyone before?" asked Crayle.

"No," replied Iker.

"OK then. It takes sharp eyes and guile. Guile and sharp eyes, Iker. The best way to learn is to watch... watch me and then you'll learn. We will go down into the town of Candara and take a look around."

Jum looked at Iker and noticed the young enthusiasm shining from his eyes.

"I'll rest here for a bit then," she said, "But don't get into any trouble."

"Of course not," replied Crayle.

"Of course not," echoed Iker.

Crayle looked approvingly at Iker and nodded.

"That's the way," he said, "Spies just watch and glean information without others knowing. That's the role of a spy. Sharp eyes and guile. Follow me."

Iker felt a tingle of excitement run through him.

"And..." said Jum, trying to get their attention, "It's hard to see far so *don't get lost.*"

Crayle jumped off the branch with Iker following right behind. He circled around twice to try to get his bearings and then glided off in the direction he thought would lead them to Candara.

When the group of friends had finished discussing plans, Tally and Kendall sat on the sledge looking subdued. The loss of Hawkeye had left Tally so upset that he could not speak without tears welling up in his eyes. He still felt that it was his fault and that he had been foolish to push the sledge so hard. He had been so excited about seeing his grandfather again, but now, after his terrible mistake, he may never see him again.

He looked out at the falling snow. It looked grey in the darkness of night. Seph reached out and stroked him tenderly. Tally appreciated his comfort but it did not bring Hawkeye back. The heavy burden of guilt and sadness weighed upon him.

Joog was looking out through the hole and turned to them to speak.

"I'm just going to have a quick scout around," he said, "I'll be back in a minute."

He flew out through the hole and then silently upwards through the falling snow, his powerful white wings cupping the icy air as he circled. His golden-yellow eyes were alert for any sign of ravens. The snow was thick as it gusted around him, then it thinned for a moment and with his excellent night vision he saw something above him. A wave of shock swept through him. He could only see it dimly at first but then it was clear. It was the black outline of another bird diving fast upon him. He fixed his eyes on it.

Joog swerved to the side and braced himself for a fight. A flurry of snow gushed past him as the bird sped downwards. Joog followed but lost sight of it through the falling snow.

Joog landed on the snow beside the hole in the tunnel wall and the bird was gone. He turned his head slowly to scan all around. A noise behind him made him jump and he spun around. Some snow moved close by and then a head popped out.

"Neville!" exclaimed Joog.

"I'm back," said Neville, looking dazed after plunging into the snow.

"Neville!" repeated Joog, "We thought... we thought..."

Joog was so thrilled to see him that he was lost for words. He took off and glided to Neville, landing beside him.

Amalek and Seph heard Neville and tumbled out of the tunnel in excitement. For a moment they gazed at Neville wide-eyed, hardly able to believe that he was alive. Then they fought through the snow towards the albatross. His multi-colored stripy scarf was around his neck with one end hanging down in front of him and the other draped behind. He was gazing at them and still looking slightly stunned after the crash.

"Oh, you two!" he said happily, "It's *so* good to see you. I thought I'd never..."

He stopped as the children wrapped their arms around him. After a moment Seph stepped back.

"What happened?" he asked, "How did you escape?"

"I just flew out," he replied.

"Sounds easy!" said Seph.

Neville looked around, "Where's everyone else?" he asked.

"In there," replied Amalek pointing toward the hole.

Joog was now hovering above their heads.

"Neville," he said, "It's great to see you but we'd better get out of the open and into the tunnel… there may be ravens about."

"Ravens?" said Neville, looking around "I thought you would have dealt with them by now!"

"We thought we'd save them for you to deal with," joked Joog, "Now, let's go in."

Neville stretched out his long wings and pulled himself across the surface of the snow with great sweeping movements. At the same time he kicked clumsily with his large webbed feet. All this movement threw up clouds of snow and it looked as if Neville was swimming on a foamy sea. After four pulls with his wings he reached the hole, folded his wings and went in followed by the children. He received another excited welcome.

Joog landed and looked in through the hole. Aram and Halo's alicorns were glowing to light up the snow-packed walls around them and the ammolite pendants were shining softly with coloured light.

"What are those?" asked Neville.

"They protect us all," said Seph, "From the spell, that is. Wizard Elzaphan sent them to us. But what about you… doesn't the spell affect you?"

"Not with this," he replied.

The ends of his multicoloured magic scarf lifted up by themselves, moved forwards and bowed to the others.

With a smile, Amalek bowed to the scarf and the others copied her.

"What happened then?" asked Seph, "How did you escape?"

"I've discovered something about the Dark Wizard Troubler that could be very important, and it helped me escape. You see, when I fell into that darkness back at Wizard Elzaphan's castle I thought that was it and I was finished. It was so dark and... so, well, so utterly miserable... horrible... and it made me despair. I wrapped my scarf around me and I'm sure that helped. It eased the pain. I could hardly see, but I felt I was falling. It seemed to go on for a long time... it's hard to say how long... and, thank goodness the scarf protected me, for I'm sure I would have died without it."

He paused, partially stretched out his massive wings and shook the snow off, splattering the others. Then he folded them again.

"In that darkness..." he continued, "Every so often, it went light and bright and *happy*... just for a short time. It was really beautiful and always surprised me, but I worked out what it was. You see, in this darkness I was really close to the Troubler... sort of in him, in his dark mind... and when it went light... well that happens when he's falling asleep and waking up. It's very short... usually a few seconds but sometimes a few minutes. But as soon as he's awake it all goes dark again."

He paused again and looked around at the bright ring of faces, all turned towards him and listening intently. He was back with his friends and it made him glow with happiness.

"Then what happened?" asked Amalek, "How did you escape?"

"Well, I took my chance during one of these light moments," continued Neville, "I concentrated really hard, and as soon as it was light I flew as fast as I could. My scarf helped, swinging out in front and clearing a way. And then, suddenly, I was out of it and in Old Howard's House with the Troubler sleeping right in front of me. Luckily he had been falling asleep when I escaped and not waking up. I crept out of the room, up the stairs and then out of a broken window."

"Neville," laughed Seph, "You climbing stairs by yourself!"

"Yes," Neville chuckled, "It was hard... especially trying to make no noise. But it's surprising what you can do when you're desperate!"

He looked around the group.

"Where's Lazuli?" he asked.

"Up there," said Seph waving his arm, "Trapped in the cloud above Candara I'm afraid... with the palace and loads of houses."

Neville looked puzzled, "How did *that* happen?"

Before anyone could answer, Neville suddenly began to shake as if facing into a strong wind. His eyes opened wide in alarm.

"Help!" he exclaimed, "It's pulling me back... I can feel it!"

All the friends moved towards him, Seph throwing himself forwards in a dive but before they reached him Neville shouted, "Oh no!" and suddenly shot up in the air. He hit the roof of the tunnel and burst through it, spraying snow all around, some falling upon the dismayed group of friends below.

When the snow had settled they gazed up through the hole. Snowflakes fell into their faces but there was no sign of Neville. He had gone!

Simron stood up and looked around at the sad faces. They had been so happy to see Neville again and they all knew what had happened. Neville had been sucked back into the Dark Wizard Troubler's mind.

"We know he's there," Simron comforted them, "We know he's alive... so there's hope... a lot of hope."

"Simron's right," said Seph, "And the sooner we get on the better."

These words helped. There was nothing they could do about Neville and so it was best to turn their minds to practical things.

"We'd better mend the hole in the roof," said Amalek trying very hard not to cry.

The children stood on one unicorn each to reach up and mend the hole. It was harder than they thought and the snow kept falling.

"Leave it," said Joog who was looking in through the hole in the side, "I'll put some branches over it. Then I'll look around out here. I want to know what's happening... where those ravens are..."

"Be careful, Joog," said Amalek.

"I will," he replied, "This hole will be easy to mend. I'll come back in through the hole in the roof if there's anything to report... if not, I'll see you at Old Howard's House... in the trees at the end of his garden. We'll all meet up there, alright?"

"Alright," agreed Amalek and Seph together.

They jumped down off the unicorns and quickly repaired the hole by building up a thin wall of snow as Joog had requested. Simron helped them.

"Let's go," he said and led the way.

The children clambered up onto the unicorns again and they moved off with Aram behind Simron, and Halo at the back so that they all had some light. Kendall pushed the sledge with a forlorn-looking Tally sitting on it. Flop walked beside Halo with Miriam on his neck.

Their meeting with the Dark Wizard Troubler, the trapping of Lazuli in the cloud and now the capture of Hawkeye, had left them shaken. The loss of Neville for the second time had been a terrible disappointment. The heavy feeling of the spell weighed upon them like a nagging pain.

As they moved, they marvelled at the quality of the tunnel. It was beautifully rounded with smooth walls and floor.

"How have they done all this?" asked Amalek turning to Kendall.

"Well there were over thirty of us building it!" Kendall replied, "We know all about digging tunnels... tunnels are our home."

"Why do they zigzag so much?" asked Amalek.

"This is how they make tunnels where we live," replied Kendall from the sledge, "They're used to building them like this. But also they are following the deepest snow drifts."

While they were travelling below the snow level, Joog was gliding through the town. The light was failing quickly as the day ended. Every now and again Joog saw a face at the window of a house, and momentarily thought he was being watched, but every time the face would turn out to be utterly still, frozen like all the other inhabitants of the kingdom.

One man was leaning slightly out of a top window. When the spell had deepened and the birds had all fallen, he had nearly fallen out, rocking slightly before coming to rest against the window frame. Now snow was piled high on his head like a tall grey-white hat, and long icicles hung from his nose, ears and chin. Joog wondered if the senses of these frozen people were working; could they still see, hear and smell? Could they feel the bitter, cold weather? Could they taste the snow as it blew into their mouths?

Spindley Tower loomed out of the grey curtain of falling snow. He landed skilfully on the very top, sinking into the layer of snow.

Above the tunnel, where the friends were travelling at this very moment, was a large group of circling ravens, the Male Squadron, with the General getting very agitated that they had found neither the enemy nor the two deserters. The compass hung loosely around his neck as he flew. As usual, Colonel Gerr was beside the General and sounded bright and perky when he spoke.

"Sir?"

"Yes, Gerr," groaned the General, feeling very frustrated at the unsuccessful search, "What is it?"

"Don't you think we should report to the Master now?"

"And tell him what?" snapped the General, "That we have failed *completely* in our search for the enemy? Should we tell him that, Gerr? Do you think that would please him? Should we tell him that we have not seen them *at all* since they ran into that wood in Summertime Kingdom... not even *one* sighting? Is that what you're suggesting?"

"No sir," replied Gerr.

There was a pause and then the General remembered something.

"What about those Candara Gems?" the General asked thoughtfully, "If we could steal those... *then* we could report to the Master." He became enthusiastic about this idea. "Yes, Gerr, you could go and steal them."

Gerr shuddered. He still had a cracked beak to remind him of his failed attempt before.

"Sir," he began, "They can't be stolen…"

"Be more positive, Gerr," the General snapped, "Go and try."

"I told you sir," Gerr persisted, "If the enemy are alive or free then the gems are protected. We need to kill the enemy first... or at least make them prisoners."

Gerr noticed something that gave him the opportunity to change the subject.

"I'm sure there should be houses along there," he said looking down at Nathan Avenue and sounding very puzzled, "What's happened to them?"

"That's strange..." commented the General, "Very strange... but the most important thing is the enemy. Where can they be? We've searched everywhere. Have you any *sensible* ideas, Gerr?"

"Well, yes sir, I do sir," said Gerr, "They may have gone another way completely. Or maybe they haven't even got here yet. Or maybe they are hiding and watching us!"

"Watching us... hmm... and hiding. I hadn't thought of that." The General perked up a little and the compass gave a little jump, "Good, good. Hiding, yes. And watching us… could be. And maybe the spies... Searle and Urrg... are helping them watch us. A bad thought but, nevertheless, a possibility we must consider. So perhaps we need to land somewhere. Now, let's have a look."

He peered down through the dark at the land as they circled above the town. Down below, directly underneath them, the party of brave travellers moved secretly in the tunnel. The snow had fallen deeper in the town than almost anywhere else in the kingdom, which made it perfect for the tunnel.

They had just turned a sharp bend in the zigzagging tunnel which meant it was heading, for a few steps only, in a south-westerly direction. They were at this moment on the turn of Nathan Avenue exactly north-west of Spindley Tower. Aram and Halo's alicorns were still glowing, lighting up their way as they walked.

"I've just thought..." began Simron, speaking quickly, "The light might show through the snow and give away where we are."

"You're right," said Aram.

Immediately Aram and Halo's alicorns faded out and they were plunged into darkness, except for the faint light of the ammolites hanging around their necks.

"What about these?" asked Seph.

"They're fine," said Simron, "They're too faint to be seen."

Up above, Gerr had seen the alicorn light.

"Sir!" said Gerr excitedly, "Did you see that?"

"What?" the General asked.

"That light underneath the snow! Down there, sir!"

"Where? I can't see any light."

"It's gone now," Gerr said, "It was there. In that street down there. Down below us. It was on and then it went off."

"Are you sure?" asked the General, "You weren't just seeing things... a reflection or something like that? Remember back in that tunnel?"

"No sir! It was not like that... it *was* there, sir. Like a short line of light running that way." He drew a line with his beak, "As clear as day it was, sir."

The General turned his head and bellowed to the following army of ravens, "Anyone see a light down there?"

There was a mixed response of 'yes's' and 'no's' which satisfied the General that there must have been something.

"Now," said the General thoughtfully, "I wonder what that could be. Got any of your bright ideas, Colonel Gerr?"

"It's them, sir! In a tunnel underneath the snow... it must be, sir!"

At this, the compass started jiggling around excitedly. The General had still lost all faith in its guiding powers so he ignored it.

"But how did they...?" the General paused to think and quickly gave up, "Still... it doesn't matter. All that matters is that... maybe... we've found the enemy!" The General was enjoying this, "So, if that *is* them, it means that they have arrived here... but more importantly, we know where they are! Go down there Gerr, and investigate. See if you can hear voices and then come back and tell me. Now... go!"

Gerr fell through the fluttering snowflakes and landed gently on the snow in Nathan Avenue where he had seen the light. His legs slipped into the snow and his body sat on the surface like a duck on water.

On the second balcony of Spindley Tower Joog was watching. He was well-camouflaged with his white and brown-speckled plumage. Neither Gerr nor the General, nor any of the ravens were aware of his presence. Joog watched as Gerr was turning his head on one side, lowering it to the snow, and listening. After a few seconds he took off and returned to the side of the General.

"It's them alright, sir," he said, "I heard them talking!"

"What were they saying?" asked the General eagerly.

"I couldn't hear, sir. Too soft and muffled."

"How can we be sure it's them though?"

"Well," said Gerr, very pleased with his discovery, "Who else could it be?"

"The Master?" said the General, "That dog, Jamaar... the Komodo dragon... Searle and Urrg, although why would they be in there? But these are the only other possibilities Gerr. Apart from them everyone else is frozen, and if it's not any of those it must be the enemy. Right then. Send down someone else to listen... who's the bird with the best hearing?"

"Decc, sir," said Gerr.

"Decc," the General nodded, "Ah, yes. He's that good flyer isn't he?"

"The best, sir. If I may say so sir, he'd be a good candidate for promotion. He's wasted in the general ranks."

"No time for that now," snapped the General, "Send him down Gerr."

"Decc, come here!" called out Gerr.

Decc flew to the front with an extraordinary twist in the air which flipped him over and back again in a flash. It served no purpose except to show off his amazing talent for flight. There was an "Ooo" of amazement and admiration from the flock.

Gerr gave him his task.

"Where's the place?" asked Decc.

They were circling above and trying to keep sight of the right place through the falling snow.

"Um…" began Gerr peering down, "There I think… just there… um… just below us… no, we've moved… just back there."

He quickly dropped below. A minute later he was back.

"Well?" asked the General.

"Voices, sir," said Decc, "I heard voices."

"What did they say?"

"Hard to hear sir," replied Decc.

The General sighed.

"But, sir," continued Decc, "It sounded like a boy's voice and a cat... I'm sure it was a cat sir. They've got that horrible tone..."

"It's them!" exclaimed the General who could not contain his excitement, "At last! Well done Decc. Now, we must act quickly. If we can find the entrance to this tunnel... well, then we can attack them *in* the tunnel. Our numbers ensure that we will prevail. They will be caught like frightened rabbits!"

"If I may say so, sir," Gerr began, "That's an excellent plan."

"Once again, Colonel Gerr," the General said, "You've done well," Gerr puffed up his chest with pride, "Now, take ten others of your choice with you... but make sure Decc is one of them. Go down and find the tunnel entrance. I will watch from above. Let me know as soon as you find it."

"Or, there is another way," volunteered Decc, "A much better way, sir."

"Yes?" asked the General.

"Smash through the snow and into the tunnel, sir."

"Yes!" exclaimed the General eager for success, "Akk and you two!" he pointed with his beak at the three ravens. "Go down there and dive bomb into the tunnel. Not too fast… it's only snow. Now… go!"

The three ravens fell through the air, tucked their wings in and hit the snow one after the other.

"They're in!" exclaimed the General, "Let's go!"

Just at that moment one of the ravens reappeared, covered in snow, followed by the other and then the third one. They flew up to join the others.

"The tunnel's not there," said Akk looking a little stunned after the crash, "It's just snow."

"Oh, no!" complained the General, "We've lost it now! Try again."

He was desperate to find them and after being so close, the disappointment made him panic. Akk was just about to go down again when he stopped them.

"No, stop!" he cried, "They'll be getting away. Quick, Gerr... as I said before, go down there with ten ravens and find the entrance. Quickly now, go!" He looked at Akk and then down below, "*And,* Akk, take those two and try again."

"But my head hurts," complained Akk.

"And mine," joined in one of the others.

The third one was too dazed to speak but nodded in agreement.

Gerr was still selecting nine other ravens to join him and Decc. The General suddenly realised they were still there.

"Go!" he boomed angrily.

They dropped through the air and then followed the direction of the line of light that Gerr had seen. They flew in a side by side formation to the south-west, just above some houses.

The General glanced around at his squadron all circling with him.

"Spread out and keep scanning the ground," he shouted at them, "The enemy could surface at any time and in any place. We need to be ready."

A little way behind Gerr's group of ravens, tracking carefully and using all his skill to stay hidden, Joog was following them. His soft feathers silently cut through the cold air. Snow was falling even more heavily now and so the General was finding it hard to see Gerr and the others. He had no idea that Joog was there.

At the same time, Joog was completely unaware that he too was being followed.

"He'll lead us to them," said Searle, "The stupid owl!"

"Yes, I know," Urrg looked edgy as they tracked Joog, "But the Master told us to stay and watch… you know, back at the house. We should never have left."

"We did watch," Searle snapped, "For a while. But you heard them talking… there's this other power… if it has the gems and it's stronger we'd be better working for that, wouldn't we?"

"But we don't even know what it is, or *who* it is do we?" complained Urrg.

"Not yet," Searle replied, "Not yet. For the moment we stick with the Master but we'll keep our ears and eyes open. We'll wait to see what happens and then *we'll* choose who to work for, OK?"

"OK," Urrg agreed, "But we'd better get back."

"No," snapped Searle, "We're searching for the enemy, remember? And anyway the Master won't wake up for a while. We'll be back before he wakes."

"Aahh!" exclaimed Urrg.

The conversation had distracted her and she had flown into a snow-covered branch. Momentarily, she was tumbling. Then she regained her flight, but her head had received a blow.

"Ssshhh!" said Searle without looking at her, "What are you doing?"

"Sorry," Urrg said, "You put me off my flying!"

She was feeling dizzy and blinked repeatedly as a trickle of blood ran into her eye. They both peered through the falling snow for Joog.

"The owl's gone now," Searle said crossly, "You've spoilt it all!"

Urrg's head was throbbing from the blow and she was beginning to feel faint. Energy drained out of her and her wings became weak. She fell from the air and crashed once again into the branches of a tree. The snow sprayed out like mist and when it cleared Urrg was wedged tightly in between two branches and could not move.

"Help me!" she screamed.

"I'll come back for you," called out Searle, "I'll follow the owl first."

"No!" called out Urrg, "Help me now!"

Searle ignored her. She flew on and between two houses looking to the right and the left for the owl. Suddenly, she felt a jolt. Something grasped the back of her neck. Sharp claws pricked through her skin and closed like a vice around her. Her wings were pointing downwards, held there by the powerful grip and she tried in vain to lift them. She was almost choking with fear as she felt herself being carried swiftly though the snow-filled air.

Chapter 9

~ The Snow-Cave ~

The group of friends had moved steadily through the dark, twisting tunnel. The light glowed from the ammolites hanging around their necks and lit up their faces with colours, but did little to tame the darkness around them. When they left the town and the deep snowdrifts behind, the depth of snow was no longer enough to make a tunnel, so they were travelling through a channel with the top open. They were pleased to be able to see better.

The snow was falling on them in large, feathery flakes. They felt they should be approaching Old Howard's House quite soon but the snow was falling so thickly that they could not see far. Then, as they turned a corner, an amazing sight loomed out of the dancing snowflakes. They had caught up with the other hares who were busily digging.

It looked like a great mass of white fur as the hares took turns to dig furiously for a few seconds. Seven would be in a row at the front, digging and scraping with their front paws. The loose snow would be kicked out behind them, or flattened and packed down by the large back feet of the other hares who were just behind them. After a few seconds of digging, the front row would drop to the back by climbing over the three rows behind them, and then seven fresh hares would take over. There were four rows of seven altogether, with two hares supervising the whole procedure and a further three others who appeared to be resting. This made up a total of thirty-two. Each had an ammolite hanging around their necks which shed a patch of coloured light on their fur.

They were also stamping their long feet on the walls making them strong and smooth. It was an extraordinary sight as they worked relentlessly at their task together.

Progress for the group became much slower now. At times they would stay right behind the hares and then they would stop, sit down and chat for a while. When the hares had created more of the channel they would catch them up again. In this way, they proceeded, moving very slowly but making sure they kept out of sight.

The day passed and evening came. They were just catching up with the digging hares again when Kendall spoke.

"I'm sure we're almost at Old Howard's House," she said "If only we could see further."

She stopped pushing the sledge and hopped towards the busy diggers, noticing some trees beyond them. She had a word with the one who was organising the digging. He was a large old hare called Darlitt who had been put in charge because he no longer had the energy of his youth. He listened to Kendall and then turned to the working party and waved to them to get their attention.

"Stop digging and listen," he said quietly, "And we do not want to be overheard, so keep your voices down."

They all stopped except for one young hare who was keen to finish the area he was working on. Darlitt pointed to him.

"Waltab," he said.

Waltab glanced up and said, "Just finishing this bit," and then carried on.

Darlitt's voice was firm. "Stop now, Waltab!"

Waltab stopped digging and looked up in surprise.

"Now come on young fellow... stop means stop, doesn't it?" he said

"Sorry," replied Waltab, sitting down on his haunches with his ears straight up and alert.

Darlitt sighed, "Your enthusiasm is a wonder to see," he said, "But your obedience..." he shook his head, "Well... it needs some serious practice."

The other hares smiled and chuckled at this.

"Now," he continued to them all, "You're doing a great job. This channel has kept us all concealed from snooping eyes, and that is *very* important. But Kendall tells me we're nearly there. So we need to take care to dig between those trees there."

They all looked towards the trees ahead just visible through the falling snow.

"Those trees are at the back of Old Howard's House," Darlitt continued, "We need to be cautious and careful. We don't want to be seen or heard... so, we slow down and make a small tunnel first. Of course the snow will be shallow under the trees so even a low tunnel will soon be impossible and it will take us out into the open. You five in the front there, and Waltab as well seeing you've got so much fine young energy; I'm giving you the job, so get to work."

They began digging a small tunnel and in a moment they disappeared into it. A little later they all hopped out again.

"That..." said Waltab proudly and pointing a paw at the tunnel, "that is the perfect tunnel."

Darlitt looked at him and smiled.

"I assume..." he began, "that means that it comes out in the right place. Is that right?"

They nodded, their long ears flopping.

"In that case it *is* perfect. Well done. Now it needs to be enlarged into a channel so that our friends here can pass through. So..."

Before he could finish all the hares began to dig and very soon the channel was dug through the trees and into the shallow snow. In the failing light, the group of friends walked through and under the trees. They were cautious, moving slowly and looking around. The hares were just in front, their white fur camouflaging them against the snow.

Night was closing in.

They found themselves, as they expected, in the trees at the end of the garden of Old Howard's House. The snow lay only an inch or two thick under their feet but they could see it become deeper as soon as the shelter of the trees ended. On the roof and windowsills of the house it lay in thick layers. The light of a flickering candle shone through one of the windows lighting up the falling snow, large flakes tumbling through the still air and landing silently on the white blanket below.

The scene was still, silent and stunningly beautiful. There was a hush in the air that was held in the stillness of winter's night and which would normally bring a joyful thrill of delight. Tonight, however, the air was also heavy with the unseen presence of the spell. A sense of doom, of impending disaster, hung around the house with an intensity that produced a tense knot in the stomachs of the brave group. They all felt it; it was the burden of the Dark Wizard Troubler's spell, cast upon their kingdom.

They all gazed out from their hiding place in the shadows of the trees. A large elm tree stood beside the house, coated with snow like everything else, and underneath its spreading branches they could see a track leading up to the back door, a waist-high channel through the deep snow. They assumed this must have been made by the Troubler. Some snow had tumbled back into the channel and was now being smoothed over by the falling snow.

"Look there," said Aram, standing just behind the children and pointing with a raised hoof, "See on the right there. That's where we broke into the house by smashing through the wall. He's repaired it."

On the back wall of the house, the hole could still be seen, but it had been blocked up from the inside with bits of wood.

Flop put his front paws on Seph's trousers.

"My paws are cold," he said, "All this terrible cold snow and cold air! Yuk!"

Seph lifted him up into his arms. "How's that?" he asked.

"Better," replied Flop, purring, "Much better."

"And how are you?" Seph asked Miriam.

"I'm fine," she replied, her nose poking out from the thick fur on Flop's neck, "Nice and warm in here."

Seph scratched the back of her head affectionately with a finger.

"I wonder where Joog is?" asked Amalek.

"Here!" said a voice above their heads.

He was perched on a branch, blending in so well with the background of snow and branches that they could hardly see him. He looked down at them like a wise headmaster.

Halo looked up and spoke. Her voice was as smooth and sweet as honey.

"Did you see anything, Joog?" she asked.

"Well, yes," he replied, "Those ravens! They were circling overhead... and then they saw your light in the tunnel. It looked like about half the group...forty or fifty of them. I saw the General with his compass."

"Oh," said Aram, "That doesn't sound good. They know we're here and where we're heading."

"It's not that bad," Joog continued calmly, "They're hunting for the entrance to the tunnel, and, of course, we covered all the holes up so there isn't one to find! Also the zigzagging tunnel sent them off in the wrong direction. So we've got a little time at least."

This was a great relief for them to hear. Joog sounded composed as he looked down at them with his alert golden-yellow eyes.

"And I've got a prisoner," said Joog nodding towards a branch in the tree. It was Searle, tightly bound to the branch with ivy wound around her. Her beak was bound too as she looked at them with her black eyes filled with fear and anger.

"She doesn't know much, but I did get out of her that the Troubler is living in Old Howard's House as we thought. He's probably in there now."

They all looked towards the house, through the densely falling snow and failing light, and at the window where the candlelight flickered. The window was misted and partly covered with snow and at that distance they could not see in at all. Just the thought that he was in there magnified their fear. If they could move away, or even just stay there hiding in the trees, it would be much easier than following Wizard Elzaphan's plan through. They knew they had to confront him and this would take all their courage.

Simron looked up at Joog.

"We have an advantage," he said, "He's sure that we're trapped in the cloud. We can surprise him. Can you fly around the house, Joog?" he asked, "Just to check for anything."

"Of course," replied Joog.

"Oh, and see if there are any tracks at the front," Simron added.

"I'll be back in a minute," announced Joog.

He jumped off the branch and glided down. His white plumage, speckled with brown, was the perfect camouflage as he skimmed across the surface of the snow on silent wings. It was dark now and only the sharpest eyes would have seen him. He circled the house, swiftly speeding through the falling snowflakes with graceful ease. He landed back on the same branch.

"Nothing... and no tracks," he said, shaking the snow off his wings.

"We'll go in then," said Simron.

His words sounded almost casual but they all knew the reality. They were about to put themselves in the most extreme danger they had ever encountered.

"But let's work it out first," he continued, "*How* we do this could be very important."

Amalek shuddered and then opened her bag. She took out a packet and held it up.

"Who'd like some Mayan beans?" she asked, "I found these right in the bottom of my bag this morning. We need to keep our strength up."

She handed around the small, brown beans as they discussed their next move.

"Now," whispered Crayle, "Carefully does it."

He was landing on the roof of The Old Mill with Iker beside him. It was night. The snow rested on the tiles in a thick layer. Iker came down where the two sloping sides of the roof met but Crayle just missed and started slipping down the roof. A little wave of snow built up in front of him and suddenly he fell over it and was tumbling. Legs and wings thrashed in a circle until the roof ended, and in a flurry of powdered snow he fell off and began to plummet.

He managed to regain his flight and flew back up to the top of the roof. He landed successfully this time with feathers ruffled and untidy, and with snow caught in among them. He stretched his wings and shook his feathers vigorously.

He was out of breath and had landed so that he was facing away from Iker.

"Are you OK?" asked Iker.

"Of course I am," snapped Crayle, "Fine. I must have landed on a slippery patch."

He turned to face Iker and then looked down with his one eye.

"Look at that icy patch there," he said, looking at the place where he had begun his fall, "No wonder I slipped."

Iker looked but it seemed to be just normal snow.

"Right then," announced Crayle, "So we've seen a light... first step of spying accomplished... spies must be aware and notice anything suspicious. Now for the second step... investigation."

"Investi... what?" asked Iker.

"In...vest...i...gation. It means to find out. And spies must move with care and do nothing to draw attention to their movements."

"Like falling off a roof!" joked Iker.

Crayle ignored Iker's comment and gave his head a little jerk to shake some snow off.

"So..." Crayle continued, "follow me."

He turned, almost slipping off again, and began trying to walk along the top edge of the roof. The snow was far too thick and so he jumped up and flew to the end where he landed. Iker followed and squeezed up beside him and they both looked over the edge and down at the top window.

The light shining from the room was changing colours with different hues which grew and faded in turn. The snowflakes caught the light as they fell past, looking magical as they swirled and danced in the air.

"What is it?" asked Iker.

"Sshh," replied Crayle, and then lowering his voice to a soft whisper, "Good question. All part of the investigation."

He jerked his beak downwards and again he nearly fell off.

"Down," he ordered in a whisper.

Crayle went first, dropping down onto the windowsill. He was very lucky with his landing and just happened to touch down gently in the soft snow. He shook his feathers and looked up at Iker.

"Come on," he whispered, "It's easy."

Iker flapped down to the sill but slipped straight off. He flew up again and this time landed safely.

"Spying needs skill," Crayle whispered, "If you want to be a real spy like me you'll need to practice manoeuvres like that."

Their black feathers were shining in the coloured light which poured out through the window. They turned to look inside but there was some snow coating the glass and so they carefully rubbed it away with the feathers on their heads. They looked in and blinked in the brightness of the light.

"What is it?" asked Iker.

Just then a figure sat down right in front of the shining light, becoming a black silhouette.

"There's someone there!" whispered Crayle, "Now who would that be? A person in a hood..."

He turned his head to one side and thought.

"I know..." he whispered with excitement, "It's that ferryman... must be! They were all coming back here... the enemy that is... and that's him. That's that ferryman."

"What about the light?" asked Iker.

"The light?" said Crayle, "Who cares about that? A light is just a light... a fancy one in this case with colours... but nevertheless just a light. No, the important thing is that we know who that is. We are spying to find out information that counts... information that is worth something."

They gazed in for a moment at the back of the hooded figure who sat completely still.

"Now," whispered Crayle decisively, "What have we learnt? We know that the enemy are here... maybe even all here in this mill somewhere. *Also,* we know that the ferryman is with the enemy. Good spying brings good results, Iker. This is the art of investigation and then drawing out sound knowledge from the facts. We've successfully completed the first four stages of spying."

"Four?" asked Iker looking puzzled and wondering what they were.

"Yes, four."

"What happens now?"

"Now we pass on the new knowledge," whispered Crayle proudly, "To him who has a special interest, namely the Master."

Iker nodded. He decided he liked being a spy. It did not seem too difficult or dangerous.

"We'll report now," Crayle said, "I don't like to leave Jum on her own... but this is too important. She'll wait for us there."

Crayle took off first and Iker followed through the heavily falling snow. They flew off into the deep darkness, towards Old Howard's House.

While the friends had been enjoying their Mayan beans, they had discussed their plans. They decided that it would be better to confront the Troubler in daylight rather than at night. They were tired and needed to sleep but there was a more important reason as well. They had noticed that in the dark hours the spell seemed to grow stronger and they could feel it now, a stifling sinister presence that hung around them like a mist in the air. To meet the evil wizard they needed to gather all their strength.

When they were in Wizard Elzaphan's castle the great wizard had talked to them about the possible ways of fighting the Troubler. Out of these discussions a plan had arisen which included the two magic boxes but now they found they had a problem; Amalek's magic star-box had been stolen by some ravens.

"*He's* got it," said Amalek, "They would take it to him, wouldn't they?"

"Yes, probably," agreed Joog, "It makes sense... but does that help us?"

"Maybe," Seph joined in, "We could get it back first and then use the plan."

"Sounds easy..." laughed Joog, "But you never know, and if we can't get the box back, then we try the plan with just Seph's box."

Simron nodded.

"We'll just have to try," he stated, "and the other problem is... the Candara Gems. If he *has* got them then it will be difficult... very difficult."

He looked around at the others with a grave expression and then smiled.

"We'll have to be... creative," he said, "but now we need to rest."

"We'll build a snow cave for shelter," offered Tally.

He was gradually feeling better after the shock of losing Hawkeye.

"Great," replied Simron, "Can you organise that please, Tally."

"We're fine out here," said Aram, "We'll sleep under the trees here."

Tally gathered some of the hares and they hopped back through the trees until they reached the deeper snow. They moved quickly to burrow in and create a cave that would shelter them through the night.

When it was finished, Tally told the others and they followed him to the snow-cave through a small entrance. They settled down for the night as comfortably as they could. The children and Simron kept their coats on as well as their gloves and hats. They cuddled up together and soon the warmth of their breath was taking away the chill of the air.

Aram and Halo had already closed their eyes and were falling asleep where they were standing under the trees. Joog stayed outside perched in the tree with his prisoner, Searle, and kept watch.

In the dark of the palace, in the cupboard under the stairs, a very strange spectacle was taking place. It was Razz and Sergeant Forr trying to walk with one leg tied together as if they were in a three-legged race. They kept pulling in slightly different directions, falling over and then complaining at each other. They each had one wing free and when one of them flapped, it would cause both of them to tilt.

They spent some time trying to coordinate their flapping and tumbled around the cupboard chaotically. It looked as though they were fighting. However, they improved slowly until they felt they could attempt an escape.

"Ready?" asked Razz.

"Nnnn," said Forr, nodding.

Forr had a pencil in his beak and they each had one wing outstretched.

"OK then," said Razz, "Three... two... one... up!"

They flapped their wings and took off. They tilted and wobbled in the air until they were beside the cupboard door.

"Now!" ordered Razz.

Forr attempted to push the pencil into the keyhole but missed. He dropped it and they fell to the floor.

"Forr!" complained Razz, "Come on!"

"Sorry," grumbled Forr, "I can't see a thing! I'll get it next time."

They tried again and failed. On the fifth try they were successful and they heard the key rattle onto the floor on the other side of the door.

Forr opened and closed his beak a few times.

"My beak," he sighed, "It's not right... and my tongue hurts."

"Right," said Razz happily, ignoring Forr's complaints, "Let's get that key."

He swept his wing under the door and managed to flick the key back towards him. After a few sweeps the key slid under the door and onto their side.

"Your turn," said Forr.

Razz picked up the key and the procedure began again. It took them four attempts to get the key into the hole and a further five to turn it.

Their last task was the easiest. They flew up to the door handle, stood on it and it clicked. A push, the door swung open and they were out.

They stumbled into the hall where it was just as dark as in the cupboard.

"Stop moving, Razz," said Forr, "Let's get this binding off first... then we're free."

Forr started pecking at the binding.

"Ow! Stop!" exclaimed Razz.

"Sshh," whispered Forr looking around, although it was too dark to see anything, "They might be still here."

"OK," replied Razz, now whispering as well, "But no more pecking. We need something sharp to cut it with, stupid." Razz took a few more steps dragging Forr with him, but Forr was still trying to peck at the twine.

"Stop it!" Razz blurted out.

"Sshh. Stop the shouting," Forr whispered again.

"And you stop the pecking," Razz whispered, "My legs are sore enough already from you!"

They struggled on along the hall until they came to the front door.

"The door's open!" Razz exclaimed with excitement, "We really are free!"

"What was all that shaking about in the cupboard?" asked Forr.

Razz shrugged. "Dunno. Earthquake? Maybe it was something to do with the Master. But we need to cut this binding off."

Razz moved back down the hall pulling Forr with him.

"Hey!" Forr complained, "What are you..."

He stopped when they bumped into something hard.

"Ow!" he exclaimed, "Hang on... it's an axe... just what we need."

The corner of the blade of the axe was still buried in the floorboards since the Troubler had swung it there. They shuffled into position so that they could rub the binding up and down the blade. In a moment the binding was broken just leaving the remains knotted to each of their legs.

They both walked around to stretch their legs, each of them dragging the small piece of twine behind. They stretched out their wings and shook them.

"That's better," said Razz. Then he stopped walking and looked blindly around. "I wonder if there's anyone here."

They paused to listen for a moment.

"Can't hear a thing," said Forr.

Razz started walking towards the open door.

"Let's go then," he said, "We'll report to the Master."

"What about the General?" asked Forr.

"I'm not reporting to *him*," replied Razz, "He gets everything wrong. No, we'll go to the top... to the Master."

They walked past the small table which was lying on its side and then peered out into the mist of the cloud. They could see the black outline of a house.

"Come on," said Razz.

He jumped into the air and flew out closely followed by Forr.

"Which direction?" called out Forr.

They glided right around the palace before Razz replied.

"I don't know," he said, "But... look down there where the ground should be!"

"What's happened?" said Forr.

"I dunno, but let's get out of here."

Razz flew down to where the ground should have been. Their flight gradually slowed until they came to a point where they could fly no further. They had reached the bottom edge of the cloud and found themselves looking down through the snow which was falling away from them.

"What?!" exclaimed Forr.

They stared down in disbelief. One minute they were flying around the palace and now, suddenly, they found themselves gazing down through the night at what looked like the ground far below. They were both stunned by it and felt disorientated, not knowing where they were.

They looked up and then down again several times.

"I think..." said Razz, "It seems strange... so strange... but I think we're... we're in a cloud!"

"In a cloud?!" repeated Forr.

"Yes," said Razz looking around again.

"And we're trapped in here," moaned Forr, "Just when things seemed to be getting better."

"I doubt that we're trapped!" said Razz, "There must be a way out. After all it's only a cloud. Let's have a search."

They flew around inside the cloud, getting more and more desperate to find a way out. They looked like two flies who are trapped in a room. They flew around all the houses and cottages and noticed people at windows frozen by the spell. Then they flew up to the top of the cloud and down to the floor of it again.

Next, they flew right around the outer edge of the cloud.

"Look!" exclaimed Forr, "An elephant!"

Lazuli looked up at them as surprised as they were.

"That's the same one," said Razz, "You know... it was with the enemy."

"What shall we do?" asked Forr.

"Nothing... come on let's find a way out of here."

They continued flying around for a while before landing again at the bottom of the cloud.

"I knew it!" complained Forr, panting for breath after all the effort, "We're trapped... trapped in a cloud."

Razz shook his head in despondency. "It's ridiculous," he moaned, "I don't understand it."

"Neither do I," groaned Forr, "What's happened? Where are we?"

"I don't know," Razz snapped, "This will take some working out..." he looked down through the snow falling away from him and tried to see the land below. "I think we're above Candara, but somehow the palace and these houses are up here too."

"What shall we do?" asked Forr.

Razz lifted his wings in an expression of dismay, "What can we do?"

Forr shook his head and snapped his beak in annoyance.

"Oh no!" he grumbled, "How can this happen!"

For a while they sat and sulked. Then Forr broke the silence.

"I'm tired," he said, "Let's rest, shall we?"

Razz could think of nothing that could be done at the moment and he really needed to rest and sleep as well.

"OK," replied Razz, "Let's go into the palace. At least we can get out of this mist."

They took off and flew through the palace door. They quickly found a room with a comfortable chair and settled down to sleep.

Crayle and Iker entered Old Howard's House through the broken window. The heavily falling snow and the darkness of the night had been the perfect cover. They landed on a chest of drawers, their claws clicking as they slipped on the smooth wood surface.

They were greeted by a fierce growl. In the dark they could not see what had made it and they were petrified. Then, a deep voice rumbled out of the darkness near the door.

"What do you want?" snapped Gratch.

"We're here to... um... to..." began Crayle still feeling terrified. Then Iker piped up with his bright young voice.

"We want to see the Master," he said.

"You can't," growled Gratch, "He's sleeping."

"But it's im...portant," said Iker.

"Who says?"

Iker did not know what to say to this so Crayle tried to put his fear aside and stepped in. Their eyes were getting used to the dark and they could now see Gratch's huge frame blocking the doorway.

"We have very important information for him," said Crayle, "About the enemy."

"Yes," said Iker proudly, "We're spies."

"We must see him," said Crayle becoming more confident now, "We've been spying on the enemy. He'll be angry with you if he hears you wouldn't let us tell him... now, let us pass!"

Gratch did not reply but reached up to the door handle with a clawed foot and opened the door. The two ravens flew through and Gratch called out to them.

"He's downstairs."

They glided down and through the open door. The room was dimly lit by a black candle which was thick with the melted wax. They headed for the mantelpiece. Crayle accidentally clipped the Troubler's head with a wing and he woke up.

"Who's there!" he said in alarm, his breath clouding in the cold air.

The two ravens landed on the floor in front of him and looked up.

"Us, great Master," said Crayle, bowing low.

Iker bowed as well.

"Ah, ravens," said the wizard, and then he snapped irritably, "Where are the rest?"

Both ravens jumped slightly at the sharp words.

"We don't know," said Crayle.

"We've... we've," began Iker, "We've been spying on the enemy, sir."

The Troubler sat up in his chair.

"The enemy? Where are they?"

"We saw one of them," said Crayle proudly, "In a mill."

"Where was this mill... is it the one in Candara?" asked the wizard.

"Yes... we saw that ferryman who tricked the General, sir," answered Crayle.

"The ferryman?" the wizard looked puzzled, "Are you sure about this?"

"It looked like him," said Crayle.

"What do you mean?" snapped the wizard, spitting out the words crossly.

Crayle was getting uncomfortable about this conversation and wished that he had seen the face of the ferryman. He should have waited longer. Then he remembered that the ferryman's face was always hidden anyway. In his confusion he began to doubt, but through fear of the wizard he decided to stick to his story.

"It looked like the f...f...ferryman..." he stuttered, "Because... because he *was* the ferryman."

"But are you sure?" the wizard hissed looking intently at Crayle.

Crayle was far too afraid to admit that he was not sure.

"Yes sir," he said decisively.

The wizard put his wiry hand to his bearded chin and wondered. This was strange. What was going on? Perhaps there were two people in the mill. Or perhaps the ferryman *was* the wizard! In that case why did the wizard want to join forces with him if he was against him? Perhaps it was a trick. He could not work it out and his brow furrowed with concern.

He turned his mind to the ravens at looked down at them standing in front of him.

"I have a job for you to do," he began, his voice was low and each word was spoken with steely precision, "Go to the Brinscally Cave, where the Candara Gems are kept. It's behind the waterfall to the west of Blue Lake. I want you to check that they are still there. If they are there, then steal them and bring them to me. If they are gone already, then come back and tell me. Understand?"

"Yes, Master," said Crayle.

"Do you know where I mean?"

"Not really sir," replied Crayle.

"Not really sir," echoed Iker.

The wizard explained how to get there and then walked to the window and opened it, pushing some snow off the windowsill outside. The light from the candle caught the falling snowflakes making them look yellow against the black background of night.

"Good," he hissed, "This is *very* important. Extremely important. Do *not* fail me.

He stood aside so that they could fly out.

"Now go."

Crayle glided out followed by Iker and they disappeared into the wintry darkness.

Underneath the cloud the Male Squadron had landed in two trees near the centre of Candara, just south of the River Tazer. The General's black compass was glowing which softened the depth of darkness around them. It reflected off the ravens' feathers in flashes of metallic blue, green and purple. The air was now still.

Around them the snow fell, silent and almost weightless, landing with the lightest touch of a feather. Such gentleness contrasted with the harsh sounds of the ravens as they cackled and talked.

The General was looking agitated and restless.

"Gerr," snapped the General, "Surely we can find them! Can't you get anything right?!"

"We looked everywhere," Gerr replied, "We tried, but…" He shook his head. "But we could not find anything."

"OK, OK," said the General, trying to stay calm, "So you failed to find *any* tunnel entrance at all."

Gerr looked sheepish.

"Yes sir," he said.

"And now…" the General continued, his voice growing more and more severe, "You couldn't even find the tunnel that we found to start with."

"Yes, s… sir," Gerr stuttered, "Yes, that is correct. But… in all this snow, sir, it's hard to find anything."

"Don't blame the snow!" snapped the General, "Wars should not be lost just because of a little snow! You had Decc with you who flies so well and hears so well, and the others... was it nine or even ten? It's not acceptable."

The General jerked his head around when he heard a sound behind him. A few seconds later the air was filled with the sound of flapping wings.

"It's the females!" shouted the one closest to them.

This caused a buzz of cackling as the females landed in the trees, finding spaces wherever they could and mixing in with the males. All together there were now about a hundred.

"What's all the noise about!" shouted the General, "Be quiet! Are you an army or a gaggle of geese?!"

The cackling died down.

"That's better," he said. Then he turned to Gerr. "Who did you put in charge of the females? You chose didn't you?"

"Er... yes sir, I did, sir. It was... er..." Gerr tried to remember, tilting his head to one side and then the other, but his mind had gone blank, "Er... er..."

"Useless," the General snapped, "Have you no memory?"

Decc was close by and called out, "It was Tull, sir."

"Thank you, Decc," the General nodded, "At least there's one bird who's been paying attention."

He glowered at Gerr. Gerr felt the insult. He did not want to fall out of favour with the General and lose his position as Colonel. He knew that the General appointed and dismissed ravens on a whim; he had seen it happen.

"Now..." the General continued, "Where was I? Oh yes, the females." He tilted his head on one side, "Who did we say is in charge of them?"

"Tull, sir," said Gerr quickly.

"Tull, where are you?"

"Here, sir," called out a faint voice from much lower down in the tree.

"What are you doing down there?" he called, "Come up here."

She flew up and landed timidly near the General.

"Well?" he snapped at her, and then ordered, "Tell me your report."

There was a pause and when she opened her beak her voice was high and nervous.

"We... we... searched, sir," she said, "As you said, sir. But we... er... didn't find them, sir."

She stopped.

"Go on," he demanded.

"And... and..."

"Yes?" the General said impatiently, "And *what*?"

"And..." she began, "And we found... um... that old man... er... the one who... you know..."

"This is ridiculous," the General said shaking his head, "Can anyone else tell me... *properly*."

Jekka was near the top of the next tree and called across.

"I can, sir," she said.

"OK, go on then."

"We found Old Howard," she began.

"Old Howard, eh?" commented the General thoughtfully, "Well... good. Tell me all about it, and quickly."

"He's escaped from Wizard Elzaphan, sir," Jekka continued, "And there was a rabbit with him called Feeni... on his shoulder, sir. She said she worked for the Master and he had told her they must go to The Kingdom Of Gems and report to him."

"But how did the Master tell her this?" the General demanded, "He's so far away from them."

"I don't know, sir," Jekka replied.

"Sounds suspicious," the General concluded.

"Exactly what I thought, sir," Jekka agreed.

"Go on," said the General, "Then what?"

"So we carried them... Old Howard and the rabbit. We left them just north of that pointed hill... you know, near the mountains. They were too heavy. We couldn't carry them any further. Then we came to look for you... sir."

"Well," the General nodded, "At least *that* was a good thing... I don't know about Old Howard and the rabbit... that's *very* suspicious. Let's hope it hasn't done any harm. Still you are back under my command now so you can't do anything else wrong." He looked around at his army and then back at Jekka.

"What's your name?" he asked her.

"Jekka, sir."

"I appoint you the leader of the Female Squadron," he announced, "Take over from... from..."

"Tull," said Gerr.

"From Tull," the General added. He glared at Gerr. "A ridiculous choice!"

Tull felt a wave of relief and fluttered down happily to the lower branch again. Jekka puffed her chest feathers out with pride.

"Now," the General continued, "We know the enemy are here... but we don't know where." Again he glowered accusingly at Gerr. "So we will sleep here and tomorrow we will report to the Master. But we must keep looking for them, so we will take turns. Jekka, appoint ten females and send them off to keep looking. And you take first watch."

"Yes, sir," said Jekka.

"And when the ten return," the General continued, "Send out ten more. That way we'll keep looking, which is most important, and we'll rest as well. Wake me if anything is seen, OK?"

"Yes sir," said Jekka with enthusiasm.

"Let's hope…" the General said earnestly, "That when we report to the Master in the morning we can give him good news."

The mention of the Master caused ripples of comments to run through the group, some were excited and some were fearful. Jekka chose and sent ten females off. The rest were very pleased to have time to sleep even though it was only half the night. They quickly shifted around on the branches and huddled together until they were comfortable. The light of the compass dimmed and then went out and they began to drift into sleep.

Clutching a lit candle, the thief moved stealthily down the dark stairs of The Old Mill. Every footstep blew up puffs of yellow dust but no sound rose as each step fell as gently as a snowflake.

The cloaked figure carried the Candara Gems. In the top room, powerful concentration had strengthened and magnified the spell, deepening its terrible force still further. Now the gems were resting deep in a pocket, wrapped up in a cloth.

On the ground floor the thief moved silently. The door creaked open. The face under the hood was expressionless with icy determination.

A moment's pause and then the hooded figure stepped out into the snowy night.

The Tazer Downs lay in the east of The Kingdom Of Gems and bordered the Kingdom Of Moone. It was a beautiful landscape of rolling hills and valleys, usually adorned with the lush green of plants and trees. Now it had been dressed with the beauty of the snow which covered everything.

The downs were dark and strangely quiet. There were no birds in the air and since the spell was cast, the only movements were the falling snow and the wind. Now the wind had completely died out to leave the air motionless. The snow floated down with a slow and gentle descent, each flake landing silently. All sharpness had been smoothed and softened from the crest of every hill to the steepest slope dropping into the valleys.

There was, however, one creature moving steadily through the hills in the thickness of night. It was Jamaar. He had crossed the border and was working his way back to his master, the Dark Wizard Troubler. His powerful legs were ploughing him through the snow. He was in territory he had travelled through before and he knew that it would not be long before the hills would end and he would be dropping down towards Whitten.

He was totally unaware that Horrik was on his trail. She was so desperate that although she was tired, she had kept going as fast as she could, stopping only to eat and drink. Step by step she was closing on him.

Old Howard was sitting on the ground and leaning against a tree. His breath clouded out of his slightly open mouth and into the icy air, lit up by a lamp which he had taken out of his bag and placed beside him on the snow. His old coat was pulled tightly around him but still he was shivering with cold. His eyes were closed and he was clutching the Hadia Stick.

Feeni was in front of him, standing in the snow which was fairly shallow under the shelter of the tree. The light of the lamp reflected in her brown eyes.

"It's so cold here," she grumbled, "Yuk!"

She hopped onto Old Howard's canvas bag which was lying beside him and looked up at him.

"Come on!" she ordered, "Get up!"

"No," he sighed, "Oy need to recover. That journey was 'orrible. Oy feel cold and ill... and it's your fault."

"Why?" asked Feeni with indignation.

"'Cos you persuaded me... remember?" he snapped, "Oy don't loike heights an' oy don't loike floying."

Under the tree they were mostly sheltered from the falling snow with just a little fluttering down on them. Old Howard crossly brushed some off his forehead.

Feeni's expression softened and when she spoke her voice was charming and mellow.

"I know... but it's alright now... you're on the ground again. We've escaped from that horrible Wizard Elzaphan and now we're free."

Old Howard opened his eyes and looked at her angrily. "Not with *this* oy'm not."

He held up the Hadia Stick and shook it at her.

"Our master will get rid of that," she said with the pretence of kindness oozing from her voice, "Then it will be alright."

"Oy need to rest. Moy ankle 'urts."

"But we need to go," she argued, and then her voice became cross again as she lost her patience, "It's a long journey. You can rest when we get there. The Dark Wizard's expecting us."

"Oy can't go... not yet," he said tipping his head back against the tree and closing his eyes again, "You go on and oy'll follow."

"That's not fair," she complained, "I can't travel in all this snow. My feet get too cold and wet... and I get tired."

"You'll 'ave to wait for me then."

Feeni stamped her foot on the bag in temper. She realised she could not change his mind and that she would just have to wait. She sat down reluctantly.

"Alright then," she said sulkily, "We'll rest a little... but not for long. It's too cold."

Chapter 10

~ Shades of Grey ~

awn broke gently upon The Kingdom Of Gems. Snow tumbled down from above; hosts of fluffy flakes, floating and swirling playfully in the fresh chill of the air. The icy-crisp weather lay upon the land like a white garment but this was just the outer face of the spell. It was a kingdom possessed.

The spell itself worked invisibly, trapping the people and animals of the kingdom and holding them firmly in its unseen presence. Now it was pressing harder to move into every living thing and leave no creature free. Powered by evil forces the spell was set to complete its absolute control.

Joog was still perched in the top of a tree at the end of Old Howard's garden where he had been watching for the last few hours. On a branch below, Searle was tied up and unable to move. She had slept too but was now awake.

"Let me go owl," she pleaded.

"No," Joog replied, "Now be quiet."

"But you can't just leave me here tied up... I'll die," she said.

Joog turned to look at her.

"You won't die," he said.

"You can't beat him," she sneered, "You know you can't... he's more powerful than all of you. He can't be stopped. You..."

"We'll never give up," Joog interrupted. He spoke with calm authority, his words sounding sharp and direct. "Be quiet."

This time Searle obeyed.

In the dim growing light everything was dull and grey; the trees, the snow-covered ground, Old Howard's House and even the falling snow. There was no joyful dawn chorus but only heavy silence weighing upon the land. This was not the silence of peace but a silence filled with a sinister threat.

The air was unnaturally still. It was eerie. Joog knew that even on the calmest day the treetops would sway slightly; today they were as still as tomb stones. It was as if the world was holding its breath; the future of the kingdom was poised on a knife edge.

Gradually the light grew and with it Joog's concern. Watching from the treetop he realised that the greyness was lingering too long. It was becoming lighter but still there were no colours. He pushed some snow off the branch he was perched on to look at the bark and at the same time he exposed a patch of moss. Both the bark and the moss were colourless, shades of grey in the grey surroundings. He shook a snow-covered twig beside him with his beak and saw that the leaves were grey too.

The spell was deepening.

The ammolite hanging around his neck provided the only colour; it still shone with wonderful clarity. Red, green and amber bathed his chest feathers. It was a splash of colour in a world of gloom. But then, as he looked at it, it faded slightly. The spell was gradually overcoming it.

He had seen the presence of the Dark Wizard Troubler draining the colours out of things close to him. Now this had spread, and maybe throughout the kingdom. He remembered also that the birds, frozen in mid-air by the spell, had gone and now he thought he knew why. They had not escaped but fallen due to the increasing burden of the spell and they were probably now buried under the snow.

The deepening of the spell was something they had not expected and even Wizard Elzaphan had not foreseen it. Joog knew that they had to act quickly but he was finding it hard to think, to move, to act. The spell was imposing itself upon him and overcoming the protection of the ammolite. It was a darkness seeping into his mind and body and he fought to keep it at bay.

They were running out of time. Joog gathered all his strength together and made himself move, lifting his wings as if through treacle and then dropping off the branch.

Once he was on the move, he felt better and he glided down to Aram and Halo. The unicorns looked up.

"Joog," said Aram, his smooth deep voice driven with urgency, "We must be quick… this spell…" He glanced around at the dull, ashen scene. "Look what it's doing."

"I know," said Joog.

"It's must be because he's got the gems," said Aram.

"Wake the others," urged Halo, "Quick!"

Joog glided into the snow-cave. He met Amalek coming out and nearly crashed into her.

"Joog!" she exclaimed, "Careful!"

"We must wake up everyone… quickly."

"Why?" she asked, "What's happening.

"The spell's getting stronger," said Joog, "Can't you feel it? Quick!"

Amalek turned back in and Joog followed. In the cave Simron was awake, as well as Flop and Miriam, but not Seph or the hares.

"Wake up, Seph," Amalek cried, shaking him by the shoulders.

When she let go Seph flopped down like a rag doll, without a movement.

"Oh, no!" exclaimed Amalek, "Seph... wake up!"

She grabbed him again and shook him even harder but still he did not wake. Then she slapped him on the face.

He opened his eyes in surprise.

"Argh!" he exclaimed, "What are you doing?"

"Waking you, Seph," she said quickly, "The spell's worse. You must get up now!"

He stood up slowly. He still looked sleepy and very untidy with ruffled hair.

"Help me wake these hares," she said urgently to Seph.

Together they tried to wake the hares, reaching down to move and shake them. They were all huddled together but they felt cold and were impossible to move. Their ammolites had lost their colour. Amalek shuddered. The hares fur was no longer soft but crisp with frost. The children moved from one to the next.

"It's no good," he said, "The spell's got them."

Amalek shook her head. "What shall we do?"

Then they saw a hare's ears suddenly stick up from the mass of grey fur; it was Tally. He jumped up and was followed by Kendall, Waltab and Darlitt. All the others remained still.

Joog flew onto Seph's shoulder. "Listen," he said, "We're all in danger, even wearing these ammolites.

Follow me... quickly now!"

The children looked at Joog, faces shocked and wide-eyed, as the impact of his words sunk in. With a great effort they all tried to get moving properly by stretching their arms and legs. They filed out of the snow-cave.

Simron came out first followed by Flop and Miriam, and then the children. Kendall and Tally were next and right behind them was the young energetic Waltab and the elderly Darlitt.

Once outside they positioned themselves where they could see the house through the falling snow.

"Everything's so dull," said Flop, "And already I feel so tired... as if I need a nap."

Amalek reached down and stroked Flop's long fur.

"Don't sleep yet," she said, "Whatever you do... *don't* sleep. You saw what happened to those hares. And we have work to do."

They were well-hidden by the trees and the deep snow which rose up in front of them beyond the shelter of the trees. The falling snow was so thick that they knew they would be hard to see from the house. They all raised their heads just above the snow line until they were peeping over. Aram and Halo stood further back in the dark shade of the trees.

"Right," said Simron, "We need to make a move."

The time had come. They had made the choice earlier when Wizard Elzaphan had asked them and they had promised. Now they had to honour that promise and see it through. This would be their most frightening moment. They had to confront the Dark Wizard Troubler.

"Look at that," said Joog pointing with a claw, "That branch there... it's near the window."

The branch was on the large elm tree near Old Howard's House and it hung near to an upstairs window on the first floor.

"We could climb the tree," said Simron, "And then through that window... yes, it could work," said Simron.

"As long as he's not in that room," said Amalek.

"But that's the whole point, isn't it?" Seph stated, "We *want* to face him."

Simron nodded.

"Yes," he said, "But we need to surprise him. If we can get into the house without him knowing... that would be good. So, Joog, can you take a look first?"

Joog nodded.

"Good," continued Simron, "If you can, check that he's not in that room. If it's all clear we can go in that way... through the window."

"I'll go now," said Joog.

He took to the air and skimmed silently across the surface of the snow. A second later and he was up in the tree and edging cautiously along the branch. The window was broken, the glass smashed completely, and he looked in through it. There was no one there. He stepped onto the window ledge, his feet slipping into the snow, and took a closer look, leaning his head inside. Lying on the floor was the huge bulk of a Komodo dragon. It was Gratch.

Joog kept still, completely still.

He tensed as Gratch growled, moved his head and settled again. His eyes were closed in sleep.

Joog relaxed.

Gratch stirred again and this time woke, opening his eyes sleepily. He remembered that he was meant to be watching and suddenly he was wide awake. He quickly pushed his great body up onto his short legs. He heard a sound and looked up at the window. The sound was Joog jumping onto the branch and then slipping away, gliding silently through the dancing snowflakes and back to the trees.

Gratch glanced up at the window and then rushed to it, his claws clicking on the floorboards. At the window he heaved himself up using his head on the window frame and then scrambling up the wall with his front legs. When his claws were hooked over the window ledge he gazed into the falling snow. His thin forked tongue slipped in and out of his mouth repeatedly and saliva dribbled from his huge mouth, some of it freezing into strands of ice. He put his snout out and turned one way then the other, sniffing the air and again his long tongue snaked out.

Then he noticed where the snow had been scraped off the branch by Joog. He stared at it.

He had heard a sound; something had moved just outside the window. Now he had seen the snow disturbed on the branch. Could it be a raven? Or something else? He knew the Prince and Princess were trapped in the cloud so it could not be them. There were only two possibilities; it was a raven or the mysterious person who he had met in The Old Mill and who had threatened his master.

Meanwhile Joog had reported to the others.

"What shall we do now?" asked Amalek.

Simron's mind was working, instantly summoning up all his experience and training as a Master of Disguise. In a flash he had a plan.

"I'll deal with it," he said, "Quick, lend me your magic box Seph."

Seph handed it over. Simron had a quick word with Aram who lowered his alicorn and created a pathway through the snow. Simron strode away from them and towards the house. They watched him go.

"How does he do it?" commented Seph, "He's so fast... and quiet..."

"And..." said Amalek as she squinted through the falling snow, "He's hard to see... where's he gone?"

Aram was now walking slowly towards the house

through the path in the snow.

"There he is Ammey," said Seph pointing.

They were crouching behind the snow and peeping over towards the house. Simron had climbed the tree and was edging along the branch towards the window.

"I ought to be there with him," Seph said, and he started getting up.

Amalek grabbed his arm and pulled him back. "No," she said, "Let him deal with it... trust him. If he wanted you there he would have said."

Seph nodded.

Simron looked in through the window to see Gratch heading for the door.

"Stop," said Simron.

His voice was different. He could impersonate any voice. This one he had only heard briefly at the border.

Gratch stopped and turned his great body in shock.

"Master?" he asked, "Is that you?"

There was no answer.

"Master?" he asked again.

Gratch was looking at a hooded figure silhouetted in the light at the window and sitting on the branch. He moved a step closer. Now he could see that it was holding a staff and therefore it must be a wizard. But somehow the voice was not his master's; it was similar but not quite the same. Then he noticed it was not his master's cloak and he knew who it must be.

"So, you've come," Gratch growled, his voice rumbling up from his great body, "I gave my master your message. Have you come to take over?"

Simron was trying to think it through. What was this dragon talking about? Who did it think he was? He had to play along and find out more.

"Yes," he said, still imitating the Troubler's voice as best he could, "I am here to take over."

"You sound like my Master," Gratch said.

"Of course I do," Simron snapped.

"Show your face," Gratch demanded, "So that I can see who you are."

Gratch stared at the figure through the window. His forked tongue slithered out of his mouth and back in again. Simron lifted the stick he was holding and whacked it down on the branch. There was a flash of golden light.

Gratch recoiled.

Simron needed to find out more. He moved closer to the window.

"Did you give him *all* my message?" he asked.

"Yes," rumbled Gratch, "He was shocked. When he heard you had the gems he... he was angry but he thought you might just be bluffing."

"Bluffing?" Simron's words were angry, "I don't bluff."

Then an appealing idea suddenly entered Gratch's lumbering mind and he acted on it straight away.

"Show me the gems to prove you've got them," he said, "Then I'll work for you instead. I'm strong and I can fight. Show me the gems."

"You're in no position to bargain with me," said Simron, thinking as he spoke, "But... I would like to have you in my service."

"Show me the gems then," Gratch insisted.

Simron paused... thinking, thinking, thinking. How could he deal with this? He had to come up with something.

"They're too powerful," Simron replied calmly, "If you look at them you'll die."

Gratch had not heard of this and he wondered if he should trust this wizard. Then Simron spoke again.

"I can show you their light," he offered.

"Yes," Gratch agreed, "Show me their light, but is it

safe?"

"It's safe," Simron confirmed, "As long as you don't look at the gems themselves."

He took Seph's oval magic box out from underneath his cloak and held it through the window. He opened and closed it quickly and a flash of bright light lit up the room for a split second. Gratch blinked.

"But the gems are coloured," he declared, "That light was white light. The light I saw in that old mill was all different colours..."

This time Simron had his answer ready. "You don't know much about the gems do you? When they're together... close together, like they are in this little box, the colours combine to make pure light, white light. When they're like this they are at their most powerful... and their most dangerous."

Gratch was almost convinced but not quite and Simron could see it.

"Alright then," Simron sounded cross again, "I'll show you." He put his hand ready to open the box again and Gratch cowered back. "You can see the gems if you really want to, but you *will* die which is good for me because I'd be rid of you."

"No!" Gratch exclaimed urgently, "I believe you... and... I'll work for you."

"Well, that's good then," Simron withdrew the box back through the broken window and took it under his cloak again. "I have a job for you," Simron stated, now in complete control, "And it's important."

"Yes Master?" Gratch grovelled, immediately taking the role.

Gratch sounded eager. He felt he had worked the situation to his favour. He was now in the service of a more powerful wizard.

"It's important," stated Simron, "*Very* important."

"Yes, Master?"

"It's something that I must deal with before taking over here. It also acts as a test for you... succeed and you can enter my service. Understand?"

"Yes master," Gratch said eagerly, "To work for you would be an honour, sir. I *will* succeed."

"Go south," Simron ordered, "Then follow the river east through the town... and keep going and going. After that turn to the north and go into the higher lands there. Then hunt. There's something there that I want you to deal with..."

"What is it?"

Simron said the first thing that came to mind.

"A dog."

Gratch was surprised. "A dog, Master?"

"Yes, a dog... now, what's your name?"

"Gratch, Master."

"Gratch," he continued, "This dog was... working for me but it was too stupid... and old... and it turned against me so I left it there. I want him dealt with before he does any harm. You like hunting, don't you?"

"Yes, Master."

Gratch was also hungry so this job was appealing to him. But most of all, he wanted to work for the most powerful wizard he could and this one had the Candara Gems. This was a step up for him.

"I love hunting," he growled, "and I can kill dogs easily."

"Good," Simron nodded his hooded head, "This one's big but it's old and slow... and almost blind. It's sense of smell is weak too... and it limps a little. So it'll be easy for you. But use your eyes. Go to a high point and look... and use your smell... but *don't* come back 'till you've found it and killed the traitor. It will be a sizeable meal for you and it'll show me your worth... then I can trust you fully and you can enter my service. Are you hungry?"

"Yes, Master."

"Well, it's meal-time for you..." said Simron decisively, "...when you've caught the dog. But I want this dealt with quickly, understand?"

"Yes, Master."

"It's very important that you get rid of it," Simron emphasised, "It's turned traitor on me. Can you climb trees?" asked Simron.

"Yes, Master... I climb well," Gratch answered proudly.

Gratch rolled his razor-sharp claws on one of his front feet on the floor. He watched as his new master climbed in through the window.

"Good... very good," said Simron, "You can go down the tree then."

"Yes, Master."

"Go now," Simron ordered, "Do well with this first job working for me and I will reward you."

Gratch walked to the window, scrambled through it and sunk his claws into the branch. Simron watched as the Komodo worked his way along the branch, down the tree backwards and into the snow below to begin his journey.

In a moment, he was gone.

While this was going on, another tunnel had been built. It was Amalek's idea. It would provide a way of travelling to the house without the chance of being seen. Tally was looking brighter again and had organised the digging. However, Darlitt was looking sleepy and his ammolite was dim; he was sitting in the snow against the trunk of a tree.

Tally worked with Kendall and Waltab who were both young and strong. Their ammolites were still glowing, which showed that they were holding the spell at bay. The three young hares disappeared into the hole they were digging and a few minutes later Tally emerged followed by the others, all panting from the exertion. It was just large enough for the children to fit into in a crawling position.

"All ready for you," Tally announced proudly, bowing to them and holding a paw out towards the entrance.

Waltab bowed as well.

"Another perfect job," he commented.

"Thanks, all of you," said Seph, still keeping his eyes on the tree, "Get down!" he exclaimed.

They all lay down on the snow and watched as Gratch climbed down the tree.

"How about that!" Amalek whispered, "The dragon's going. How did Simron do that?"

Seph smiled, "He's amazing. He can talk his way through anything. Remember how he confused the ravens? I bet he used some disguise..."

"Oh no!" interrupted Amalek suddenly, "The spell's got Darlitt."

She turned to Tally.

"Tally?" she said, and then in alarm, "Tally!"

Seph looked round. Tally was still, completely still. Kendall and Waltab and were both unmoving as well. Their ammolites had the faintest glow left and then, like a dying candle flame, they flickered out. Amalek reached out to grasp Tally. He was cold and his fur was as hard as wire.

Tally had felt the spell, like a dark mist swirling through him, sweeping him away. His sight faded to black. He felt as helpless as a piece of paper caught in a hurricane.

He dimly heard Amalek shout his name and wanted to reply but could not. Then he heard something else, much closer; a voice that sounded loud in his ears.

"KYWAY, Tally, KYWAY," said his grandfather.

The world came back into view. The black changed to white and he realised it was the white of the snow. He felt warmth flow through him, into his legs and head and body. He was back.

"Tally," soothed Amalek with relief.

She lifted him up, wrapped her arms around him and hugged him. Seph was looking at Kendall and Waltab who remained motionless, like grey rocks. They had been taken by the hideous power of the spell.

"It's got them," said Amalek.

"And it's getting stronger," said Seph, "We must get going before it's too late!"

They could feel the pressure of the spell forcing itself upon them; it was harder to move now and the glow of their ammonites was fainter.

"Come on Ammey!" Seph urged, "We must go… now!"

She nodded and looked around at Aram and Halo.

"We'll stay here," said Aram, "We'll keep watch."

Halo nodded her fine silver head, shedding a spray of silver sparks from her mane.

Flop was already in the tunnel and Amalek and Seph crawled in after him with Tally between them. When they were halfway through, Flop slowed.

"Keep going, Flop!" Seph said cheerily.

"Sorry," he replied slowly and then stopped.

"Flop!" said Seph, "Are you alright?"

Seph caught him up and reached out a nervous hand. His finger tips touched and quickly recoiled. It was like receiving some terrible news; Flop was cold to touch and his silky-soft fur was as hard as stone.

"What's happening, Seph?" asked Amalek from behind.

"Flop's frozen," he answered.

Amalek's heart sank.

"What about Miriam?" she asked.

"I'm just moving up to find out..." he said, "Oh no... she's frozen too!"

There was nothing they could do but leave them there. They squeezed past, scraping on Flop's frozen fur, and carried on. It was like moving through treacle but they forced themselves forwards knowing that they would soon be emerging near the tree.

"Oy'm tired," grumbled Old Howard as he pushed and forced his way through the snow towards his house.

"Stop complaining," snapped Feeni crossly in his ear.

"Woy's everything so grey?" asked Old Howard.

She was sitting on his shoulder. They were both coated with snow and Old Howard's progress was very slow. Feeni looked around.

"I don't know," she said, "We'll find out when we get there. And we'll be there soon... if you don't keep stopping all the time. Just keep going."

Amalek and Seph emerged from the tunnel and climbed the tree. Tally sat on Seph's shoulder. When they were on the branch they found Joog there.

"Are you two alright?" Joog asked softly.

"Yes," they said together.

"Just about," added Amalek.

"Be strong," he whispered, "The kingdom depends on you two."

"You're coming in with us?" asked Amalek.

"Not yet," he replied.

"But we need you," whispered Seph.

"I know," Joog whispered, "I will be with you soon, but I need to stay out here for a while in case the ravens arrive. I'll join you inside."

He flew off silently, circled the tree and then landed near the top where he could hide in a mass of leaves. The ammolite hanging around his neck flickered but held its colour in the grey surroundings.

The children and Tally climbed in through the broken window and joined Simron inside.

"Well done," whispered Simron to the children.

"And well done to you," whispered Seph, "How did you get rid of the dragon?"

"Easy..." laughed Simron, "It took some help from Aram and your box..." he pulled it out from under his cloak and handed it to Seph.

"Thank you..." he began but stopped when he heard a noise outside.

In a few seconds the sound had grown louder. It was a flock of birds.

"Ravens," whispered Amalek, her shoulders giving a little shudder of fear.

A nasal command cut harshly through the thin air.

"Land in that tree by the house!" commanded the General.

The sound of flapping wings grew as more and more ravens landed in the tree, a great fluttering of black shapes among the branches.

"Quick, get down!" whispered Simron, "Under the window here."

The ravens cackled and screeched with eager sounds as they landed. Aram and Halo were watching all this from the deep shade of the trees at the end of the garden.

"What shall we do?" asked Halo softly.

"I don't know," replied Aram, "There are so many of them."

Halo lifted a hoof and placed it down again. "We've got to do something," she whispered.

"Let's get closer to the tree," Aram replied, "I've got an idea. But we'll have to move very carefully not to be seen."

They started moving slowly through the trees.

The General had landed on the side of the tree closest to the house. Gerr was beside him. Joog watched them from above and stayed completely still. The ravens had not seen him and neither had Aram and Halo who thought he had gone into the house with the others.

"So, Colonel Gerr," asked the General, "We're sure that they're travelling by tunnel, aren't we?"

"Yes sir."

"But…" the General lifted one of his feet and proudly tapped the compass around his neck with his claws a couple of times, "I don't know. We couldn't find any entrance and we can't even find the place where you saw the light in the first place. Do you think they were tricking us?"

"That would explain why they've disappeared, sir," said Gerr, "But I did hear voices. And so did Decc. So they were in a tunnel then."

"Muffled voices, Gerr… unidentifiable voices… it may have been anyone. Could have been voices from the grave for all we know."

"But, sir," argued Gerr, "Decc was sure it was a cat. Anyway, who else could it be? And also, *because* we can't find them they must be in a tunnel."

"I suppose so. But that's the worst thing. If they *were* in a tunnel, and we found them back there…" he jerked his head back toward Candara, "It's a *disaster* that we let them get away. Anyway, we'll wait here 'till they arrive, then we'll strike." He looked down at the others, "Akk and Rakka!"

"Yes, sir!" they chorused.

"Go and tell the Master that we've arrived."

"Why us?" complained Rakka. After his last meeting with the Troubler he was terrified of him, "Can't Gerr go?"

"No!" cried Gerr, sounding very alarmed by the idea, "He asked you."

"Or Forr," Rakka continued, "He could go. After all you made him a sergeant and…"

"Stop!" shouted the General, "Stop grumbling and go and do it."

Rakka jumped reluctantly off a branch and took off followed by Akk who looked just as unhappy.

"And Decc?" the General looked around the group, "Where are you?"

"Here sir," came a voice from the mass of ravens.

"You're the fast flyer aren't you? Scout the area in ever-widening circles and tell me immediately if you see the enemy or the Master, for he may not be here in the house."

"Yes sir," he replied and took off and circled around the tree.

"Bigger circles than that!" shouted the General.

Aram had moved faster than Halo. He was now right under the tree but she was still working her way around the patch of trees that ran right around the garden.

Then she trod on a branch which broke with a crack.

The ravens stopped chattering and they all looked towards the sound. Over a hundred pairs of evil, black eyes stared at Halo.

"It's the enemy!" screeched the General, "There's a unicorn! Get it! Get it!"

All together the ravens raised their wings ready to take off and attack. At the same time Aram plunged his alicorn into the trunk of the tree. A fizz ran up the tree and along all the branches.

The ravens felt it and fell back onto their branches in shock.

"Attack! Attack!" shouted the General.

"Attack!" shouted Gerr.

They tried again to take off, lifting and flapping their wings in panic. As hard as they tried they could not take off. Their feet were stuck to the branches of the old elm tree by its sap and as they flapped more furiously, wings and feathers and heads and beaks were getting stuck too.

"Gerr!" screeched the General, "Do something!"

He glared at Gerr, who immediately started pecking frantically at the sap on the General's feet.

"Come on, Gerr!" shouted the General.

Gerr threw all his energy into the job but his beak just bounced off the rubbery substance.

"Be careful!" the General complained, "I don't want to end up with a broken… aaah!"

Gerr had missed the sap and given the General a vicious peck on the leg.

"Idiot!" the General shook his wings in anger and pain, "Stop! I told you to be careful. My leg! If it's broken you lose your position!"

Gerr was so carried away that he gave one last peck and his beak got stuck in the sap on the General's foot. Here the conversation ended because the General was too angry and in too much in pain to speak, and Gerr could not open his beak which was stuck in the sap.

"What's happening?" asked Seph.

Simron lifted his head above the window frame and peeped out. It was a commotion of noise and panic with ravens flapping, pecking and trying to fly off the tree.

"They're stuck in the sap," whispered Simron to the others, "They can't fly."

The ravens cackled as they struggled to fly in vain. After a while some became quiet as they gave up. They glowered and squawked in anger. Occasionally, one would try to jump off the tree only to fall back pathetically. The old elm tree looked as if it was covered with black leaves shaking in the wind.

Then Rakka and Akk returned.

"What's all the fuss about?" asked Rakka as he swooped down.

"Don't land!" shouted the General but it was too late for them to stop, "What's the matter with you?! Couldn't you see that we're all stuck?"

Rakka and Akk flapped furiously and Rakka managed to rise off the branch, stretching the sap like elastic, but then the sap pulled him back. He bumped down onto the branch looking more dejected than ever. Then Decc appeared over the house and swooped down towards the tree.

"Don't land!" screeched the General again, just as Decc perched on a branch and his feet sank into the sap.

"You idiots!" the General exclaimed, sounding near boiling point, "Now we're all trapped."

"No sign of the enemy sir," said Decc brightly.

"Well, thank you," heavy sarcasm dripped from the General's words, "Now we can all relax. Wonderful. The enemy are nowhere to be seen," he mocked and he looked this way and that with his beak hanging open to give him a gormless expression. Then, in his frustration, he gave his black compass a vicious peck.

The compass knocked into his chest feathers and then clicked open. The General watched in amazement as a two-tailed scorpion climbed out and balanced on the top. There was a pause as it looked up at him. The General was so surprised that he did not move. The other ravens looked on in stunned silence.

The scorpion moved suddenly and scuttled quickly up the chain making a metallic clicking noise, spread its wings, and flew onto his head.

"Gerr!" he blurted, "Where's it gone?!"

"On your head, sir!"

The General shook his head in panic and it was thrown off. Its wings whirred and it landed on the trunk of the tree, ran into a hole in the bark and disappeared.

"That was a scorpion, wasn't it Gerr?" he asked.

"A scorpion, sir... yes...with two tails and wings."

"It must have been living in the compass all this time!"

"Yes sir."

"Well, it's a good thing it's out then," he commented.

The General shook his head in disbelief. He looked at the compass. It hung loosely on the chain around his neck and he snapped it closed with a claw and his beak.

"Perhaps it'll start working properly now," he said and then turned to look at Rakka. "Rakka, did you find the Master?"

"No, sir," replied Rakka.

The General then seemed to slip into deep dejection as he thought about how the Master would return to find them all stuck in a tree. He imagined the fury that the wizard would vent upon them and realised that this was probably the worst thing that could possibly happen. The ravens stopped talking. Their cackling gradually subsided and all was quiet once more. They just sat on their branches, prisoners of the tree, and looked down sulkily at the snowy garden below.

Just above them, well-hidden by leaves, perched Joog. He had seen and heard everything. He had felt the sap ooze from the bark and now he tried to lift one of his feet. It was firmly stuck. He could no longer fly in to join the others and this concerned him. He considered trying to fly and see if he could break free but if it failed it would give away his position so he decided he would have to wait.

The thief approached Old Howard's House from the south-east. The figure was huddled under a dark-hooded cloak, now dotted with grey from the large snowflakes which were falling in the lifeless air.

Moving under the trees, the snow eased and the layer on the ground was shallow. Suddenly walking was easy. The trees here provided the perfect cover for a cautious approach to the house.

The house came into sight through the trees. The thief saw the mass of ravens on the tree and paused. The next move needed to be right.

The thief dipped a hand deep into a large pocket and fingered the cloth containing the Candara Gems. The thrill of such power brought instant excitement but the thief was too cunning to be carried away by this. The power would be used with icy precision.

The Prince, Princess, Simron and Tally had slipped through the door and into the upstairs hallway. Simron closed the door very quietly behind them. For a moment they paused and listened.

The house was silent.

They were acutely aware of the intense chill hanging in the air. It was uncomfortable then but now it had deepened. It was on the verge of being unbearable. It was a dark presence which deadened all life in its dullness; it smothered all joy, delight and other bright qualities. They had never felt so uneasy and vulnerable.

As well as this, it was getting harder to move. Now they were in the house they were finding that they had to force their movements even more. It felt like walking through sticky honey.

They looked along the hallway. It was colourless. A thick layer of dust, disturbed by earlier footsteps, coated the floor and surfaces. It was not an inviting place to be in.

Their ammolites still hung around their necks, glowing gently with coloured light. Simron opened a pocket on his belt and took out a metal spike with a twist on the end. He inserted it into the keyhole and worked it around until he felt the lock turn. He glanced at the others and whispered softly.

"We don't want ravens breaking free and coming after us do we?"

"Definitely not," whispered Amalek.

"How did you get rid of that creature?" asked Seph.

"Easy," whispered Simron, "He played into my hands... he thought I was someone else." Then he smiled, "I sent it off far away to the east hunting for an imaginary dog! The trouble is, it sounds as though there is someone else here, another fallen wizard."

The children's eyes opened wide in shock.

"Another wizard!" exclaimed Seph, "Where?"

"I don't know," whispered Simron, "In the kingdom. But it's worse than just that. It seems he might have stolen the Candara Gems."

Amalek's jaw dropped in shock.

"Stolen the gems!" whispered Seph in amazement, "That's terrible."

"Does it affect our plan?" asked Amalek.

"Maybe... maybe not," Simron whispered, "If it's true then maybe it's better if the Troubler hasn't got them. Anyway, we have to stick to the plan as best we can and just be ready for anything. But we must act quickly before things get worse."

They slipped their shoes off and left them by the wall so that they could creep silently along the wooden floorboards. Tally moved stealthily beside them on his padded paws. Simron turned to the children again.

"It's all up to you two now," he whispered, "You're the ones who have to do this... you have to face him. I can only help, and I will to the best of my ability. Remember the important things… the way to beat a wizard is through his weakness. Through greed he will fall. Through his greed you can trick him. Stick to Wizard Elzaphan's plan."

Amalek and Seph nodded.

"You need *all* your courage and *all* your strength. And remember..." He paused, and when he spoke his words sounded as clear and fresh as birdsong in the early morning. "Real strength is found within."

They nodded again and felt ready, and then Simron led the way.

They listened at the doors to the other upstairs rooms and on hearing nothing Simron knew there was no one there. As they went he locked the doors.

"How can you tell?" asked Seph in a whisper.

"It's a mixture of instinct and senses," replied Simron.

They crept down the stairs. Occasionally a step would creak and they would all stop. They moved slowly through the hall, pausing at each door to listen. One door was ajar and when they paused outside Simron again shook his head.

"He's not here," he whispered.

"The cellar door," commented Amalek, "We haven't tried the cellar."

Moving on dusty socks, they reached the cellar door. Again Simron shook his head.

"That's it then," whispered Seph, "He's not here."

"Do we wait for him?" asked Amalek.

Simron nodded, "Yes, which is good. We can really surprise him now."

Then he looked thoughtful.

"But there is one other place to look," he whispered, "The attic. I saw an entrance in the ceiling upstairs."

"Right," Seph acknowledged, "We'd better check then."

They moved to the foot of the stairs and began to climb.

Outside, in the shade of the trees, Aram and Halo watched the house through the thickly falling snow. When Aram spoke, his voice was deep and smooth yet there was an anxious edge to it.

"I wish we knew what was happening inside. Perhaps we ought to be in there too."

"Maybe," replied Halo, nudging him affectionately with her beautiful silver head, "But someone needs to watch. We don't even know if *he's* in there… and he might return."

"Yes, you're right of course," he agreed, "And I am concerned about those ravens... we need to keep an eye on them."

Aram had seen some of the ravens trying to struggle again and a few seemed to be having some success. They were beginning to work themselves free from the sticky sap. Aram was watching these particularly closely.

Suddenly, a raven rose off the branch attached by one strand of sticky sap which stretched like an elastic band and snapped with a crack.

In a flash Aram was up and into action. His powerful back legs kicked hard into the ground and propelled him forwards across the snow towards the tree. Snow sprayed up around him as he surged forwards. It was a dramatic sight with Halo springing into action beside him and their manes leaving a trail of silver and gold sparks behind them. The ravens cackled and shouted at them.

Aram pointed his golden alicorn at the raven that had broken free and shouted.

"Feathers!"

Its feathers disappeared and it fell to the ground with a desperate cry and smashed into the snow.

Four more were now rising off the branches. Then one was free. It was Halo this time who shouted.

"Feathers!"

It plummeted with a frightened whimper. The other three struggled until they broke free and rose from the tree with amazing acrobatic flying skills. Then there were more ascending through the snow-filled air. Aram pointed his golden alicorn at another and shouted again.

"Feathers!"

Its feathers disappeared and it fell; a black, wrinkled, skinny, frightened thing, squawking and screeching into the deep snow. Halo aimed her shiny silver alicorn at another.

"Feathers!" she shouted.

It fell, spinning into the snow. More and more rose from the tree. Aram and Halo were quick and alert to point their alicorns and shout "Feathers!" at them, and black featherless ravens continued to fall out of the air.

"Get the owl!" screeched Decc.

Joog had been spotted. He rose out of his hiding place in the tree with a long line of sap still attached to one of his legs. Decc and five others were already right behind him. The sap held Joog back and then snapped. He was free and shot forwards but it was too late. The ravens swarmed around him, pecking at him viciously. Joog fought back, using his claws and beak.

No longer flying, they all fell through the air, a swirling mass of black feathers with Joog in the middle. They crashed into a tree to the south-east of the house, spraying powdery snow into the air. He felt a blow to the head as he hit the trunk and passed out. His limp body fell through the branches.

The thief looked up and stepped quickly back. Joog fell to the ground splattering snow over the thief's boots. The ammolite faded to the slightest glow.

Decc and the other ravens rejoined the army who were gathering for a mass attack. There were now thirty or forty of them in the air. They were cackling and shouting eagerly. The commanding voice of the General rose above all the others.

"Attack! Attack!" he boomed.

Inside the house everything was still. The friends were standing on a stepladder which Seph had found in the cellar and brought up. Simron was carefully opening the hatch to the attic. The ammolites around their necks glowed in colours upon the wooden ladder, but they were even fainter now, fading like the last moments of an evening's twilight. They were running out of time.

When the hatch was open they felt the temperature drop sending a shiver down Amalek's spine. Simron knew there was someone up there and he lifted a finger to point above.

He pulled himself up. Light shone through the hatch from below in a pale beam but the rest of the room was dark. Behind him Seph climbed up and then Amalek with Tally in her arms. Seph had his oval magic box in his pocket.

The chilling atmosphere engulfed them. The air was icy. It felt like entering another world, a dim world where everything was held in heavy gloom. A shiver ran down Amalek's back as she put Tally down and grabbed Seph's hand for comfort. Seph gave her hand two quick squeezes for reassurance.

Staying perfectly still, they looked around. They had moved out of the light of the upstairs hall into the windowless attic. At first, most of the room was too dark to see anything but then their eyes began to adjust. Gradually things became clearer. There was a table. And was that a chair? As they gazed across the dusty floorboards they saw two black objects. Was that a pair of boots?

Then they heard a sound. It came from the far corner of the attic but in the silence of the room, in the chilly thin air, it was perfectly clear.

Someone was breathing.

Long breaths flowed slowly in and out. The oppressive presence filled the room like thick black treacle and once again they found it was invading their minds. It pressed upon them, weighing them down and seeping into their beings.

Their eyes became used to the darkness and with the help of the ammolites they could see more clearly now. The room, which was large and which stretched across the whole of the house, was very plain with hardly any furniture on the bare floorboards. There were no windows in the sloping ceilings and the main source of light was the square hole through which they had entered. The glow of their ammolites dimmed further.

Then something small and bright and golden suddenly lit up on the far side of the room.

"What's that?" whispered Amalek very softly.

It was shining like a star in the darkness now and from its light they could see that it was on a shelf. It was glowing brighter and brighter until it was lighting up the room, casting long shadows. In its light they saw a large armchair, and as the light grew brighter still, they could clearly see a figure sitting in the chair. It was dark against the light behind it, black and sinister, and rising and falling gently as each breath flowed in and out. The breath hissed in frosty clouds to hang there briefly and then fade. The head was tilted back and in sleep the lower jaw had dropped leaving the mouth slightly open. Although the chair and the figure were mostly a dark silhouette, the light caught the pale grey forehead which looked as ghostly white as a corpse.

Their fear deepened, like the turning of a powerful vice squeezing the life out of them. The menacing deathly atmosphere that filled the room was the presence of the Dark Wizard Troubler.

Amalek and Seph took a step in front of Simron and Tally. It was almost impossible to move now, and they had to force each step with all their energy. They paused to summon up courage and then continued to creep cautiously forwards.

Chapter 11

~ A Purple Robe ~

Outside the house the General was leading the army as they circled above. The attempt to attack Aram and Halo had been abandoned because over twenty ravens had been made featherless and fallen to the ground. Even with the mass attack the unicorns were too quick and none were getting through. Circling above, they were out of danger and had time to plan what to do next.

The ravens had felt the presence too and knew that their Master was in the house. The General had sent Decc down to investigate and to try work out where their Master was. They needed to find a way in.

"He must be in danger," said the General, "Otherwise... why are the unicorns guarding the house?"

"Because the enemy are in there, sir?" asked Gerr.

"Exactly... well at least it's possible... and if it's possible then we have to act on it. We must act to protect our Master."

"What about the unicorns, sir?" asked Gerr.

"Forget about them," snapped the General. Then he looked down. "Ah... Decc."

Decc was returning, flying up to them at high speed. With a clever twist in the air he slowed and turned, ending up just below the General and flying at the same speed.

"What's your report?" snapped the General.

"I think he's in the attic sir," said Decc, slightly out of breath, "The Master, that is."

"Why?" asked the General.

"Because his presence is stronger there sir," replied Decc, "And also I can see through windows to all the other rooms and he's not in any of them, so he must be in the attic, sir."

"Good work Decc," the General complimented.

"Also I checked for ways in, sir," Decc continued, "Every way is closed and locked. There's one broken window but inside the door is locked."

"In that case," the General added, "We must assume that all the doors are locked... so there's no point breaking windows to get in. What do you suggest?"

Gerr answered quickly, still frightened of losing his position to Decc. "Down the chimney, sir?" he offered.

"And where would that get us?" snapped the General crossly as if it was the most ridiculous suggestion. Gerr made no reply so the General answered his own question. "Into the rooms, that's where. And all the rooms are locked, remember, Gerr?"

"Yes, sir," Gerr replied, cringing.

"I suggest through the roof sir," said Decc, "We need to blast our way through... but once a tile or two is broken then it's easy... usually just some soft stuff and thin wood underneath, sir."

The General clearly liked this idea.

"We're going in through the roof!" the General shouted to the army.

Once again the ravens furthest away could not hear clearly.

"What did he say?" they muttered to each other.

"I think it was, 'We're going into the hoof,'" said one.

Another immediately piped up, "Which must be a way of attacking the unicorns."

Most of the remaining army fell towards the roof, while a group of six dived toward Aram and Halo. These quickly lost their feathers and spun helplessly to the ground.

Inside the house, in the attic, the children continued creeping gingerly towards the Dark Wizard Troubler. Amalek and Seph were side by side with Tally between them and Simron right behind.

They kept their eyes fixed on the wizard as they took one step at a time. With great care and effort they were moving without any sound, their socks silent on the dusty boards.

They were half way across the room when a tap on the roof made them stop. Silence. They started stealing forwards again. Then another tap. The Troubler stirred, coughed and settled. When they were just a few feet away from the wizard, there were more taps and scratchings on the roof, so they paused again.

"Ravens," mouthed Amalek to Seph, pointing to the roof.

Seph felt his oval magic box in his pocket with one hand and looked around at Amalek's face lit by the light shining from the shelf.

"Ready?" he asked in the softest of whispers.

Amalek nodded.

They took another cautious step. Now they were so close to the sleeping wizard they could reach out and touch him.

A small hole appeared in the ceiling just above their heads as the frantic ravens tried to break through and a few fragments fell to the floor. The noise broke through the wizard's deep sleep making him stir but a pause in the sounds allowed him to settle again.

Seph took another step. He was right beside the Troubler. The air around the wizard was freezing cold and Seph felt it on his skin like an icy north wind that cuts into the flesh. The hostile atmosphere was stifling his breathing, his chest tightening; the life was being squeezed from him. He felt like turning back, escaping, running, anything to get away, but his legs would not move.

He glanced at Amalek and their eyes met. She pointed at the black compass that hung on the chain around the Troubler's neck. This was a chance to disarm him of the mysterious weapon.

The tapping on the roof continued as Seph slowly reached out his hand, moving towards the black compass which lay on the wizard's chest, rising up and down with his breath. Seph's hand moved closer. He held his breath. The tip of his finger touched the black chain. It was like touching ice.

Amalek was looking at the light on the shelf and when she realised what it was she felt a gush of delight spring in her heart. It was her magic star-box; it had broken free from the ivy binding. The lid was open and golden light streamed out.

A loud rattle on the roof made the wizard jerk in shock and the compass bumped into Seph's hand. The Troubler's eyelids flickered open. He was awake. His long black hair turned white, his robe became purple with shining silver stars, and his face looked radiant and happy. Instantly the heavy atmosphere lifted.

This was the time that Neville had told them about; the short time between being asleep and awake. Seph recognised the opportunity and so did Amalek, who whispered to him.

"Get the compass... now, quick... get it!"

They knew they only had a short time. Energy flowed into them and moving was easy. Seph grabbed at the compass hanging around the Troubler's neck. The wizard straightened up in his chair. Seph had judged it perfectly and his hand closed tightly around the cold black compass. He felt it move and shake by itself as he pulled the chain over the wizard's head. He had it!

The Troubler looked confused. He looked blankly at Amalek in front of him, and then at Seph, and frowned. Seph took his magic box out of his pocket with his other hand and opened it.

Amalek ran to the shelf and grabbed her box, snapping it closed. The light disappeared and the room dimmed, lit now only by the light shining up through the hatch.

The wizard was now staring at Seph with eyes of clear hazel and his face alarmed with confusion.

"What's happening?" he said.

In panic, he pushed Seph away and the Prince fell to the floor. Then the stars on the wizard's robe faded away and the purple darkened to black. His eyes deepened to the depth of the night. His confusion dissolved into an expression of anger and he stared down at the Prince with eyes that pierced into him like daggers.

Amalek ran to Seph's side, pulling him up.

"Look away!" she shouted.

"No!" said Seph, keeping his eyes fixed on the wizard, "No, we must face him."

"You!" the wizard said in a voice that was unruffled and biting in its intensity. He stood up slowly. Tally hopped forwards and between the children.

The Troubler glared with eyes that drilled through them.

"Do you think your little efforts can beat me?" he sneered, "Is this the best you can do?"

Seph was clutching the compass behind his back. The wizard noticed immediately.

"And you've stolen a compass," he ridiculed, turning his attention fully to Seph, "That was a mistake which can only do you harm... serious harm."

Seph felt the compass click open in his hand and the icy touch of tiny legs in his palm. In panic he dropped the compass and shook his hand. The scorpion gripped on and its double sting swung down. Simron saw this from behind and struck the scorpion with his hand. The blow sent it flying through the air and into the far wall. At the same time he kicked the compass away. Both thudded into the wall, passing straight through and leaving two small holes.

The wizard scowled at Simron, hissing at him, "Get back!"

Simron stepped back. The wizard slipped his hand under his shirt and pulled out another compass which hung around his neck.

"You are trespassers in my kingdom," he snapped, spitting out the words out with venom at the children, "And now... you'll pay!"

He grabbed his staff and stepped towards them. They cowered back in fear with Tally between them. The wizard lifted his staff and slammed it onto the floor with a heavy thud. The garnet gemstone flashed with deep red and then black. The wizard vanished.

Amalek and Seph felt all the burden of failure fall upon them. They fell to their knees in deep despair. Their plan had failed and the darkness of the spell was seeping into them. Coldness entered their limbs and crept into their bodies. They strained to move. They felt the frost forming on their faces, and then down their neck and onto their bodies. Their arms and legs were heavy and cold. The ammolites hanging around their necks lost their colour and glow, and then faded to grey.

Outside, the ravens were almost through the roof. The General's voice boomed out a command.

"Up, now! Follow me."

In a couple of seconds the army had skilfully swirled up above the house, gathering and hovering in a huge mass.

"Right! Colonel Gerr… you go in first." The General voice was fast and urgent, "One good dive should get you through. But go in with great caution and find out what's happening in there. Then fly out and tell me so that we can all go in and deal with the situation. Go!"

In the attic Amalek and Seph were utterly still, kneeling on the floor, their skin pale with frost.

"No!" screamed Tally as loud as he could, "KYWAY!"

The children heard his voice as faintly as a whisper, like a far-distant cry. In it they also heard a primitive heart-breaking call for help. Tally's scream contained a desperate cry from the whole kingdom. All the pain of all the creatures trapped by the spell was somehow contained in the sound.

Tally's cry hit at the heart of the spell, weakening it and jolting the children out of its grip. They began to move their arms again as they stared at the place where the Troubler had been.

Suddenly, there was a tremendous crash above their heads and Gerr came smashing through the roof. Like a black arrow he flashed downwards from the ceiling. He hit something and instantly the Troubler reappeared. Gerr's beak had plunged through his black cloak, piercing through the middle of one of the black stars, and deep into the leg of the Dark Wizard Troubler.

"Aaaaah!" the wizard screamed in pain, and he grabbed at the struggling, flapping Gerr with both hands, "Idiot!" he yelled.

His staff fell to the floor and rolled away.

He watched it go. He grabbed Gerr with two hands and pulled the raven out, releasing a longer cry of pain.

"Aaaaaaaahhhhhhhh!"

His black eyes flashed with anger and he flung Gerr across the attic and then stared down in shock at his wounded leg. Gerr scudded across the floorboards and crashed hard into something metallic at the far end of the attic. It was a cage.

Hawkeye was inside. He was weak and exhausted but managed to lift his head and tried to move. He was too

unsteady and his head fell back feebly.

Gerr flew back across the room and shot out through the hole in the roof. He reported back to the General and quickly told him what had happened.

"I've had enough of you!" the General boomed at him in a fury.

"But sir," he pleaded, "I didn't see him at all... I don't know why. He wasn't there and then he was..."

"You have harmed the Master..." the General snapped harshly, "There is *nothing* worse that you could have done! You are demoted... get out of the army!"

"But, sir..." he begged.

"Go!" the General commanded.

He flew off reluctantly in disgrace.

"I appoint you Decc," he announced, "You are my new Colonel."

"Thank you sir," said Decc proudly.

"We'll fly in," ordered the General to the rest, "And serve the Master."

Inside the house the Troubler was clutching his leg. Blood was dripping from his cloak onto the floor. He let go, looked at the blood on his hand and scowled. Then he clutched his leg again and looked around. He was looking for his staff. The red glow of the garnet gem was easy to see in the semi-light; it was lying on the floor out of reach.

Amalek and Seph were staring at him with a new determination. Their ammolites were glowing again and the frost on their faces was melting and looking like beads of sweat. Behind their backs they each held their magic boxes. Both boxes opened together, a crackle of energy passed between them and then they closed again.

"We'd like to bargain," said Seph, his voice clear and resolved.

At this moment the General flew down through the hole with great care to go nowhere near the wizard. The other ravens began flocking in, one at a time in quick succession.

"At your service, Master," announced the General landing on the floor.

The other ravens were gathering all around him as they poured in. The wizard kept his eyes fixed on the Prince and Princess.

"Wait," he snapped sharply to the General, "Don't do anything unless I say... anything at all. Understand? Nothing!"

"Yes sir," said the General.

"And keep your birds under control."

"Yes sir."

He turned to the children.

"I don't bargain," he growled, glancing again at his staff.

"Listen to me," said Seph, surprised at how strong his own voice sounded, "The bargain might interest you. We give you the Candara Gems... and in exchange you dissolve the spell and leave the kingdom."

The wizard's eyes opened wide at the mention of the Candara Gems. He was desperate to get them. His mind worked fast, planning his next move.

"General?" he said, still keeping his gaze riveted on the children, "Bring me my staff."

The General moved.

"No!" commanded Seph and the General stopped moving instantly, "No staff. We deal with this right now... as we are."

The wizard looked angry.

"Show me the gems then," he demanded.

"No," Amalek said in a calm, strong tone, "End the spell first and then you can see the gems."

"You know I can't do that," he hissed, "How can we make a deal if I don't know that you really do have the gems? Show them to me and then I'll do it. It's a good bargain... the gems for the kingdom... a fair exchange... but if you want your kingdom back you must show me the gems first."

Seph nodded.

"Alright then..." said Seph, "One quick glance."

Seph brought his box out from behind his back and so did Amalek. The wizard watched intently. Together they opened their boxes. Light flooded out and filled the drab room with beams and sparkles of rainbow colours.

The wizard's black eyes glinted in the light of the gems and he pushed his head forward greedily.

"Open them a little wider so that I can see the gems properly," he demanded.

The children opened the boxes and the wizard peered in. There they were, just as he had seen them all that time ago in the cave. The blue sapphire and the purple amethyst were in Seph's box and the red ruby was in Amalek's. At the sight of them his desire rose stronger than ever.

At that moment Crayle's head appeared through the hole in the ceiling.

"The gems are gone!" he announced to the wizard, "They're not in the cave."

"The gems are gone!" echoed Iker's voice from behind, "Not in the cave."

Amalek and Seph looked up. The wizard immediately took his chance and dived at them. He judged it perfectly and knocked the boxes out of their hands. As the boxes fell to the floor the gems rolled out and rattled across the wooden boards away from the children.

They all dived at them but the wizard was much closer and got there first, reaching out and greedily grasping at them. He felt a thrill as his hand closed around the ruby. The other gems lay there invitingly and he swept them up in his other hand. This was the moment he had been waiting for ever since he entered this kingdom.

He squeezed his hands around the gems and gripped them tightly. His heart thumped with excitement; at last the gems were his!

He looked up to see the Prince and Princess picking up their magic boxes and slipping them into their pockets. He needed his staff and stepped towards it. Then he stopped abruptly; there was a tingle in his hands and he knew something was wrong. He opened his hands and stared in disbelief; the gems were gone.

At that moment, everything changed.

The floor beneath them disappeared and they found themselves dropping through the air, falling gently and floating like feathers. The walls of the house had gone… the whole house had gone! After a few seconds, they landed lightly in a sprawled muddle on the ground with all the ravens scattered around them.

In the trees, just to the south, the thief was watching. Joog's body was lying close by, a trickle of dried blood on the white feathers of his head.

When Old Howard's House had suddenly disappeared, the surroundings were transformed. In that second, life burst free from the hideous grip of the spell. A million shades of colours flooded back into the kingdom to decorate the rich scenes throughout the hills and the valleys. The snow sparkled in the sunlight for a brief moment and then was gone. The tops of the Snowpeak Mountains were still capped with snow but everywhere else, it vanished. Birdsong filled the fresh air and thronged through woods and forests as new as any dawn chorus. Animals, suddenly free to move again, sniffed for subtle scents and padded across leafy glades. Cows, horses and donkeys began grazing. Insects buzzed in the warm air.

The Kingdom Of Gems was reborn.

The thief was devastated by this sudden unexpected change but only briefly, recovering perfect poise in a few seconds. Already a new plan was forming to adjust to the new situation.

The thief started moving forwards to find a better place to watch, but stopped and stepped back towards Joog, crouched down over him and looked intently at the ammolite. Its magical glow had gone completely now. The thief reached down and ripped the ammolite and its silver necklace from his neck. Standing up, the ammolite was dropped into one pocket while a hand slipped deep into the other to grip the gems.

The thief moved forward into some large bushes, and then, with eyes as cool as ice, continued watching.

Chapter 12

~ Butterflies ~

"To the trees!" ordered the General.

The ravens took off and were flying around in a confused flight above everyone's heads. They bumped into each other in turmoil as they swirled in a random way, not knowing what had happened.

"Order!" shouted the General, "Get some order into your flying... Colonel Decc, tell them!"

"Order!" shouted Decc.

Then the General's whole body shook and he began changing shape. "Aaah... what's happening... something's happening to me... I feel... terrible... Aaah!

He was rapidly becoming smaller and so were the other ravens.

"Help!" he cried, "Stop it, someone! Quick!"

Panic gripped him and he thrashed the air with his shrinking wings. His black compass, empty since the scorpion had crawled out of it, slipped from his neck and fell to the ground below. When it hit, it broke apart, the lid coming off and rolling away.

A muddle of flustered flapping completely took over the chaotic group. Then, with a little popping sound, one of the ravens turned into a butterfly. A second later another changed and in a moment the air was filled with popping sounds. Within a few seconds the whole army had become a fluttering cloud of butterflies.

No one noticed the scorpion a little distance away. It was the one that Simron had knocked off Seph's hand and had passed through the wall. It was digging a small hole. Its legs worked with lightening speed as it dropped out of view. It reappeared to grab the chain of the compass and then popped back, pulling the compass after it. The earth covered it up and it was gone.

Aram and Halo rushed out from under the trees. They stopped when they saw the Dark Wizard Troubler watching them, their hooves skidding on the grass. The wizard stood up, gripping his leg again as pain shot through it. His face wrinkled into a deep frown and his lower jaw pushed forward aggressively.

"That is enough!" he shouted, turning to Seph and Amalek, "Enough!"

His hands were covered with blood after holding his leg. He lunged towards the Prince who turned to get away and slipped out of reach. The wizard crouched slightly and then dived at him, like a wild animal pouncing on its victim. He caught Seph by the ankle with one hand and the Prince fell, ending up stretched out on the ground. The Prince kicked back with his other foot, knocking the wizard's hand off his ankle, and he wriggled free.

Amalek leapt at the wizard from behind, holding him around his neck. He shook her off and went after Seph again who was just getting up.

Suddenly, Joog appeared in the air. Some of his white feathers were matted with dried blood as he swooped down. He had recovered consciousness and immediately raced to help, dipping towards the Troubler's head. His sharp talons scraped across the wizard's cheek and drew blood. The wizard moved fast and struck out at Joog, hitting at him with his fist. Joog was too fast, glided up and turned for another attack.

Seph was right next to a curved wall of glass which had suddenly grown up from the ground. The Prince reached out to touch it and his hand passed straight through. The wizard leapt at Seph with all his might just as Joog dived at his head, knocking him sideways. The wizard landed and was on his feet in a second and watched Seph crawl away. He dived after him again but hit something hard - something invisible. His face thudded against it and he fell back in shock, falling onto the ground and clutching his face in pain.

His nose was bleeding now, as well the cuts inflicted by Joog's sharp talons, and the blood ran down into his black beard. He reached out a hand and felt the cold touch of the glass wall. He moved his hand over it and then, as he looked closely, saw a glint of sunlight reflecting in it. He banged on it with a fist in anger, and found it was solid and strong. He stood still, staring at it and calculating what to do.

He looked again for Amalek and saw her rushing out through the glass. Struggling to his feet, he glanced around. The glass was now totally surrounding him in a circle three metres across, a cylinder rising straight upwards from the ground. His eyes flashed around it and then up. Just above his head, about two metres high, the glass spread out horizontally, then turned back to curve in a dome above; he was trapped inside a large glass mushroom. Old Howard's House was gone and this now stood in its place.

The butterflies had swarmed up to the top of the mushroom, fluttering around each other and then passing out through the glass.

The wizard banged again on the glass and a dull thud echoed around the mushroom. Looking around with flashing eyes, he saw that everyone else was outside the mushroom now except for Hawkeye who was lying in the cage. The old hare's body was stretched out as he lay on his side too weak to move. His eyes were open and alert. He was watching everything.

An idea sprung into the Troubler's mind. His temper and frustration rose up inside him like lava in a volcano.

His staff was lying nearby, and he quickly snatched it up. He lifted it and then thumped it down hard on the ground in temper but nothing happened. He looked at it; it appeared the same with the huge red garnet gemstone on the top but there was no glow and no power. He shook it in frustration and then using it like a walking stick he hobbled towards Hawkeye.

Tally saw what was happening and immediately hopped back in through the glass towards hie grandfather. It was a race to the cage. The wizard got there first, clutched the cage by the handle on the top and swept it up into the air. Hawkeye slid across the floor of the cage and rattled into the bars.

"Stop!" the wizard shouted at Tally.

Tally skidded to a halt.

The Troubler's leg was so painful that he had his foot off the ground and was supporting his weight on his staff. He tucked the cage under one arm to free the other one, opened the cage door and reached inside. He grasped Hawkeye around the neck.

"Keep back," the wizard growled, and then shouting louder to the others, "All of you!"

Everyone stood still.

"Let me out of here and this hare will live," he cried, "Otherwise... say goodbye to it now."

"We can't let you out," replied Seph, "We don't know how to."

The wizard shook the cage.

"*How* do I get out!" he snapped aggressively, "Tell me now!"

"It's a spell," said Amalek shaking her head and spreading her hands.

"Alright then," the wizard growled.

He paused to composed himself. His cunning mind instantly produced a plan.

"I'll take one of you instead of the hare. You choose. The Prince or the Princess for the hare. One of you. *Now!"*

The wizard shook the cage again as a threat and Hawkeye's body bumped up and down.

Seph stepped towards the mushroom.

"No!" exclaimed Amalek.

She rushed to grab him by the arm but he slipped through her grasp. Two steps and he was through the glass and inside the mushroom.

"Seph!" cried Amalek, and then pleaded, "Come back."

Seph was some steps away from the wizard but facing him with a purposeful stance. He gave the slightest of glances at Tally and then Hawkeye. Then he settled his look directly at the Troubler.

"You can't escape," Seph said.

"Come here," hissed the wizard, "And I'll let the hare go."

"I don't trust you..." began Seph.

Suddenly, Tally leapt forwards. At the same time Hawkeye jerked his neck loose from the wizard's grip and bit him on his finger. The wizard cried out in pain and dropped the cage. Joog swooped from behind him and knocked into his head. Then Tally leapt forwards and dived for his staff, knocking it away. The wizard lost his balance and fell. Seph was there, grabbed the cage with Hawkeye inside and ran out through the glass. Tally followed.

Seph put the cage down on the grass and Tally was beside it in a moment.

"Thank you for that," said Hawkeye, sighing with relief, "Great work!"

Tally was overjoyed.

"But don't just stand there looking at me," Hawkeye joked, "Help me out of here."

The Troubler struggled to his feet and looked around. All the others, all his enemies, even the weak Hawkeye who had been locked up in a cage, were all outside the circular glass wall and he was the only one left inside. Joog flew silently down to land on Amalek's shoulder.

The terrible truth dawned on the Dark Wizard Troubler; he was trapped in a glass prison. He slumped against the glass wall, hating what had happened, hating being defeated, and hating the Prince and Princess and the group of animals who had done this to him.

Then he remembered something and hope flashed through his mind. The black compass was still around his neck and he stood up. He was sure that this, with its magical powers and the indestructible quality of the metal, would smash through the glass. He flung it as hard as he could into the glass. It passed straight through and skimmed over the grass to disappear into some bushes at the end of the garden.

He watched it go and then leant against the glass wall. His plan to rule the kingdom was in shatters. He let his back slip down the wall until he was sitting. A dark, sullen mood invaded his being, as he brooded on his situation. Weariness overcame him and he closed his eyes.

At that moment, Neville suddenly appeared. He was in the air beside the wizard's head. He glided out of the mushroom, passing through the glass with a slight hiss of air, and touched down.

"Neville!" cried Amalek and Seph together.

Their faces were beaming as the watched him coming in to land. His great webbed feet were the first to touch, tilting back and skidding on the grass. His magic scarf flowed behind him.

After a few seconds he slowed, his heels digging in then catching to send him rolling forwards. A spectacular tumble followed until he hit a mound which lifted him into the air for a second. He crash-landed onto the top of a bush and was left sitting on it. He shook his feathers and turned his head to look at the children. Then he slowly sank into the bush and was gone. Everyone was staring when his muffled voice came from underneath the leaves.

"I'm down."

The thief had observed all this from the cover of the bushes without anyone knowing. The scene had been dramatic and it meant that everything had now changed but the thief remained unruffled and calm.

One thing, however, stayed the same. Deep in the thief's pocket laid the most important prize of all - the Candara Gems.

The thief paused, before turning and slipping away through the trees.

Crayle and Iker had been on the roof when Old Howard's House vanished from beneath their feet. They were terrified and flew off to land in the closest tree. From this excellent view they watched their Master being trapped in the glass prison.

"This is bad," Crayle said, shaking his head, "Very bad. Let's find Jum and then decide what to do."

They flew off together. She was waiting for them on the same tree in Silvermay Forest where they had left her the day before. She was huddled on the branch looking frightened and agitated.

"Jum!" called out Crayle as they glided towards her.

Jum looked up and her relief was clear to see.

"Oh," she sighed as they landed, one on either side of her, "Thank goodness... thank goodness... oh, thank goodness you're safe."

She put a wing around Crayle while Iker cuddled up to her on the other side.

"Of course we're safe," said Crayle.

"It was fun!" piped up Iker brightly, "I like being a spy!"

"But what on earth has happened," Jum said, "I mean... everything's coloured again, and birds are singing and flying around... has the spell gone?"

"Yes," replied Crayle looking crestfallen, "It's over. The war...." he dropped his head in resignation at the terrible thing he had to admit, "The war... is lost."

Jum looked at him wide-eyed.

"You mean..." she began, sounding excited and overjoyed at the news, "You mean... there's no more war, no more army, no more fighting?"

"Yes," Crayle confirmed glumly, "But it's not something to be happy about... we lost."

Jum turned to Iker.

"And you're alright are you?" she asked him tenderly.

"Oh, yes," he replied perkily, "We spied on a man near a light... and Crayle fell off the roof..."

"Ssshhh," said Crayle, not wanting Jum to hear about that.

Iker carried on with enthusiasm. "Then we reported to the Master... and he sent us to spy on some gems... but they weren't there... then we told him... but he's in a glass mushroom now..."

"A glass mushroom?!" exclaimed Jum, "What do you mean?"

Together they told her all about what had happened.

"Well," she commented when they had finished, "This is the best news I've had for a long time. This Master that you worship so much... what right has he got to come here and take over a kingdom?"

Crayle was looking at her dumbfounded.

"If you ask me," she continued, "He got what was coming to him... selfish man! And now that we're free of him, and that General, we can go."

"Go where?" asked Crayle.

"To the tree, of course," she said, her face alight with excitement, "That tree near Munden. Remember how nice that was... it's perfect for us!"

Crayle looked around. He felt lost. All of a sudden things had changed, he could no longer spy for anyone and he did not know what to do.

"Are you coming?" Jum asked Iker.

"Yes, please," he replied with glee. Then he leant forwards and looked past Jum to Crayle. "And can you teach me more about spying?"

Crayle closed his eye and nodded reluctantly.

They were all silent. Crayle was finding it impossible to accept that the Troubler was beaten and that his dream of being a spy was over. He needed something to do. As he thought about training Iker, he began to realise that it could be interesting work. This would be something to fill the void. He could teach him all he knew. They could go on practice missions to spy on unsuspecting sparrows, cows, horses or anything. Maybe people living in Munden. It would not mean anything but would be almost like the real thing, and then, if a war arose, they would be prepared for the important task of spying on the enemy.

"OK," said Crayle, "I'll teach you all I know... everything. How to be an accomplished spy. But you'll have to be disciplined and do what I say. It'll be tough... getting up early and going on planned missions. So, young Iker, do you think you can do it?"

Iker was thrilled.

"Yes," he said without a shadow of doubt.

Jum felt happy inside.

"Let's go," she said.

The friends were gathered around the giant glass mushroom. The stately, strong figures of Aram and Halo were standing side by side behind them. They gleamed with gold and silver in the morning sun. They all looked in at the Dark Wizard Troubler. Gradually, the truth was sinking in; they had beaten the evil wizard, the Dark Wizard Troubler. There he was in front of them, trapped and unable to do any harm to anyone or cast any spells. He had been so powerful but now all that was gone. His pale thin face was bruised and smudged with blood from his nose. Joog's claws had left cuts running down one cheek and his leg was badly injured by Gerr's beak.

As they looked, he glanced up at them and his black eyes pierced into them with ice-cold hate. The children staggered back into Simron. The Troubler held his intense stare for a moment. Suddenly, he moved and was up on his feet. The children stepped back again in shock. Aram and Halo stepped forwards, their alicorns pointing through the glass wall. The Troubler laughed and slipped to the ground again, pulling his cloak around him and over his head. Then he was still.

Aram and Halo relaxed and stepped back.

"It's alright," comforted Simron, "He can do that as much as he likes… he's a prisoner now and can do no harm."

"I know," said Amalek, "It's just that it seems as though he could walk out. I have to keep reminding myself that he is trapped in there."

"But why…" began Seph, "why is it a mushroom?"

Simron laughed. "That's just like Elzaphan! He's a great, great wizard and he's serious when he needs to be. But he has a wonderful sense of humour! He couldn't resist this."

They all relaxed and laughed at the sight of the huge glass mushroom in front of them. Only two parts of Old Howard's House remained. Firstly, a circle of the wooden-boarded floor which filled ground inside the circle. Secondly, the cellar stairs which could be seen through a hole in the floor.

The Troubler looked out from under his cloak. He noticed the hole with interest. He pulled himself up and then using his staff he hobbled to the hole and descended the stairs. He found two small rooms; a toilet and a bathroom. He briefly glanced into these but what interested him most of all was something at the foot of the stairs. It was his large block of gold. He had cut one small piece from it and given it to Old Howard as a bribe. It was lying at a strange angle, balanced on a corner and leaning against the bottom steps. It had somehow survived the change.

Then he looked more closely. It was not glinting with the brightness of gold. It had turned to iron and a yellow hue of rust blotched its sides. He grunted with annoyance, climbed up the stairs and leant against the glass wall again. He felt a warm breeze on his cheek which made his mood darker still. He was trapped inside the mushroom when even the air could pass through. He sat down and pulled his cloak around him and over his head.

Outside the glass prison and throughout the kingdom the atmosphere had changed from gloom to joy, from fear to freedom, from misery to happiness. The friends standing around the mushroom heard the wonderful sound of life all around them. Birds were flitting around in the air, released from their frozen state. They were singing their joy.

Now that the spell had been dissolved and the clouds had cleared, the sun shone brightly down on the land and reflected off Blue Lake, Lake Clase-Moy and Hazy Pond. Rivers flowed again and life in the water and on the riverbank awoke as if from a winter's hibernation. Streams gushed with fresh water and Boon's Brook gurgled happily once more to tumble into the River Gem.

The lively flow of the Gem Falls, for so long frozen into a wall of ice, was freed into a fluid cascade of water which plummeted down with a roar which announced its return.

The white mountain hares of Summertime Kingdom were hopping around on the grass. Neville had emerged from the bush, dragging a few twigs behind him, and joined Tally and Hawkeye on the grass. Tally had helped Hawkeye out of the cage. The old hare was very weak and unable to walk.

"We'll get the sledge for you, Gramps," said Tally perkily, "We can pull it along on the ground."

"Thank you," replied Hawkeye, "You're a brave young hare. You have done so, so well. Your parents would be proud of you... and so am I."

"I just did what I could," Tally replied.

Hawkeye nodded with a smile and an affectionate twinkle in his eye.

"And what you did is very good. And as well as helping this..." he waved a paw at the land around them, "you showed all the other hares what a hare can do... how a hare should behave. You showed them all that a hare can fight for what is good and true, and make a difference."

Tally gazed lovingly at his grandfather. "Thanks, Gramps," he said, "But without KYWAY I could never have done it."

Hawkeye held up a paw. "That may be true, and KYWAY has served me through the years. But KYWAY is yours now. I've helped you, yes, nudged you in the right direction. Now you must use it yourself."

Tally nodded.

"I'm tired," Hawkeye continued, looking at Tally and dropping his head onto his stretched out paws, "Very tired. I need to rest... just for a while, before we go."

Flop, with Miriam on his neck, joined the others by the mushroom. Joog had landed on Seph's shoulder and Amalek leant against her brother and was wiping the blood off Joog's feathers.

"Are you alright?" Amalek asked.

"Oh, yes," Joog replied, "Just a little bump on the head."

"That's it then," said Seph, looking at the Troubler's huddled shape.

The tall figure of Simron stood just behind the children.

"Yes, that's it," he confirmed, "Except there is the mystery of the missing Candara Gems.... and..."

"And our parents," Seph said sadly.

Amalek did not speak but her eyes filled with tears. She sighed and then glanced towards Candara. Beyond the town she could see the hill of her home looking strange and incomplete without the palace seated on top. Simron put a comforting arm around each of the children. Then he noticed something.

"Look at that!" he said, pointing up.

They all looked to see an amazing sight. The dark cloud, which had been hanging over the town, began to dissolve and a house slowly dropped from it and began floating down towards its street below. Then another appeared, and another until there were more than thirty houses drifting gently, floating like hot air balloons, all descending and returning to the streets below. They could see people leaning out of windows and looking confused and frightened at what was going on.

House after house touched softly down until they were all settled back, but not in the right places. Later on, this caused some confusion because the house numbers were all muddled. The rearrangement also created arguments, some of which carried on for years. People found they had someone else's garden; tidy, well-cultivated gardens were now overgrown and vice versa.

The cloud dissolved away completely to leave the palace in full view. It started descending, looking bright and beautiful in the clear blue of the sky, graceful in it's smooth movement and majestic in structure. Each of the tall pinnacles was topped with an unfurled flag as if in celebration and the whole thing turned slowly as it floated down towards its place on the hill.

Amalek turned to her brother.

"Lazuli's in one of those, but what about our mother and father?" she said tearfully, "Where are they?"

Seph immediately turned to the wizard and demanded harshly, "Where are the King and Queen?"

Huddled under his cloak, the wizard remained still and silent. Then Simron tried.

"You have nothing to lose by telling us, have you?" he asked, "Are they alive? Where are they?"

No answer.

"What about the Candara Gems?" asked Simron, "What do you know about them?"

The Troubler did not move.

Simron sighed. "We'll get nothing out of him."

He beckoned to the others to step back from the glass prison so that they could talk without the Troubler hearing them. Joog was still on Seph's shoulder, his yellow eyes glowing in the sunlight.

"What do we do?" he asked, "He's the only one who knows where they are."

"We search for them," began Amalek. She wiped a tear from her eye. "We search until we find them."

Joog nodded. "We'll search the kingdom. From above I can spot most things... and with all the guardian owls..."

"It will still be difficult!" said Flop, "It's a big place, you know."

"It *will* be difficult," agreed Aram, his strong golden body glinting in the sun, "But we'll ask all the creatures and people in the kingdom to help... I'm sure they'll all want to join the search."

Hawkeye had been listening to the conversation and he opened his eyes.

"Tunnels!" he called out.

They all looked at the old white hare. He was still lying down beside Tally and although he was tired his eyes were bright with life.

"Underground," he continued slowly, "He could have hidden them beneath the ground. The King and Queen... and the gems. It would be a good place, wouldn't it now? I know there are tunnels here. Do you have maps?"

"No," replied Seph, "They were lost years ago."

"Perhaps you could try to find them," Hawkeye suggested, "In the meantime we'll do our best to discover the tunnels. The gems will be extremely difficult to find. Have we any idea where they might be?"

"None," said Simron, "They've been stolen... and the question, the other question is - who stole them?"

"If it's the Troubler," began Amalek, "He may have hidden them. But I don't think so because when we tricked him he really thought we had the gems. So it must be someone else."

"So we are looking for the gems," said Seph, summing up, "*and* someone with them *and* our parents."

Joog was on his shoulder now. "It's not an easy task," he began, "But we'll try."

"Alright," said Amalek keen to get organised, "So we've got to search above ground *and* below. Let's get started."

"Right then," said Joog decisively, "Hares underground... Hawkeye? Can you organise the hares please?"

"Yes, but with Tally," Hawkeye replied, looking perkier every minute, "We'll do it together. Is that alright, Tally?"

"Yes Gramps, of course," he replied.

Hawkeye had a plan already developing in his mind. This was like old times when he was a young hare and his adventures took place when was battling against Gugeol. Now he was out of the oppressive presence of the Dark Wizard Troubler he could feel the fragile weakness was lifting off him and his energy was returning. Although his body was old he began to feel young again.

"Neville and I will organise the search from the air," continued Joog, "And it is up to you, Amalek and Seph, to be in charge of the search on land. That's everything covered." Joog's eyes shone golden. "We just need to get on with it."

"There's also the Komodo dragon," said Simron, "I sent it off to search for a dog in the east…"

"What dog?" asked Joog.

"There isn't one," Simron smiled, "I sent it off to search for a dog that doesn't exist. I thought that would keep it busy for a while!"

Seph looked at Simron with admiration. "It's great the way you do things like that. But you made me think of that huge dog that chased us. What about that?"

"Simron killed it!" squeaked Miriam from Flop's neck, "Simron killed it! One swipe with his oar!"

"But the Komodo," Simron continued, "We'll keep an eye out for it."

"We'll go back to the palace first," said Joog, "We all need a proper meal… and a wash! Then we'll begin the search from there."

The whole group, including all the mountain hares, set off to the palace. Seph was riding on Aram while holding Tally and Hawkeye in front of him. Amalek was on Halo with Flop and Miriam. Simron strode beside them.

Flop was very pleased that the cold weather had ended and purred loudly. They heard a noise behind them and looked back to see Neville attempting to take off.

He was waddling across the grass, building up speed until he was running with his head pointing forwards and wings outstretched. He had to slow when he reached the trees at the end of the garden. He turned and tried again, running back towards the mushroom. He began to lift until his webbed feet were just touching the ground with each step.

"Look out!" called Amalek.

He lifted just off the ground and flew straight into

the mushroom. He passed through the glass and towards the Troubler who looked up and saw him. Neville veered as the Troubler leapt up at him, grasping at him with an outstretched arm and catching hold of one of his legs. The wizard was lifted off his feet and they met the glass wall with a bump.

Neville slipped through and the Troubler was forced to let go and fall to the ground. Neville glided gracefully and smoothly up into the air without a flap.

"Made it!" he cried as he glided over their heads.

"How about a riddle?" called out Seph from Aram's back.

Joog joined him as he circled above their heads and began to sing.

> "I tap, tap, tap a rhythm out,
> sometimes fast, sometimes slow,
> I weave about and in and out
> always down below.
>
> "At breakfast, lunch and supper too
> then to the dining-room I come,
> I never touch the food as such
> or lick it with my tongue!
>
> "We come in many different sizes
> and many varied colours too.
> We're black or green or red or cream,
> or purple, white or blue.
>
> "We rest at night and work by day,
> you'll always find we live in pairs.
> We move about - inside and out,
> and up and down the stairs."

I Tap, Tap, Tap

"I tap, tap, tap a rhythm out,
sometimes fast, sometimes slow,
I weave about and in and out
always down below.

At breakfast, lunch and supper too
then to the dining-room I come,
I never touch the food as such
or lick it with my tongue!

We come in many different sizes
and many varied colours too.
We're black or green or red or cream,
or purple, white or blue.

We rest at night and work by day,
you'll always find we live in pairs.
We move about - inside and out,
and up and down the stairs."

~ NEVILLE'S 7TH RIDDLE ~

He then flew off with Joog towards the palace leaving them discussing what the riddle could be. The unicorns galloped towards Candara leaving Simron behind, surrounded by the mountain hares. They lolloped along with him.

When the unicorns entered Candara, they were immediately surrounded by a group of children who gathered around to greet them.

"Look everybody!" shouted one of them, "It's the Prince and Princess!"

The town was busy. Many people, as well as all sorts of animals, were out in the streets. They were confused about what had happened and were talking to each other and trying to work it all out. When they heard the excited

cries of the children and they saw the unicorns and the others they gathered around and began cheering and asking questions. Amalek and Seph answered as best they could.

The word spread quickly through the town that the Prince, Princess and the others were the heroes, the ones who had freed them from the evil spell, the ones who had risked their lives and fought the Dark Wizard Troubler. The people of the town left their chattering and lined the streets to cheer and clap. Some sang and danced around the unicorns as they walked together through the streets.

This carried on right the way through the town. As they were moving along Nathan Avenue they heard a wonderful sound; it was an elephant trumpeting. Then Lazuli appeared, walking out from Link Way and then breaking into a run when she saw them.

"Lazuli!" cried Amalek.

"Why did you desert us?" joked Seph.

She laughed and in a moment she was beside them. She looked up at Seph and Amalek on the unicorns.

"You did it!" she exclaimed, "You did it!"

Seph reached out and patted her on her head.

"Where is he?" she asked.

"He's trapped in a giant glass mushroom now!" he said.

"A good thing too!" stated Lazuli, "But a mushroom?!" Then she laughed, "That sounds like the doing of Wizard Elzaphan!"

As they walked together they exchanged their stories. They passed along the last street and out of the town and then up Palace Path towards the palace.

"Home!" said Amalek, but her voice was dampened by a deep sadness which felt like a knot in her stomach. "If only our parents were here to enjoy it too."

As they approached the palace, the full impact of the loss of the King and Queen hit the children; they felt heartbroken.

The palace stood back on the crown of the hill in the morning sun, its many spires pointing to the clear blue sky. Some windows were open letting in fresh air for the first time since the spell was cast.

Soon they were entering the palace gardens through the wrought-iron gates which hung on the huge gateposts. This is where Aram and Halo had stood perfectly still for over three hundred years. The path led to the front door, flanked by the smooth flat lawns which extended to the trees of Silvermay Forest.

The unicorns hooves clip-clopped up the path to the front door. They left the children and the others there and then went to graze on the grass. When the children stepped inside, they felt the happy atmosphere that filled the palace when they were growing up. They were home.

Joog and Neville were already there and Simron and the hares arrived a little later.

After eating in the kitchen, they began the search for the King and Queen as well as the missing Candara Gems. They decided to start in the west from Charin Road. They would try to cover the areas from the Heather Heights right up to the Vale of Gems. This would include Charin and the Plains of Wilrack. The Wellspring Woods and all the land around Old Howard's House would have to be searched another day. It was a massive task which took place on three levels; on the land, in the air and underground. People, animals and birds all took part.

Joog called a meeting of his elite group of owls - the Guardians of the Kingdom Of Gems. There were thirty of them of many different types and they each had a look-out post somewhere in the kingdom. For most it was a tree but always situated with a good view of the surrounding area. The owls now dotted the side of the palace on ledges and window sills. There were Barn Owls, Great Grey Owls, two Sooty Owls, another Snowy Owl and a couple of speckled Short-eared Owls. Marli, the tiny Elf Owl, was the smallest. They chatted until Joog's voice rose above.

"Firstly, it is wonderful to see you all again," he announced, "but there is something extremely urgent to do. The King and Queen are lost and we need to find them. We need to search thoroughly."

"Where do we look?" asked one.

"We think the Troubler has hidden them and we don't know where," Joog replied, "They could be anywhere, dead or alive. We will work in areas across the kingdom. It could take days."

On hearing this, there were mutterings among the owls. Joog continued.

"And there's something else," he continued, "You've all heard the legend about the Candara Gems?" There were soft hoots of interest. "Maybe some of you know already… but the legend *is* true. The Candara Gems do exist. But they have been stolen and now we have to find them. They may be hidden... or someone may have them, but we have no idea at all who that is. So, our task is difficult and we need to be at our most alert as we search."

He paused and looked around at them.

"Let me know straight away if you find anything."

He told them which areas to cover and then took to the air.

"Good luck!" he shouted.

The owls all rose and flew off in different directions.

By the time the sun was setting the whole area had not been covered and no one had found the King and Queen. The search went on after sunset until Amalek and Seph reluctantly called the search off. Joog sent the message around to tell everyone involved, including Hawkeye and Tally, who had started the search for underground tunnels.

It was not long before everyone had settled down to sleep for the night. In the morning there would be energy to resume the search.

After the search had been called off for the night, two ravens took off from a tree in Silvermay Forest. They had been hiding there since the palace fell from the cloud and now that it was dark they felt it was safe to travel. Their black feathers were the perfect camouflage.

"Keep up," said Razz, "We need to be quick 'cos the Master may need us."

"Maybe," said Sergeant Forr, "But the spell's ended hasn't it? It's over."

"We don't know," Razz snapped, "It all seems to be back to normal, yes. But maybe he got away or something. Surely he's too powerful to be beaten. Come on... the sooner we get to the house the better."

They flew in a straight line towards Old Howard's House, above the Flatsage Farmlands, across Charin Road and some trees, and finally across Shaky Field.

"Where's the house?!" exclaimed Razz, who was still slightly in front.

It was hard to see in the dark so they were not aware of the glass mushroom at all but they could see the circle of the remaining floor. They could also make out the shape of a person. They swooped lower.

"It's the Master!" exclaimed Razz with excitement, "See, I told you he'd be OK."

"Is it him?" asked Forr, squinting his eyes as he gazed through the night.

"Of course it is!" scorned Razz, "Come on. Let's report to him."

Forr was still hesitant.

"I don't know..." he began but Razz was already dropping out of the air and down towards the wizard.

Forr watched him go and then blinked in astonishment. Razz suddenly changed. One second he was a raven and the next he was shrinking. A second later he had turned into a butterfly. Forr froze in fear and began to fall through the air. He tried to recover, started flapping his wings and began to rise again.

What had happened stirred in him a distant memory. He could feel what it was like to be a butterfly fluttering on the breeze. It was no clearer than that, but the thought of turning into one now terrified him.

Forr rose in the air and flew away as fast as he could. He had no plan about where to go; his flight was driven by panic and fear. The warm air rushed through his black feathers as he flew along the dark line of River Tazer and then over the Wellspring Woods.

When he reached the border he hesitated, flying along it for a while. Then he decided: he turned west, crossed the border and kept flying.

Chapter 13

~ Relbuort Cottage ~

The moon shone on the glass prison, reflecting here and there. The mushroom of glass acted like a lens to focus the rays and created a soft glow inside.

Just after midnight the Troubler finally fell asleep. He had found some blankets in the bathroom below, wrapped himself in them and curled up in the centre on the wooden floor. He was filled with feelings of hate and revenge and he searched his mind for a solution. However, after a while, tiredness won over his thoughts and sleep took him.

In a dream he had the Candara Gems in his hand but when he opened his hand they turned into butterflies and flew away. He felt the anger and pain of this loss all over again and was relieved to be woken up by a noise outside the mushroom.

He stared out into the dark, listening intently. Something was moving in the bushes close by. Then he saw it; a black object was moving towards him. He sat up and when he saw what it was he relaxed and leant against the glass wall.

It was a raven, as black as the night. It walked towards the glass mushroom and when it was within a few feet it bowed, dropping its head low to the ground. It was Gerr.

"Master," Gerr said respectfully.

He was cautious and stood back from the glass. He had seen what had happened to the others.

"I thought you had all gone," the wizard commented, sounding surprised, "Are there others?"

"I don't know Master," replied Gerr, "I think I might be the only one left."

"But, there *might* be more..." the Troubler said thoughtfully, "This is interesting. What's your name?"

"Gerr," he replied, and then, disregarding the fact that the General had demoted him and thrown him out of the army altogether, "Colonel Gerr, Master."

"What do you mean 'Colonel'?"

"I was appointed Colonel of your army for my good service," Gerr said proudly, "The General appointed me. And now, because the General has gone, I feel that if I am to continue in your army, and I am the highest ranking surviving officer, I should be the new General... Master."

The wizard was surprised, "But you're the only one left!"

"Exactly my point, Master," said Gerr, "And if you want me to continue in your service, well, I will, Master, if I am the General."

"But you'll be General over no-one!" said the Troubler shaking his head, "There is no army to be the General of!"

"I don't mind," persisted Gerr, "And anyway, in the future, I might recruit an army."

"Alright, alright," said the Troubler impatiently, "I appoint you General... General Gerr… happy?"

"Yes, Master!"

"Good."

The Troubler felt a glimmer of hope. Without getting up he shuffled over across the wooden floorboards until he was right beside Gerr and stared at him through the glass, with penetrating black eyes.

"Now, here are your orders, General Gerr," he hissed, "I want you to do a very special task. It will involve your best efforts."

He leant his head as close as he could to Gerr until it was resting against the glass and then continued, this time in a whisper.

"I want you to go to the palace and spy on them. Find out what you can... but *don't* be seen. Understand?"

Gerr nodded as he was given his orders.

"Go now," snapped the Troubler sharply, feeling the exciting taste of hope.

"Yes, Master," Gerr replied, opening his wings.

"Wait!" the Troubler exclaimed. Gerr folded his wings again.

The Troubler was still for a moment, listening. He had heard a movement in the bushes.

"Who's there?" he demanded.

The bushes rustled and out walked Jamaar. His powerful frame was gone. When the spell had been dissolved his body had turned back into the skinny dog he had been before. He looked again like a wandering mongrel but with half his tail missing from when Horrik spat at him. He moved towards the Troubler.

The wizard looked at him with a puzzled expression. Then he recognised him.

"Jamaar!" he cried out in surprise, "Is that you?"

"Yes Master," replied Jamaar, wagging the remaining part of his tail.

The wizard had been sure that Jamaar had died falling down the Silver Well. The dog approached closer.

"Stop!" ordered the wizard, "Don't come through the glass else you might be trapped like me."

"Through the glass, Master?"

"Yes, I'm trapped in here."

"How did you get in there?" asked Jamaar.

"It was those children…" he began crossly, "And… but how did you get here? What happened to *you*?"

"Well, Master," Jamaar began, "I fell into the well and then woke up in…"

"Stop," the wizard snapped, "It doesn't matter now. You can tell me later. I've got a job for you… a very important one. It's perfect now that you've turned up. Are you listening carefully?"

"Yes Master," Jamaar replied.

Then the Dark Wizard Troubler noticed something.

"But…" he began, glaring at Jamaar, "Where's my compass? You've lost it haven't you?"

Jamaar jumped back in shock at the sudden fury of the accusation, "Master, I don't know where it went," he pleaded, "When I woke on the beach it was gone."

"What beach?"

"In the Kingdom of Moone, Master."

"The Kingdom of Moone?" he scowled, "What were you doing there? Look, I want that compass back. I *have* to have it!"

He was shaking with anger. He wanted a compass again and bitterly regretted throwing his last one at the glass and losing it.

He forced himself to calm down.

"Your task is to find the compass you have lost, but first there's another job for you to do."

"Yes, Master," Jamaar said keenly, glad the problem of the lost compass had not been pursued any further.

"Good," hissed the wizard. He was spitting out words now with excitement and desperation. "You must dig me out of here. There's a bathroom under here… see down that hole… so you aim for that and I'll be waiting down there for you to come through."

"Yes, Master," Jamaar repeated.

Jamaar liked this idea. He loved digging and although he felt tired after the long journey he started digging straight away.

He tried a couple of times in different places but the ground was too hard. On the third attempt his paws slipped into the earth easily and he was off, kicking out the earth behind him.

Suddenly they heard a voice from the trees at the end of the garden.

"Help," called out the voice plaintively, "Help me, please!"

Jamaar carried on digging and the wizard turned to Gerr who was still obediently standing near the mushroom.

"Gerr," the wizard ordered, "Go and investigate."

Gerr took off and flew towards the voice.

It was dark, especially in the trees, but the voice continued pleading for help and guided him to it. There, tied tightly to a branch with ivy, was Searle. He landed beside her.

"Ah haa!" he said, "Searle… one of the deserters. And how did you get into this mess?"

"That owl," said Searle sounding despondent, "You know, one of the enemy. But I think they've forgotten about me. Quick now, untie me."

"Not so fast," Gerr wanted to be in control of the situation, "You know I'm the General of the army now?"

"Where is the General?" asked Searle, "And the all others?"

"All gone! All turned back into useless butterflies. So I am General Gerr."

"Who said?" snapped Searle.

"The Master," Gerr said proudly, "He appointed me just now. So you can't argue with that, can you?"

"Where is the Master?" asked Searle, who could not see the glass mushroom or the prisoner inside through all the foliage of the tree. She had heard all the commotion going on earlier, and had seen the house disappear. Then she had heard and seen everything come back to life around her. She knew that things had gone terribly wrong but she did not know how.

"Why does that matter?" Gerr retorted, "I am in charge now and I will release you and re-enroll you in the army. As long as you serve me well I will forget the matters of desertion and spying and..."

Gerr was desperate to be the General in command over at least one raven.

"Spying?" Searle looked surprised, "Never!" then she snapped, "Why are you accusing me of that? It's ridiculous! I've never spied in my life! I'm not serving under you!"

"Then I won't let you go."

Gerr turned to go.

"Wait!" shouted Searle.

Gerr turned back.

Searle looked at him pleadingly. "Remember how we worked together when we went to get the gems for the Master? We were equals then."

"Don't be stupid!" said Gerr, "That's ages ago. I am the General now. So, will you join my army or not? Last chance."

"Yes, alright," said Searle reluctantly, "Now set me free, please?"

"OK," replied Gerr, "Then I'll send you off on your first duty."

"OK, OK," said Searle impatiently, "I agree... I'll do it. Now, set me free... pleeease."

Gerr started pecking at the ivy and soon he had broken the stem. The ivy loosened and unravelled easily and Searle slipped out. Immediately, she flew off at top speed, and before Gerr realised what was happening she had disappeared into the night.

"Stop!" Gerr shouted.

He flew after her for a moment but she was gone so he returned to the wizard and landed beside the mushroom. To his surprise he found that the wizard had gone too!

Then he heard the sounds of digging and remembered what was happening. He walked over to the hole and looked in. He could not see Jamaar and realised he must be nearly through.

The wizard was waiting in the bathroom. He had tipped over the sink which fell with a crash and smashed some of the floor tiles. Using various other things to hammer and dig at the floor he managed to clear an area and dig a hole in the soft earth underneath which was big enough for his body to squeeze through. He looked down into this hole in the floor and sat down eagerly to await the arrival of Jamaar. His head was over the hole so that he would be ready as soon as Jamaar appeared.

Jamaar was really enjoying the dig. This was the first time he had dug a hole since his form changed from a thin homeless dog into a mighty hulk of ferocious muscle.

Now he was thin again but he was still a good digger. Also, because he was thin the hole could be smaller too.

In no time at all the hole had turned into a small tunnel, and soon he was underneath the glass mushroom. Now he was ready to dig upwards. He continued with enthusiasm and energy.

As the Troubler waited and watched, one of Jamaar's front paws suddenly appeared through the earth right below him. His black eyes shone with glee.

"Yes, Jamaar!" he cried in excitement, his thin evil voice echoing slightly in the bathroom, "You're through!"

A thrilling feeling ran through him. He would soon be free. He grabbed the paw and pulled. But he pulled too hard and toppled backwards, crashing onto the floor. He recovered quickly and looked for Jamaar. To his horror, Jamaar's leg, the leg he had pulled out of the earth, lay in front of him.

"What's happened?" he thought and then called aloud, "Jamaar!"

He moved to the hole and looked down into it. There was Jamaar, who was gazing up at his master through the glass; two pairs of black eyes met in a terrible moment of realization. Neither of them knew that the glass passed underneath the mushroom as well. The paw and half the leg had passed through the glass and then could not pass back. When the wizard had pulled it, the leg had been sliced off with a cut as clean as that of a falling guillotine.

The wizard saw the panic in Jamaar's eyes and then heard his muffled cry.

"Master!" shouted Jamaar retreating backwards down the tunnel, "No!"

He moved backwards with difficulty as he had to push with one leg. The remaining stump was bleeding badly and staining the earth as he moved. The throbbing pain made him whimper as dismay took over his mind.

Like a mad, wild animal, he pushed and fought until he had forced his way backwards to the surface.

He collapsed and pushed his wound onto the cool grass. The pain eased a little but it was bleeding badly. The Troubler had climbed the stairs and was back in the mushroom again. He was clutching the leg in one hand. He looked out to see Jamaar backing away.

The wizard picked up his staff and hobbled towards him. When he had moved as close to Jamaar as he could he sat down by the glass.

"Jamaar," he said calmly, "It was an accident... it wasn't my fault. Neither of us could know..."

Jamaar was in shock. He stared at the Troubler as he continued to retreat, walking backwards. Then he turned and started walking off as best he could on only three legs, stumbling and limping, leaving a trail of bright red blood behind him.

"Stop! Wait!" called out the evil wizard frantically, standing up by the glass, "I will help you. Don't go!"

Jamaar hardly knew what he was doing. Without turning or speaking he was through the trees. He found himself thinking of going back to the Kingdom of Moone, to that land he had passed through and liked. He would live there now and be free to come and go as he wished.

The Troubler flung the leg into the air. It passed through the glass with the sound of a puff of air, spinning as it flew in an arc. It landed in some bushes, and by some extraordinary influence of fate, or maybe evil attraction, it landed right on top of the black compass the Troubler had thrown out before.

The lid of the compass clicked opened, pushing the leg up slightly. A two-tailed scorpion scuttled out, spread its wings and flew onto the top of the leg. It plunged both stings in and the leg began to change, the fur smoothing and turning blacker still.

The Troubler felt lost. He was used to being in control but now, trapped in the glass prison, things were happening that he could do nothing about. He had to find a way to escape. He knew that with the departure of Jamaar he only had one last chance and that rested fully with Gerr. He looked out to see Gerr looking in at him.

"Well?" the wizard asked, "What was that noise about?"

"It was Searle, Master," he replied, "She'd been tied up in that tree. But she deserted first and was spying for the Prince and Princess."

"What?!" the Troubler exclaimed in astonishment, "Bring her here."

"She flew off," Gerr explained, "I freed her and then she flew away."

The wizard thought for a moment.

"We can't do much about that now," he growled, "But you do what I said before… go and spy in the palace. Alright?"

Gerr nodded.

"Go!" the wizard shouted, "Now!"

Gerr jumped at the sudden command and took off. He completely forgot about the glass mushroom and slipped inside without a sound. In horror, he realised the terrible mistake he was making, and tried to turn back but it was too late. With a soft 'pop' he became a butterfly, circled the mushroom in an upwards spiral and then fluttered away through the roof.

The Dark Wizard Troubler watched from below, screwed up his face in annoyance and thumped the glass wall in anger.

A morose mood engulfed him, like an incoming tide, and yet it did not take him over. Part of him was poised, ready to grasp at the slightest opportunity to escape.

Jamaar was beginning to recover from the terrible shock. He tried his best to limp along on three legs and after a while, he began to get used to the different rhythm and he started walking faster. Quite naturally his walk turned into a run. His lighter body was now an advantage.

Recently he had had his share of pain. He had received three heavy blows to his jaw; firstly by Halo's hoof, then by the Ferryman's oar, and finally when he fell down the Silver Well and hit his chin as he toppled in. But this new pain was the worst of all.

He was extremely angry that he had lost a leg but at the same time, in a strange way, he felt uplifted. It was the feeling that he was now free to do what he wanted. This was exciting. He found that from time to time he was almost able to ignore the pain where his leg had been severed. At other times the pain would make him grimace and clench his teeth as he ran along with his unusual three-legged gait.

He was worried about losing blood and knew what he had to do. He needed to get some Rock Verthus leaves, a herb well-known for its healing properties. He knew where to find it growing in the Flatsage Farmlands and so he headed straight there.

The darkness of the night was subdued by the light of the moon which meekly gifted the land with a silver glaze. The moon hung in the clear sky, paper-white amidst a sea of stars. The Kingdom Of Gems was glowing with a stunning night beauty as if to pronounce her new freedom.

Jamaar was not interested in this lovely scene. He was concerned with his leg and the healing herbs. As soon as he found the field of Rock Verthus, he ran into it and pushed the stump of his leg into the leaves. He immediately felt the cool soothing effect. He stayed there for a while until the herb stopped the bleeding.

He set off again on his journey but then changed his mind. He was just cutting across the path that leads up to the palace, when he thought of something that he felt he must do before he left the Kingdom of Gems. He moved into the cover of bushes and trees and followed the path towards Candara. Slipping into the town without being seen, he climbed and slipped down the muddy bank to the River Tazer. The water flowed past silently.

The moon reflected on the surface as a path of shimmering white light on the murky pitch-black water. In the night, the river looked dark and dangerous and he shivered at the thought of entering it. Glancing around to check he was not being watched, he caught his breath as he carefully lowered himself into the cold water. He turned into the flowing current and began to swim upstream. His leg was throbbing now but the fresh cool water had a wonderful soothing effect.

He soon reached the back of Relbuort Cottage, 17 Nathan Avenue. It was difficult to clamber out onto the grassy bank especially with only three legs. It took him several tries but finally he made it. He stood for a moment wondering how to proceed. He wanted to find out why Darsan Lopery had in his possession a black compass with a wizard's coat of arms on it. It obviously belonged to a fallen wizard: it was not quite the same as the Dark Wizard Troubler's coat of arms but remarkably similar.

He wondered how Darsan had got it and what he was planning to do with it before it was stolen? It also crossed his mind that Darsan might be a wizard himself, hiding his identity for some reason.

He did not know how to find the answers and so he sat down behind a bush to think about it. He needed to watch and see how Darsan acted. After a couple of shakes of his body to spray off some of the water, he walked quietly up to the house. He jumped up onto his hind legs and used his remaining front paw to try the handle. The handle dropped, the door swung open and immediately he heard voices.

He stood completely still. The front half of his thin body was through the open doorway, with his good leg on the floor. A drop of blood fell from the remaining stump of his other leg. He tilted his head on one side and listened intently. The voices were coming from upstairs.

Jamaar knew it must be Darsan and Harraine. He moved into the dark room and the voices became clearer. He took a couple of steps further into the room and found he could hear what was being said.

"But what do you mean?" asked Harraine.

"I mean," replied Darsan, clearly very upset, "That the dog... the dog called Jamaar that you insisted on befriending and offering a home to... the dog must've taken it, that's if you didn't take it and then lose it yourself."

"I haven't," snapped Harraine, almost shouting, "I already told you that."

Jamaar thought that maybe they were talking about the black compass that he stole. Light shone into the room through the open door on the other side. As he was listening, he crept across the carpet, leaving a wet muddy trail and a few more drops of blood. He passed the desk and moved stealthily out of the room to the foot of the stairs. There was an oil lamp fixed to the wall halfway up the stairs which flickered gently. Now he could hear the voices clearly.

"Well then, it's *your* fault," said Darsan, raising his voice to make the statement sound final, "You wanted the dog and it's led to this..."

"You're actually blaming me, are you?" Harraine exploded, "*You* are blaming *me* for the loss! Ridiculous!"

There was silence for a moment. Then she spoke again, but this time the words were too soft for Jamaar to hear.

Jamaar stood at the foot of the stairs listening keenly.

Suddenly there was a crash followed by the sound of fighting. Feet scuffled and then there was another crash. Darsan staggered backwards into view at the top of the stairs. He balanced precariously at the very top, throwing up both arms and one leg in front of him to try to keep his balance. For a split-second it worked but then his balance went. With a cry he fell, toppling backwards and into the air.

Jamaar blinked as he smashed onto the fourth step from the top and then tumbled like a rag doll all the way down until he lay, unmoving, in front of Jamaar. Darsan's hand went limp and a small box fell from it, rolling onto the floor beside him.

Harraine appeared at the top of the stairs in her wheelchair and gasped with surprise when she saw Jamaar. In the lamplight her face looked pale and tired. Their eyes met and both froze as thoughts of panic rushed through their minds.

There was deathly silence. For a moment the passing of time seemed to be suspended. Everything was still. It was so silent that you could have heard a feather tumbling through the air.

Harraine broke the silence.

"Jamaar!" she exclaimed in surprise, "What are you doing here?"

Jamaar did not answer.

"What's happened to your leg?"

Just at that moment another drop of blood fell from it and splattered on the floor.

"Jamaar," she said again, holding her hand out to point at Darsan, "It was a just a terrible accident!"

Still Jamaar said nothing. He did not know what to say. He looked again at Darsan.

"It was just an accident," she repeated, "Oh, how terrible! Jamaar! Just a silly argument about nothing. I didn't mean to kill him!"

Jamaar looked up the stairs at her.

She spoke again, this time calmly. "He was blaming me because of what *you* stole, so it's your fault this happened."

Jamaar was shocked. He did not like the sound of this. She was right - he had stolen it, but surely she could not blame him for the murder of Darsan!

"You need to give it back," she continued, "Whatever it was you took… you must give it back."

"Give it back?" he asked.

Even if he wanted to, it was gone, carried down the well on Horrik's foot.

"You do have it, don't you?" she asked anxiously.

"I..." Jamaar hesitated, "I… I don't know… no... it's lost."

Thoughts flashed through his mind. Perhaps he should run and escape as quickly as possible.

"I shall have to report this…" Harraine began.

Jamaar looked at Darsan and noticed he was still breathing. Maybe he was just unconscious. Then Jamaar decided. He did not wait to hear the end of the sentence. The small box was so near that he grabbed it in his mouth and turned and ran.

"No, wait!" cried out Harraine in a panic.

Jamaar scampered away, into the room, skidding as he turned and crashing into a small table. Running fast on three legs was not easy. He got up and hobbled as quickly as he could across the carpet and out.

Harraine's distraught voice was screaming now but Jamaar was well away and it faded behind him. He was managing an awkward gallop now and quickly crossed the lawn.

He skidded down the bank and plunged into the water. When he surfaced he swam as fast as he could with the current helping him along. He was swimming in a panic and a wave of water splashed through his mouth and washed out the little box he was carrying. He saw it floating on the water and he snapped at it but missed. Then it was gone. He forgot about it and anyway he had no idea what was inside. It was probably nothing of importance.

In another minute he was out. He ran out of the town, across fields and towards Silvermay Forest.

The compass was lost, and now with Darsan Lopery possibly dead, he realised that he may never know the answer to his questions about this mystery. He had tried to find out and in doing so he had been virtually accused of murdering Darsan.

Silvermay Forest was not far now so he tried to ignore his leg which was throbbing with pain. He decided he would carry on running until he got there and then he would rest under the cover of the trees. The feeling of being free to do as he wished began to return and this spurred him on.

Soon he entered the forest which he knew so well. His leg was bleeding again and leaving a trail of drips on the ground. He hurried past a few trees towards a sheltered place where he used to sleep sometimes as a wandering stray. The throbbing pain became even worse and he began to feel dizzy. He managed to reach a grassy area under some overhanging trees and stood for a moment wincing in pain. He looked around at the dark shapes of the trees and saw them begin to swirl in front of his eyes. He collapsed onto the grass and passed out.

The dawn arrived fresh and clear in The Kingdom Of Gems. A big red sun peeped over the horizon to cast long shadows from the trees and buildings. In the valleys, the darkness lingered, drawing out the night as long as possible, whereas the hilltops were painted with the pink tint of the sunrise.

Since the morning before, when the spell still held the creatures of the kingdom prisoner, the land had been transformed. No longer did the heavy poisonous atmosphere of the spell infect the land. The snow had all gone and once again life hummed with vitality in every corner of the kingdom.

The palace was also buzzing with life. It was as if everything had received an extra boost of energy to get things going again. Things were gradually being restored to how they were before, as the people who worked in the palace were cleaning all the rooms. The thick layer of dust that coated the floor and furniture took some work to remove but it was already proceeding well.

In Candara, Whitten and Charin, life was also returning to normal. Many were preparing to search again for the King and Queen but the necessities of life demanded that some resumed their normal jobs. Shops were opening, farming was restarting as usual and craftsmen were picking up their tools once again to practice their fine skills. While all this was happening there was much talk about the extraordinary events that had taken place.

However, something had changed and it affected every person and creature that lived in the kingdom. Since the spell had been dissolved there was a feeling of uncertainty in the air. The initial jubilation was already fading and as people busied themselves with their jobs and with the search for the King and Queen, they were irritable and impatient with each other. The same applied to the animals.

This was the effect of the loss of the Candara Gems. Before the spell was cast the gems were in their rightful places in the cavity in the wall of the Brinscally Cave. There they protected the inhabitants of the kingdom in many ways. At the same time, the good living of the people and animals protected the gems. It was a strong mutual connection which forged the kingdom and the gems together in goodness, but that was now broken and the consequences were being felt.

Bright rays of sunlight shone through the gold-framed windows and lit up the Round Room. The table was spread with plenty of food on a blue tablecloth but not much was being eaten. The mood around the table was subdued.

"Things aren't right, you know," said Joog, perched on his branch which hung by the table, "The kingdom needs the Candara Gems."

"I know," commented Amalek, "And with our parents lost it'll never be the same."

"We'll find them, Ammey," comforted Seph, "I'm sure we will... then it will be all back to normal again."

"We must hope," said Simron, "We're all hoping. And Joog's right, the loss of the Candara Gems affects everyone. And remember my conversation with the Komodo dragon? It said about how some other wizard had taken them?"

Joog was perched on his branch by the table.

"I'll visit the Brinscally Cave," he said, "To see if there are any clues there. It's easy for me to fly through the Gem Falls and into the cave."

"And I must go back to Summertime Kingdom soon," said Simron.

Amalek looked up from her food with a surprised expression. "When?" she asked.

"Not just yet," Simron replied, "I told Wizard Elzaphan I would... as soon as possible. But as the gems and the King and Queen are missing I will stay a little longer. When I go, then Lazuli and Neville should come too. We're all needed back there."

Joog looked at Simron, his golden-yellow eyes catching the morning sun which was streaming through the window. "And when do you think Wizard Elzaphan will come here? He needs to deal with the Troubler some time."

Simron nodded, "Yes, he'll come. I don't know when... but the Troubler is safe in his glass prison at the moment."

"I'm not hungry," said Seph.

"Neither am I," agreed Amalek, "Let's get the search started."

She gathered some food together and put it in a bag ready to give to the Dark Wizard Troubler and then they descended the stairs and out onto the front lawn.

Joog flew straight off to the Brinscally Cave and the search was resumed in the west of the kingdom. Amalek and Seph set off, riding on Aram and Halo down Palace Path and heading for the Wellspring Woods to search there. They would check on the Troubler on their way.

They approached the glass mushroom across Shaky Field at a trot. The sun reflected off Aram and Halo in gold and silver, and sparkled on their manes which flowed in the breeze. Their hooves thudded on the grass as they carried the two children with ease.

They slowed to a walk and passed into the shadows of the trees, the children ducking to avoid some low branches. When they were out in the sunlight again they were close to the mushroom. The morning sun gleamed brightly on the glass.

Around the mushroom was a circle of flowers, several plants deep, which displayed many different colours and shapes. They all had their flower heads bowed as if in sadness and when the children were close they could hear tiny sounds coming from them which sounded like crying.

"They're suffering," said Aram, his voice strong and clear, "They're suffering because he's suffering and brings such misery around him."

He nodded towards the Troubler who was huddled in his blankets on the far side of the mushroom. He had his back against the glass. His face was badly bruised and cut from the various blows he had received. He opened his black eyes and glared across at them.

A chill ran through the children. The wizard held them in his steely stare and they felt drawn into his darkness. Aram pawed the ground uncomfortably with a golden hoof.

"Don't look at him!" he commanded, "Look away now."

They tore their eyes away, looked down and immediately felt better.

Beyond the Troubler were the holes that Jamaar had dug in the night but the children did not notice them. They were still on the unicorns' backs and Amalek turned to her brother.

"I don't know why we're bringing him food," she said crossly, "He won't even tell us where are parents are."

Seph sighed. "I know," he said, "But *we* can't be cruel just because he is."

"Food!" called out Amalek sharply.

The Troubler remained still and silent. She threw in a bag of food which passed through the glass with a soft 'phoo' sound and bumped onto the wooden floor. Seph slipped off Aram's back, rolled a glass bottle of water into the mushroom, and then mounted again.

Seph turned to Aram.

"What happens to him now?" he asked.

"He stays here until Wizard Elzaphan comes," Aram replied.

"What if he escapes?" asked Amalek.

Halo replied, her words as smooth as liquid gold, "He can't. It's his own evil that traps him in there... that's why *you* could walk out but he can't."

Halo turned and walked up the garden and through the trees at the end. Aram followed. In front of them was an area of flat land leading to the Wellspring Woods. The children held on as the two magnificent unicorns built up speed from a trot to a canter. Then they broke into a gallop and soon the wind was whistling through the children's hair as the ground sped past.

Amalek and Seph were pleased to be travelling so fast because they were anxious to continue the search for their lost parents. It was not long before they were in the woods and working their way methodically through the trees.

The late morning in Candara was fairly quiet because most people were helping with the search for the King and Queen. The air had been pleasantly warmed by the intermittent showing of the hot sun from behind slow-drifting clouds.

The event that had happened at Relbuort Cottage was the talk of this little town; a town where everyone knew everyone else. This meant that nothing stayed secret for long. In Corten's Bakery in the High Street, Jethrynne Corten was doing an excellent job of spreading the news, and when Merryl Chardley entered her shop it was another opportunity.

"Have you a large granary please Jethrynne?" asked Merryl.

Merryl was John Chardley's wife, the town's beekeeper who also looked after Spindley Tower. The wonderful smell of freshly baked bread filled the shop.

"Have you heard about Darsan Lopery?" was Jethrynne's response, who was keener on spreading the gossip than selling bread, "Up an' left Harraine, he has! Just like that! Gone!"

"What! Old Darsan... left Harraine!" exclaimed Merryl, as astonished as everyone else, "I don't believe it!"

"You mayn't believe it, but it's true. As sure as I'm standing here, I tell you. She's distraught, is poor Harraine, beside herself with worry. An' her in a wheelchair an' all... it's just not fair."

Jethrynne reached up to take a large granary loaf from the shelf behind her. She put it into a brown paper bag and handed to Merryl who put it into her shopping bag. Merryl inspected the rows of cakes on display on the counter.

"I'll have three of those tarts there as well, please," she said, pointing to a cluster of strawberry tarts.

Jethrynne put them in a paper bag and handed them across the counter, "He's just gone and left her, and after all those years together!"

"But where's he gone?" Merryl looked puzzled, as she put the tarts in her bag.

Jethrynne lowered her voice, "No one knows," she answered, clearly enjoying the gossip, "It's a strange one this is. Harraine says she's no idea. She went to bed early and in the mornin' he was gone. But it must be a woman."

"Darsan? Left Harraine for another woman?" Merryl looked truly amazed now, "Not old Darsan. Now *that* I really don't believe. Who'd have him anyway? The grumpy old devil."

She took a six dib note from her purse and handed it to Jethrynne.

"Thank you," said Jethrynne and handed her the change in several coins, "Well, I know what you mean, but what else could it be, I ask you? A man disappears overnight and his wife's distraught. Read between the lines, Merryl."

"I would rather not jump to conclusions myself."

She turned towards the door, as if to go and then hesitated.

"Have the Guardian Owls been looking?" she asked.

"Yes. They've been searching everywhere since mid-morning. They're out looking for the King and Queen really but they're keeping an eye out for him at the same time. But it's mysterious 'cos they've found no sign of him at all... but that's because he's cunning! Those birds have great eyes, and yet, no sign of him. It's suspicious, that's what it is."

"Well, I suppose we'll have to wait and see," said Merryl, "Anyway, thanks for the bread," she said as she turned to leave, walked to the door and opened it.

A horse and carriage clattered past outside. As she left, another customer came in and just before the door closed she overheard Jethrynne's opening line.

"Have you heard the news about the Lopery's?"

In this way, by word of mouth, the strange disappearance of Darsan Lopery was known by everyone in Candara. Several people called on Harraine but they found that they were unable to console her in the misery of her loss. Many saw her looking out of her window with a tear-stained face as they passed the house, and felt sorry for her sad and unresolved misfortune.

The undulating land of the Tazer Downs looked beautiful. The slopes were adorned with many shades of green resting calmly beneath the midday sun. It was an area of gently rolling hills and shallow vales dotted with occasional trees as well as substantial woods. To the east it bordered the Kingdom of Moone.

Gratch had followed Simron's instructions, fully believing that he was working for a powerful wizard who possessed the Candara Gems. He wondered what had happened the day before when suddenly the kingdom changed and everything sprang into life around him and the snow disappeared. He knew that this could only mean one thing; the spell had ended. This was puzzling but he trusted that his new master had something to do with it and he was glad that he was now working for him. Maybe his new master had carried out his threat to beat the Dark Wizard Troubler and destroy his spell.

He had been told to hunt the area for a dog and the best way to do this was with his fine sense of smell. He smelt with his long forked tongue, stretching it out to sample the air so that when it returned into his mouth it carried information about any scent for a wide area around him. In this way his sense of smell was very acute.

His hunting was methodical. He decided that if he moved in a straight line as far as possible, cutting across the downs from south to north, then he would be likely to pick up the dog's scent. If this did not work then maybe he would zigzag across.

So far he had not found the dog and it did cross his mind that perhaps he had been tricked. After all what evidence did he have about his new master? He had been shown the gems but he had not actually seen them. He had not even seen this new wizard's face. Really he knew very little.

He was in a valley walking through some trees with these doubts and questions turning in his mind, when suddenly his tongue picked up something; it was the scent of a dog. It was faint but definitely there. He moved to his right, lined his great body up in the right direction and began to move cautiously. Within a minute he came to a path and stepped onto it. His tongue snaked out and in several times. A dog had definitely passed this way.

For a while he kept testing the scent that he had picked up, dropping his head close to the ground, his tongue sliding out and then in again. The scent was faint but he knew that the dog had been here within the last day.

He tried to work out which way it had been moving, but this was much harder. Then he heard a sound along the path behind him and moved into the trees to hide and watch. His bacteria-filled saliva, already dribbling out of his mouth, began to run even more. He was about to satisfy his hunger with a sizeable meal. If it was not the dog approaching him now along the path then he would probably get a meal anyway.

As the sounds became louder he crouched low to the ground and got ready to pounce. Now he could hear the feet thudding on the ground and he could tell that this creature was larger than a dog.

The pounding feet were close now and Gratch got ready. When it suddenly appeared he opened his eyes wide in surprise. It was another Komodo dragon and he leapt out of the trees in front of it.

The dragon reared in shock and skidded to a halt.

"Horrik?" asked Gratch.

"Gratch!" exclaimed Horrik.

They were both astonished.

Horrik shook her great head in disbelief, "What are you doing here?"

"I'm looking for a dog," said Gratch, his voice deep and powerful.

Horrik was surprised again, "So am I!" she said, and then her voice turned into an angry growl, "He's called Jamaar. I hate him and I'm on his scent."

"But *I've* been sent here to hunt for a dog and kill it," said Gratch, "Maybe it's the same dog."

Horrik looked puzzled. "Who sent you then?" she asked.

"A wizard," Gratch growled, "A powerful wizard… he's stolen the gems… he's got the Candara Gems."

Horrik looked surprised and then puzzled and so Gratch tried to explain.

"He's not Kasimir... your wizard," he said, "But I'm here in this kingdom because I got Kasimir's staff and brought it here for him."

"I bet he was pleased," commented Horrik.

"He was... very," began Gratch, "But I don't understand about this other wizard..."

"Neither do I," she growled back, "Everything's hard to understand." She looked along the path. "What I do know is that I want to kill that dog," she growled, "I don't want him getting away. If you come with me we can talk about everything as we run."

"That's a good idea," he agreed, "And the dog you're after may be the dog that I'm after. I'll help you kill it."

"That..." growled Horrik with hate, "won't be necessary. I want to do it all by myself."

Gratch suddenly noticed the two black compasses hanging around Horrik's neck.

"I've seen those before," he commented, pointing at them with a claw, "But only on a wizard... and you've got two! How did you get them?"

"I found them," she replied, "They're guides, I think, and they light up when it's dark."

"What else do they do?" asked Gratch.

"I don't know... let's go."

They began to run along the path side by side and talked in deep growls to each other as they ran. After a while they decided that after they had found the dog they would try to find out what was happening by returning to Old Howard's House.

"We'll work together," concluded Horrik.

"Alright," Gratch agreed. Then he asked, "And share the dog?"

"If you insist," Horrik growled, "But *I'll* kill it."

They carried on following Jamaar's scent until they could see Whitten just beyond a hill. They wanted to avoid being seen and so they were glad that the scent turned south-west. It led them to the banks of the River Tazer where Horrik assumed Jamaar must have swum across. They swam the river easily, their bodies wriggling skilfully through the water. At the other side the scent had gone.

Horrik moved around, growling with frustration.

"I've been following Jamaar all this way," she complained, "And now we've lost the scent."

She flopped down in a gesture of despair.

"What shall we do now?" she groaned.

"We've got to find out what's going on," Gratch answered, "We need to know who's winning out of the two wizards... and why the spell has gone. So let's go back to that house. Maybe the dog's there anyway... then you can kill it and we'll get our meal."

This gave Horrik some hope that she would still get revenge over Jamaar and they headed off together.

After Searle had escaped in the night, she had flown straight to the Wellspring Woods to hide. She nestled down in the branches of a tree among the leaves and slept there. The dawn chorus arrived and Searle woke up. She stayed where she was as morning came and went, and now, in the mid-afternoon, she began to wonder what she should do next.

Everything had gone wrong. She did not know what to do and she was afraid. Gerr had told her about all the other ravens turning back into butterflies and this terrified her. She was afraid this might happen to her at any moment.

As she huddled on the branch, she heard the sound of voices calling out some distance away.

She wondered who this was so she took off and flew towards them. The voices grew louder, so she landed and peered through some leaves and branches. It was the Prince and Princess calling out as they searched for their parents.

She heard something move behind her and when she spun around she jerked her head up in shock. It was Urrg.

"Urrg!" she exclaimed, keeping her voice down, "I've been looking for you."

"Yeah," she whispered sarcastically, "Likely story."

"Honest, I have," Searle whispered, "I've been looking everywhere."

"You left me stuck in that tree," retorted Urrg, and she jabbed her beak at Searle in anger.

"I had to," pleaded Searle, "It was too dangerous."

"It was dangerous for me too," Urrg stated.

"Anyway, you're free now," Searle whispered cheerily, "But what are you doing here?"

"I'm following..." began Urrg, whispered proudly "I've been following that Prince and Princess all the way from the town. I followed them past the Master in the mushroom thing, and then to here."

"Mushroom thing?" Searle asked.

"It's a great big... a big thing... made of glass. Or it seems to be... well, shaped like a mushroom... but see-through... and the Master's inside it and he can't get out! But never mind about that... I'll explain later, OK?"

Searle nodded and looked through the branches to see the children on Aram and Halo. The two beautiful unicorns were walking through the woods.

"Let's steal something from them again," Searle suggested, "You know, like we did before."

"And remember what happened before?" objected Urrg, "I nearly got all my feathers blown off, that's what. It's too difficult."

Searle was looking down intently.

"But they don't know we're here," she whispered, "We'll surprise 'em... It'll be easy."

"No," Urrg objected, "Those unicorns are dangerous. It's too risky."

"Not for me," she said, "Watch."

She swooped down and landed in the lower branches of a tree. A moment later the two unicorns walked in front of her. Amalek was just passing when Searle flew out of the tree as fast as she could, accelerating towards the Princess. She ducked and Searle grabbed her shoulder bag in her beak and lifted it away.

The attack had been so quick and unexpected that it took them all by surprise. It was a skilful and well-executed theft.

"Hey!" shouted Amalek.

Halo turned, and then Aram, but Searle was already gone, hidden by the trees as she sped away.

Urrg was right behind her.

"Well done," called out Urrg.

Searle could not reply as she had the strap of the bag in her beak.

They flew until they were out of the woods and flying towards the Plains of Wilrack. They glided down to land on a grassy area.

Searle let go of the bag and it fell limply onto the grass showing a bulge where the contents were. A buckle held the flap closed.

"Let's see what we've got," Searle said.

"What's that?" asked Urrg, pointing at the bulge with her beak.

"Dunno," Searle replied.

They both walked right around the bag looking at it. Then they walked around again.

"Well, go on!" bossed Searle, "Have a look inside."

"*You* got it," Urrg looked hesitant, "So *you* can look first."

"Are you afraid?" asked Searle.

"Are you?" Urrg retorted.

"Of course not," replied Searle.

"Then you look!" said Urrg, feeling she had turned the argument around.

"Alright, alright," said Searle.

She gave it a tentative peck with her beak and when nothing happened she pulled at the strap passing through the buckle. It loosened and she peeped inside.

"It's the star-box!" she exclaimed.

"What!" Urrg was so excited she jumped in the air and flapped her wings, "We've got it back again! This is better than we'd hoped for!"

"But remember how hard it was to catch?" said Searle.

"And how it blew me way up into the sky!" added Urrg, looking afraid again.

"And," said Searle thoughtfully, "the thing is... what do we do with it anyway?"

"Yeah, that's true," said Urrg, her initial enthusiasm deflated, "Our Master is trapped and we don't know how to use the magic."

"Well, in that case," said Searle looking at the bag, "Let's keep it locked up in the bag for now. Pull the strap, Urrg."

"No, you," said Urrg taking a step back.

"You're such a coward," Searle said glaring at Urrg, "I took it from the Princess and I opened it. So you owe me one and anyway it's your turn!"

Urrg realised she had no choice and she stepped forwards very cautiously and lowered her beak slowly towards the bag, but as she did it moved. She jerked back in shock.

"Quick!" screeched Searle, "Before it escapes!"

Urrg grabbed the strap but the star-box was already half out. It slipped through the opening and snapped at Urrg with its hinged lid. Urrg dodged back.

"Grab it in your beak," yelled Searle.

Urrg dived for it but again the star-box was too quick, opening its lid like a mouth. Urrg saw the danger but could not stop and her head went right inside the box.

"Help!" she cried. Then, somehow, amazingly, although she was much bigger than the star-box, she disappeared inside it and 'snap!' went the lid. Urrg was gone.

"Urrg!" cried out Searle.

She moved quickly away from the box, running as fast as she could and then taking off, flapping frantically and flying towards the plains with the magic star-box right behind her giving chase.

The search went on through the afternoon and into the evening. The sun fell from the sky and then through the horizon, and night settled on the kingdom bringing a resigned feeling of failure; the King and Queen had not been found and there was no sign of the Candara Gems. In spite of all the many helpers it was a huge area to cover making the task seem impossible.

Aram and Halo carried the Prince and Princess to the palace and then grazed on the lawn. In the Round Room a large supper was served and Amalek and Seph ate well and then went to bed early.

Amalek went into her bedroom feeling weary and ready for sleep. She placed a flickering candle on her bedside table, sat on her bed and looked out of the window. She could see the lights dotting Candara and was pleased for the people there who were living life normally again.

She turned and lifted the sheets ready to get into bed when something caught her eye. It was a glint of gold on the end of the bed. She leant over and when saw what it was a surge of joy ran through her. It was her magic star-box.

She picked it up and wondered, and then opened it. She looked inside and smiled. Closing it again, she walked over to her window and holding it outside opened the lid again. Out flew two butterflies which fluttered harmlessly away.

Chapter 14

~ Amalek's Room ~

usk faded the dim light into night. The moon lifted slowly above the horizon to throw her delicate light across the kingdom. The curved top of the glass mushroom caught the moonlight to shed a pale illumination below. Around the glass prison, the flowers were still drooping their heads in sympathy with the painful dark mood that hung around the Troubler. Their bright colours had been tamed to shades of grey, a faded echo of their former glory.

The Troubler was lying on his blankets and had one wrapped right around him so that even his head was hidden. The blanket rose and fell to the rhythm of his breathing as he slept soundly.

Nearby, walking across Shaky Field, Old Howard looked a weary figure, but with a resolute expression on his face. He still hated the Hadia stick with passion but he had no choice but to grip it constantly to avoid the pain. Feeni sat on his shoulder and he was looking forward to arriving back at his house. The journey from the Marshes of Macaroone had been very difficult for him. His ankle was swollen and he had to make frequent stops to rest it and as well as this, he found the weight of Feeni an extra burden he would much rather do without. Since the spell had gone, they had made efforts not to be seen, travelling through wooded areas whenever possible. When the snow disappeared they feared that the Dark Wizard Troubler had been beaten, but they needed to find out.

They had crossed the River Haze at Whitten Bridge and then moved under the cover of Silvermay Forest where they had slept a night. Then they journeyed cautiously on until finally they were nearly at their destination.

Old Howard clutched the Hadia Stick in his hand which was helping him to move his portly figure along while taking weight of his injured ankle.

"Just through those trees," he said to Feeni.

"And about time too!" she said crossly, "You've taken *so long* to get here!"

"And you've done nothing," complained Old Howard.

"Put me down," Feeni bossed.

Old Howard was pleased to oblige so he stooped down and she ran down his back and jumped onto the ground.

As they passed through the trees Old Howard received a huge shock. He expected to see his house looming out of the darkness but it was not there! They passed through the trees and out into the open and he was even more shocked. He walked towards the mushroom

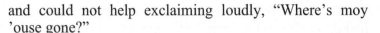

and could not help exclaiming loudly, "Where's moy 'ouse gone?"

His loud comment woke up the Dark Wizard Troubler who had been dreaming that he had escaped from the glass mushroom and standing on the top of Point Hill gazing at a wonderful view of the snowbound kingdom. When he woke his dream dissolved and there was a brief moment when he had a flowing white beard and purple robe. In an instant, he changed; his selfish desires appeared in his cold heart and he was possessed by evil again, his hair and robe blacker than the night surrounding him.

Old Howard's mouth dropped open with astonishment when the wizard poked his head out of the blanket to see what was going on. The Troubler looked equally surprised to see Old Howard.

"Where's moy 'ouse, Black Oiys?" Old Howard asked again.

The Troubler just stared back, so Old Howard raised his voice in anger and boomed at him.

"Where's moy 'ouse?"

"Don't ask me," replied the wizard calmly and quietly, recovering from the sudden awakening and the shock of seeing Old Howard, "You should look after your property better."

"Oy rented it to you!" Old Howard's plump cheeks shook as he shouted. "And now oy demand it back and moy rent in gold!"

The Troubler frowned.

"Listen," he said, his voice sounding icy calm, "If you have to blame anyone it's the wretched Prince and Princess - they took your house. Go and ask them and leave me alone."

Old Howard looked around.

"But where is it?" he said holding out his hands in a gesture of puzzled despair, "Where's moy 'ouse gone to?"

"It hasn't gone anywhere," snapped the wizard, "It's just gone. And I'm not paying rent for a house I'm not living in and doesn't even exist," the wizard snapped, "Go away!"

Old Howard's face flushed red with fury and he kicked at some of the flowers in anger. He took a step closer to the glass mushroom and was now just a few feet away. The moon was reflecting on the glass and he suddenly noticed the mushroom. He took one more step towards it and glared at the wizard.

"And what about the riches you promised me? What 'appened to them? Oy did what yer said and what did oy get...?" His voice rose again. "Nothing!"

He lifted his Hadia Stick and swung it at the glass mushroom. He expected it to hit it hard but instead it passed straight through. He lost his balance and spun around, falling forwards and through the glass.

On seeing this, the Troubler laughed mockingly.

"You're an idiot, but a very entertaining one."

He stared at Old Howard as he lay there in front of him. The smile left his pale face and his voice became cold and cutting.

"And, don't forget, you were a failure. Your memory can't be that poor, can it? You failed in all the tasks I set for you... every one. And then you ran off like the coward you are! With that you forfeited all the favours I would have given to you, and the gold too. And where is the bar of gold? Because you failed... I want it back."

For Old Howard that was the last straw, and just as a kettle of water eventually reaches boiling point, his temper and frustration bubbled up inside him and he was ready to explode.

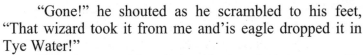

"Gone!" he shouted as he scrambled to his feet, "That wizard took it from me and'is eagle dropped it in Tye Water!"

For the Troubler it suddenly made sense. He remembered his dream of falling into water and hitting a bell, the famous Glyifild Bell, on the bed of a lake. This was the bell that had been used to cast a powerful spell over Summertime Kingdom years before. It was lost and now he knew where it was; in Tye Water. But what use was this to him now? He would think about this later.

He looked up to see Old Howard coming at him brandishing a stick. As he swung the Stick, the evil wizard was suddenly very fast and rolled out of the way. Old Howard crashed to the floorboards.

"Ha!" laughed the Troubler, "More entertainment! Thank you! Thank you! It gets very boring in here."

Old Howard struggled up and lurched at the wizard holding his walking stick in front of his rotund body with two hands like a heavy sword. He lunged and caught the wizard a glancing blow on the cheek with the stick. Old Howard nearly overbalanced again, staggering past the Troubler and receiving a hard kick on the knee which sent him tumbling towards the glass wall.

He crashed into it making the whole mushroom wobble and vibrate, and then bounced off it and fell onto the floorboards again. He just had the strength to lift a fist and bang on the glass. Horror filled his face as he realised that he was trapped inside the glass with the worst company he could imagine.

Feeni had watched all this from the shadows of the trees. She hopped out towards the glass mushroom and sat a little distance away, looking in. Her ears pointed straight up and twitched this way and that.

"Ah, Feeni," said the Troubler, "You've done well."

Feeni was at her most charming, "Thank you, Master," she said, "I try my best for you... my very best."

"Good... good," he said, "I have a job for you... a tricky little job... but one that could be very important."

"Yes Master," she said.

Old Howard was sitting up now. "Where's moy 'ouse?" he grumbled at the wizard.

"Don't start that again," the Troubler snapped, "Be quiet!"

He turned back to Feeni.

"I've got to get out of here," he said, scowling as he looked up at the glass mushroom sweeping over his head, "And you could help. I want you to go to the palace and find out what you can. You'll have to find a way in without being seen. Then listen and look, and you may discover something that will help me get out. And find out about the Candara Gems. Then come back and tell me."

Feeni stared back at him.

"Hold on," she snapped, "And what do I get out of it? I'm risking my life for you... and that's worth a lot."

"What do you want?" he hissed.

He was not used to this and it made him feel uncomfortable. She was bargaining with him and he had to follow her demands.

"I want gold," she said,

"Alright," he agreed.

"And jewellery."

"You can have it," he said, "So..."

"And..." she continued, holding up a paw and interrupting him, "I want to work for you - with you... that's if you escape of course."

"Alright... yes," he agreed, "When I'm out of here you can work for me. So, go now. The night is the best time for breaking into the palace."

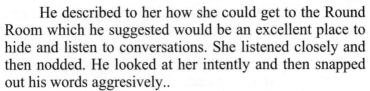

He described to her how she could get to the Round Room which he suggested would be an excellent place to hide and listen to conversations. She listened closely and then nodded. He looked at her intently and then snapped out his words aggresively..

"So, go now," he commanded.

"Yes Master," she replied.

She hopped quickly back into the trees.

When Feeni had left, the Troubler suddenly thought of something. He got up, leaving his blankets in a muddled heap, and hobbled across the floor using his staff for support. He descended the stairs to the block which used to be gold but now looked like rusting iron. He placed his hand on it, hoping it would work.

"Feeni?" he said, "Can you hear me?"

He heard nothing.

"Feeni?" he shouted.

As he expected, it had stopped working. Everything had been taken away from him. He rubbed his hands together to remove some rust and then slumped down onto the iron block and thumped his hand onto it in frustration.

Feeni looked up at the palace as it towered above her. She was in some trees in the gardens at the back and planning her move. She was alert and ready.

It looked like a difficult task, even for a small rabbit, because at a first glance all the doors and windows seemed to be closed. She could try to jump up to the door handles of course but for her that was a difficult jump and with paws it would be hard to turn the handle.

Then she saw the perfect way in for her. It was a catflap. She kept low as she scurried across the grass. The catflap was in a door and she went straight through. She was in.

The palace was quiet. Everyone was asleep. She moved along the hall and then up the stairs with her padded paws making no sound. She followed the Troubler's directions, through hallways all lit by the occasional candle. The doors in the palace were easy for her to open because every door inside the building had a handle for humans as well as one lower down for the cats of the palace, Tilly and Flop.

As she moved she was observing everything and noting things that might be useful to her task. She stopped at the foot of a set of six steps. There was a door at the top with a sign hanging there. On it was written:

AMALEK'S ROOM

She was not good at reading so she stared at it, slowly working it out. A candle flickered behind her casting her shadow on the steps.

"*Am...a...lek's Ro...om,*" she read. This was followed immediately by another thought. "*Jewellery! There could be jewellery in there.*"

She loved jewellery and the thought struck her that she might as well make the most of being here and steal

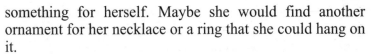

something for herself. Maybe she would find another ornament for her necklace or a ring that she could hang on it.

She crept up the steps to the room. At the top she paused and then put her paw on the lower handle and pushed down. With a nudge of her head the door opened. The room was dark. Amalek would be asleep.

Feeni took a few cautious steps into the room and listened. The sound of slow breathing came from the bed. It must be the Princess sleeping.

She looked around as her eyes adjusted to the darkness. She spotted the dressing table and stepped quietly towards it. The necklace around her neck made a little 'chink' as the ornaments bumped each other and she stopped completely still.

Then a noise to her right made her jump. The world exploded. Something hit her from above and then she was tumbling out of the room and down the steps.

She landed with a bump but something cushioned the impact. It was Tally who had leapt upon her and then clung to her back as they rolled down the steps. He had landed on the floor with her on top of him.

She jumped away.

The blow had taken the wind out of Tally and he lay there for a second. Feeni spun around to see him lying there. The fire of anger lit her eyes and she leapt at him. He saw her coming and with a kick of his legs rolled out of the way. She slid into a table leg and a vase of flowers fell off the table just missing her head and smashing all around her.

Amidst the broken bits of vase, the scattered flowers and the splattered water they faced each other.

Their eyes met.

A flower was resting on Feeni's paw and she flicked it into Tally's face. He jerked his head to one side but it had been enough to distract him and Feeni attacked, pouncing forwards and biting at him. Her teeth caught his leg. Feeling a sharp pain he pulled away. Blood trickled from the wound and Feeni spat out some white fur.

"You even *taste* horrible," she hissed out the words with hate.

Hawkeye was just behind Tally now.

"KYWAY, Tally," he said. "KYWAY."

Feeni attacked again but this time he was too fast, turning and thrusting his back legs towards her as hard as he could. He hit her square on the side with his legs and she flew across the room, slipping on the water and crashing into the wall. Tally was upon her and together they flew across the hallway, biting and scratching at each other in a frantic blur of brown and white fur.

Amalek's head appeared around the door, looking wide-eyed at the scene.

"What's happening?" she said, turning to Hawkeye.

"He can deal with it," Hawkeye replied confidently.

Suddenly, Tally and Feeni broke apart and were staring at each other. Feeni cowered away from him. He was bigger and taller, and he stepped towards her aggressively.

"What are you doing here?" he snapped.

This comment sparked off Feeni's cunning mind and when she spoke she sounded weak. She looked at him with a pitiful expression.

"I just need somewhere to stay," she said, "It's cold outside."

"Why are you here?" he demanded.

"As I said, I just need somewhere to sleep," she said innocently, "Somewhere that's nice and warm... that's all. I'm just a poor little rabbit."

"Maybe..." Tally said doubtfully, "But it's warm outside now. And what were you doing in her room? You came here to steal didn't you?"

"No, I'm just a poor little rabbit," she repeated.

She could tell he did not believe her story. Now she needed to run. Amalek guessed what was she was thinking and moved to block her way

Tally glanced at Amalek and Feeni was quick to take her chance. She took off, bumping into him first and knocking him sideways. She slipped past Amalek's legs and then scampered away.

Tally followed with Amalek behind. Feeni had a start on them and she sprinted away at full pelt. She had left all the doors open and she just had time to close the first one behind her before Tally got there. He was faster than her and once he had got past the door he began reduce the gap.

Feeni passed through another door and closed it behind her. Tally raced towards it, skidded to a halt and reached for the handle. As he did Feeni kicked it open as hard as she could with her back legs. It whacked Tally on the head and sent him crashing into the floor.

By the time Tally was on his feet again and looking through the open door, Feeni was gone. She was running down the main stairs. He felt dizzy and could only lie where he was. The chase was over.

Amalek, who had been just behind, rushed up to Tally.

"Are you alright?" she asked.

"Yes," he nodded, "But, she got away."

Other people and animals were waking up. Doors were opening and with sleepy faces looking out to see what was happening. Feeni descended the stairs, ran along the hall and out through the catflap. She slipped into the trees and stopped to get her breath back, licking some of her wounds. She was lucky not to have been badly injured.

What would she do now? She was afraid of the Dark Wizard Troubler and reporting her failure to him. He would be angry. She decided she would hide in Silvermay Forest and then plan what to do.

A door of the palace opened. Simron and Amalek looked out with Tally at their feet. Feeni was gone.

"What was it up to?" asked Simron.

"Just after somewhere to sleep," replied Tally, "Or so she said. But I don't believe that."

"What do you think then?"

"I think..." said Tally, "That she was a common thief trying to steal something."

"My jewellery," commented Amalek.

"Did she get anything?" enquired Simron.

She shook her head. "No, I don't think so."

"Good," Tally said, "That's something. But shall I follow?"

"No," Simron said, "I don't think it's worth it. You've probably frightened her off for good. How's your leg?"

Tally held it up for Simron and Amalek to take a look.

"It needs attending to," Simron commented, "and so do some of those cuts. Come on."

They closed the door on the night-time world outside.

Horrik and Gratch were on the move. They had a short sleep a few hours on the southern outskirts of Silvermay Forest. When they woke they still felt they needed more sleep but wanted to push on, so they set off through the night under the cover of darkness. The gentle glow of the compasses helped them see their way as they ran to Payli's Bridge and crossed the River Tazer.

Turning due west they powered along at a good rate, passing just to the south of Candara. Finally they headed north again, swimming back over the river and entering the trees near Old Howard's garden and the glass mushroom.

They paused to rest for a moment and get their breath. The light of the compasses reflected on their shiny scales.

Horrik's yellow forked tongue slithered out of her mouth and stayed there, wriggling in the air. She growled in contentment.

"Jamaar!" she rumbled.

Gratch put his tongue out too and nodded. "It's the same scent... it's here."

"No," said Horrik, "It's too faint. But..." she lifted her head and her tongue weaved in the air again, "it's been close by... definitely... but it's difficult... it's all mixed up with other scents... it's not clear enough to follow."

"So, what now?" asked Gratch.

"Find the dog," growled Horrik.

"The dog… yes," Gratch nodded, "But also I should be reporting to my Master and you to yours."

"But that might make us enemies!" Horrik's tongue slithered out and in, "We don't know, do we? It depends what's happened. We don't know who's in charge here. After all, the spell's gone. Our masters might have fought and... one beaten the other... or they might have both been beaten... or... Well, we don't know do we? We don't know anything."

"Let's watch the house then," Gratch's deep voice echoed in his great body, "Before we do anything we need to know more."

"And Jamaar..." Horrik said, "might be at the house."

They crept through the trees until they stopped and stared in surprise at the glass mushroom. A bright highlight from the moon reflected on the surface of the dome and they could see two people inside.

"The house has gone!" whispered Horrik in astonishment.

"Who are those people?" asked Gratch in a whisper.

"That's Old Howard sleeping there," whispered Horrik, "But the other... it's all wrapped up in blankets... it could be my Master, or yours, but I can't tell."

"This is bad," Gratch shook his head, "I can feel it. Maybe we should just leave."

"Let's watch first," Horrik whispered, "Find out what's happened. And *anyway*..." Her voice became a hateful growl. "Jamaar's been here." Her tongue snaked out again. "The scent is stronger here, but not strong enough to follow it. But he might return. I'm not leaving until I've killed Jamaar!"

"Alright," Gratch agreed.

Dawn was approaching as they moved back into the trees and quickly found a dip in the ground underneath some ferns where they could hide. They were tired and soon fell asleep.

Old Howard had sulked for most of the night in his new abode. He struggled to come to terms with everything that had happened to him. When he had escaped from the hut on Keill Island, he thought that things would improve for him. He desperately wanted to get back to his house and carry on living as he had lived before. Now everything had become much worse and the disappointment was almost too much to bear. He was trapped again but this time there seemed to be no chance of escape.

Also he had to keep holding the dreadful Hadia Stick to avoid the pain which wracked his body when he let go of it. Sometimes it would slip out of his hand as he slept and then the pain would wake him up and he would desperately grab hold of it again.

He did not even have a bed and the Troubler had taken all the blankets so he lay on bare floorboards. Thoughts had circled in his mind endlessly trying to work out some sort of plan but in the end he had realised there was nothing he could do to change anything and he began to cry.

After sobbing with misery for some time he finally fell asleep.

When he woke up, the sun was rising and the dawn chorus was resounding all around him. He looked out of the glass prison through blurry eyes and saw Amalek and Seph looking in at him. Aram and Halo were standing just behind them.

Amalek had brought some food for the Dark Wizard Troubler and they were astonished to see Old Howard in there as well. They thought he was still back at Wizard Elzaphan's Castle.

The flowers around the mushroom were still all bowing their heads in misery.

"Old Howard!" exclaimed Amalek, "How did you get in there?"

"Oy fell in," he grumbled, "Let me out... let me out now."

"We can't," answered Seph.

"Let me out," he pleaded, "An' where's moy 'ouse gone?"

"We can't let you out," repeated Seph, "This glass prison is to trap *him*," he nodded towards the Troubler who was still asleep in the centre, "Not for you... but now that you're in there there's nothing we can do."

Old Howard stared at them. His bottom lip began to tremor with anger and frustration. He opened his mouth to speak but then he changed his mind and his expression softened. Despair took over and he started crying again. He slumped down to the floor beside the glass.

"Do you want some food?" asked Amalek.

Old Howard did not answer and so Amalek threw the bag of food through the glass.

"Share it between you," said Seph, "Come on, Ammey, let's go."

They turned to go and stepped through the dew-laden grass to Aram and Halo. They mounted the unicorns and rode off to join the search for their parents.

Old Howard cried for some time and when he finally stopped he saw the bag of food in front of him and ate some.

For once his mind was not busy scheming or worrying which was very unusual for him. The crying had released some of his pain. He sat up and leant against the glass wall. Looking around he soaked up the scene and listened to the birds singing. He felt better than he had for a long time.

Then he saw something that he had noticed before. Feeni had warned him to ignore it when they were in the

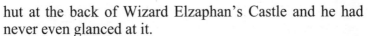

hut at the back of Wizard Elzaphan's Castle and he had never even glanced at it.

He was looking out at the flowers that surrounded the glass prison when his eye was caught by something shining brilliantly into his face. He looked down to see that it was coming from his stick.

The sun was reflecting brightly off the silver band on the middle of the stick. He drew the stick towards his face so that he could study it more closely. This was the first time he had paid it any attention. He saw it as a burden that he hated, a curse beyond measure.

He looked at it and began to see some words, beautifully engraved in the silver band. It was a poem and it spiralled down and around the silver. Then he found himself reading it:

Shun greed, Old Howard, and embrace
Generosity's more gentle ways.

Let your selfish frozen heart
instead of hate, true love impart.

Of all you have, give all you can
and you'll be known a wiser man.

Smile on those whose paths you cross
and leave them with more gain than loss.

As sure as winter wilts away
when spring awakens longer days,
then you will live a life of grace
in Generosity's kind embrace.

Old Howard was stunned. He was amazed that it was addressed to him. To read a poem was something

The Hadias Stick

Shun greed, Old Howard, and embrace
Generosity's more gentle ways.

Let your selfish, frozen heart
Instead of hate, true love impart.

Of all you have, give all you can
And you'll be known a wiser man.

Smile on those whose paths you cross
And leave them with more gain than loss.

As sure as winter wilts away
When spring awakens longer days,
Then you will live a life of grace
In Generosity's kind embrace.

completely new for Old Howard so he read it right through again. He turned the stick in his fingers to follow the words, and as he did he began to feel even better.

He was not sure what that meant. What were 'Generosity's more gentle ways'? He had been generous before, but that was so long ago in his childhood, and when it was not returned to him he gave it up and became bitter.

The words were changing him; just as the rising sun gradually melts the frost and ice of the chilly night, so was Old Howard's heart being thawed by the magic of the poem. He enjoyed the feeling of being lighter and happier so he read it for a third time.

Once again, the tears came and he cried like a little child, this time with guilt. The burden was almost unbearable as he looked back at his past actions. For the first time, Old Howard was realising what he had done.

He continued sobbing most of the day. Occasionally he would read the poem and then cry with regret, and wished he could go back in time and change his actions. The flowers around the mushroom drooped even more. Each time his crying stopped, he would read the poem again.

Evening approached. Old Howard was just reading the poem again when he suddenly fell back into the flowers. He jumped up in surprise. He was outside the mushroom! He slowly reached out his hand towards the glass and very gently touched it. He could feel nothing. He made a tiny movement with one finger and it went through. He saw the Hadia Stick lying on the floor inside and smiled. There was no pain.

His feelings towards the stick had changed from hate to love so he reached his arm through the glass, picked it up and pulled it out.

Old Howard's smile turned into a beam and his joy suddenly burst loose. He began jumping around and dancing in a very random fashion, looking as if he had no sense of coordination at all.

"Oy'm free!" he cried, "Oy'm free!"

Old Howard's abandoned celebrations woke up the Dark Wizard Troubler. For a moment his hair was white, and then darkened into black. He was on the other side of the mushroom and he sat up with a frown on his pale face.

"Stop all that noise!" he yelled.

Old Howard stopped and stared at him. Their eyes seemed to lock together. The expression on the wizard's face turned from anger into surprise. He stood up and strode towards Old Howard, holding him in his gaze.

"How did you get out?" he snapped.

"Oy don't really know," replied Old Howard. The happy beam had gone from his face. "Oy was leaning against the wall an' then oy just fell out."

The wizard stepped towards him and Old Howard recoiled, taking one step back. The glass wall was between them. Slowly the wizard reached out his hand and touched the glass; it was as solid as ever. He slapped his hand on it which made a smacking noise. Then he thumped it with a fist and the thud echoed around the mushroom.

"*How...* did you do it?" he demanded.

"Oy told you," said Old Howard nervously.

"No you haven't," the Troubler's words were sharp and intense, "What happened before you fell out?"

Old Howard thought.

"Oy was reading the Stick," he replied.

"Reading the Stick? What stick?"

Old Howard held it up. His hand was shaking with fear. Even though he was free and the wizard was trapped inside, they were standing so close and the glass seemed like no barrier at all. The Troubler had his eyes fixed on

Old Howard and saw something extraordinary happening; Old Howard's eyes were changing. In a few seconds they transformed from black to grey and then into pale blue. The wizard shuddered.

"What do you mean... reading the Stick?" he hissed.

Old Howard felt stronger but still his reply was a frightened stammer. "There's a... there's a p...poem on it."

"Show me," the wizard demanded.

Old Howard was caught by the Troubler's icy stare. He held out the Hadia Stick. As soon as the end of it passed through the glass the Troubler grabbed it and pulled. Old Howard fell forwards through the glass and stumbled onto the floor. He landed face down in front of the wizard who stood on his hand. Old Howard cried out in pain.

"Now," the wizard hissed dropping his head down close to the back of Old Howard's, "Tell me the truth... *how* did you get out?"

"Oy... oy... oy..."

The Troubler pressed his foot down harder.

"Ow! Oy read the poem and then oy fell out," he blurted out quickly, "That's what 'appened. 'Onest."

The wizard held the Stick up and began to read.

"Shun greed, Old Howard, and embrace..." He looked down at Old Howard and growled at him, "What is this?" Then he continued reading. "Generosity's more gentle ways... let your..."

He paused and reached out to touch the glass. It was still hard.

"This is ridiculous!" he snapped, "I'm not reading this rubbish!"

Suddenly the Stick moved by itself, slipped out of the wizard's grasp and whacked the Troubler hard on the leg. He lifted his leg in pain and Old Howard's hand was released. Immediately, Old Howard rolled over and scrambled through the glass and out of the mushroom. The Stick gave the wizard another whack on the leg and then floated out of the mushroom to Old Howard. He caught it with delight. The Hadia Stick, which he had hated so fiercely, now felt like his best friend.

Without looking back, Old Howard turned and walked towards the trees in the direction of Shaky Field. The Troubler watched him go and then sat down in the middle of his glass prison and bowed his head deep in thought.

The big search had moved today across the kingdom and to the east. The Flatsage Farmlands, Silvermay Forest and also the Marshes of Macaroone were being covered. In these marshes a man could be swallowed up in a matter of seconds and they hoped the Dark Wizard Troubler had not thrown the King and Queen in there, but they had no way of knowing. The Great Mountains would also present a major challenge.

The search proceeded on the land, in the air and also underground where any tunnels could be found. The day had passed without success and as the sun was setting the search was called off for the night.

Amalek and Seph rode up to the palace on Aram and Halo. The unicorns liked to spend the night outside on the front lawn where they were happy grazing and sleeping on the grass. They had no need to graze but enjoyed the fresh grass.

Seph dismounted and patted Aram on his golden side.

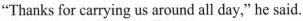

"Thanks for carrying us around all day," he said.

Amalek jumped down off Halo.

"Do you think we'll find them?" she asked.

Halo dropped her fine silver head and answered, "We'll try again tomorrow. There are still plenty of places."

The front door opened and Flop came out. His fluffy tail was up as he ran to greet them. They went in together and the children headed straight for a comfortable lounge where they could rest for a while.

It was a few hours later when Flop burst in.

"Quick!" he said, "Something's happening in the cellar. I've got Tilly and my kittens out."

"What's happening?" asked Seph as they ran towards the door.

"There's banging... from underneath the floor!"

They rushed down the main stairs to find a gathering of men in the hall. These men had the job of becoming guards and soldiers if needed but usually spent their days doing ordinary jobs around the palace or in the gardens. When the banging had started they quickly picked up their swords and ran to the downstairs hall.

"Into the cellar!" commanded Seph who fearlessly led the way down the steps.

Amalek followed amidst the swarming mass of men.

As soon as Seph was down the banging stopped as a wooden floorboard smashed upwards and a hand holding a rock appeared. Seph jumped back.

"Guards!" he shouted, "Swords ready!"

They quickly surrounded the broken floor.

No one moved as a face appeared at the gap in the floorboards.

"Seph!" exclaimed the King.

"Father!"

All the men got to work using their swords to force up the floorboards so that there was room for the king to get out. Seph and the men grasped his arms and pulled upwards, and amidst a cloud of dust he was lifted out of the hole. His clothes were tattered and dirty, his silver hair was grey with dust and he looked tired.

Everyone looked expectantly down the hole for the Queen. She emerged in a similar state and Amalek rushed into her arms. The King and Seph joined them and they hugged and kissed together in the sheer joy of each others company.

"We thought we might never see you again," said the Queen tenderly.

"So did we," said Amalek.

"And the Troubler?" asked the King, "Has he gone?"

"He's trapped," said Seph with glee, "In a glass mushroom!"

"What!?" laughed the King, "A glass mushroom is something I have *never* heard of before!"

He thought for a moment and then laughed again, "Wizard Elzaphan!"

The Prince and Princess smiled and nodded.

"So you beat him?" asked the Queen.

"Of course!" chorused Amalek and Seph together.

While they hugged, some of the men were looking down the hole in the floor. They saw a line of steps falling away into the darkness below. As they were looking down, one of them accidentally kicked part of a broken floorboard down the hole. It rattled down the steps until the sound faded away.

The reunited family left the cellar. The first thing the King and Queen did was to have baths before climbing the winding stairs to the Round Room where the table was set for a meal. Amalek and Seph were at the table with Flop

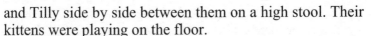

and Tilly side by side between them on a high stool. Their kittens were playing on the floor.

Aram and Halo were grazing on the lawn and Joog was in a tree waiting for all his guardian owls to report to him after the search. Joog was delighted to see Neville approaching on the wing. He was gliding above the Flatsage Farmlands and in a moment he was passing over some trees and coming into land on the lawn.

He hung his great webbed feet beneath him to act like windbreaks to slow him down. His long wings adjusted with tiny movements to hold him level. In spite of this, when he touched down he was still travelling too fast. His heels skidded onto the grass and he sped across the lawn, looking like a surfer on the ocean waves.

Joog took off and flew above him.

"Are you alright?" he called out.

"Of course," replied Neville.

He was heading for some trees, so he attempted to turn but lost balance. With a cry he fell and then rolled, with his wings thrashing the ground in a tumble of white feathers. He came to rest under a tree, stood up and shook his feathers.

Joog landed beside him.

"That was one of the worst landings I have ever seen!"

"Thank you," replied Neville, "I appreciate your…"

He stopped suddenly and looked across the lawn.

"Look!"

He was gazing in astonishment at a most surprising sight. It was Old Howard walking up Palace Path.

In the Round Room they were eager to exchange accounts of what had happened. Amalek and Seph went first, helped by Flop, until the King and Queen had heard all about it.

"It's an amazing story," commented the King, "Your courage has saved the kingdom." He glanced out of one of the gold-framed windows. "Look at that. Everything is right again."

The Queen had tears in her eyes as she looked at her children. "What you have done is the most wonderful thing... so courageous. I can hardly believe it."

"So, tell us your story," enquired Amalek.

"Our story," began the King, "Is not so courageous... no, we relied upon luck. It was extremely frightening though. Being frozen by the spell was... like being in a dark sleep and being dimly aware of what's happening around you... very dimly. And not being able to do anything at all. It was scary. The Troubler dropped us down The Silver Well."

"The Silver Well?!" exclaimed Seph, "That explains why we couldn't find you. But how did you survive that?"

"Well, as we were being dropped down the well we knew what was happening but only just. We could hear and see and feel very faintly. So we knew what was happening. First I was dropped down the well, then the Queen. But as I fell…"

There was a knock at the door and in walked Old Howard using his Hadia Stick to support the weight on his injured ankle. Immediately everyone jumped up in surprise. Old Howard stood there beaming at them.

He had never been to the palace before and in fact he had never wanted to go until today. Many other inhabitants of the Kingdom - humans, animals and birds -

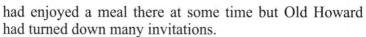

had enjoyed a meal there at some time but Old Howard had turned down many invitations.

They watched as he stood in front of them, his expression falling into one of deep sadness.

"Oy've come 'ere to apologise," he said, "Oy've been a fool... a selfish old fool. But now..." Old Howard's head dropped in shame, "But now oy feel bad... very bad about it all. Oy 'ave 'urt so many people. Oy don't think oy'll ever recover or be able to repay you all..."

Tears welled up in his eyes as he was overcome with emotion. He suddenly felt like a broken man.

Amalek and Seph walked over to him and helped him to a chair by the window. In spite of all that had happened they felt sorry for him now.

"What happened?" asked Amalek.

"It was this stick," he said, holding it up, "It's got a poem on it... and it's written to me."

Amalek took the stick and read the poem aloud as they all listened.

The King laughed. "That's typical of Wizard Elzaphan! He knew that was just what you needed."

"It's strange, you know," Old Howard began, looking up at the King, "Oy carried it all that toym without seein' that writing! It was there all the toym... in my 'and! Oy could've read it any toym and 'ave been free."

The Queen went over to him.

"Come and eat," she invited him, "We've been offering you meals for years... I hope you'll accept now."

"Well, yes Your Majesty," he replied.

He got up and sat down again at the table.

"This is an 'onour," he said, "To eat with you good people. But what can oy do to put all moy wrongs right?"

The King scratched his white beard thoughtfully.

"Hmm. There are jobs that need doing," he said, "So you could work for me. Your first job could be on

Spindley Tower - carrying materials up to repair it. It will be tough…"

"Oy don't care," Old Howard said, welcoming the idea, "Oy'll do it."

"Good. And you'll have to report to me..."

"It would be an 'onour, Your Majesty," he said as he smiled and bowed his head, "Oy would be 'appy to follow your advoyce on everything. Thank you greatly."

Chapter 15

~ Marli ~

Night descended upon the kingdom and everyone, all the people and creatures involved in the search, were in their homes and resting so that they could resume in the morning.

A while earlier Joog ordered his Guardian Owls to continue the search a little longer. The news of Darsan Lopery's disappearance was now well-known and Joog had decided that they should concentrate their search around Candara. This way they could look out for Darsan as they searched for the gems, and anyway, there could be a connection. They expected to find some clues at least to help explain where he had gone.

The night sky was dotted with owls gliding silently in circles above the town. Their powerful eyes scanned the land below, and whenever they saw anything unusual they would swoop down to investigate. Joog had organized them to work in particular areas, including of course Relbuort Cottage, and the plan was to gradually move outwards from there so that every piece of land would be covered.

It was not long before Marli saw something. She was a pigmy owl and only about the size of a sparrow, but her eyes were as good as any of the others and she could fly at speed in short bursts. She swooped down to inspect something reflecting the moonlight. It was nestled in some long grass growing in the river in Candara, just along from the bridge over the footpath.

She glided down, landed beside it on the bank and looked down between the blades of long grass growing from the river. It was a small wooden box, painted blue. The moonlight was reflecting as a bright dot of light on the metal of the hinges.

Marli hovered above and then flattened some of the grass with her feet. She reached down and tentatively nudged the box with her beak. It was probably nothing of any importance, but she was intrigued to see what was inside. It looked as though it could contain some jewellery, perhaps a ring, and she imagined a young man about to propose marriage to his girlfriend accidentally losing the engagement ring which he had bought with a year's savings.

Because she was so small, she wondered how she could carry it to the bank but when she tried to grasp it in her talons, her sharp claws pierced the wood. As she rose, she found to her surprise that it weighed nothing; it was like lifting a feather. This was very strange and she flew with it to the bank.

She dropped it onto the grass, skilfully unhooked the catch of the lid with her beak and opened it. The sight inside made her gasp with surprise. The pupils of her round yellow eyes contracted as they met a display of bright shining colour. Inside were three gems, picking up the light of the stars in the night sky and reflecting it back with greatly enhanced luminance.

The three gems were blue, purple and red, but in the meeting of these colours many hues and tints were created. She had never seen anything like this and knew straight away that these gems were special. She gazed at them for a moment. Her feathered face was covered with white and brown speckles but now it was a kaleidoscope of colour.

"The Candara Gems!" she thought with excitement, *"I've found the Candara Gems!"*

She quickly closed the box, picked it up in her talons and flew off through the night to report to Joog. He was in the top of a tree in the palace grounds. He saw her coming and called out.

"Marli!"

She landed beside him.

"What have you found?" he asked.

"This," said Marli lifting her foot and placing the box carefully and proudly on the branch.

"A box?" asked Joog, looking quizzical.

"Yes, but it's special," Marli sounded excited, "For one thing... it weighs nothing! And look inside and you'll see why it's so spacial."

Joog gazed at her with interest and then picked up the box with his much larger taloned foot. She was right; it was completely weightless.

Marli could not contain her excitement and blurted out, "It contains the Candara Gems!"

"What?" Joog raised his head in surprise.

"I think so anyway," she added as Joog undid the catch, "Take a look."

Joog opened the lid. The coloured light shone out and bathed everything around, including the two birds.

Joog sighed with relief.

"Yes," said Joog calmly, "It's them."

As he moved the box to inspect them carefully, the coloured light danced on his face and reflected in his eyes.

"Only the Candara Gems shine like this, Marli," he said, his eyes transfixed on them, "No other gems have the same amazing light. Well done. This is a wondrous find. What you have found… it's the most important thing you will *ever* find! But, where were they?"

"Near Candara, over there," and she nodded in the direction.

"Near Candara," he repeated, "How did they get there I wonder."

He shook his head and looked thoughtful.

"But where?" he asked.

"In the river," she replied, "Caught in some long grass."

"We'll take them into the palace," said Joog, "The King and Queen will be very pleased. Come on."

They took off and flew up to the Round Room.

The bushes under the tree where Joog and Marli had been talking, rustled. Feeni's head appeared. She looked all around and then hopped off towards the glass mushroom.

When Jamaar had collapsed in Silvermay Forest two days before, he nearly died. The loss of blood coupled with all the effort of running on three legs left him weak and exhausted. He lay there unconscious for the rest of the night and when he did finally come round it was well into the next day and he was shivering with a fever. His wound was becoming infected and it seemed likely that he would not survive. He needed some Rock Verthus leaves but he was too weak to move.

He opened his eyes from time to time and saw the trees around him but his mind was so confused he was not sure where he was.

Through the rest of the day and the next night he felt hot with the fever and panted continuously. He dropped in and out of restless sleep. However, when dawn rose on him for the second time his wound was healing and the infection was gone. He began to feel better. Through the day he just lay on the grass recovering. Night came and he fell asleep.

When he awoke, midnight had passed and he felt he was strong enough to continue his journey to the Kingdom of Moone. The night sky was a black dome above him, scattered with crystal-bright stars. A few clouds wandered across, occasionally hiding the moon but when it came out he could see quite well. The night was warm and he felt much better.

He was desperately hungry now and decided to go back to Candara because he knew the ideal place where he could steal some food. It was dark but he knew his way well and he had become used to walking and running on three legs.

Soon he was scavenging for food at the back of some shops in Candara. As he foraged around in dustbins and boxes his noises echoed along the deserted street. Everyone was sleeping.

When he had eaten his fill something stirred in him to pay one last visit to the Dark Wizard Troubler. He still felt that the wizard was his Master and this was drawing him back. He followed this pull until he arrived in the trees to the east of the glass mushroom.

He crept through some bushes until he could see the Troubler clearly huddled under the blankets. The moon came out and reflected on the glass mushroom in a sheen of silver light.

Suddenly he felt something move under one of his paws and he jumped in surprise. He stared down in shock and amazement. It was his leg, his severed leg! He reversed back into the bushes to get away but the leg moved after him, hopping as if controlled by a puppeteer. The moonlight reflected off it and Jamaar caught his breath in surprise. The leg was no longer furry but smooth and black.

It hopped towards him again and he cowered back. Suddenly, it moved swiftly at him, swishing through the air. He heard a click and felt a touch of cold on his wound. He looked down. The leg had reattached itself. Now he could see it was made of black metal.

He put his weight on it. It held. Then he lifted it up and wriggled it around, lifting the metal paw up and down and then turning it. It worked as normal. Moonlight glinted on its shiny, deep black surface.

Jamaar felt good. He was thrilled to have four legs again.

A sense of great power passed up through him. He felt he could conquer anything, and it was a feeling he recognised; it was the same when he started working for the Dark Wizard Troubler and now it was back. But it was stronger, much stronger. Coupled with this, he was being pulled by an irresistible urge to be serving his Master again and felt he would fight for him with his life.

Suddenly, pain racked his body as if he was about to explode. He squeezed his eyes closed in agony. The pain ended and he opened his eyes to find that he had become the muscular hulk again that he had enjoyed before. He was taller once more, as well as broader across his chest and back. His jowls were powerful again and his legs bulged with muscles.

He moved forwards and looked out through the bush and again something moved near his feet. He looked down to see a black compass. It clicked open and out came a two-tailed scorpion with a pair of wings folded on its back. It stopped and looked quickly around, moonlight glinting on its bone-hard body. After a few seconds, it turned towards the glass mushroom and began scuttling over the ground. Jamaar watched it go.

When it was halfway there, it stopped as if it had heard something. It tapped on the ground with its large front pincer. The earth moved just beside it and out climbed another scorpion. It pulled out its black compass on the chain and then left it on the ground as together they ran over towards the mushroom.

When they reached the glass they passed inside and then immediately turned back. In the silence of the night Jamaar heard them clicking and scraping against the glass.

He wondered if he should wake up the wizard but he decided he would wait and watch to see what happened. He lay down comfortably in the grass. His tired eyelids dropped and in a moment he was asleep.

Jamaar woke to the sound of voices and opened his eyes. The sky was lightening now as dawn approached. His head was resting on his paws and he moved his metal leg to check it was still working. Then, very slowly to avoid being seen, he lifted his head to look through the leaves of a bush towards the glass mushroom. He could see the Dark Wizard Troubler and the back of a hooded figure, and they were deep in conversation.

On the far side of the mushroom, behind the Troubler and hidden from the hooded figure, the two scorpions were busy cutting through the glass with their pincers. They were about two feet apart and had cut straight up for a few inches. Although they were working with great speed, their progress was very slow.

"Where are the gems now?" asked the Troubler, gazing intently through the glass wall at the hooded figure.

"I don't know," the figure replied, "The dog took them."

"What dog?"

"A dog... just a dog," the figure answered, "They were in a box and the dog stole them."

Jamaar could just about hear the hooded figure's words. He strained to listen, stepping cautiously forwards but making sure he was still hidden. The conversation was about him and the box he had stolen had contained the Candara Gems!

Then he noticed that the figure was holding a staff with a large gem on the top. It was a wizard.

"You let a *dog* take them?!" hissed the Troubler angrily, "The gems were stolen by a dog? Well, we must find the dog. Have you tried to find it?"

"I've tried, yes, of course," the figure snapped, "Of course I've tried."

"What does this dog look like?" the wizard asked.

"Black," the figure replied, "And with a leg missing..."

"Jamaar!" exclaimed the wizard, "That's *my* dog, Jamaar! But why was he stealing the gems... I don't understand..."

"That dog is bad," the figure said, speaking louder now. Jamaar thought he recognised the voice and stretched his head forwards a little more. "That dog's no good. Not trustworthy. It's the second time he's stolen from me... he stole my..." The voice stopped suddenly.

"Yes... stole what?" the Troubler asked.

Jamaar suddenly stepped out of the bushes. The hooded figure turned quickly and saw him.

Their eyes met.

"Jamaar?" questioned Harraine, sounding surprised. Her face and hands were ghostly white and her eyes pierced him with a glare that oozed evil. "That *is* you, is it? You're bigger... and your leg. What's happened to you?"

"It's me," growled Jamaar.

She looked surprised but continued.

"Jamaar, good dog," she said with mock friendliness, "Come here and we can talk."

"I want to tell my Master about the gems..." Jamaar said.

A sound behind him made him jump and turn his head to look. Horrik's huge frame loomed out of the darkness, saliva dripping from her mouth as she lurched towards him with a swift movement. He turned to face her as she lunged for him with a snap of her cavernous mouth. Before he could pull away, her jaws closed around his black metal leg. Horrik cried out in pain as her teeth scraped against the metal. Jamaar's felt no pain and his leg slipped free.

Horrik thrusted her great head forwards again but she was more cautious now. Jamaar was still afraid and backed away. He held his leg out in front in defence.

Harraine suddenly swung her staff through the air. Green light flashed from the huge jade stone on the top, scattering green frost on the ground and crackling like a firework.

Jamaar cowered to the ground and Horrik stopped her attack.

"What's going on?" demanded Harraine, her voice harsh and stinging.

"Horrik!" exclaimed the Troubler who was staring out from the glass mushroom.

Then there was another rustle in the bushes and Gratch appeared, pulling his huge form forwards on clawed feet.

"And yet *another* one to join the party," Harraine exclaimed with surprise.

There was a moment when everyone was trying to work out what was happening.

"I am at your service," said Gratch to Harraine, his deep voice echoing in his chest as if in a great cavern, and he dropped his head in a small bow, "I am ready to serve."

His tongue flicked out and then in. Harraine stared at him, and her eyes narrowed as she tried to work out she should accept. Then she smiled.

"A good choice," she said, "The best choice you have ever made."

On the far side of the mushroom, the two scorpions were still cutting away at the wall. The Troubler glanced back at them and this had an immediate effect; although they were already working at an amazing speed, with their legs moving faster than the eye could see, they somehow managed to speed up even more. No one else had seen them.

Horrik then spoke. Venomous saliva dribbled out of her mouth and her voice husky and slow. "I will serve too but I need to kill Jamaar first. He tried to kill me... and we are very hungry."

Jamaar looked terrified and cowered lower but then he remembered what his black metal leg had done. He leapt at Horrik and struck her with his new leg. It knocked her sideways and she cried in pain.

Harraine laughed.

"Looks like you've met your match," she said.

Horrik looked at Jamaar with hate and roared at him. She drew her head back and then jerked it sharply forwards, spitting at him. Jamaar dodged and the deadly saliva hit a small bush making it sizzle and smoke.

"Stop!" hissed the Troubler from inside the glass mushroom, "We work together!" His voice carried a power that forced them all to listen to him. "We work together. All of us. Do you hear?" He glared at Horrik. "All of us. I'll need some questions answered, especially from you."

He turned to Jamaar, nodding at him. "That leg makes you *really* one of us. Now you've got that you can't go off on your own little schemes anymore. You have to serve *me*." Then he turned to Harraine and said again with irresistible authority in his voice, "We must all work together."

"That's right," she said, "Together we are strong... we will all gain from it."

The tension relaxed and Jamaar and the two Komodo dragons stepped towards Harraine. Horrik glowered at Jamaar and he shook his head slowly at her as if to say 'you can't get me now.' Then he lifted his metal leg, waved it threateningly at her and walked around Harraine to hide behind her.

"We will work together…" continued Harraine, her voice seething with evil. She turned and glowered at the Troubler. "But… with *me* in charge."

The Prince and Princess closed the palace door and walked across the dew-covered lawn towards the unicorns. Dawn pressed upon the dying night. The morning star was dissolving into the brightening sky and some birds had started singing.

Amalek had prepared some food to take to the Dark Wizard Troubler. The children had started doing this every morning and they enjoyed riding the unicorns down Palace Path to the glass mushroom. She had woken Seph and with a little persuasion because he was always still in bed at this time, he had managed to get out of bed. Now he was up and had shaken off his sleep, he was enjoying the fresh early morning sights and sounds.

Aram and Halo saw the children coming and started walking towards them. The unicorns' powerful forms moved with fluid grace and stood out against the darkness of the trees behind them. Halo shook her head and silver sparks flew from her mane, shining brightly in the fresh morning twilight.

The children greeted the unicorns with delight, patting them on their strong flanks. Seph ran his fingers along the spiralling surface of Halo's alicorn. Then he mounted Aram, and Amalek swung up and onto Halo's back.

"To the glass mushroom?" enquired Aram.

"Yes," Seph replied, then turning to his sister, "Have you got the food for him, Ammey?"

"Yes," she nodded and patted her bag, "It's in here."

"I hope Wizard Elzaphan can come soon," Seph commented, "Then he can sort out the Dark Wizard Troubler."

"That would be good," Amalek replied, "Even though he's locked in there he still gives me the creeps."

"I know," agreed Seph, "But at least he is trapped. He'll have to just stay there for a while."

Aram and Halo started walking down the Palace Path. Amalek reached out and stroked Halo's silver mane; it felt as smooth as silk.

"Halo?" asked Amalek.

"Yes?" Halo replied, her voice clear and gentle.

"You know how you come to life when the kingdom needs help?" Amalek began, "Well, now that the danger is over…" she paused, finding it hard to ask the question and fearing the answer, "will you become statues again?"

"Of course," Halo replied kindly, "But don't think about that now. Just enjoy today."

As soon as they had passed through the gates, the unicorns gathered speed and broke into a trot.

The Troubler had not reacted to Harraine's statement but just stared through the glass at her. She had turned to Horrik and Gratch and demanded that they work under her command. They had agreed.

The Troubler was keeping an eye on the scorpions with an occasional discreet glance. They had just completed the three sides of the square they were cutting out of the glass and had met in the middle of the horizontal cut. With a whirr of their wings, they dropped and started cutting the last side of the square which was next to the ground.

Harraine reached down and patted Jamaar on the head with an icy-cold hand. Her voice was soft and kind. "Where are the gems?"

"I don't know," he replied.

"*You* had the box," she stated, her voice quiet but firm, "therefore, the only question is, where is the box now?"

"I dropped it," he said.

"What?!" she looked shocked, "You dropped the gems? The *precious* gems?"

"I didn't know what was in the box, did I?" pleaded Jamaar, "I didn't know. I lost the box when I was swimming in the river. It was in my mouth and then it was gone."

"So, *if* we believe you," she said sarcastically, "They are lost... somewhere in a river. So it's impossible to find them. That's very convenient." Then her voice turned hard and cutting and she gripped one of Jamaar's ears and pulled upwards. "Now... tell me the truth. Where have you hidden them?"

"He's telling the truth," said the Troubler with certainty.

"How do you know that?" Harraine asked, turning to face him.

"The leg," he replied, "With that leg he *has* to serve me."

Harraine nodded and released Jamaar's ear.

"Alright," she said, "But he'll serve me now. What he is saying then, about the river... means that the gems are lost."

The Troubler stepped towards the glass.

"And trying to find them in the river is impossible."

A noise made him stop. They all turned as Feeni hopped out of the trees towards them.

"They've got the gems," she said, "They've got the gems in the palace."

"How do you know that... and who are you anyway?" asked Harraine.

"She works for me," the Troubler said.

"I listened, as you wanted, Master," Feeni said hopping forwards and closer to the glass mushroom. She sat on her back legs and then bowed low to the wizard, "And I heard; an owl found them in the river and took them to *the* owl... the snowy owl... so *they've* got them."

"Anything else?" he asked, and then sarcastically, "Any more good news?"

"They are searching, Master," Feeni continued, "For the King and Queen."

"And have they found them?"

"No," she replied.

"Well that's good at least," he sneered, "And they won't find them either. Apart from that... it's all one big disaster." His voice was quivering now with controlled anger. "*They* have the gems... my spell's destroyed..." He kicked the glass wall in frustration. "But... but... even now, all is not lost."

"I will be out soon," he continued, his voice now utterly calm, "And now we're all together we can conquer this kingdom again. I like it here." He looked around. "But with all that has happened it makes *them* more powerful. It'll need a strong spell and..."

"You forget already," Harraine interrupted aggressively, spitting out the words, *"I* decide things now... and anyway, you're in there, in prison, and useless to anyone..."

She paused. He glowered back at her. Her words seemed to hang in the icy air between them.

"But, yes, working together..." she continued, "if you ever escape, then yes, you can join me. But with *me* in charge... I will take this kingdom…"

At this moment the scorpions finished the square of glass and it fell outwards and onto the flowers. The Troubler turned quickly, lay down, pushed his staff through the square hole first and then slipped lithely through. He was free!

Harraine's eyes flared with anger as she watched him through the glass as he stood up on the other side of the glass mushroom and grabbed his staff.

His feet crushed some flowers as drab shades of grey spread around him and a wave of deeper coldness bit the air. His breath hissed out in clouds. Harraine watched him intently.

The scorpions flew around the stem of the mushroom and back to their compasses. The Troubler followed the one that flew into the bushes, striding quickly after it. It got back into its compass and pulled the lid closed. The Troubler grasped the compass and hung it around his neck on its chain. The other scorpion was back in its compass now as well and the wizard picked it up and slipped it around his neck where it clinked against the first one.

Harraine held out her hand. A deep frown etched into her pale forehead. "And one for me?" she asked impatiently.

The Troubler bumped his staff gently on the ground to check it was working again. The huge garnet gem flashed red and lit up the area around.

"You must learn…" he hissed at her, "Who is *really* in charge here."

Their eyes were fixed on each other like two wild animals about to fight. The Komodos, Feeni and Jamaar all backed away.

"I have told you…," she began.

The Troubler stepped towards her, leaning forwards with hostility. She lifted her staff and a green flash burst from the jade stone. He staggered back, knocked by the blast. She moved to attack again swinging her staff and releasing a sweeping flash that sent him reeling and he fell to the ground. He lifted his staff but she was too quick. Another green flash hit him and sent him skidding across the wet grass.

In a moment he was on his feet. Harraine stepped towards him again but this time he was much too fast as he lifted his staff and pointed it at her. The red flash was brighter, exploding from the garnet in her direction. The impact threw her to the ground and she cried out in pain.

He pointed his staff again and another flash hit her. She cried out once more, unable to get onto her feet and holding up her hand in submission.

"Stop, stop!" she cried.

He strode towards her, glaring with angry disdain. He pointed his staff at her again and bent down until his head was close to hers.

"Never…" he hissed softly, shaking the staff as a threat, "Never… *never* test me again. Understand?"

Harraine cowered beneath him.

"Alright," he said, his voice sinister and cutting with an ultra smooth tone, "I think we know who's in charge. Don't we?"

She stared up at him but did not reply.

"*Don't we?*" he snapped.

"Yes," she grovelled sulkily.

"You work for me now?"

Her face was hard with anger as she made one small, reluctant nod.

"Good," he sneered.

He straightened up and looked around at everyone.

"You all know I'm Master here?" he asked.

They all nodded and made sounds of agreement. He turned his attention to Horrik.

"How have you got two compasses?" he asked her.

"I found them Master," she growled back.

He stepped towards her, grasped the chain of one of them and pulled it over her head and off her scaly neck. He inspected it, turning it over in his hand. He saw his coat of arms but was shocked to see a Komodo dragon on the top right instead of the crescent moon. He knew what this meant. Before he made the journey to The Kingdom Of Gems one of his compasses had been stolen. This was it. Only a wizard or a witch would have the power to change the coat of arms and the only reason for this would be to change the compass and make it theirs. Someone had begun this change.

He looked up and glared accusingly at Harraine who was on her feet again. Then he looked back at the compass. He stared intently at it, and as he did the Komodo dragon changed back into a crescent moon. Then he tossed it to Harraine who caught it.

"Put it on," he commanded.

She obeyed. She had been put in her place and she did not like it. The Troubler checked the other compass that still hung around Horrik's neck, studying the coat of arms, and saw that it was his. Then he lifted one of the two that were around his own neck and hung it over Gratch's great head.

"Good," he said and looked around at the others, "Now we are all together."

"What about me, Master?" asked Jamaar.

"You don't need a compass, dog," he said, "Because you've got that metal leg."

Feeni hopped forwards.

"And me?" she asked, "I need a compass too."

"No," he said firmly, "Around you're neck you have a piece of gold…"

"It's gone rusty now, Master, like iron."

"Of course," he hissed, scowling with annoyance, "But you also have a gem which came from this." He pointed to the huge red garnet gemstone on the top of his staff. "It came from here when this stone was cut."

"But…" she looked puzzled, "I found it… it's mine."

"No, it's mine," he snapped, "It's a loan from me to you… so be thankful! It makes you one of us."

When the garnet gemstone for his staff had been cut some time ago, he had sent seven pairs of ravens on journeys with a specific task to complete. He gave each pair a bit of the garnet, a little gem, which had been chipped off the large stone. He directed the ravens to drop them in different kingdoms knowing that whoever found them would be affected by them; their minds and hearts would be polluted with his evil.

In his search for kingdoms to take over, he would have his own accomplices already in the kingdoms. Feeni was the first one he had made contact with. Already, she had served him well.

He glanced around. It was light now. The sun's first morning rays were catching the top of the glass mushroom. Suddenly, the wizard jerked his head around in alarm. The sound of hooves on soft earth made them look towards Shaky Field.

"Quick!" said the Troubler.

He moved over to Gratch and pulled himself up onto the dragon's back.

"Master," growled Gratch, "This is an honour."

"I want to come too!" said Feeni.

"Of course," the Troubler replied leaning down and grabbing Feeni by her ears, making her squeal in pain as he swept her up and onto Gratch.

"Harraine," ordered the wizard, "You ride on Horrik."

Horrik bent a front leg and Harraine clambered up.

"And Jamaar too," ordered the Troubler, "On Horrik's back. Quick!"

Horrik churned inside with anger at Jamaar as he leapt towards her back. She moved sideways and he crashed onto the ground and rolled over.

The Troubler glanced behind to see the unicorns trotting through the trees.

He struck Gratch on his neck with his staff and commanded, "Go!"

The two Komodo dragons were very fast runners and they accelerated into the trees to the south with Jamaar running after them. They crashed through some bushes, flattening them as they thrust their way through.

At that moment, Aram and Halo came out of the trees and towards the glass mushroom.

"He's escaping!" exclaimed Amalek, pointing, "Look! On a Komodo!"

" But how did he get out?" blurted Seph.

"It doesn't matter," she cried, "Let's get after them!"

Aram and Halo pursued, running straight into the glass mushroom and out the other side, and then into the trees. They were closing already and the children were leaning forwards and holding on tightly to the unicorns' flowing manes.

The Komodos stopped suddenly and turned to face the unicorns. Jamaar stood beside them baring his teeth. The Troubler wielded his staff in one hand and swung it through the air. A blast of red light flashed and hit a tree which snapped off near its base like a matchstick and fell in front of Aram with a mighty crash. Aram could not stop in time and he skidded into it sending Seph flying off and falling into a patch of ferns.

Halo swerved to avoid Aram and her alicorn plunged into the tree trunk and stuck there. Amalek was also thrown off and landed close to her brother.

Harraine pointed her staff now and this time green light flashed towards Aram who defended himself with a flash from his alicorn. The Troubler sent another dazzling explosion of red light towards the golden unicorn. Again, Aram defended himself and then sent a blast at the wizard who leant to one side, avoiding the main force of it.

"Aahh!" he cried as it fizzed around him and he glared furiously at Aram.

The children were on their feet just as Jamaar attacked. The huge dog was slavering at the mouth as he leapt into the ferns, growling and staring threateningly at them. Seph stepped towards him, grabbed a large stick and held it out in front of him with two hands, pointing it at Jamaar.

"Run Ammey!" Seph shouted, "Run!"

She ran towards Halo.

Jamaar lunged forwards at Seph and bit through the stick as if it was a matchstick. Then he swung his metal leg at the remainder that Seph was holding. It was ripped from Seph's grip and sent spinning away. Seph backed off, still facing Jamaar, stumbling away with feet slipping in panic. Jamaar got ready to pounce, his legs charged with energy.

"Dog!" shouted the Troubler, "Leave them! Follow!"

Jamaar was wild with hunger and out of control, and he ignored the command.

The Troubler turned to Harraine and shouted at her, his words fast and urgent.

"We'll go... the power is too even here now. It's too risky. South is the quickest way out of this kingdom. Then we'll go west to Gugeol."

"I want to go to Agulta," argued Harraine.

"I decide," he hissed at her.

"But..." she began.

"No!" he shouted.

He glared at her with an intensity that silenced her.

"We go to Gugeol," he snarled.

Meanwhile, with untamed ferocity, Jamaar leapt at Seph. Seph grabbed another stick but fell onto his back and Jamaar landed on him, his front paws pinning him to the ground. Jamaar bared his teeth again and growled, droplets of his saliva spraying onto Seph's face.

A flash from Aram headed towards Jamaar and he lifted his metal leg in defence. The bolt of gold light hit it, knocked Jamaar sideways and then shot up into the branches of the tree which burst into flames. The huge dog jumped up and slammed his metal leg down into Seph's ribs. Seph winced in pain.

"Seph!" cried Amalek, "Seph!"

"Dog!" shouted the Troubler even louder, "Leave them! Now!"

Jamaar glared down at Seph, baring his teeth and growling. Then he obeyed his Master, overwhelmed by the command, and reluctantly pushed off Seph to run to the wizard. The Troubler kicked his heels into the sides of Gratch to make him turn. Horrik and Jamaar followed and they all bolted out of the trees and towards the river.

Seph struggled onto his feet, holding his ribs, and bending forwards in pain. He staggered to Aram, stepping onto a log and then ignoring the pain as he hauled himself onto Aram's back.

"Are you alright Seph?" asked Amalek.

"Of course," he replied bravely, and then shouted urgently, "Come on! After them!"

Aram turned.

"Halo!" he exclaimed.

Amalek was helping Halo who was straining to pull her alicorn out of the tree. Suddenly, it came loose and they both fell back.

Amalek jumped onto Halo, "Let's get after them," she shouted, "Come on!"

They galloped out of the trees and towards the River Tazer.

"Amalek! Seph!" called a voice from above.

They looked up to see Joog gliding silently on outspread wings with Neville beside him and his long multicoloured stripy scarf flowing behind.

"Joog!" exclaimed Amalek.

The children felt strengthened by the presence of the two birds who swooped down until they were just above their heads. Then Amalek heard a squeak. She held on tightly to Halo's mane as she glanced down to see Miriam climbing out of her pocket.

"Miriam!" she said in surprise.

The tiny harvest mouse climbed onto Amalek's shoulder and clung on with her sharp claws while the two birds flew above them. She had just woken up.

"What's happening?!" she squeaked, "What's happening?!"

"We're chasing the Troubler," Amalek replied, "He's escaped."

The unicorns dropped down a slope and approached the River Tazer. They saw the Komodos swimming across, climbing out on the other side and then turning to look back. The unicorns reached the bank and stopped, looking over the water at the Komodos.

The Troubler swept his staff through the air and sent a shaft of dazzling red light sizzling above the river. Aram and Halo both dropped their alicorns and sent blasts of light to intercept it. Gold, silver and red light met in an explosion above the water which bubbled and steamed with the heat.

Harraine then sent a green blast fizzing low across the surface, turning the water to ice which crackled as it fractured and split. Before the blast reached the other side the unicorns intercepted it with more flashes from their alicorns.

"Go!" shouted the Troubler.

The Komodos turned and ran southwards, still taking the quickest route to the border. Once they were out of the kingdom, a right-hand turn would take them westwards towards Gugeol.

The land sloped up into Heather Heights and the Troubler knew the border was not far away. Jamaar powered along beside them.

The unicorns ran straight into the river, their feet smashing into the newly-formed ice. It was a struggle, as the green ice gathered around their feet, gripping their hooves and sending freezing cold up their legs.

The children held on tightly. Gradually, the unicorns fought their way across until they reached the other side and leapt onto the bank. They could see the Komodo dragons racing up the hill in front of them, now well ahead.

Joog and Neville glided above, staying close to Amalek and Seph. They were watching and waiting for any opportunity to help. Up ahead, the Komodos reached the top of the hill, dropped down a gentle slope and rose again up the next hill. Their powerful legs pounded the ground to thrust them along at a good pace.

The sun cast a bright morning light upon the slopes of the hills which were tinted with the purple of the heather. Across this tranquil scene, the Komodos moved with dynamic energy. They were charged with primordial power and the two wizards made the most of it, urging them on with shouts of "Get along!" and "Keep going!" and "Faster!" If they slowed at all they would receive a stinging blow from the wizards' staffs.

Jamaar enjoyed having his powerful body back again. His legs were so strong that he could easily keep up and his black metal leg was untiring.

The unicorns ran with all the power of thoroughbred horses and a lot more. Their muscles forged them through the heather with masterly control and strength but at the same time they were moving with sublime grace. They were intent on catching up and were closing all the time. It was a race to the border.

The gap closed until the unicorns were within striking distance. They lowered their horns to attack. A crackle of light, like gold lightening, flashed from Aram's alicorn. Before it reached the fleeing Komodos, the Troubler had intercepted it with a flash from his staff. Halo tried and this time Harraine fended it off. Then one of Aram's flashes got through and hit Feeni, just catching her on her back. She cried out and tumbled off Gratch, spinning through the heather in a fast roll.

Just in front of them, the land changed suddenly from the heather-covered hills into a flat rocky plain. This was the border, marked by the abrupt change.

"We're at the border," Halo called out, "We can go no further."

Both unicorns sent another shaft of light flashing from their alicorns. Halo's hit the Troubler in the shoulder with a flash of silver light and he cried out in pain. Aram's hit the invisible border in mid-air, exploding like a firework.

The Komodos and their riders hurtled across the border into the Kingdom of Sumlaire, with Jamaar right behind them. Aram and Halo pulled up and tried to stop before the border, their hooves sliding on the heather. Halo stopped just in time but Aram stumbled, his legs folding under him as he crashed down. Seph tumbled off just before Aram skidded over the border.

"No!" cried Seph.

He could do nothing about it. Through the dust-filled air he could see Aram; he was only just over the border, no longer a powerful creature full of life, but lying on his side as lifeless as a rock.

Joog was now hovering just above and Neville was swooping down, his magic scarf trailing behind him.

Just ahead, the Komodos skidded to a halt on the dry rocky earth, throwing up clouds of dust around them. Feeni had managed to hop across the border, the fur on her back badly singed and one of her ears bleeding. She stared back at Halo with fear and then turned to see Aram lying in front of her, a lifeless golden statue.

The Komodos were breathing heavily after their long run; breath hissing out in misty clouds from their nostrils. Jamaar was panting. For a few seconds, as the dust settled, they stared at each other across the border.

One of the Troubler's arms was hanging loosely by his side, the shoulder shattered by Halo's bolt of light. He winced in pain and then turned his attention to his pursuers. His gaze drilled into them with icy force. The children felt numb inside but were strong enough now to resist it.

"The strength lies within," Seph said quietly to his sister, "Remember? We can stand up to him now."

Amalek nodded, feeling strong.

"Yes," she said quietly.

She whispered something to Miriam and lifted her magic star-box out of her bag.

The evil wizard glanced down at Aram, spat on him in disgust, making a sound of hollow metal, but it was a pure note which rang out beautifully like a drop of water in a still pool. The wizard winced.

"Crush it's skull, Gratch!" he ordered.

Gratch lifted one of his powerful clawed feet and smashed it down on Aram's head. This time the sound was louder but equally beautiful; it was a perfect chord ringing in the air. Aram's head was undamaged.

Gratch looked puzzled. "Shall I try again, Master?"

"No!" snapped the wizard quickly, "Stupid animal! Can't you hear it... that sound... it's taking our power!"

Then he looked at the others again and his black eyes filled with hate.

"You think you've won, don't you?" he sneered.

"We have," stated Seph defiantly, "It's over."

The wizard frowned and shook his head. Then he hissed slowly and deliberately, "No... this is not the end."

Jamaar was glowering intently at them across the border. He looked fierce and eager, as if he could hardly stop himself leaping across and attacking. Gratch opened his great mouth and released a loud roar at them which shook the air so much that it seemed to shake their bones. Horrik scraped the rocky earth with her claws; she was ready for action too.

The Dark Wizard Troubler looked down at Feeni and Jamaar.

"On the dog's back," he snapped.

Jamaar lay down to let Feeni clamber onto him. Then he stood up.

The wizard rested his staff on Gratch's back and reached down with his good arm. He grabbed Feeni by the ears again. She squealed and kicked her legs.

"Keep still!" ordered the wizard.

"It hurts!" Feeni exclaimed.

Feeni managed to stop wriggling and the wizard placed her on Gratch's back. He took hold of his staff again and looked back across the border. Then he slowly lifted his staff.

They knew they were defenceless. There was nowhere to escape and nothing to hide behind.

The wizard suddenly ducked as something caught his eye. Joog was diving at him from above. He just had time to lift his arm in defence, and Joog glanced off it. He rose through air, leaving a couple of his feathers floating near the Troubler's head. The evil wizard lifted his hand to his cheek where he felt three deep parallel scratches oozing with blood.

He looked back across the border where Seph was struggling towards Aram, finding it hard to move after Jamaar's blow to his stomach.

"No, Seph!" cried Amalek from Halo's back.

Seph stopped.

Joog had circled and was attacking again. The Troubler pointed his staff at him, releasing a dazzling ray of red. A quick movement with his wings and Joog had dodged the blast. Harraine fired a green shaft of light at him which also missed and soared high into the sky.

Then Halo joined in, sending a shaft of silver light flashing from her alicorn towards the wizard but it smashed into the invisible border, spraying light in all directions.

The wizard laughed.

"You are powerless!" he exclaimed.

Joog was upon him again. The wizard saw him just in time, swinging his staff at him and hitting him on the side with a thud. In a flurry of feathers, Joog was sent spinning to the ground. He lay there, unconscious.

The wizard lowered his staff and pointed it at the Prince, and then at the Princess. They were at his mercy and he wanted to savour his moment of success.

"Before I dispose of you..." he began.

"I'll do it!" cried Harraine, pointing her staff across the border.

"No!" the Troubler barked, with the full force of his evil authority, "I'm dealing with this."

She glared at him and then stabbed out her words aggressively. "Do it quickly!"

"I will," he replied, "But before our friends are gone, forever," he hissed, "They have a right to know what will happen to their beloved kingdom because they won't be here to see it again." His eyes seemed blacker than ever as he glared at the prince and princess. "I will cast another spell, more powerful. The kingdom, and all it's riches, and the Candara Gems... all this will be mine. I will rule here..."

"Get on with it!" interrupted Harraine impatiently, "I'm not waiting any longer!"

With one quick movement, she lifted her staff, aimed at Seph and released bolt of green light straight at him.

At the same moment, Neville appeared. He had been rushing towards them, descending from above, his great wings outspread and his magic scarf draping below. The end of the scarf was curled up, and riding in it was Miriam, with a pile of gold dust all around her.

Miriam swept some gold dust out to intercept the bolt of green light; the timing was perfect. The bolt hit the gold dust and was deflected, shooting instead towards the Dark Wizard Troubler. He started lifting his staff but was too late. It hit him in his injured shoulder, a mixture of the icy green blast and gold dust.

"Ahhh!" cried the wizard.

He dropped his staff, and his face twisted in agony. He grasped his shoulder with his hand but the green ice had already entered through the wound. It spread like ink into blotting paper. A moment later, he was frozen, as still as a tombstone. Then, gradually, he became translucent, like green frosted glass. In eerie slow motion, he began to fall forwards, the ice cracking on the surface with a thousand tiny fractures. He slumped onto Gratch's neck, with one arm either side, and balanced there.

Harraine immediately took command.

"South to Agulta!" she ordered, "All of you!"

Horrik turned her huge frame and started running southwards. Gratch followed, carrying the Dark Wizard Troubler's slumped lifeless body, as well as Feeni, on his broad back. Jamaar was right behind them.

Amalek slipped off Halo's back and rushed over the border to Aram. Seph struggled across, holding his stomach.

"This side," said Seph, "We'll push him back over the border... come on!"

They put all their strength into the job but after the third try, they only managed to move him slightly. They paused to gather their strength and saw one of his hooves twitching with life. It had passed over the border.

"Oh, good, good!" exclaimed Halo, "Well done."

She dropped her head, gripped his hoof between her alicorn and her hoof, and with great ease, pulled Aram back across the border. As he crossed over, life rippled through his golden body and he scrambled onto his feet.

"Thank you," Aram said, his voice as rich and smooth as liquid gold.

Amalek had picked up Joog and carried him back to the others.

"Joog," she said anxiously, shaking him, "Joog!"

He opened his eyes and said, "I'm alright... I'm fine." He lifted up his head with a jerk, remembering what had been happening. "But, where's the Troubler?"

"There," said Amalek, pointing across the border, "He's dead."

For a few moments, they gazed across the great plain in front of them in silence. They could still see the Komodos and their riders heading south, now just tiny figures throwing up a cloud of dust as they moved. They grew smaller until eventually they were out of sight.

Neville was gliding above them now without a flap, his great wings outspread as he worked the air currants. His scarf, now longer than ever as if in celebration, flowed behind him with Miriam peeping out.

Seph held his side and stomach, and sighed with a mixture of pain and relief.

"He's gone," he said.

Amalek beamed at him. "It's amazing, isn't it? I can't wait to tell Wizard Elzaphan."

Aram smiled, and spoke kindly. "You two can be extremely pleased about what you've done," he said, "And what about little Miriam?! The smallest one of us did the most important job!"

"And Joog," added Halo, "And Neville. What a group of heroes! It's a great achievement."

Joog looked comfortable in Amalek's arms. "We've beaten him twice!" he hooted, "Ow! My ribs!"

Amalek stroked him affectionately and very gently on his back. Halo lifted a hoof and dropped it back to the ground.

"You've all been wonderful," she said kindly.

Seph nodded contentedly and tried to climb onto Aram's back.

"I'll help you," Amalek said.

She lifted Joog onto Halo's back as she slid off. Then she helped Seph.

"Thanks," he said, "I think it's my ribs too."

He smiled at Joog. "We'll need lots of looking after."

"Lots!" agreed Joog, who laughed again and then grimaced.

Seph patted Aram on his broad neck. "We could never have done it without you... it was everybody all together."

"Where's Neville?" asked Amalek, looking up.

Joog laughed and then winced. "Ow! I ordered him to stay in the air. Something told me this was not the time for one of his wonderful displays of worst landings ever!"

They all laughed.

"Can you fly?" asked Seph.

He jumped off Halo's back, glided in a small circle and landed on Seph's shoulder.

"Painful," he commented, "But not too bad."

Neville swooped just above their heads and Amalek felt the warmth of his magic scarf brush her cheek. Miriam jumped off and landed on Amalek's shoulder.

"Well done, Miriam," she said, "You were amazing!"

The tiny harvest mouse snuggled up to her neck.

"How about a riddle?" Neville called from above.

The children laughed. They felt the happiness that relief brings.

"Yes, Neville," replied Seph, "Sing it to us."

Neville opened his great beak and sang:

More Attractive Than A Flower

"No human eyes will ever see
my form because I have none,
I have no size, I have no eyes,
I have no mouth or tongue.

I'm neither large, nor am I small,
I'm always here and there.
I can't be found below the ground
or above and in the air.

To call me nothing would be unfair.
I act with awesome power
throughout all space, in every place,
more attractive than a flower.

Without a movement I move all things,
whether large or small.
With invisible force I steer the course
of a galaxy, planet or ball."

~ NEVILLE'S 8TH RIDDLE ~

*"No human eyes will ever see
my form because I have none,
I have no size, I have no eyes,
I have no mouth or tongue.*

*I'm neither large, nor am I small,
I'm always here and there.
I can't be found below the ground
or above and in the air.*

*To call me nothing would be unfair.
I act with awesome power
throughout all space, in every place,
more attractive than a flower.*

*Without a movement I move all things,
whether large or small.
With invisible force I steer the course
of a galaxy, planet or ball."*

"That's difficult," said Seph, "Any ideas Ammey?"

"Not yet," she replied, "We need to hear it a few times... but it sounds *very* mysterious!"

"I'll tell you what," Seph said with a twinkle in his eye, "We'll try to solve it later, but now... race you to the river!"

"What about your ribs?" asked Amalek, climbing onto Halo's back.

"We'll still beat you!" he smiled, "Won't we Aram?"

"Easy," Aram joked.

Aram and Halo both took up the challenge and burst into action, and like springs released they accelerated away across the heather. Joog took to the air and flew side by side with Neville. They enjoyed a perfect view of the race from above.

Chapter 16

~ The Time Has Come ~

Amalek and Seph rode up the Palace Path on the two trotting unicorns. Joog and Neville had flown on ahead; Joog landed in a tree by the palace and Neville had crash-landed onto the grass. Aram and Halo slowed and then stopped when they reached the palace gates.

"The time has come..." began Aram as the children slipped off the unicorns' backs and landed gently on the ground.

They both looked at Aram who lifted his proud golden head and continued.

"The time has come. The Troubler is dead, the gems have been found and the kingdom is restored to peace. We have done our job."

The children had dreaded this moment. They knew it would come but they had tried to forget about it. The time had come to say goodbye and tears filled their eyes.

"But…" said Amalek, "we want you to stay as you are."

Halo looked at Amalek with loving eyes.

"I know," she said kindly, "And that would be wonderful, but it's not the way these things work. There's no choice about it, I'm afraid."

"I'm sure," began Aram, "that we'll meet again... I mean when we are called into action once more. But it will only be, unfortunately, when some kind of trouble arises and we are needed to fight against it. As statues we can still hear you and see you... we will watch and wait for the time when we are needed, so it's not so bad."

"We are happy to do this you know," said Halo gently, "It's a wonderful job we have. Being statues for a while is not like being caught in a spell! It's like having a rest... a very peaceful rest... and that's no problem for us. We rest and wait, and we're happy to wait as long as necessary. You'll come and see us from time to time and tell us the news?"

"Yes, of course" said Seph.

"And remember," said Aram, "We can always hear you."

"Yes," replied Amalek.

Hearing the unicorns talk and explain it was very comforting and she stopped crying. She wiped the tears away with a sleeve.

"Good," Aram said kindly, "So you won't forget as you grow older... we *will* hear you although we can't speak or move at all. Now go, and when you see us next, we will be statues again, but statues with a difference."

Amalek and Seph hugged the unicorns around their necks and stroked their manes.

"Good-bye then," Seph said.

He did not want to let go of Halo's neck. Amalek buried her face in Aram's golden mane and began to cry again. Seph was crying too but managed to let go and put his arm around his sister's shoulders.

"We must go," he said to her, "Come on, Ammey."

"I know," she said and they turned to walk away. "Bye," she said, trying to sound cheerful.

"Good-bye," said Aram and Halo together, then

Halo added, "Don't be sad."

They began to walk up Palace Path towards the palace.

"Oh," called out Halo, "Just one thing before you go."

They stopped and turned to listen.

"If danger does arise then you must let us know immediately. The sooner we find out the better."

Seph nodded.

The Prince and Princess turned back towards the palace and started walking again.

"You know, Seph," said Amalek, "I want them to come to life again, so badly, but... I don't want another troubler coming here!"

Seph smiled at his sister. "I feel the same," he said, "It's a strange situation. But we'll visit them every day."

"Definitely," Amalek was smiling now through the sadness, "And we can tell them the news... especially the bad news!"

"It might be tempting to exaggerate that a bit, Ammey!"

Amalek laughed. Then they saw Joog flying towards them. He swooped down and brushed Amalek's cheek with the tip of his wing.

"See you in the Round Room," he said as he rose in the air towards the high spire.

He had been witnessing the scene at the gates and this gesture and his cheery words somehow told them that everything was alright.

"Joog is amazing, isn't he?" Amalek said.

"The best," Seph agreed, "The very best."

At the door the children glanced back and saw the two unicorns jumping up onto the gate posts, first Halo and then Aram, and then rearing up on their back legs. Before their weight had pulled their front legs down, they became motionless.

"They are statues again," said Amalek.

"And now that it's happened..." said Seph, "And with all they said, it seems alright."

"I know what you mean," Amalek smiled, "It's meant to be. We'll visit them tomorrow."

Amalek opened the palace door and stepped in followed by Seph. The door closed behind them.

The next morning, dawn arrived bright and clear in The Kingdom Of Gems. The rain-dampened land glistened in the early morning sun with the joy of a new day. There was a different feeling in the air today because the finding of the Candara Gems and the death of the Dark Wizard Troubler had restored happiness and peace to the land. The warmth of the sun was like a healing hand to the kingdom recovering from the terrible spell. Bright rays glanced through the trees of the Wellspring Woods and Silvermay Forest where life was teeming everywhere. Blue Lake was without even a whisper of a wave and its mirror-like surface reflected the Snowpeak Mountains to perfection. The mountains themselves proudly overlooked the wide and wonderful landscape of a kingdom enjoying peace.

The people in Candara, Whitten and Charin woke up this morning with a joy in their hearts that had been missing since the spell had ended. The gems were already enriching their lives with the best qualities which would bode well for the future. Everything seemed to have been revitalised with goodness.

The inhabitants of Candara Palace were also enjoying the peaceful, happy feeling. They were going about their various tasks in good humour. In the Round Room the conversation around the breakfast table was happy. There were eight at the round table. The King, the Queen, Amalek and Seph were all there, as well as Flop and Miriam, Tally and Hawkeye. They were sitting on various chairs, stools and cushions. Joog's branch was there but this morning it was vacant.

A window was open, letting in fresh air and the sound of birds singing. Amalek looked across the table at her father.

"We still haven't heard what happened to you," she said.

"Oh yes," said the King, "I told you that we were thrown down the Silver Well, didn't I?"

"Yes," she agreed, "But that's all."

"Alright then," he nodded, "As I fell, the effect of the spell faded… it didn't extend right under the ground. I think the Troubler overlooked this… and so by the time I hit the deep underground lake I was free. I plunged deep before rising to the surface. It was…"

He looked up as Joog glided silently in through the open window, tucking his wings in skilfully and landing on his branch.

"Neville's just coming," he said.

"How are you?" asked Amalek.

"Oh, I'm fine," Joog replied happily, "I can't move properly with these broken ribs, but it will heal. Seph, how are you."

"Same thing!" he answered, "Three broken ribs, but for a good cause!"

"An excellent cause," commented the King, smiling at his son proudly.

They all looked towards the window to see Neville appear. He had to draw his great wings in, almost to his body. He crashed onto the table and slid along carrying with him the table cloth, bowls, cutlery, a variety of pots, a teapot, a jug of milk, cups and glasses. The whole lot fell off the end of the table with a great crash and the tablecloth wrapped around Neville as it fell.

They all rushed past the table and surrounded the tablecloth with all the broken bits of china scattered on the floor.

"Are you alright?" said Amalek looking alarmed and concerned.

Neville's head popped out from the cloth.

"Fine," he replied, "I think I misjudged that one… sorry. A slight problem with the landing. If only I'd had a little more room. And sorry about the breakfast!"

"Your landings," said Seph, smiling, "Are always equally bad but always great entertainment!"

Everyone laughed and helped to untangle Neville from the tablecloth. Then they helped clear up. More breakfast, new pots and bowls, and another tablecloth were soon brought and everything was laid out again. When everyone was settled again the King took out a small box from his pocket and placed it in the middle of the table among all the breakfast things. It was the Candara Gems.

The finding of the gems was a great relief but had left them wondering what had happened. No one knew the details of how they had been stolen and then ended up in a small box in the river. There were ideas and suggestions and they all pointed to Harraine of course. The protection of the gems stopped any intruder stealing them, but as she was a resident of the kingdom she could have done it.

The Queen reached out and opened the box. The gems shone out gloriously with their red, blue and purple brilliance, reflecting from shiny objects and refracting through transparent ones. The colours intermingled to produce a multitude of hues and shades which dotted the room everywhere. It was a spectacular display.

"Look at them!" the King remarked, gazing at the gems with admiration, "We've got them back. If only they could tell us the story of how they got into the river."

His thinning silver-white hair looked as though he had forgotten to comb it again. The Queen was sitting beside him and she patted his hair affectionately.

"We know it must have been Harraine who stole them," said the Queen.

"It's incredible that she's a wizard!" Amalek exclaimed, "And we knew her as an old lady in a wheelchair!"

"A good disguise," commented Seph, "Yes, she must have taken them. It must be her. The Troubler couldn't… it had to be someone living here."

"I always thought there was something strange about her," the Queen added. "And how did the gems get in the river?"

"And what about Darsan?" asked the King, "Where does he fit into this? Has he been found yet?"

"No," answered Joog, "There's no sign of him."

Amalek suddenly remembered something.

"Your story," she said looking at her father and then her mother, "We *still* haven't heard it. Can we hear it now?"

"Of course," the King replied, smiling, "Where was I? Oh yes, when I fell down the well, I became free from the spell and I splashed into the lake. When I came to the surface…"

The door opened and Simron entered and sat down.

"Ah, Simron," the King said, "I've been wanting to ask you... any thoughts on the gems? How do you think they were stolen and how did they get in the river?"

Simron leant forwards and studied the box, his face lit up with all the colours of the rainbow.

"They're *so* beautiful," he commented and leant back. Then he smiled. "If you pass me a slice of that toast which smells so good... then I'll tell you my thoughts."

"Of course," laughed the King, "To hear your words of wisdom, a slice of toast is a small cost!"

"Thank you," he said, taking the toast, and spreading it with butter and honey, "As you have thought already, Harraine must have stolen them. She's a wizard who has lived among you with a hidden identity. No one suspected?"

They shook their heads.

"We didn't see much of her," said Amalek.

Simron nodded and took a bite of his toast. "Mmm, delicious," he commented, "But... how the gems got into the river... that is a puzzle and I don't know the answer."

The King looked around at the gathering and smiled. "Perhaps we'll never know the exact details of what happened. But the gems need to be placed back where they belong... and as soon as possible. Are you well enough for a trip to the Brinscally Cave, Joog?"

"Yes," said Joog.

"And Neville, Lazuli and I must leave after breakfast," said Simron, "We've a long journey to cover, although I must say it's much easier now without all that snow to contend with."

"And without a spell," added Neville.

"And without ravens," Seph said.

"Yes, you must go," the King nodded, "But we'll miss you."

"Will you sing a riddle to us, Neville?" Amalek asked, "Before you go."

"I'd love to," he agreed.

They had finished breakfast now, so they made space for Neville to stand on the table. He waddled on until he was surrounded by the bright shining of the gems.

The King laughed.

"It looks as though you're on a stage," he joked.

They all moved their chairs back. Flop sat on a low table by the window which was one of his favourite places; for a large part of the day he could enjoy the heat of the sun. Miriam was settled cosily on his neck.

When they were ready Neville bowed to his audience and his large bill accidentally tapped on the table. The children giggled. Both ends of his scarf rose in front of him and bowed too. He opened his bill and began to sing.

> *"I move with vigour twice a day*
> *and sometimes more than that.*
> *My body's thin, I help you grin,*
> *my hair's cropped straight and flat.*
>
> *"I have no legs to walk around,*
> *no eyes to look and see,*
> *no wrists or arms, no hands or palms,*
> *no face to show it's me.*
>
> *"And yet you use me every day*
> *and shake me from my dream*
> *when you appear to find me here*
> *so I can help you beam.*
>
> *My body's colour could be any,*
> *my hair is often white,*
> *I'm born to serve 'round every curve,*
> *with a mirror to help your sight."*

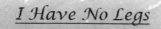

I Have No Legs

"I move with vigour twice a day
and sometimes more than that.
My body's thin, I help you grin,
my hair's cropped straight and flat.

"I have no legs to walk around,
no eyes to look and see,
no wrists or arms, no hands or palms,
no face to show it's me.

"And yet you use me every day
and shake me from my dream
when you appear to find me here
so I can help you beam.

My body's colour could be any,
my hair is often white,
I'm born to serve 'round every curve,
with a mirror to help your sight."

~ NEVILLE'S 9TH RIDDLE ~

It had rained heavily overnight in Summertime Kingdom. The rain swept across the land bringing a very welcome drink to trees, plants and animals. Just before dawn it had petered out leaving the land drenched. It had not only provided a thirst-quenching drink but had also washed everything, leaving a fresh sweet smell in the air.

Crayle, Jum and Iker took shelter in an old barn on the outskirts of Munden. They found an open window to the upper room which was filled with hay. As dawn broke Iker was the first to wake up. He looked out of the open barn window and smelt the fresh air. He felt a little surge of excitement inside and stood up.

Then he stretched his wings and said out loud, "I'm a spy."

Crayle and Jum were huddled together in the corner. Iker did not realise they were awake and watching him.

"Not yet, you're not!" said Crayle, "You will be... but there's training to do first."

"Yippee!" exclaimed Iker jumping again and kicking up some strands of hay, "Training! What happens today?"

"We settle in," said Jum, "There's lots of work to do in our new tree first."

Crayle looked disappointed. "But I need to start training up this young rascal."

"OK then," said Jum sweetly, "Tree-work in the morning and spy-training in the afternoon."

This seemed to satisfy everyone. Jum led the way out through the open window and then flew in a straight line to the tree she had set her heart on for so long. They were soon sitting on a branch high in the tree and looking at it. It was perfect.

The tree divided into three large branches creating a bowl shape in the trunk. It was filled with water after the rains of the previous night and a few twigs and leaves were floating on the surface.

They soon cleared the water by flicking it out with their wings. They had just started building a nest when they heard the sound of flapping wings. Looking up, they saw two golden eagles coming down to land on a branch on either side of the nest. It was Harris and Quint.

The ravens panicked. Crayle flew up in the air, hit his head on a branch and fell straight down between the tree branches and got stuck. He tried to pull himself out but failed. Iker and Jum flew into each other and then tried to disentangle themselves. It looked like a fight with black wings flapping and feathers flying.

"Stop!" ordered Harris.

Jum and Iker stopped at once and looked at the eagles with terrified glances.

"We're not in the army," blurted out Jum, "Not any more. Not at all."

"We were," Crayle joined in, still stuck in the centre of the tree, "But now we're not. That's all over."

"We're spies now!" announced Iker loudly.

"Sshh," said Jum, "He's just young... he likes playing at being a spy!"

With great enthusiasm Iker said, "But I *am* a..."

Before he could say 'spy' Crayle pecked him on his foot.

"Ow!" said Iker.

"We're just..." began Jum, "We're just planning to live quietly in this tree here. That's all."

"No fighting?" asked Harris.

"No... none," said Jum.

"What about the fight just now?" asked Quint, winking at Harris, "We've just seen you fighting."

"No, no," pleaded Crayle, "That was just a mistake. You frightened us."

"Looked like a fight to me," said Harris, "But if you're sure..."

"We're sure," said Crayle and Jum together.

"Absolutely sure," said Jum nodding.

"So you'll just live here quietly?" asked Quint.

They nodded.

"Alright," said Harris, "I don't know how you've done it, but somehow you seem to be different from the other ravens."

"Thank you," said Crayle and Jum together.

"Wizard Elzaphan knows you are here," stated Harris, "I will be calling on you regularly and some of our sparrows will be watching you. So, behave yourselves!"

The eagles gave them a threatening stare and then took off back to the castle.

A few weeks later, when autumn was overcoming summer like an incoming tide, Amalek and Seph sat on Halo and Aram in the twilight. The wind gusted around them as if in a hasty rush to pull the last of the golden leaves off the trees. Most of the boughs had lost many leaves now but on this evening, autumn was working hard to strip them bare. Crisp dead leaves danced in the wind in their multitudes, swirling giddily as they tumbled towards the damp earth.

Rain drops, chilly and large, had just begun to fall, splattering fresh and cold on the children's faces and chinking metallically on the hard, gold and silver bodies of the unicorns.

"We'd better go in," said Seph loudly so as to be heard above the swirling wind.

Amalek was thinking about Aram and Halo.

"I sometimes wonder…" she said, "I know they said they will be able to hear us… but sometimes it's hard to believe."

"I know what you mean," agreed Seph, "But we must believe because they told us. They would never make it up… you know them. They're probably listening now."

A strong gust of wind whirled some leaves around them.

"Let's go," said Amalek.

They slid down off the unicorns and onto the gateposts. Seph patted Aram and Amalek stroked Halo on her nose. The unicorn statues felt cold and wet.

Suddenly both children looked across at each other with excitement. Amalek spoke first.

"She winked at me!" she said.

"And Aram looked at me!" Seph said smiling., "His eye turned!"

They gazed at the beautiful statues and waited. Nothing else happened; they were completely still again.

Seph turned back to Amalek and grinned at her and she beamed at him. They jumped down off the gateposts, landed on the path together and then stepped onto the sodden grass. The wind and leaves swirled around them in a spiral of excitement and joy.

They began laughing with happiness and trying to catch the leaves, until they collapsed to the ground and lay on their backs, the raindrops splashing on their smiling faces.

Epilogue

After the Candara Gems had been replaced in the Brinscally Cave behind the Gem Falls, The Kingdom Of Gems became a peaceful place again. The red ruby, the blue sapphire and the purple amethyst rested once more in their rightful places in the cavity in the wall. The brilliance of their shining colours gleamed and sparkled gloriously in their secluded home. This splendour shone like their fine qualities and the kingdom was protected once more. Everything was back to normal, almost as if nothing had happened at all.

Simron, Neville and Lazuli returned to Summertime Kingdom where they were needed to help Wizard Elzaphan. Old Howard worked hard at his new job repairing Spindley Tower. He reported to the King who gave him his weekly wages for which he was extremely thankful.

Darsan's disappearance remained a mystery and Harraine's dramatic departure left behind her the stunning revelation that she was a wizard. With Relbuort Cottage vacant it was the perfect place for Old Howard to live and he was happy to move in. He kept his Hadia Stick with him at all times and read the poem every day. The transformation was remarkable and he soon became a well-liked character in Candara.

The mountain hares left to return to their home in the Becci Mountains. Seph and Amalek put wheels on Hawkeye's sledge and he was pulled along with Tally sitting beside him. All the hares were keen that Tally would be their new leader with the wise Hawkeye guiding him. This would need the approval of the other hares who had not made the journey and so when they got back, there was a successful vote.

The friendship between Flop and Miriam continued and they would visit each others families regularly. The unusual bond which had formed between a cat and a mouse was passed on to the new generation; the wonderful sight of the kittens and the baby mice playing together was frequently enjoyed by Amalek and Seph.

The glass mushroom remained where it was. No one knew what should be done about it and so the King decided to wait until Wizard Elzaphan came to visit the kingdom. In the meantime, it stood as a reminder of the events that had happened, like a monument to the Dark Wizard Troubler's spell and his defeat. It attracted a constant flow of visitors, both animals and people, who looked at it in wonder. Children loved to play in it, running through the glass and acting out the events that had happened there.

Joog continued to lead The Guardians of the Kingdom. He recruited another ten owls because he felt that the border could be watched more thoroughly by forty owls rather than thirty.

Princess Amalek and Prince Seph visited Aram and Halo every day. Their confrontation with the Troubler had strengthened them, bringing a deeper level of courage, honesty and other good qualities.

While The Kingdom Of Gems enjoyed peace and happiness, it was not the same elsewhere. Beyond its borders, to the east and to the west, evil forces were gradually awakening. The creeping desert continued its steady movement across the Kingdom of Moone and towards Summertime Kingdom. The power of Gugeol was rearing up and would soon be ready to strike.

Bonus Story

This is a short story related to The Kingdom of Gems trilogy. This story takes place prior to any events in the trilogy itself.

This is an example of one of the stories you will receive by being part of the KOGworld™ membership.

Make sure you are a member of KOGworld™ so you don't miss out on other short stories like this.

Bonus Story

~ The Somon ~

This event happens in Stellen 564, three years before the Dark Wizard Troubler entered the Kingdom of Gems and cast his spell.

I t moved through the trees as silently as a shadow. Then it paused, looking around quickly with eyes alert for the slightest movement. Stooping down, kneeling on one knee, it listened. Its semi-transparent human body was green-tinted in the sunlight and then the colour shifted to blend into the background. It became hidden from view.

After a moment it stood up and started moving again across the damp ground. Now it was visible, but only just, a movement among the colours of the woods. Its progress was swift, faster than a human sprint, and almost without sound. It stopped suddenly when it heard voices. The colours on its slim body adjusted and again it faded from sight.

"… called you all here…" said Joog, "Because I am appointing some more owls to join us. They will be here in a minute or two. This kingdom is a large place… and we need a few more to cover it all and do our job well. There will be five more joining us."

There were murmurings of surprise from the twenty-four owls who were perched in the trees and all facing Joog. They turned to each other as they discussed who these five owls might be.

"Temon and Dinty," said Lorder, a Great Horned Owl, his deep voice echoing in the woods, "Without doubt… they're as reliable as the seasons."

"Yes, I agree," replied Fearn, a Barn Owl, "But don't forget Claw. Now he's grown up he's a good strong flyer."

"What about Humm," said another.

"And Terb…"

The chattering petered out and stopped as the five owls arrived, gliding in on their silent wings and landing in a row beside Joog.

"Here they are," Joog commented, lifting a wing to indicate the row of owls on his right, "You probably all know them, but just in case… this is Temon and Dinty, Spec and Mima, and Claw."

The owls nodded and chorused their approval by hooting. Joog lifted a foot and spread his toes to quiet them down.

"Good," he said, "I knew you'd approve and give them a good welcome. We are now thirty. These new Guardians will take up their posts straight away. Temon and Dinty in the furthest north-east corner of the kingdom where there is an old wooden tower. Some of you may know it… it's called Thurby Tower and is perfect for the job. Spec and Mima will watch from the far north-west point although they will still live by the Great River Sween, and Claw will take the far South-east corner in a strong, young poplar. I've been worried about these places for some time, but now…" He turned his head to look at the new recruits. "Now I feel we are covering the whole kingdom…"

Joog stopped suddenly, sensing something. He looked down, his eyes alert, scanning the woods below. All the other owls looked down as well.

"What is it, Joog?" asked Lorder.

"I don't know," said Joog quietly, "Just a feeling really… that something… or someone… is down there. I don't know… probably nothing, but I'd like to check anyway. We'll all have a fly around down there and scan the area, and if there's nothing there... then up to the palace. The King wants to talk to us."

Joog raised his wings and glided down, followed by all the others. Without a sound, they weaved in and out of the trees, staying watchful for anything unusual. It was an extraordinary sight to see so many owls together.

The somon stayed completely still, blending in so perfectly with the background that it remained unseen, even to the sharp eyes of the owls. This was an occasion when it was glad to be a somon. Most of the time it was racked with pain and misery, but now it was smiling with satisfaction as the owls flew by without seeing it.

Suddenly, the somon saw an owl flying straight at it. It was Lorder. If the somon moved, it might be seen, so it stayed still, hoping the owl would miss it. Lorder dipped, and without knowing, headed directly at the somon's head.

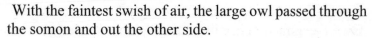

With the faintest swish of air, the large owl passed through the somon and out the other side.

"Alright," announced Joog, "There seems to be nothing here. Strange. But we'd better go. To the palace!"

Joog led and all the owls flew silently behind him. In a moment they were all gone.

The somon waited a few minutes. Then it moved. Now it was visible, but only just, darting rapidly through the trees. It passed out of the Wellspring Woods and followed the River Tazer until it came to East Bridge. It slipped underneath to hide until dark.

Night descended but still the somon waited under the bridge. When midnight was near it emerged, climbed up the river bank and then it paused.

"Who am I?" it thought, *"What am I?"*

It stared through transparent eyes at the ground. Confusion filled its mind and despair was close. It knew that it had known the answer to these questions but now the memory had gone. It had happened before many times but it could not even remember that.

Then the memory stirred.

"Yes!" it whispered aloud, "I know… I am a somon! I was human… then I died. Before I died I was…? I was…?"

The somon tried to remember. Then it realized that this was a question it could never answer. It had thought about it before for long periods and sometimes it seemed the answer was very close, but it could never quite remember.

"I am a somon," it whispered to itself, "I am a somon."

It felt normal again. Looking around, it realised why it was here. From a huge distance away it had smelt

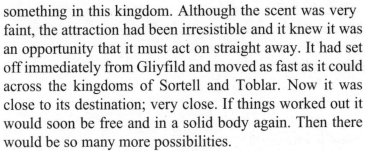

something in this kingdom. Although the scent was very faint, the attraction had been irresistible and it knew it was an opportunity that it must act on straight away. It had set off immediately from Gliyfild and moved as fast as it could across the kingdoms of Sortell and Toblar. Now it was close to its destination; very close. If things worked out it would soon be free and in a solid body again. Then there would be so many more possibilities.

It followed the scent along the river towards Candara. At Ayder Water, it paused again. It was almost intoxicated by the smell, and excitement swelled in its chest. It moved on quickly, flitting through the shadows of the night with hardly a trace. In Candara, it stayed close to the river, on the northern bank.

It crossed Nathan Avenue, almost invisible as it slipped through the night; the merest shadow in the moonlight. Then something made it stop abruptly; it had spotted an owl on the top of Spindley Tower. It was Joog.

Joog still felt uneasy. He was sure he felt something earlier in the woods and was making sure the town was safe.

Below, the somon was now completely still. It did not want to take any chances; this was too important.

After a while, Joog decided to head back to his oak tree in the Wellspring Woods. Maybe whatever he had sensed was still there. he would have a scout around.

He jumped off the tower and glided through the fresh night air. he followed the river towards the woods.

The somon watched Joog go and continued following the scent. Sometimes it jumped over fences and sometimes passed right through objects that were in its way. It glided through the sleeping town unnoticed.

Soon the smell became overbearing and it knew it had reached the place. It flitted across a lawn and to the back of a cottage. It knew this was the end of its journey because the smell was no longer a scent to be followed. It was all around.

The somon was now filled completely with the desire to claim the most treasured possession that one of its kind could ever steal; a human body.

It passed through the wall and into Relbuort Cottage.

Note from Jasper

Did you wonder what the General meant on page 140?

"What do you mean, disappeared?" asked the General, "He can't just disappear like a somon in the night, can he?"

Now you know!

'The Somon' is an example of one of the stories you will receive by being part of the KOGworld™ membership.

To get access to more stories just like this from
The Kingdom of Gems "world", make sure
you are a member of KOGworld™

As an owner of The Glass Prison, you get a FREE
Level 3 KOGworld™ membership!

If you are not already a member, you can unlock your
FREE membership by using this special link below:

www.TheKingdomOfGems.com/gp-world

Unlock Code: TPX348GP8

(special link for Glass Prison owners only)

Author's Notes

Thank you for reading The Glass Prison. I've had a
wonderful time writing the Kingdom of Gems trilogy. It has
taken years of extremely enjoyable creative work and it's
great that you have shared the adventure with me.

If you enjoyed the trilogy, you will be glad to hear that there
is much more to come! Even though officially this is the last
book in the trilogy, this is not the end of the series...

There are already two other Kingdom of Gems books well on
the way, and on top of this, I will constantly be adding new
short stories in the Kingdom of Gems series to the
KOGworld™ membership site.

Some of these short stories will be adventures about the
characters you know and love, some will introduce new
characters and some will reveal the answers to mysteries
contained in the trilogy you have just read.

If you're not yet a KOGworld™ member, you are entitled to
a FREE level 3 membership because you are an owner of
this book. To join, you can find the website along with a
special 'unlock code' on the very last page of this book.

Many thanks for reading this trilogy, and I look forward
to sharing more adventures with you in the future and
reading your comments in the KOGworld™ members
area!

SPECIAL THANKS for their enthusiastic support for THE KINGDOM of GEMS Trilogy.

Beth Attwell

Josh Scott

Suzan Lacey

Alex Silvester

Veronica

Isobel Gannaway

Luke Moroney

Cullum Attwell

Julian

Selsted Church of England Primary School, Kent.